Katelyn Brawn

I want to dedicate this project to someone very important to my life, a girl with a lot of substance! I love you Courtney!

Chapter One

England 1537 A.D.

"Ivyana? Ivyana?" Rachel called out into the night. It was unlike her mistress to run off alone in the middle of the night. "Milady where are you?" She paused at the sound of the trees rustling above her head. She sighed aloud and planted her hands on her hips and looked up. "Ivyana!"

"Not here." a voice drifted from the tree above.

"How did you even get up there?" Rachel demanded.

Ivy rolled her eyes and jumped from the limb nearly fifteen feet above to the ground below. "It's not that hard." she said once she landed.

Rachel gripped her chest and said, "You are not to frighten me like that. What are you doing out here mistress? It is nearly midnight. You need your rest."

"Well I do have a full day tomorrow do I not?" Ivy said, her tone sarcastic as she pulled her shawl closer around her shoulders.

Rachel rolled her eyes and said, "Please do not pity yourself, it is quite unattractive." She rubbed her arms vigorously and said, "Get inside now, it is cold out here."

"Do I not have the right to be upset?" Ivy demanded. Rachel sighed and turned and looked at her, bidding her to go on. "I am being sold, I have the right to be angry."

Rachel rolled her eyes. "You are not being sold, you are to be married."

"To a horrible man!" Ivy argued.

"You have never even met him." Rachel said crossing her arms.

Ivy let out a laugh. "Yes and that is so much better." She sighed aloud at Rachel's vacant expression. She was tired but Ivy did not care. "I have heard he is not a good man."

"We cannot know that for sure considering that we have never met him." Rachel said with a sympathetic sigh.

"Why is father doing this to me?" Ivy asked, the pout of a child spreading across her face.

Rachel shook her head slowly. "Milady you are a Duchess and that title is the last thing your family has. Your father has gambled away your dowry, all of his inheritance, everything. The only way your father could find you a husband is because he will receive the title."

"What does he do again? This man I am to marry." Ivy asked.

"May we continue this conversation inside? I am very cold." she asked, her tone growing with irritation. Ivy kept her feet planted. Rachel rolled her eyes and said, "Fine, he is a boat builder. No title to speak of but very rich. Which is exactly what your father wants him for."

Ivy shook her head. "The Duchess of Lentenworth to marry a lowly shipbuilder. It is embarrassing."

"Stop complaining, it makes you look older." Rachel said with a roll of her eyes. "I am tired, I am going inside and much like you I have a busy day tomorrow. Go to bed, and I am not suggesting this, I am telling you."

Rachel left her then and wandered back inside the home.

Ivy crossed her arms and huffed aloud. She had grown up along side Rachel, the two were only weeks apart in age and yet Rachel always acted as if she were wiser and older than Ivy. Ivy hated that. She sighed aloud and pulled her shawl even closer around her and walked back inside.

"Begging your pardon milady," Rachel said to Ivy the next afternoon. "But your father requires you. Your betrothed has just arrived."

Ivy rolled her eyes and placed her needlework to the side. She held her hands up in front of her and shook her head. They were covered with prick marks from the needle. "I am so poor at this."

She turned her hands toward Rachel who shook her head. "You will never learn will you?"

"Apparently not." Ivy said with a laugh. "Have you seen him yet?"

"Who?" Rachel asked inspecting Ivy's hands closer.

"The shipbuilder, what is his name again?" Ivy asked.

Rachel did not raise her eyes. "Marcus, Marcus Lecruex. And no I have not seen him yet, but your father does require an audience with you before you meet him."

"Fine." Ivy said rubbing her hands together. She followed Rachel down the hall toward the grand hall. The manor had become eerie in the past years. Ever since the dismissal of most of the house staff it had become quiet. Her father sat at the far end of the room and did not rise as she approached him.

"Father?" she said when she was upon him. His chin was

resting on his fist and he was looking away from her.

"Tomorrow is a very important day child, you understand that do you not?" her father asked, twirling the ring around his pinky finger.

"Of course father." Ivy said, folding her hands in front of her.

"It is very important that you make him happy Ivyana. We cannot afford for you to ruin this." her father said, his eyes still focused away.

"I won't, I promise." Ivy said, her eyes focusing downward.

He rose his gaze then and looked her once over. "Your beauty will take you far in this marriage, but it cannot do everything. You will actually have to do some work in it."

"I understand." Ivy said, her eyes still focused down.

He rose quickly to his feet and put his hand under her chin and raised her gaze to his. "It has only been the two of us for a long time Ivyana. I am sorry that it had to come to this but I see no other way. We need this."

"I understand father." Ivy said, her face absent and emotionless.

"He is in the parlor, if you are ready to meet him." It did not come across as a suggestion to Ivy. So she simply nodded and followed her father into the next room.

Her pulse quickened as they walked. With each step she could hear her heartbeat in her ears. Her father paused before the double doors and took in a deep breath. The doors swung open and much to Ivy's surprise the room was full of people. She had not planned on this. She had intended it only to be the three of them. Embarrassment flared within her and she flushed a deep red. Her father grabbed her elbow forcefully and hissed in her ear, "Stop blushing! You look like a whore."

Her body's first instinct was to blush deeper but she resisted and took a deep breath until she mellowed to a pale pink. "I apologize father."

Together they walked through the crowd, all eyes upon her as she walked toward the front of the room. She scanned the crowd, trying to determine which could be him. The faces all looked the same, like all the ones she had always seen in her life, but as she reached the end of the crowd one was different. He stood off to the side, away from the group as if wishing not to be seen, but she had seen him. His eyes were focused downward, away from her, but at the moment she spotted him his head snapped up, faster than she could see and his eyes, his piercing eyes, locked on hers. For what could have been no longer than a second she stopped and held his stare with her own. Her breathing silenced and muscles relaxed as an overwhelming calm mixed with a feeling of inhibiting dread rushed over her. The moment was over as quick as it had begun as her father eased her forward with his hand against her back. She broke her gaze but she could feel his eyes on her as they moved.

She stopped in front of a man only a few years older than she. He was tall and brawny for a man of his stature. His skin was the color of copper, no doubt from years of working in the outdoors building his ships. His sandy blonde hair hung in his eyes that she could see were a deep set brown. He was attractive by any woman's standards, but there was something about him that was unsettling to Ivy. Her father stood by her side and bowed to the young man, who returned the gesture. The two then turned to Ivy. "Marcus Lecruex I would like to introduce to you my daughter, Ivyana Duchess of Lentenworth. Ivyana, this is Marcus Lecruex, your future husband."

Ivy's insides curled at the sound of the word, but she held her distain away as he bowed to her. "Pleasure to meet you milady." his voice was deeper than she had expected.

She sighed quietly and curtseyed low. "The pleasure is all mine sir." The awkwardness of the following moments of silence made Ivy's cheeks begin to flare again. She breathed deep to calm herself. She raised her gaze and saw Marcus staring at her, his brow furrowed. Had she done something wrong?

Marcus turned to Ivy's father to make a request. "My lord I wonder if you would allow me a moment alone with my betrothed?"

A gasp sounded around the room at the sound of this and Ivy's eyes grew large at the concept. An unmarried woman alone in a room with a man? Such a thing would never have been asked for if he knew their customs. He had obviously not spent any time among people like herself.

Ivy's father leaned in and said, "That is not done here. I cannot leave the two of you unaccompanied."

"Of course not entirely alone my liege," Marcus said smoothly. "My man servant will stay with us." He snapped his fingers in the direction of the far wall, toward the man she had locked eyes with. Ivy's breath caught in her throat as he nearly floated toward them. "Rudolph will stay in the room for the duration." Rudolph gaze had locked on Ivy again. She had never seen such audacity in a man, to stare right at a nearly married woman, while her husband-to-be stood in between them no less.

Ivy's father glanced between the three of them and then gave a sharp nod of his head. "As you wish." He turned then to his audience. "Ladies and gentlemen, let us retire to another room." And just like that all shuffled through the doors. Her father may have ruined the family fortune, but he could still command a crowd.

When all had filtered out and only they three remained inside Marcus rolled his eyes and hissed, "Go stand back over there Rudolph."

Rudolph bowed his head and said smoothly, "As you wish." His voice was like the touch of the softest satin mixed with the taste of creamy milk she missed from her childhood. The sound nearly made her knees buckle. He floated on air back to wall from which him came but locked his eyes on her.

Marcus crossed his arms over his chest and said, "Stand up straight girl." He began to walk in a circle looking at her up and down, making her stomach twist. She was not a show animal. "How old are you?"

"I am nineteen." she said simply. Her eyes wandered over to Rudolph and his arms were crossed across his chest, a disapproving look on his face, but he was not looking at her. He was looking at Marcus.

Marcus huffed in disgust. "You are older than your father promised. He said you were fifteen. I knew you were older." He stopped in front of her and lowered his face close to hers. She could almost feel a heat coming from Rudolph's direction as he did this. He was angry. "Listen here girl, I am only here, marrying someone like you, for the title it will bring me. Otherwise I would never marry anyone like you." He laughed at the last part as though it were in any way humorous.

Normally she would have pulled herself away, cowered inside while he said such horrible things. But there was something about that moment that made her brave. "And make no mistake shipbuilder, I am only marrying you for your money. Obviously not your breeding."

He just stared at her for a moment, flummoxed she assumed, and thought she had won. The thought only lasted a moment. Before she could think of anything else he had raised his hand and slapped her hard across the face. She fell to her knees. Within what seemed a second Rudolph was at her side gently helping her to her feet.

"Leave her." Marcus demanded. "Let her see what will happen if she defies me."

"No." Rudolph grumbled as he helped Ivy the rest of the way up. Their eyes locked again, this time much closer together. Her breathing became more labored as his stare intensified. Again the moment only lasted a second before Marcus grabbed Rudolph's arm forcefully and pulled him away from Ivy.

Rudolph did not seemed phased by this gesture as Marcus began to shout. "What did you say to me?"

Rudolph did not speak at first, only stared deep into the eyes of his master. "Release my arm." Rudolph said, his voice so smooth it nearly forced Ivy off her feet again. Slowly Marcus began recoiling his fingers. "Now go away." Rudolph finished. Marcus did not speak but turned on his heel and sped in the other direction.

"Are you all right?" he asked turning back to her. He had not spoken to her yet, only around her. She could not muscle a vocal response, her throat was too tight for her to speak. She nodded her head slowly up and down. He let out a sigh and relief and a smile spread across his face that nearly stopped her heart. "Good."

"That was very foolish." she said, somehow finding her voice. "Standing up to your master like that. You did not have to do that for me."

"I am not afraid of him." Rudolph said, his voice signing with what must have been a laugh.

"But he is your-" Ivy began.

"He is not." Rudolph said, at the sight of her confusion he sighed and explained, "I am not here because I am forced to be. He calls me his servant so he will look more important to you and your father. If anything he is in my charge."

"How is that?" she asked.

"I am his supplier. For the ships he makes. I supply him with everything he needs to do it. Without me there are no ships, so no money, and he would not be here."

"Then why would you pretend to be his servant?" Ivy asked.

He shrugged. "He is my friend and he asked me to." He placed his hand gently on her arm and said, "But I will warn you milady, you must be careful when you are with him. Especially alone." It was something she did not want to hear. Something she had hoped would not be true. However Marcus had struck her in the presence of a witness. What would he do when they were alone? Rudolph could sense her fear and felt the need to comfort her. He put a palm against her cheek and that same overwhelming calming sensation she had felt before came rushing back. She closed her eyes and absorbed the feeling. "I do not tell you this to make you afraid, only to keep you aware. I will never be far away. I promise you that."

"Why would you make me such a promise? To someone you do not even know?" she asked easing her eyes open again.

He shook his head slowly and said, "It is something about you I suppose."

"What?" she asked, her eyes wide with amazement. "What about me?"

"I do not know." he said. She seemed confused, he did not. "But I feel it and I have learned to trust what I feel."

The following moments were quiet and he did not recoil his hand from her cheek. Suddenly he pulled it away and took a step backward, folding his hands behind his back. The next second the door behind them opened and her father walked back in. "Is there a problem? Where is Marcus?" he asked.

"He retired early sire. In preparation for tomorrow." Rudolph said calmly as Ivy focused on her breathing.

"Ivyana are you all right?" her father asked turning his attention to his daughter.

"I am fine. Just feeling a little faint." she said with a smile.

"Perhaps you should go to bed. Tomorrow is too important for you not to be at your best." her father suggested.

"That is a good idea father, that is what I will do." she smiled again and turned to Rudolph. "Good evening Master-"

"Stoker, Rudolph Stoker." he finished for her with a bow. "Good evening to you milady."

She curtseyed to him and her father and then took her

leave. She took a final glance at Rudolph and then went on her way.

Something about the man enticed and frightened her, but something greater inside pushed the fear away and left only the enticement that she could not ignore.

"Milady, milady." Rachel whispered quietly the next morning as she shook Ivy's shoulder. Ivy stirred then flipped on her side, away from Rachel. Rachel huffed loudly and grabbed the blankets over Ivy and pulled hard.

"Vile woman!" Ivy shrieked, shielding herself from the sudden, overwhelming cold.

"The day calls milady. You would not answer so I answered for you. Up please, we have a lot to do." Rachel said pushing the covers to the base of the bed.

"If I do not wake, it is not real. Only a nightmare." Ivy said digging her face into her pillow.

"It is real whether you wake or not. Now get up or I will force you up." Rachel said grabbing the pillow harshly from Ivy's grasp.

"You are evil, you know that right?" Ivy said crossing her arms over her chest.

"And yet you keep me around anyway." Rachel said pulling Ivy up by her arms.

"Because I must. I have not been given any alternative." Ivy said with a groan.

Rachel laughed. "Even given the chance you would not get rid of me. I am too valuable to you." The two shared a laugh as Rachel pulled Ivy to her feet. "All right enough of this. You need a bath." Ivy rolled her eyes but went along willingly if for no other reason than she knew resistance would be futile. Rachel always got her way sooner or later.

She bathed and had her hair brushed till dry and then she dressed. The gown was made of the most expensive silk and beaded with real crystals. It had been her grandmother's wedding dress and it hurt her to wear it. Such a beautiful garment for such a sad day. Her veil had been made by nuns in a nearby convent and is spread down her back and onto the floor. It was tradition in her family for her to keep the veil over her face until the ceremony's end. This suited Ivy fine. It meant she not truly lay her eyes on her soon to be husband until the last necessary moment.

"If it is of any comfort to you, you do look beautiful." Rachel said as she straightened Ivy's train at the back of the church.

Ivy sighed aloud. People had always paid her the same compliment. She was beautiful and it was truly something she could not deny. She had dark, curly, red hair that hung about her back. Her body was petite but womanly, with curves in the perfect places. Her eyes were a deep set emerald that could envy the depths of the ocean. And while she knew that others saw her as a beauty, she shied away from her looks, feeling insecure about herself.

Her face flushed a bright scarlet and said, "Thank you Rachel."

"Are you ready now milady?" Rachel asked raising back to her feet.

"No." Ivy said with a roll of her eyes. "But I suppose I must."

"Yes, you must." Rachel said with a smile.

Ivy took in a deep breath as the doors before her swung

open. The room was full of faces she did not recognize. They were blank, emotionless as she traveled down the aisle. At the end he waited for, his expression as cold as the rest of them. As a child she had always seen herself marrying for love, a utopian idea she knew, but it was always what she had dreamed. Those thoughts ended when her mother died. Ivy had been six and was the only heir to her father's title. Most widowed lords would have married again, unfortunately there was no woman of high enough standing who would take the risk of marrying her father with his gambling ways. So, it was understood that when she did get married it would be of the greatest convenience to her father, and that fate was about to become a reality.

When she reached him she caught a familiar set of eyes behind him. Rudolph stared intently at her as if he was starring inside her and she could not pull her gaze away. The voice of the priest was the only thing that could grab back her attention.

"Dearly beloved," he began. "We are gathered here today to join the Duchess of Lentenworth and Marcus Lecruex in holy matrimony." Her heart rate began to speed to the point that she could feel the beat in her ears. "Do you Marcus Lecruex take Ivyana, Duchess of Lentenworth to be your wedded wife?"

"I do." Marcus said his voice cold and vacant.

The priest then turned to Ivy and said, "Do you milady, Duchess of Lentenworth take Master Lecruex to by your wedded husband?"

She swallowed hard and was silent longer than she should have been. The room boomed with silence as she held her tongue and finally breathed the two simple words that everyone waited for,

"I do."

The priest took in a sigh of relief and said, "I now pronounce you husband and wife. You may kiss your bride milord."

They turned and faced each other, his eyes were so cold it made her shiver. He lifted the veil from her face and placed his hard lips against her cheek. She placed her hand upon his and together they faced the congregation. And that was it, her fate was sealed, whether she was happy or not.

Chapter Two

For the first year of their marriage things remained the way they had started. Cold and absent. He did not touch her. Finally, after the urgings of her father they consummated their marriage and Ivy became pregnant. Nine months later she gave birth to beautiful baby boy. Steven. He became her entire world, the only thing that mattered. Once she was pregnant her husband turned back to his old ways and ignored her completely and so it stayed for the two years that followed. Ivy had hoped that it would not bother her, she didn't want him in the first place. But it raised a question that Ivy did not want to ask. He was a man after all, if he was not receiving satisfaction from her then from whom?

"I do not know what to do." she said one day to Rachel. "Everyone always says how beautiful I am and what a lucky man my husband is and yet he will not even touch me. My father would like there to be another child. I am already twenty-two years old how much longer I can wait."

"Give it time milady. When it is meant to happen it will." Rachel said running a brush through Ivy's hair.

"How much time do I give Rachel? We have been married already three years and he has only touched me once. Once!" She sighed deeply and stared at her reflection in the mirror. "And where does he go every night? Instead of coming to me he goes somewhere else. What did I do?"

"Do not be ridiculous. You have done nothing and you know that. As to where he goes every night, that is a question I can not answer, but I doubt it is about you."

"How can you say that? How could you know?" she asked.

Rachel was silent for a moment and as she opened her mouth to speak a knock sounded at the door. "Good morrow." Rudolph said, a smile spread upon his face. In the years that had passed she had become impossibly close to Rudolph. There had always been something about him that had made her feel safe and it was a feeling that never wavered. "I was wondering Miss Rachel if you could give her ladyship and I a moment alone?"

Rachel exchanged glances with both Rudolph and Ivy before bowing her head and leaving the room.

"What can I do for you Rudolph?" Ivy asked, the first smile of the day spreading across her face.

"Nothing of any urgent importance. I just wanted to talk to you." he said, smiling again. "You have seemed upset recently. I have been worried about you."

"I thank you for your concern, but it is nothing for you to worry about." she said, her eyes focusing downward.

He placed a finger under her chin and raised her eyes back up. "Please tell me."

She felt the overwhelming compulsion to be honest, even though her head told to keep it quiet. "I want another child Rudolph. I love my son, but I should have more that one. The mother in me needs another, but Marcus will not touch me." She caught her words in an instant and wished she had not said them. "I am sorry that was out of place for me."

"Not at all," he said with a shake of his head. "Your husband is an odd one. I have known him a long time."

"What are you not saying? No one ever tells me anything."

she said with a pout.

"It is hard to explain milady."

"Ivy. Please call me Ivy." she said, her voice still sad. She needed his friendship now, not his dutiful candor.

He smiled brightly and whispered softly, "Ivy."

The silence grew deeper and more intense between them. His hand remained about her face. His face moved closer to hers as he said her name again, "Ivy." She felt the need to resist him. She was a married woman and it would be so wrong. But something about him pulled her closer. Before she could resist any further she crushed her lips against his and her resistance melted away. She pushed her fingers through his hair and her kiss intensified. So quickly, she nearly missed it as he tore away from her. What happened next was so fast she at first thought she had imagined it, but it was too strange to be unreal. She could have sworn that is eyes changed from those of a person to those of a cat. Her own eyes grew wide upon the sight and she leaned back and away from him. "I am sorry milady." he said, his voice torn and anger, with himself, not her. "I should not have done that."

"I wanted you to." she said tears forming in her eyes.

He turned back around to her and his face was so sad it made her want to cry harder. He shook his head slowly and said, "No angel, do not cry, please do not cry."

He wiped away a tear from under her cheek with his thumb and left his hand against there. She felt herself succumbing to him again, but found the strength to resist him. "I have to go." she said, her voice breathy as she ran out the door.

She traveled through the corridors of the castle looking for Rachel but she was no where to be found. She wiped the tears from her eyes and moved to the kitchen. "Have you seen Rachel."

"She left just a moment ago milady." the cook said with a smile.

"Where did she go?" Ivy asked.

"Toward town. You could probably catch her if you wanted to." the cook said.

"Thank you." Ivy said with a smile. She grabbed her cloak and hurried down the road. Finally Rachel came into view, but too far for her to see Ivy. She decided to just follow quietly. They entered a part of town that Ivy had never been to before. She bowed her head and walked quickly, averting the eyes of the many men who looked her way. She watched as Rachel headed toward a tavern. She was meeting a man. She had not told Ivy any of this. The two had always shared everything. It was only when she got just a bit closer that Ivy discovered why. The man that exited the tavern and took Rachel in his arms, was familiar, too familiar. It was Marcus. She could not breath. He kissed her hard on the mouth, unlike he had ever kissed Ivy. He touched Rachel like he had never touched her. Ivy felt instantly sick. Her oldest friend, how could she betray like this? Ivy felt like she should leave, go home and pretend like she had seen nothing, but her heart would not let her do so. Before she knew what was happening her feet were carrying her to the room which they had entered. She pushed the door open so forcefully that it hit the wall with a loud crash. Rachel and Marcus looked at her in astonishment and then Rachel turned to shame.

"Ivy," Rachel said, her voice so quiet it was almost inaudible.

"What is this?" Ivy demanded.

"None of your concern." Marcus said, his voice smug as if he had done nothing wrong.

"I did not mean to hurt you Ivy." Rachel said rushing to Ivy's side.

"Are you joking?" Ivy said, taking a step away. "How could this not hurt me?"

"I have known him a very long time, long before the two of you even met. I have always loved him and I did not know what else to do." Rachel pleaded. It had been lies, everything lies.

"He is my husband Rachel. How could you?" Ivy said, emotion catching in her voice.

"Do not speak like this is such a betrayal to you," Marcus began. "You do not love me, and I do not love you. Do not make this a problem, it is not."

"It doesn't matter Marcus," Ivy screamed as she moved toward him, growing angrier with each step. "You took a vow and you have broken it. What if I were to do that? You would not be so cavalier then would you?" He did not speak at first. Then she made her mistake and punched her fist as hard as she could into his chest.

Anger rose inside him from the tips of his toes to the top of his head. His face flushed red and his breathing became more labored. Slowly she realized what she had done and grew frightened. "Rachel," he said, his eyes locked on Ivy. "Leave."

"Marcus-" Rachel said trying to protest.

"Leave!" Marcus said. The boom of his voice made Ivy begin to shake. Fearful for her own life Rachel fled pulling the door shut behind her. The slam of the door turned on his rage. He threw her against the wall. "Would you like to hit me again my wife!" he shouted. He slapped her hard throwing her to the ground, her lip was bleeding. He kicked her in the stomach, once, twice, three times. He pulled her up to her feet and said, "You want me so badly to touch you; is this enough for you?"

"You bastard." she muttered.

He banged her against the wall three times, each time hitting her head before holding her there. The pain was more than she could bear. He balled a fist and she braced herself and he hit her twice. She fell to the ground again. He kicked her once more and laughed. "You have brought this upon yourself. You are the only one to blame." His voice was so far away. Her vision was hazy and she did not notice him leave. Her breathing became harder and harder. She could feel herself succumbing to the peaceful end, anything that would stop the pain but it was in the moment that she wanted it the most that strong familiar hands pulled her up.

"Ivy!" he shouted, his voice absent of its music, so different from what it had ever been. "Ivy, stay with me please."

"Rudolph," her voice was breathy. "It hurts Rudolph, it hurts too much."

"I should have followed you sooner, but I thought you would not want me to. Then Rachel came back alone and was so upset."

"I am cold." she said. She could taste the blood in her mouth and felt the pain from every region of her body.

"Do not give up, don't." he demanded. He searched his brain for any way to save her, any way other than the one plaguing his mind. He pulled her up close to him and whispered in her ear, "I can save you. If you want it me to."

"How?" she asked.

"I am not like most people Ivy. I have not been for a long time." he said, emotion catching in his throat, this was not something he had ever told anyone.

"I do not understand." she said, the pain growing stronger inside her.

"I am not human, not anymore." he said, his voice nearly disgusted with the confession.

"What are you saying Rudolph?" she demanded, dragging her eyes open.

"Do you want me to save you?" he asked, unable to answer her question directly.

"I-I" she said, her voice trailing off.

"Ivy! Ivy!" he shouted, shaking her vigorously. She was slipping farther and farther away and the decision was left to him. He had been here before, seen people dying, more than he could ever count, but had never come close to doing what he was considering now. But this was different, he knew that. In that moment he made the decision for her. He could not lose her. A single tear, the first he had shed in nearly three centuries rolled down his cheek as his eyes changed to those of a cat and pulled her hair away from her neck. "I am so sorry," were the only words he could find to say as he clamped his teeth down hard on her neck and started the process of making her into what he was. A vampire.

Chapter Three

She had never had this feeling before. Every part of her body burned and ached and yet she had never felt such relief. Every inch of her tingled with this mixture but all of it settled in her throat, it felt as if it was aflame. Her eyes shot open and she had never seen so clearly. She could see the dust that floated through the air and focused to the point that it moved slower than the passage of time. She could see the smallest cobweb in the farthest corner of the ceiling. All things she could never have noticed before. She took in a deep breath and nearly panicked as it whistled through her, giving her no relief at all. She felt a hand on the top of her head, her own went zooming to grab it, it moved so fast she did not see it. Panic began to run through her as she sat up just as fast. Her head started zipping from side to side, her mind trying to absorb the situation but to no avail. Familiar hands were placed on either side of her face steadying her, making her still.

"Calm down." Rudolph said softly and yet powerfully.

"Calm down?" Ivy said, shocked at the sound of her own voice. It was musical, just like his. "Calm down? What has happened to me? What did you do to me!"

She locked her eyes on his face and it was more shockingly beautiful than she remembered. His face was tense as he forcefully pushed her down with both his hands. Anger stewed inside her, how dare he touch her. After what he had done, whatever it was he had done.

She linked her hands around his wrists and said, "Let me go." His eyes grew wide at the strength of her grip. With one heave she threw him across the room with only a flick of her wrists. He hit the wall hard and she gasped aloud. In the blink of an eye she was by his side again. "I am so sorry, are you all right?"

"I am fine, you have to monitor your strength. You'll be much stronger than me for a spell of time." he said rising back to his feet.

"What-what are you talking about? I don't understand. What is going on!" she shouted, her voice sounding like a song even with her anguish.

He sighed aloud, his face torn. "You have to understand Ivy. I-I would never want this for you, or for anyone, but you were dying and I had to make a decision for you."

"What did you do?" she demanded.

"I made you into what I am." he muttered looking down at his hands.

"What are you talking about? I do not understand." she said, pacing back and forth. "And what do you mean into what you are? What are you?"

"How old do you think I am Ivyana?" he asked, his eyes still locked on his hands.

"What does that have to do with anything!" she demanded.

"I am trying to explain, just answer the question." he said with a sigh.

She shook her head, this was ridiculous and pointless in her mind. "I do not know, twenty-five I suppose, something around that."

He laughed a little to himself, a sad and absent laugh. "And what would you say if I were to tell you that I am three hundred and forty-seven years old?"

Her face went blank. She slowly settled down to the floor

beneath her feet. "What? That is ridiculous."

"Do you know anything about vampires Ivy?" Rudolph asked, sitting down next to her.

Slowly she turned to look at him. Her mouth fell open slightly as she stared. "The nightwalkers? I have heard stories, but such things are not real." She shrunk away from him, hurrying, too fast into the corner. "Are they?"

"Do not be afraid, I am still me." He said, reaching out toward her.

She pushed even farther away and he recoiled his hand. "I do not understand, you are one of these things? How is that possible. They are just stories."

He shook his head slowly. "No Ivy, they are not just stories. We are real." His focus turned to the floor. To say what else must be said he could not look her in the eye. "And I am sorry but I am not the only one anymore."

It took her a moment to process what he was saying but when it came to her she went into a panic. "You mean me? No! It cannot be true, it is not true! You are wrong!"

She hurried to her feet and made a break for the door. Just as she reached it he shouted at her. "Stop!" his voice was so different. It was like a wave that moved through her and froze her feet in place. She could not move. He sighed aloud and said, "I don't want to have to do that, but you have to listen to me."

"What-What did you just do?" she demanded.

"I am your creator. If need be I can force you to listen, but I do not want to have to use that power over you. Just listen to me on your own." he urged. "It will all be all right if you just listen."

"All right?" she questioned. "You made me into a monster and yet you say it will be all right? Why did you do it? Why did you not just let me die?"

"I could not." he whispered, his eyes still focused downward.

"Would not." she corrected, folding her arms across her chest.

"No, I would not place this fate on anyone if it were not what I thought was necessary." he said placing an arm on her shoulder, she did not shrink away. "From the moment I saw you I knew you were different. I saw in you what I know my creator saw in me."

"Must you always talk in circles Rudolph?" she asked, her body feeling weak.

"Come inside and I promise I will explain it all to you." he said, his voice soothing and musical again.

Ivy nodded her head slowly and turned back into the room. He motioned for her to sit in a chair beside him, but her feet would not carry her that far as she slowly melted to the floor beneath her. He sat beside her.

"I suppose the best place to start is the beginning." He sighed aloud and began the story. "Ever since there have been humans there have been vampires. Our exact origin is unknown but it is understood that we all began as humans. I am sorry to say that your human side is gone, and with the passage of time you will lose more and more of it. The memories of what it was like to be a human will go too and all you have left is the vampire." Her face fell at that. He looked down at that ground and continued, "Our rules are simple ones. No going out in the daytime-"

"Because I will burst into flames?" she gasped,

remembering the horror stories she had been told as a child.

He laughed aloud, that story never ceased to amuse him. "No, not exactly, it makes us weak and will eventually kill us if we're in it long enough, but sorry to disappoint you there are no flames." His laugh silenced slowly as he turned back to the business at hand. "Other than the sun, the most important rule is never revealing yourself to a human. Their fragile states could not take knowing what we are and it would raise too high a panic and put us all in danger."

"That makes sense." she said, her eyes focused on the floor in front of her.

"There are also certain abilities that come with being a vampire. Besides the speed and strength which you have already seen, you have the ability to read the minds of other vampires."

"At any time?" she asked, her voice almost amused.

"Yes." he said.

She focused hard and said, "But I cannot hear what you are thinking."

"That is because as your creator I can choose to keep you out and I'm taking that choice. Any other you can hear." he said.

"Why are you keeping me out?" she asked.

"Personal choice. You are the only vampire I have that freedom with." he said.

"All right." she said, with a slow nod of her head. "What else comes with being this?"

"That leads into what I do." he said rubbing his hands together.

"You have a job as a vampire?" she asked.

"Yes, I have a rather important job. You see it is the responsibility of the creator to guide the newborn vampires, to teach them of our ways. However some vampires decide that they do not want the responsibility and thus leave their newborns rogue. I cannot begin to explain to you how dangerous that is, the way you tossed me across the room, imagine doing that to an unarmed human. My job as your creator is to teach you to hunt correctly, to stay hidden and obey every other rule, but unfortunately some vampires create and then neglect the responsibility and that is where I come In. I am what we call a prowler. I intercept the rogue vampire before they can do any harm and then I do everything that a creator is supposed to do for them. And then when they are ready to go out in the world I help them get established. When all of that is done I go after the rogue creators and bring them to their own justice."

"What does this have do with me?" she asked.

"I am a prowler and I created you." Rudolph said, as if it was all the explanation she should need. She just stared back and waited. "So, I am to train you to be one as well."

"What if I do not want it." she said, twirling her hands together.

He shook his head and said, "You do not have a choice I am afraid. I told you that I saw something in you, you have the spirit of a prowler and you would be the first female, but I know that it is there."

"I am scared, I do not want this." she said burying her face in her hands.

"I know that you don't, but I will help you. I promise I will teach you everything you need to know." he said taking one of her hands in his. He secretly missed the warmth of her skin, but would never tell her so. She didn't need that now.

"My throat burns." she murmured.

He smiled and pulled some of her red hair back from her face. "I can fix that." He reached around her for a goblet he had hidden under the bed. The smell of it was intoxicating to her, she nearly ripped it out of his hands and gulped it down. The taste was unlike anything she had ever experienced in her life. It was rich and thick and it took her a long moment to realize what she was drinking. Blood. Her human response would have been total repulsion but this new response, her vampire response just craved more of it. When the goblet was empty she extended it back to Rudolph, her eyes pleading as she said, "More, please more."

"In due time my dear, in due time." he said, taking the goblet back and placing it where he had gotten it. "Do you feel any better."

She nodded slowly. "Yes, a bit. What about my life? My human life?"

"It is gone. You are no longer the Duchess of Lentenworth. You are just Ivy."

"What about my family? What do I tell them?"

"I am sorry Ivy, but you cannot see them again. They will not understand what you are. Remember you cannot expose yourself to humans."

"But my son, my Steven." she said a silent cry echoing in her voice. "I cannot leave my baby."

"You must." Rudolph said simply and strongly, turning his gaze away.

"Then what am I supposed to do now?" she asked.

"You should get used to your new abilities first, then we will begin your training and adapt you to live among humans again."

She pulled her knees up to her chest and just stared ahead. Adapt to living among humans, which she no longer was. How could it be possible? Only days before she had been a powerful married woman with a family and a life and today she was no one, not even a person. Gone.

It took her nearly two months to learn what he had to teach her. The rules were simple and yet whenever he would bring her blood, where he got it from she did not know. The craving for it would be so intense that he hesitated allowing her out to hunt. But the time came when he knew he could not wait any longer.

"Just do as I say Ivy. Do not get too close to anyone before I give you permission." he demanded, his eyes darting back and forth as they ventured out.

She rolled her eyes, the cabin fever she had been experiencing had been so great that she thought she was going mad. She had not come even close to accepting what was going on. The fact that she was this creature was unsettling and still crazy to her, but she was ready for real blood from a living creature and the closer that they got to the humans the more she began to realize why Rudolph had been so strict in his rules. "I can feel their heartbeats." she murmured as a strange feeling rushed through her, settling in her mouth. Slowly two fangs began to push their way through her gums, it was painful but she was so surprised that she did not notice the pain. Her eyes began to switch from their normal gaze to an intense glare and she noticed even more than before. These were the eyes of a predator.

He grabbed her wrist and turned her to face him. "Control yourself. If you are not ready we do not have to do this yet. We can wait."

She took in a deep breath, still unable to adjust to the lack of relief it gave her, and shook her head. "No, I have to do this sometime."

"All right." he said nodding his head, he knew that he had to learn to trust her, but being his first creation was like being his first child; he felt the need to be more protective of her than anyone. And the way her felt about her personally did not help matters much either.

"You did not tell me about the fangs." she said as they slowly retreated back into her gums. She was much more knowledgeable of the pain this time around.

"You will adjust to the pain. They only come out come out when you are ready to feed or when you feel threatened." he said as they slowly paced forward. So much of what they had practiced was doing things as a human. It was incredible how much she had lost so quickly of her human side. She moved too fast to even appear human. It had taken her days and days to master just moving at a human pace again. She also had to master breathing and blinking normally because neither action gave her any relief any longer and so she did not find the need to do them on her own. He had trained her for everything.

"Why did they not come out before? It is not the first time I have been hungry or even had blood." she asked.

"It is not just the need to feed, but also the fact that you can sense them, feel their hearts beating. It is why your eyes changed into your predator side, you can feel your prey near and you are ready to hunt.

"We have talked about this. This is when you need the most control of all." His body stiffened then and his eyes closed. Suddenly she could sense what he was feeling. She could hear the heartbeat. It was close.

Her teeth began to protrude again and her eyes quickly switched. He grabbed her arm as a growl rumbled deep inside her. "Easy." he said simply. The heartbeat grew louder and louder and louder until Ivy thought she would go mad from the sound. And then the heartbeat's owner rounded the corner and Ivy pulled back. It was child. She could have been no more than twelve or thirteen at most. Her clothes were tattered and her cheeks were dyed with a makeup of some sort. "Is she a prostitute?" He nodded, his eyes locked on the young girl. "She is just a child."

"She will not be missed." he said, his voice cold and hungry.

"But-" she said, trying to ignore the girl's appetizing heartbeat.

His head flipped quickly toward her, his catlike eyes lit with fire. "Where do you think I got the blood for you? This is what you have to do if you want to survive."

She was frightened by him, but she knew he was right and she knew he was hungry as well. "All right." she said her eyes turning back to her predator side.

A smile appeared in the corner of his mouth. "Wait down the end of the alley. I will bring her to you."

And so she followed his instructions. She walked to the end of the dark alley and she waited. Within a matter of minutes Rudolph was walking back toward her, the girl a few paces ahead. She looked calm, too calm. It was not until she saw Ivy that her expression began to change. Ivy's eyes were still catlike and her fangs were exposed.

"Oh God!" the girl shrieked. "Please do not hurt me, please!"

Ivy's eyes flicked up to Rudolph as she tried to ignore the girl's flushed cheeks. The blood was calling to her.

"Think of her as an animal Ivy, not a person. The first is always the hardest." he said, keeping his feet planted in place.

"Please, please." the girl pleaded. "I will not tell anyone I saw you, I just want to go back with my mother. Please." she pleaded.

"Stop talking!" Ivy demanded. She was food, not a person, just food. The thought resonated in her mind like a chant, over and over. She took a step forward and then another. She thought the girl would move, try and run, but she did not. She seemed paralyzed with fear. She reached out and touched the girl's cheek, the heat nearly burned her skin but she did not recoil her hand. She pushed the hair away from the girl's neck and could see the blood as it rushed through her veins. She looked up at Rudolph and he smiled, "It is all right, go on." She bared her teeth and closed her eyes and just before she clamped her mouth down she whispered a nearly silent apology to the girl.

The heat of the girl's blood as it rushed down her throat was incredible. She had never experienced satisfaction like this from any substance before. The girl struggled at first, but her resistance faded quickly. Ivy dug her teeth deeper and deeper into the girl's neck until the girl stopped moving all together. Her body went limp in Ivy's arms, and the vein went dry. Ivy's eyes focused back to normal and her fangs quickly retreated into her mouth and she began to shake.

"Take her." she muttered, her voice breathy as she stared at the lifeless body. "Take her Rudolph!" she shouted again after he didn't move.

He took the girl in his arms and carried her away. She began to shake and melt to the ground. Before she could reach it he was by her side again. "The first is always the hardest love." he said pushing some of the hair away from her face.

"I am a murderer." she said with a sob. "I killed that poor girl."

"Food Ivy, she was just food." he said, his voice musical, trying to sooth her.

"How can you be so cold? She is dead and I killed her." she said, her body shaking.

"Food." he said again, calmly. "Just food. If you think of them as people it will destroy you. You have to eat."

"Did you take her away? Far away?" she asked, her eyes still focused away.

"Yes, she is gone." he said pushing another strand of her red hair behind her ear.

Ivy shook her head slowly. "I do not know what is worse, the fact that I just killed a child or that all I can think of is doing it again."

He sighed heavily and said, "I promise you it gets easier. As I told you, your first kill is the hardest."

She hoped it was true. She hoped that she could get to the point where the need to eat did not repulse her. And as the days passed it did get easier and she felt less and less sympathy for those she had to kill. Finally the day came where Rudolph allowed her to hunt on her own.

"Remember what I have taught you." he urged as she prepared to leave. "Do not be seen and take someone who will not be missed."

"I understand Rudolph." she said with a smile as she eagerly moved around him.

He grabbed her arm and said, "Be smart, be careful."

"I will, as long as you let me truly do it on my own. I will know if you follow me." she said, her voice cold and hard. Letting go was not something Rudolph did easily.

"I promise." he said. She could tell that he meant it. Which would make what she was planning even worse for him. She was supposed to take someone who would not be missed, but she had a specific target in mind and ever since her change she could not let it go. She had made it her goal to think of other things all day long. One of the traits of a vampire was the ability to hear the thoughts of the others, but he could not know this one task she had in mind so she pushed it away, far away. "But please just be careful." he insisted again.

"I will." she said the corners of her mouth turning up in a smile. "I will be back soon."

She turned and walked off into the dark of night. The street lamps had just recently been lit which helped to light the way. Her vision switched to predator so that she could see better in the dark. She moved quickly through the streets. She could sense no heartbeat close by, so she moved with a vampire's speed.

She stopped dead about thirty feet away. It was the same, nothing had changed and yet everything was different. She was at her home, only it didn't feel that way anymore. Rudolph was right, the human side of her was dead, but before she could put her that life to rest there was one matter she had to settle. She moved to the back of the house and looked for the correct window. She bent her knees and sprang to the upper balcony with one leap. She landed with barely a sound. Her teeth pushed outward and her focus increased. She moved slowly and silently into the bedroom. She stood over the bed ready to pounce but hesitated, there was something she did not expect. Marcus was not alone, he was with Rachel. Rage ran through her, he was sleeping with her, in Ivy's bed. She clamped her hand hard over Marcus's neck and with one yank threw him against the wall. Rachel awoke and opened her mouth to scream but with immeasurable speed grabbed her around the neck and tossed her next to him like a child's rag doll.

"Do not move." she said to them both in a hushed tone.

"Ivyana!" Rachel gasped, her voice breathy almost inaudible.

Ivy reached out and grabbed Rachel's left hand to examine the gold ring on it. "Well, congratulations are in order it seems." Ivy said, her tone sarcastic, she would take her time with this. "Duchess."

"Ivyana, I thought you were dead." Rachel said.

"Thought? No, you hoped I was dead, in fact I think you

were planning on it. Was this all part of your plan from the beginning?" Her eyes darted quickly to Marcus who was just staring at her like a wide-eyed deer. "Surprised husband?"

"What are you?" he said, panic rising in his voice. The sound of his quickening heartbeat enticing her with every passing moment.

"Well, when you left me for dead I was found by someone else. Someone who gave me a new life." Ivy said, almost as if she was admiring this new existence she had been given.

"What are you saying?" Rachel asked, a tear escaping her eye, it angered Ivy.

Ivy grabbed her by the throat hard and banged her head into the stone wall once, not hard enough to do any real harm, it was not time for that yet. "Don't you dare cry. Not after what the two of you have done to me. Don't you dare shed one tear." She released her grip on Rachel's neck and gasped for breath. Ivy turned to Marcus. "To answer your question my dear I have become a walker of the night. A vampire."

"Good lord." Rachel said with a tearless sob. "Please don't hurt us."

Ivy shook her head slowly. "You were my friend Rachel, we grew up together, how could you do this to me? Betray me this way?"

"I am so sorry, if I could take it back I would." Rachel said, her body shaking with fear. The thumping of her heart too much for Ivy to ignore.

"But you cannot." Ivy said simply before latching her teeth onto Rachel's neck. She drained her faster than she had ever drained a human, she was not the most important target. When she was finished Marcus had hurried to his feet and was trying to get the door. She stepped in his path.

He fell to his knees and began to beg like child, "Please, please Ivyana have mercy."

She shook her head quickly, wiping Rachel's blood from her chin and said, "Not tonight my husband, not tonight." She took her time with Marcus, savoring the sound of his screams and as they eased into nothing and then finally to the total submission of his body. When she was done she let his body fall to the floor and took in a sigh of relief. It was done. She looked at them both, her job had been sloppy, their blood covering the floor. In the moonlight it looked nearly black. She had to make it look like an attack. She bared her teeth and lifted Rachel's throat to her mouth, she closed her eyes and ripped the flesh from ear to ear. She moved to Marcus and before doing the same thing said, "Only God can give you mercy."

She had wished to stay entirely in this angry moment, relish in her kill, but something pulled the attention away from that. At the far side of the room a cry sounded from a small bassinet. Steven. Tears, more than she had ever cried in her life, filled her eyes as she walked over to him. Gently she lifted him out of the cradle and laid him in her arms. His cries silenced instantly, he still knew her. "Oh my dear boy." she said biting her bottom lip. "I love you more than anything in this world. Mother has to go away and I am afraid you will never see me again, but I have a new journey in life. I will watch you grow from afar and watch you marry and have your own children and their children, and their children." The cries erupted at the thought of what her existence had become. She could not bring herself to call it her life, it was not a life anymore. The baby reached up and touched her face, his little eyebrows pushed together as he caressed the cold surface, he knew now that she was different. She pressed her wintry lips to his forehead and felt him shiver. She placed him back in his cradle and slowly withdrew her hand from him. "I love you, forever." and she truly meant it.

She walked to the balcony and took a final glance at what she had done, as she turned back around she said a silent farewell to the life she had once had. She was no longer the Duchess of Lentenworth, no longer a wife or a mother, she was simply Ivy. She was at peace.

When she returned to Rudolph's home she was not surprised to see him waiting for her.

"How did it go?" he asked, his hands folded in his lap.

"Fine." she said simply, her eyes focused away.

"Any problems?" he asked, his voice devoid of its music.

"Of course not. we have done this enough times with you to know what to do." she said.

"Who did you pick?" he asked, something in voice that she could not recognize.

"No one of consequence, a prostitute I assume." she said, tying her hair back with a leather strap trying as hard as possible to think of other things, he would find out eventually, she could not hold it in forever, but now was not the right time.

He slammed a fist against the arm on the chair and said, "Do not lie to me." In a second he was face to face with her, his eyes on the side of the predator inside him. "I know what you did."

"You followed me?" Ivy asked, her voice disgusted at the

betrayal.

"Of course not, I did not need to, I knew where you would go. You are vengeful at heart, I knew the moment I changed you that you would go after Marcus the first chance you got. And no mattered how hard you try to push it from your mind I can still see it there."

"It was not just Marcus, Rachel as well." she said settling on the bed across from him. "He married her, so quickly and I just lost any sanity that I had left and I slaughtered them both. Without mercy."

"I understand why you did it Ivy, but you have to leave the human emotions out of this, because you murdered them." he said sitting beside her.

"You said it wasn't murder, they are food." she said, her sad eyes focused on the ground.

"Answer me this then, did you kill them for the blood or did you kill them just to kill them?"

She thought over his question and she realized he was right, for the first time she saw the difference. She was a murderer. "Get it out of me. Get the blood out of me!"

"It cannot be done, it is a part of you now I am afraid. Accept what you have done and move on from it. And never lie to me again." he said rising up from the bed and moving to the windows, sealing them for the daytime. "Get ready for sleep."

She laid her head against the pillow and tried to shut her eyes, while she no longer dreamed her mind was plagued with thoughts of their faces and their final moments. She knew in that moment that it would plague her forever.

She was awakened with a startle the next evening, right at twilight. "Wake up." Rudolph said shaking her shoulder.

"What are we doing?" she asked, startled by the quick awakening.

"Today you learn how to be a prowler." he said pulling his jacket up over his shoulders.

"Is there a rogue?" she asked pulling on her boots.

"Just created." he said. "Are you ready yet?"

"Yes." she said following him out the door. "How do you know? About the rogue I mean?"

"I can feel it." he said simply turning down the closest alley. "I will train you to feel it too."

They twisted through alleys and down streets, and she assumed they were close when his speed became faster and faster. "Do as I do." he said suddenly as they pounded down the cobblestones of a dead-end alley. At the end there was a young boy his eyes wild and crazed as he darted back and forth to the two walls of the alley, so fast she could barely see him even with her predator eyes. The boy could have barely been an adolescent. Two bodies lay around him, lifeless, dead.

Slowly Rudolph walked toward him, him palms open and out at his sides as if to show that he meant the boy no harm. "Do not come any closer!" the boy screamed.

"I am not here to hurt you, just to help you." Rudolph said, his voice so seraphic it made her head spin.

"You cannot help me." the newborn shouted. "No can help me! Look at what I am!"

"I understand." Rudolph said, taking another cautious step forward. "That is what we are as well. Your creator has abandoned you, but we will not abandon you."

"I do not want you. I do not want this." he screamed.

"Neither did I, nor did she." Rudolph said, his voice calm and soothing. "What is your name?"

"Victor." he said, stopping his quick, jerky movements.

"Victor." Rudolph repeated with a smile. "This is hard to process I know, and it does not make any sense to you now but I promise it gets better, less difficult to handle, but you have to let me help you."

"Why would you help me? You have no reason to." Victor asked, his voice slower than it had been.

"It is was I was designed to do. I want to help you." Rudolph said, taking another more confident step forward.

"Do you not say anything?" Victor asked, looking back at Ivy.

"I am learning, to do what he does." she said softly.

He seemed comforted by her, she supposed because she was newborn as well. "Does it really get easier?" he asked her.

She smiled and nodded her head. "Yes, yes it does."

He nodded slowly and turned back to Rudolph. "Fine, help me."

Rudolph smiled and put a hand on Victor's shoulder and led him out of the alley, his grip strong so that Victor could not slip away. As he passed Ivy he said, "You will be an excellent prowler my girl." Ivy smiled and followed behind because she hoped he was right.

Chapter Four

"Mr. Lenox, when can we expect your next book?" a reporter asked as Casper left his office building.

"Mr. Lenox? Honestly Mikey does that joke ever get old for you? It's not like we haven't been friends since childhood." Casper said with a laugh pulling his sunglasses over his eyes.

"Fine, but seriously man, you haven't published a book in like two years." Mikey said putting his notepad back into his pocket.

Casper shook his head and lit a cigarette. "I don't know man, I liked writing about the supernatural before it became cool, it's been kind of hard to get inspired recently." The extended the pack of cigarettes to Mikey who took one happily.

"Thanks man, you know Belinda goes through my pockets making sure I don't still have these." Mikey said taking a long drag off the cigarette. "Oh sweet mystery of life at last I've found you." he sang out.

Casper laughed aloud. "I still can't believe you got married man. You're completely whipped by that woman of yours."

"I'm not whipped, I just realized it was time to grow up." Mikey said.

"Grow up? We're twenty-five years old." Casper said with a laugh.

"Yea, but I was ready to be an adult and if my wife doesn't want me to smoke then I won't." The two glanced at the cigarette in his hand. "Well at least as little as she knows."

Casper laughed and said, "Sorry but I could never see myself married."

"Married? Man you've never dated a girl for more that five minutes, I don't ever see you as getting married either."

"Uncool man, I've been living with Gloria for three months." he said crossing his arms across his chest.

"Yea there's the source of a good relationship. What do you see in that girl anyway?" Mikey asked with a laugh.

"What did you come to bust my chops about anyway?" Casper said, trying to laugh off his comment.

"The public wants to see Detective Alan Williams again. They like the whole vampire and crime mixture, it's very in right now." Mikey said throwing the cigarette to the ground.

"Dude I told you, I liked writing all that years ago before it was cool, you've known me forever, do I seem like the kind to fit in with the crowd?" Casper said with a roll of his eyes.

"Well, I also wanted to give you something." Mikey said reaching into his pocket and pulling out a tattered paperback.

"You giving me reading material Mike?" Casper asked turning the book over to read the back.

"This chick's officially the new big thing in vampire fiction." he said stuffing his hands in his pockets.

"It's become its own genre?" Casper asked with an aggravated disgust. "What is the world coming to?"

"I'm going to say that's a rhetorical question." Mikey said with a laugh. "But she's good, really good. She kind of goes back to old school vamp fiction, you know crosses and coffins and all that." he said.

"All this is wonderful Mikey, but what exactly does this have to do with me?" Casper asked opening the back flap of the book and reading the author biography.

Mikey shrugged his shoulders and said, "I don't know, she lives in the area, I thought maybe you could take a meeting with her and get back to your roots, you really got to start writing again man."

"Well I appreciate your opinion Michael but I think I'll read it first and make my own damn opinions about how good it is." he said turning away with a smile.

"Give my love to the vixen." Mikey said walking along his own way.

"Give my regards to the old ball and chain." Casper said with a smile walking in the opposite direction towards his apartment building.

He put his key in the lock of his apartment and had the overwhelming feeling that he should just run the other way and never look back, but being the dumb-ass he was he turned the doorknob anyway. The music of Patsy Kline filled the apartment which was another bad sign. Patsy was Gloria's angry music. Then another bad sign, just about the worst he could get, she came out of their bedroom pulling a suitcase behind her.

He thought she'd be angry, start throwing things, at least that was how his last girlfriend had left things. She sat the suitcase upright and crossed her arms over her chest. "I thought you wouldn't be home until later."

"Is that what you thought or what you were hoping for?" he asked walking into the kitchen. He pulled out a glass and a bottle of vodka and began to pour.

Gloria rolled her eyes and said, "There's a shocker, that's the first place you go."

"Screw you Gloria." he said with a gruff tone, downing the glass of vodka.

"Is that how you respond to everything Casper? Just shut down and shut me out?" she asked putting the bottle back in the fridge.

"You're the one leaving Gloria, don't put it on me." he said leaning against the counter.

"Would you like to know why I'm leaving? Or do you just want to stew some more?" she asked with a shake of her head.

"Does it even matter Glor?" he asked pulling the bottle back from the fridge.

She rolled her eyes again. "I love you Casper, I really do, but I don't even know who you are anymore. I started dating Casper Lenox one of the greatest young authors of our time and now you just bitch and complain about how what you wrote became popular. But that's the problem with your writing Casper, if you want to call that a problem, that's not the problem with you."

"What is the problem with me Gloria?" he asked taking a long dramatic sip from the bottle.

"You're afraid, actually you're scared shitless! You're so frightened that someone is going to outdo you in your field that you've just completely given up. I didn't fall in love with this guy, whoever you are. If you're willing to bring the old Casper, the real Casper, I'll stay with you. But you this way is just too hard. Can you do that? Be you again?"

"Get out." he muttered, his eyes focused downward and as far from her as he could.

"Casper," she said taking a step toward him.

"Get out Gloria." he said his eyes snapping up to meet hers, his gaze so angry he could barely stand it. "Get out! Just get out of here!"

"Fine." she said grabbing her bags and rushing to the door.

He grabbed the bottle and drank half of it down without a breath. What did she know? She wasn't a writer, she wasn't anything. He drank the rest of the bottle down.

An hour later after finishing the vodka and two beers, and a little stint of throwing it all up, he was nearly passed out on the couch. He rolled on his side and the book Mikey had given him caught his eye. He reached over and grabbed it. *The Prowler* it read, farther down the cover he saw the name, I. Ana Lyons. He wondered for a moment what the "I" stood for but quickly moved on. He flipped the book over to read the synopsis again, it was apparently something about a vampire who was the police for vampires, what a ridiculous concept. He wanted toss the book aside and not look at it again, but something kept it in his hands. Maybe it was what Gloria or Mikey had said to him, or maybe he really was desperate to get back to writing roots, or maybe he was just really drunk (that seemed like the most likely possibility). He tried to deny the truth of the latter but the more he racked his brain the more he discovered its validity. So he flipped the book open, and three hours later he was still reading, so engrossed in the story that he couldn't put it down. As he read the last page he closed it and sighed aloud, rubbing his eyes. "Well I'll be goddamned." he muttered. "That was really good." He moved to his computer and typed in the name, it brought up a few fan sites but nothing about her or where she was. He reached over and grabbed his phone, he quickly dialed the number of his publisher and waited while it rang. "Nora," he said when she finally picked up.

"Who is this? Casper? There's a voice I haven't heard in a long time." she said with a laugh.

"Very funny Nora." he said rolling his eyes.

"What can I do for you Casper?" Nora asked. "Any chance you have a new manuscript for me?"

"Not today." he said with a depressed sigh. "I was actually wondering if you could help me find someone."

"Gloria not work out?" Nora asked, her voice not surprised. "There a few very cute copy editors here."

"No she didn't, and that's not what I meant." Casper said pouring himself a glass of water. "I'm looking for an author and since you seem to know everyone I though you could help me."

"Who we looking for?" Nora asked.

"I. Ana Lyons." he said, reading her name off the book cover.

"Sure I know her. We publish her." Nora said with a laugh.

"I thought I was the only vamp author you had." Casper said, trying not to sound offended.

"Well honey I would have loved to just keep you but you haven't given me anything in a while and well the genre is really in right now."

He rolled his eyes. "I know, I know, it's all about vampires. Can you give me some info?"

"What do you want?" she asked.

"Just want to meet her, talk to her about her book." Casper said popping open a bottle of aspirin, the headache from the massive amount of alcohol was setting in.

"Which one?" she asked.

"There's more than one? Vampire books?" he asked swallowing the two pills.

"There are six books in *The Prowler* series and I think she's planning on putting out a few more." she said with a smile in her voice.

"Wow." he said simply. "I have to meet this lady."

"Well, one condition." she said with a slight pause. "I have I to come with you. She's a little awkward with strangers."

"Okay. That's fine." he said.

"Okay, meet me at Fisher's tomorrow at noon sharp we'll go from there, an please do not be late you know that I hate to wait."

"See you there." he said with a smile as he hung up the phone.

The next day Casper pulled in the restaurant's parking lot a few minutes after noon and Nora was patiently waiting inside her car.

"You're late." she said as he got in the seat next to her.

"I know, there was this raccoon and he jumped in my car window and I had to fight him with my bare hands. And then-"

"You're a bastard." Nora said with a laugh at his sarcasm.

"I try." he said with a laugh of his own. "Why again did you feel like you had to come with me? I am a big boy you know."

"Ivy doesn't get out much." she said curtly.

"Ivy?"

"Oh yea, her first name is Ivy, that's the 'I' in her pseudonym." Nora said her eyes focused on the road. Nora was an interesting specimen to behold, he always forgot how beautiful she was until he was right next to her. Her hair was yellow, not blonde, yellow. She had dark eyes and the palest skin he had ever seen. She sat so serenely as she drove, something about her always seemed unreal to him, something he couldn't put his finger on. "Anyway she probably wouldn't open the door for you alone."

"So she lives alone then?" he asked, his eyes still locked on her, it was hard to break them away.

"No, not exactly." Nora said with a smile. She glanced over at Casper who was eagerly awaiting a further answer. She sighed and said, "Five people live with her."

"Family?" he asked.

"Not exactly. They've been together, all of them, for a long while so I think they act like a family, but they sort of work for her." she said trying to explain it the best she could without actually telling him anything.

"Okay," he said, not fully understanding, but he was able to tell from Nora's body language that that was all she had to say, or all she could, he wasn't sure which.

As they pulled up in front of the writer's home Casper couldn't help but let his jaw drop open. It was huge! He assumed it had been a plantation at one point from the architecture of the house, but he had never seen one like it in Baltimore, in fact he had never seen one like this in his life.

"Most important thing," Nora said pulling him back to reality. "Do not stare at them."

"What do you mean?" he asked with a furrow of his brow.

"You stare at me, don't stare at them." she said, he looked confused which made her laugh. "Please you're a subtle as a train wreck. But don't stare at them and make me regret bringing you here."

"Okay, okay." he said, confused and baffled but trying to make Nora happy, whenever she talked for a while he always had the need to make her happy, it was a quality in her voice that made him do so.

The two got out of the car and walked to the door, Casper opted to stay behind her and let her lead the way. She knocked on the door so softly he doubted anyone had heard it, but sure enough a moment later the door opened to a smiling face.

"Nora!" the young man shouted embracing her in hug. He was as pale as Nora, if not paler his skin was almost gray. His short blonde hair was gelled into spikes and his blue eyes sparkled. His smile was so wide that it revealed a set of shockingly white teeth that were nearly blinding to Casper.

"Hi Leo, how are you?" Nora said with a smile returning his embrace. "Do you mind if we come in and get out of sun, it's rather warm out here."

"Sure, come on in." Leo said with a bright smile.

Suddenly another young man appeared in the doorway, blocking the entranceway, his eyes were not as friendly as the other's had been. "Who is this?" he demanded.

"Peter you know Nora." Leo said with a roll of the eyes.

"Of course I know Nora Leo, I mean who are you?" Peter demanded turning his attention to Casper. The young man had dark curly hair that hung in his eyes which made it hard for Casper to see them and that was unsettling for him, but he remembered what Nora had said and averted his eyes before it could be considered staring.

"This is Casper." Nora said, staying calm. "He's one of my authors and he was inspired by Ivy and wanted to meet her."

"Ivy's busy." Peter said with his arms crossed.

Leo began to laugh and said, "No she isn't, I was just in there with her, she's not doing anything."

Peter stared intensely at Leo who began to shrink down next to him, his smile disappearing. "Leave him alone," Nora muttered. "Twenty minutes in and out, that's all I ask." she said to Peter.

Peter glanced down at Casper, who was trying very hard not to stare. "Fine, twenty minutes, you handle them Leo." Peter said turning away from the door.

Casper let out a deep sigh of relief as he walked away. Leo laughed and said, "Yea Peter's kind of a hard ass, but you get used to him."

"Yea, I'm sure." Casper said.

"Come on in." Leo said opening the door a little further. He wrapped his arm around Nora's shoulders as they walked through the house. It was like being on tour at the White House. It was majestic and beautiful and so old-time, it was cliché but they just didn't make homes like this anymore.

He looked to his right where two women were playing chess, with three full boards, their hands moving so quickly Casper nearly missed it. Nora laughed at them. "Grace, Mollie is this the game to the death?"

"Always." one said, never breaking her gaze from her opponent's.

"She's in her office." Leo said releasing Nora's shoulders and backing away.

"Are you not coming?" Casper asked him, beginning to regret the decision of going to this place at all.

"No, no we don't go in there unless we're invited." he said with a smile.

"Don't be scared." Nora whispered to him.

"I'm not." he said, trying to sound confident even though he knew he was failing at it.

Nora smiled and knocked. From the other side the door a musical, woman's voice said, "Come in Nora."

"How did she know it was you?" Casper asked.

"Security cameras." Nora said pushing her way through the double doors of the office, Casper looked but saw no cameras.

In the chair across the room sat a woman more beautiful than anyone he had ever seen. She had long, curly, red hair and eyes that sparkled so bright. She was so beautiful he could not look at her for too long, he found himself starring and finding the need to look away only having his eyes pulled back to her.

"Nora?" she said her voice so beautifully musical it pulled at his heart.

"Ivy, this is Casper Lenox, he's one of my authors." Nora said in a calm and even tone, he could hear a bit of music in her voice as well, he had never noticed it before.

"It's a pleasure to meet you Ms. Lyons." Casper said extending a hand to her. She did not acknowledge him. Her hands were folded atop her desk and she stared intently at Nora, her sparkling eyes brimmed with anger.

"He just wanted to meet you Ivyana." Nora said.

Ivy shook her head slowly and turned to Casper. "Mr. Lenox can you give Nora and I a moment?"

"Sure." Casper said, his gaze darting back and forth between Ivy and Nora. He walked quickly to the door, shutting it behind him.

When he was outside and out of hearing range Ivy began to rant. "Nora, what the hell are you thinking? You brought a human to my home? A human?"

"What does it hurt Ivy? He's been one of my best vampire authors, one of my biggest sellers and he's been in a funk recently and I just thought-"

"Thought what? That his meeting a real vampire would get the creative juices flowing? Why didn't you just take him home with you?" she asked in a sarcastic tone.

"Of course not Ivy," Nora said with a roll of her eyes. "I just think because you do have the experience in this arena you could help him."

Ivy stared at her blankly. "I don't have time for this, we actually have work to do, and for your information I have a newborn upstairs, could you have picked a worse time to do this? Once you came in here I sent the girls upstairs to help Alex keep her subdued. Damn it Nora you remember what it was like to be newborn, do know how dangerous it is to have a human here."

"I understand all that Ivy, believe me I do, I just-I just wanted you to help him. And for the record he called me about you not the other way around." Nora said grabbing her purse off the floor.

"Really?" she said, caught off guard by this. "Why?"

"He read the first book in your vampire series and wanted to meet you, I think he wants some tips, get him back to the writer he was. It's everything to him Ivy and I worry he won't get it back."

Ivy rolled her eyes and said, "I'll give him ten minutes, but then you have to take him away from here and don't bring him back."

"All I want is ten minutes and I promise I'll get him out of here." she said with a smile. "Casper, come back in." she said just loud enough for him to hear.

Ivy was across the room before he opened the door, searching through her book shelf. She found what she was looking for and tossed it to him. "This is you right?" she asked.

"Yea," he said with a smile. "You've read my books."

"I've read a lot of books." she said sitting back in her chair. "Have a lot of free time."

"What do you think?" Casper asked sitting back in the chair he'd abandoned.

She ignored him for a moment and turned to Nora. "Nora dear can you give us a minute?"

"Sure, I'll be right outside." she said casting Ivy a weary look. *Don't do anything stupid Ivy*, she thought.

Wouldn't dream of it, Ivy thought in response, a smile spread across her face.

She followed Nora to the door and whispered, "It'll be fine

Nora." She shut the door and walked back to her desk and Casper waited patiently.

"You have an interesting viewpoint Mr. Lenox-"

"Casper," he interrupted.

"Mr. Lenox," she continued. "This is one of the first books I ever read that made vampires like real people. Integrating them into society, an interesting choice."

"Thank you-" Casper said with a smile.

"I don't believe I said that was a compliment. You definitely strayed from what's traditional. Why?" she asked settling back in her chair.

He shrugged. "I don't know, I guess I just wanted to do something different."

"Why haven't you written anything recently?" she asked gripping his book in her hands.

"I guess I just got annoyed with what vampire culture became. I liked it when it was different, something strange really and when I started seeing thirteen year old preppy girls so engrossed in the culture it just turned me off." he said with a sigh.

She smiled, really smiled. "Well there's something we agree on. I hate what people perceive vampires as, I'm sure in reality they'd be much more like what you wrote."

Watch it Ivy, Peter thought from the next room over.

I'm fine, she hissed in her head.

He's just reminding you not to get carried away Ivy. Grace reminded, trying to ease the tension.

"Well then why do you write the old school stuff?" Casper asked.

"Just because I find the obsessive culture ridiculous doesn't mean I don't like the fiction. It's been popular that way for so long for a reason." she said. "I feel like you and authors like you have just screwed up everything we've worked for."

Watch it Ivy! Peter nearly shouted in her head.

"What are you talking about?" he demanded.

"Nothing," she said shaking off the voices in her head. "You came here for advice right?"

"Well, kind of, I just really liked your book." he said, leaning back in his chair.

"Well here's all the advice I can give you, start thinking about why you became a writer in the first place and run with that. Screw the culture, screw everyone and just write." She wanted to say more, push him farther, but the intercom interrupted those thoughts.

"Um Ivy-" Leo's voice said through the grainy speaker. "Our guest is awake, and she would really like to see you. Perhaps it would be best if Mr. Lenox and Nora left."

"I think you're right." she said, her eyes locked on Casper. *Come get him Nora*, she thought and instantaneously Nora walked through the door.

"Let's go Casper." she said grabbing his arm.

Can't hold her much longer boss. Grace thought as Nora pulled Casper from the room.

"What are you talking about? We were just getting started." Casper said as Nora dragged him away.

"Stop dragging your feet, let's go." Nora nearly screamed.

Get him out of here Nora! Peter shouted.

Then a new voice entered their minds, it was desperate and frantic and had discovered Casper's presence. *BLOOD, BLOOD, BLOOD!* the voice shouted over and over and over again.

She waited until Nora and Casper were safely out the door before she bolted up the stairs making the paintings on the wall shake. She nearly ripped the door from its hinges making her way inside.

"You let the human go!" the newborn shouted her predator eyes brimmed with rage and her fangs protruding from her mouth. Alex had one arm and Leo had the other and yet it was an effort for them to hold her. "How could you do that!"

"Calm down April." Ivy said with a roll of her eyes.

"Calm down! Calm down! How can I do that! I'm so thirsty!"

"Mollie, bring me the blood." Ivy said to the girl in the corner.

Mollie walked to the refrigerator at the far corner of the room and pulled out a vial of blood. She tossed it across the room to Ivy, she twirled it in her fingers. Ivy pulled off the top of the vial and tipped it toward the newborn's mouth. She coughed on the contents.

"It's cold!" she shouted.

"It's all you get." Ivy said tipping it further until it was gone.

"More," April groaned.

Ivy tossed the empty vial to Grace who was standing clear across the room. "Not yet, first you'll answer a question."

"What do you want?" April moaned, her eyes aching for more blood.

"Who created you rogue?" she demanded.

"I don't know, I don't know." April cried, the poor girl could not have been more than fifteen years old and while Ivy pitied her she could not give in until she got what she needed.

"Was it male or female?" Ivy asked coldly, not allowing her emotion to overtake her.

"Female." the girl said, racking her brain for the memory. Ivy understood why it might be hard for her to remember, the pain of the change was something all vampires tried to forget.

"Did she say anything to you?" Ivy asked.

"I don't-I don't know." she said her eyes darting back and forth frantically searching for the answers that Ivy required. "Please I need the blood."

"Think April, think." Ivy demanded.

April took in two deep breaths, a human source of comfort that would do nothing for her now. "She said something, I can't-I can't remember it."

"Think!" Ivy said again.

"Her name, she told me her name." April said searching and searching for the answer.

"What was it?" Peter now asked from the other side. He so desperately wanted to be what Ivy was, he tried to be actively involved in every rogue's interrogation.

She closed her eyes and waited a moment, then suddenly her eyes flew open, she did not focus on anything in particular as she murmured the name, "Emily." At the sound of the name Alex dropped her arm and stumbled backwards. A foolish mistake. Feeling the second of freedom the rogue moved faster than even the other vampires could and made a lunge for Ivy.

Chapter Five

"What was that Nora?" Casper demanded once they were back in the car. "We finally start talking and you pull me out."

"I told you she was strange." Nora said her hands tensely gripping the steering wheel and her eyes focused forward. "She needed us to go so we had to go."

"I don't understand what happened." he said with a sigh.

"Did you get anything constructive out of it?" Nora asked, trying to turn the conversation away from commotion at the house.

He sighed aloud and said, "She pretty much just said forget about everyone else and just write for me."

"Sounds like good advice to me. And I have known Ivy for a very, very long time, I would listen to her." she said with a smile.

"So what I just sit down and write, that's your solution?" he said. "I could have figured that out on my own without going to the crazy house."

"Well that's what you got, and it's not my solution it was hers." Nora said pulling into Fisher's restaurant. "Give it a shot man." she said as he got out of her car. "It couldn't hurt to just start writing again."

"See you later Nora." he said as he shut the door to her car and wandered back to his own.

He unlocked the door of his apartment and flipped on the lights. It was darker now than it had been before. The walls seemed bland and white and pale, perhaps it was appropriate for the author of vampire stories to live in a place that could remind him of his subjects. He walked into the small office in the back of his apartment, he walked around the desk and sat in the chair. His poor computer almost seemed happy to see him like a long lost friend. He turned it on and as it roared to life his thoughts switched to Ivy and the people who lived with her. There was something about them, something unusual, something amazing. They were shockingly beautiful, they glided on air when they walked almost as though they were flying, their voices came out like honey and the most shocking sight of all was in their eyes. He swore when he looked into them they literally sparkled and seemed to beckon him in to them. Even as he spoke to Ivy he felt himself pulled to her, it was strange and fascinating. His monitor beeped to life and he smiled, he had missed it too.

He opened a new document and laid his hands upon the keys as if it were a piano and he was about to create the musical masterpiece of his life. Her words fluttered though his mind then *Just write*, and he did. He wrote of an angel, different from what he normally wrote, but perhaps it was time for a change. He knew it would lead back to vampires, that was what he knew, but it was nice to start from somewhere new…

Eight hours later he had a hundred pages, whether or not they were complete crap he wasn't sure, but he didn't really care. His protagonist was a fallen angel who had been changed to a vampire and walked the line of the delicate balance between heaven and hell. It was interesting, it was different and he had just writing it, not thought about it, or over thought it like he tended to do. And it was because of Ivy. She gave him a simple piece of advice, one it seemed like anyone could have given him but she was the one to say it. He had been wallowing for the past two years, angry that others began to love what he loved, how stupid was that? He had to thank her for it. He could remember how to get to her home, it was true Nora drove incredibly fast, but he was in no hurry he'd find it. He could just call Nora and ask her but he figured she'd insist on coming with him again and he didn't need a babysitter. He grabbed his keys and flash drive, maybe she'd like to read what he'd written, and ran out the door…

April lunged for Ivy's throat but Ivy was faster. In a moment that was too fast for even the seasoned vampires to see, Ivy had April on the floor with a knee in her back and her hands pushing on her shoulders. "You see young-blood," Ivy began, increasing her hold on the girl. "You may have the brute strength of a newborn, but I have five-hundred years of experience on you. Do not cross me."

"I'm sorry." April said, her voice muffled by the floor.

"I know you are. Will you behave?" Ivy asked, the strain of holding down the newborn taking a toll on her.

"Yes." April insisted. Ivy couldn't know for sure if it was the truth, but she didn't have much of a choice, she couldn't hold her much longer. Slowly she stood up, releasing the girl, the others in the room took a stance incase she decided to pounce again.

"Mollie," Ivy said keeping her eyes locked on the newborn. "Perhaps you could get April another vial."

Mollie nodded, even though she knew no one was looking at her and walked slowly to the fridge, her eyes too still locked on April. She grabbed a vial from the inside and held it in her hand. "Toss it to her, quick." Ivy said, waiting to see what the girl would do. Mollie knew what she meant, she wound back and threw the vial as fast as she could, with practically no movement April caught in her hand, her reflexes were sharp. She popped off the top and drank the contents quickly.

"Do you really survive on this?" she asked, her face tight as if she'd eaten something sour. "It's disgusting."

"You get used to it." Alex said from the other side of the room. He sat curled up in the corner. He was angry at himself for letting go of the newborn, putting his boss, friend, sister in danger, putting them all in danger. But when she had said the name, Emily, he lost it. It was a name he never wanted to hear again. Emily had created him as well, she had a habit of creating vampires and leaving them rogue and prowlers like Ivy were left to take them in, that's why he had stayed with her so long, he wanted to stop those like Emily.

April turned her attention to him and asked, "I can sense your presence better than the others, why?"

Everyone was silent, it was clear he was not going to answer that. Peter decided to do it for him. "You're siblings in a way." Alex glowered and growled at him. "Is it not true my brother? You were created by Emily as well."

"You were?" April asked.

"Why do you think I dropped your arm?" Alex asked, his voice ridden with disgust. "I don't make mistakes like that, but you caught me off guard."

"Calm Alex." Ivy urged with a smile. "Everyone is all right."

"But have you never longed for the blood straight from a human, hot, thick blood. Oh God I can nearly taste it now." April said her fangs protruding as she did. The others around the room began to do the same.

"Calm yourselves." Ivy's voice bellowed, pulling them all to reality. In the blink of an eye she had the girl pushed against the wall. "Let me explain something to you newborn," she began, her eyes filled with rage. "I have killed more people in my years than you can imagine but I will not do it now, I will not take blood from humans, not when we live in a world where there are other options. We can buy blood now, just like buying groceries." Her mind drifted back to Rudolph and what he had told her the first night she killed that first girl. "They are not just food," she said emotion catching her off guard. "They are people, just like we all were once. I will not kill another." She released the girl who seemed so confused, but did not say a word. Ivy turned to her followers, "Give her two more vials then lock it up." She turned on her heel and bolted from the room.

She settled in her study, she flipped on her computer and brought up a game of solitaire, anything to distract her. A soft tap came at the door and she paused with her game. *Come in Alex.*

"Ivy, I am so very sorry, I should have been in complete control of the situation and I wasn't, I cannot tell you how sorry I am." he said standing at the back of the room.

"Weren't these games more fun when we actually played with cards?" she asked, her eyes back to her computer, beckoning him closer to sit in the chair across from her desk.

"I suppose they were." Alex said, he was one of the older vampires that Ivy had in her company.

"How long have you been with me Alex?" she asked her eyes fixed on the pictures of cards on her screen.

"Well, it was right at the end of the Civil War, so

one-hundred and forty-five years, give or take a few." he said trying to figure out where this conversation could be going.

"And we've probably had about a hundred rogues come through here since then yes?"

"I suppose." he said glancing down at his hands, a human mannerism that they had been trained to acquire as well as blinking and breathing on a normal basis, they did these things out of habit now not necessity.

"Have you ever faltered before?" she asked, her hands now folded atop her desk, her eyes focused on her comrade.

"I suppose not." he said in a whisper, but she could hear him clearly.

"Suppose nothing, I know you have not. You were caught off guard is all, did you think I couldn't stop her?"

"Of course not, you're more capable than all of us together, but just hearing that name, we have to get her Ivy." he said his voice sad. Like many of them Alex despised his creator for turning him into the monster that he saw himself as. Rogue creators had to be brought to justice, they had captured many, but Emily was different. She was slowly becoming Ivy's white whale, she was quick and smart and to this point had averted every attempt any prowler in the world had tried to catch her. Ivy was determined though, they would get her she knew they would.

"We will Alex, I can feel it. It just might not be as soon as you'd like." she said with a sympathetic smile. Alex had a good heart, metaphorically speaking, she was so glad to have him.

Suddenly Alex's head flipped to the side. "Do you hear that?" he asked her.

Ivy focused her hearing on sounds outside the house. *Ivy I think someone is coming*, she could hear Mollie think.

Goddamn him! Peter thought.

Who is it? Grace asked in her head.

That damn author Nora brought here! Peter shouted in his thoughts.

"Not good." Ivy said aloud. The newborn had a sense of his blood already, it would be too hard for her resist. *Peter and Leo stay with the girl, the rest of you with me!*

Wouldn't it be better if I was with you? Peter demanded.

No! Follow my orders Peter, do not cross me. Keep the girl subdued, give her more blood if you have to. Ivy commanded.

As you wish. Peter thought simply, his inner voice defeated.

In the next moment Mollie and Grace were waiting at the door of her office along with Alex. The four walked quickly, fast even for them, to the front door and out onto the lawn. "We just need to get him out of here."

"We understand." Mollie said her voice calm and even, necessary for this moment.

Sure enough a moment later a car came up their long driveway, he was smiling, human eyes couldn't have seen it from where they were, but they could. "Do not frighten him or give him any reason to suspect anything." *Why did I let him inside?* she thought. It was meant to be a private thought, but sometimes no matter how hard they tried nothing could be private.

You couldn't have known boss. Mollie thought trying to comfort her.

Thank you Mollie, but it's my job to know these things. Ivy thought her eyes narrowing as he pulled in front of the house. He stepped out of the car his smile wide and bright.

Get him out of here quick! Leo urged. *The newborn already senses him.*

"What are you doing here?" Ivy demanded as he walked toward her.

"I took your advice and it really worked, I think I've got a good project going here and I just wanted to thank you." he said, his smile bright. She was angry, he could tell that, but even in anger she was the most beautiful thing he'd ever seen.

"Ever heard of a telephone?" she asked, her voice sharp and angry.

"I didn't have your number." he said.

"Nora has it, you should have called her. You should not have come here." she hissed.

Ivy! Get him out of here! Peter shouted in his mind. *She's strong!*

"You need to go." she said grabbing him forcefully by the arm and leading him back the car.

"You have quite a grip." he said, trying to ease into the fact that she was really hurting him.

Too late for that! Leo's mind shouted. *She's coming your way.*

Just then the window two stories up shattered and April came barreling through it. "I can hear it!" she shouted. "I can hear his heart beating."

"Get back inside!" Ivy shouted to her, knowing she had no power with her, she was not her creator.

"You've killed before, you said so yourself, why can't I have just this one?" she said her eyes fixed on Casper.

"What the hell is going on!" he screamed.

April turned to him and said, "The most beautiful sound, a human heartbeat." Her eyes had changed and her fangs were out. With one leap she pounced for him. It was Mollie who hit her away. The others moved into their predator mode as well and circled the newborn.

Ivy turned to Casper, her catlike eyes burning with anger. "You should not have come here." Ivy crotched down into her hunting position and circled around April. "Stop this now!" she shouted at her.

Not a chance. She turned to Casper again and Ivy could tell that there was nothing that would keep her from him now. The most important part of taming a rogue was keeping them away from fresh human blood for as long as possible, the battle had already been lost there. April sprung again for Casper, only this time Ivy put herself between the two and growled feverously.

"You will not take him," she bellowed, her voice devoid of it's music.

The two jumped for each other, rolling around on the ground, April trying to bite at Ivy's throat, Ivy just trying to maintain control. The others stood around and watched, there was nothing they could do, or that they knew to do. It was a challenge from the newborn, they could not interfere unless Ivy let them. Casper was the only one to not stand amazed. He didn't understand what was going on, but at that moment he couldn't think about it. He ran to his car and popped open the trunk. He searched for something, anything that could help him now. He realized that he still had the camping equipment from a trip he'd taken with a few friends a week back. He rustled through the bag and grabbed a wooden pole they used for the tent. If these people were what he was beginning to think they were he could only hope that this would help. He rushed around the side of his car and the two were still rolling around on the ground, the others still circled around them, unmoving. They did not notice him. The crazy one was atop Ivy now, without thinking he ran toward them, and still none of them noticed. He held the pole above his head and pierced through her back where he knew her heart should be. She stopped moving. He thought that was all, but it was not. In the next moment it was like she exploded, the red of her blood almost looked unreal, as if it was taking from a box of crayons. Ivy remained motionless on the ground, covered in the remains of the rogue. The others moved then, Peter, who had joined the group along with Leo, grabbed the pole from Casper's hands and flung it away with a flick of the wrist, Casper watched is shatter to splinters on a tree about a hundred feet away.

The two girls stayed with Ivy, helping her slowly up, while all three men gathered around Casper. *Put him in my office*, Ivy thought, unable to form the words with her mouth.

Peter wanted to kill him, that much was obvious, but he would not disobey her. He grabbed the back of Casper's shirt and carried him inside.

Get Nora here now! Ivy screamed in her head. Leo opened his cell phone and dialed the number quickly, she was too far away to hear the thought for herself.

The girls took Ivy upstairs. She stood motionless in the

bathroom as they removed her clothes and stuffed them into a bag, they would burn it later. Mollie turned the water on in the shower, cold or hot really made not difference, her temperature wouldn't change anyway, but in classic human fashion the hot water was meant to be soothing. The two helped her into the bathtub. She did not have it in her to stand. They washed her hair and her skin, both still dressed in all their clothes, but it would never be enough she thought. She had only ever seen two other vampires killed in her life, both by Rudolph and both had been by decapitation, never staking, staking was too messy. She had never been so close either, it had frightened her. But what frightened her more was the wonder of whether the human had really meant to kill the rogue or had it been and accident, was he really aiming for Ivy? And even worse a human had just killed a vampire which would mean They would be coming, the thought sent shivers down her spine.

She changed her clothes and tied her crimson, wet hair into a knot at the base of her head. As she walked down the stairs the door of her home swung open and Nora walked in. *What happened?* Nora wondered, staring intently at her friend.

Your little author killed the rogue. Ivy said, even the tone in her head was cold, sometimes the things Nora did drove Ivy out of her mind.

Nora threw a hand to her mouth to keep in the gasp that wanted to come out. "You were one of my successes Nora, a rogue who conformed to human society, how could you put us in danger like this?" Ivy shouted at Nora.

"I don't understand, why would he come back without telling me?" Nora asked.

"He never should have been here in the first place!" she screamed so loud it made the room shake. "Stupid girl! Stupid!" She moved very close to Nora, uncomfortably close, it made Nora uneasy. "They will be coming now, I know it."

Oh god. Nora murmured in her head. "Have they made contact?" she asked aloud.

"Not yet, but they will, a human just killed a vampire, of course they will." she said. Ivy turned on her heel and walked quickly to her office. Five vampires stood around one human in a chair, he looked petrified, not of them, but of her. "We need to talk in the other room." Ivy said to her family. She looked down at Casper and said, "You, don't move."

The seven vampires stood around the dining room table, a simple prop of course. "We need to kill him." Peter insisted. "If we just get rid of him They won't have any reason to come."

"What did I teach about killing a human, if you have to do it what do you choose?" Ivy demanded of him.

"Someone who won't be missed." Mollie answered for him.

"That's right, and trust me people will miss him. He has a family, he has a career, for Christ's sake the man has fans! They will notice if he just disappears." Ivy said growing impatient.

"Then what do you suggest we do Madame Prowler?" Peter asked, mocking in his voice. "You're supposed to have all the answers aren't you?" Ivy glowered at him, of all of them Peter had been with her the longest, since the early 1800's and he was cold to her because she denied him the one thing he always desired. Her. It was not a requirement in anyway for her to take a mate and after the way she had left Rudolph she did not want one. He was angered by her refusal, in his thoughts he saw the romantic idea of them prowling together, forever. It might possibly be that way, together forever but he would never be her mate and it caused his defiance toward her.

"We will wait." she said calmly and evenly.

"Wait for Them to come?" Leo asked.

"It's one human and we are the only other witnesses, They will probably only send one." Ivy said with a sigh, again out of habit not relief.

"How are you so cavalier about this?" Peter demanded.

"Calm down." Alex said with a roll of his eyes. "You're always so dramatic Pete."

"Maybe if you had seen it coming, we would not be in this situation." Peter hissed in response. Alex gaze lowered, if for no other reason than he knew Peter was right.

"Perhaps we should see what Casper actually knows," Nora began, trying to help the situation. It was all her fault after all. "He may be in shock, we might be able to convince him that he didn't see what he did."

Ivy shrugged. "It won't convince Them but it might ease me a bit." She began to move to the door and the others followed, she whipped around quickly stopping them dead. "But I will talk to him alone."

"What?" Peter demanded.

"If I need sarcastic, cruel comments Peter you will be the first I beckon to." she said, her eyes dark and cold. The others snickered.

"Fine." Peter said, his teeth clenched together.

She paused momentarily before opening the door, when she did he was sitting rigid in the same position she'd left him in, just like she'd told him to. She glided on air to her own chair, there was no real reason to put on the human act now. He looked like a scared kitten, his face had lost all color and his eyes were wider than she'd ever seen on any human. "Breathe." she commanded and he did so.

"What-What-" he mumbled unable to form his thought, she waited patiently for him to find it. "What was that?" he finally got out.

"What are you talking about?" she asked, calm and cool as if nothing had happened.

"Out there, with that woman-" The memory rushed back to him. "I killed her, I killed that woman."

Nerves began to bubble inside Ivy, but she kept calm. "Did you hit your head? You didn't kill anyone." That much was true in one sense considering vampires were technically already dead.

"No, no I killed her. She was going to hurt you and I had to stop her." he said frantically. So, he had not been aiming for her at all, that was a relief at least. "I don't understand what happened, she jumped from a window, high up and she didn't even have a scratch. And you-" he paused and looked up at her, Ivy's grip on the arms of her chair was so strong they were snapping under her grip. "You were like an animal. Your eyes, something was wrong with your eyes."

"You don't know what you're talking about." she said through her clenched teeth. She was able to keep her thoughts silent until that moment. *He knows.* With that the room filled with the other six, so fast she nearly missed it.

Peter's eyes had changed and he was ready to kill him. "Pull back Peter, now." she demanded. Slowly his teeth pushed back and his dark eyes settled back to normal.

Casper glanced around the room and had the realization that should have been clear earlier. How could he have missed it? The ungodly beauty of their faces, the grace with which they walked, the paleness of their skin, the music of their voices. The eyes and teeth. Nora's impatience to get inside out of the sun, Ivy's anger at his humanization of the creatures he wrote about. How could he not have seen it? He knew it should not be true, that such things could exist but in that moment his life's work became a reality, he sat inches away from them. A room full of them. Vampires.

It was in this moment that Ivy wished she could hear the thoughts of humans too, not just other vampires. He sucked in a shallow breath of air and she knew what he was thinking. He had put it together. Mollie and Alex now bared their teeth and changed their eyes along with Peter. "Stand down." Ivy said calmly and evenly, but even she could sense Casper's quickening heartbeat, she could see the blood run through his veins and even she found it appetizing. She was still a vampire after all. "Stand down." she said again, and they did. She may not have been their creator, but unlike April they respected her and valued her as a parent, a friend, a mentor whatever they needed. Their faces changed back to normal. "We will wait for Them to come before with make any rash decisions."

Casper for some ridiculous reason felt brave at that moment and turned in his chair until he met Nora's eyes. "How could I not know? I've known you for so long."

"I didn't want you to know, no one knows. And I'm sorry to have put you here." she said emotion catching her voice.

"What-what do you mean?" he asked flipping back to Ivy.

"Do you know what we are?" Ivy asked, avoiding his first question.

"Vampires?" he said with a smile.

She snapped the sides off her chair. "It's not something to smile at. This is serious."

"I'm sorry." he said quickly, his eyes wide with shock watching the hundred pound woman snap the sides off an armchair.

"What would happen to you if you killed a human?" she asked, her eyes focused down on desk.

"I'd go to jail I suppose." Casper said with a shrug, trying to stay calm even though he knew he was a in a room of creatures ready to kill him.

"Well, we have our own systems, you killed a vampire today, that comes with consequences." Ivy said with a sigh.

"But I saved you. How can I get in trouble for that?" Casper demanded, his voice becoming squeaky and frantic.

"And I do appreciate that that is what you think you were doing, but you didn't choose wisely." Ivy said, her attention focused on her hands.

"But I kept her from hurting you," he turned to the others looking for some support, but seeing nothing but resentment (and despair from Nora and even Leo). "They just stood there, I tried to help."

"Did you really think that's what we were doing? Nothing?"

Alex asked.

"Like all six of us couldn't handle one little newborn, ridiculous." Peter said in a grumble.

"I don't understand." he said, completely baffled. "I don't understand!"

"She challenged me, it was pride thing." Ivy said, her eyes still fixed on her hands. "I wanted to save her, I could have subdued her and if not I had five other vampires ready to rip off her head if she made the wrong move."

"How was I supposed to know that, you were all so painfully still, how was I supposed to know that they weren't just in shock and that you weren't really in trouble."

Ivy shrugged. "I don't think you could have known-"

"You shouldn't have been here in the first place!" Peter shouted, more to Nora than to anyone. "We have had such a good thing here, how could you ruin that."

"It's not her fault, don't yell at her." Casper snapped.

Peter moved closer, his eyes narrowed, to about an inch from Casper's face. "Do you really want to go up against a two-hundred year old vampire human? Because I'd be willing to take you out myself. Save the family some heartache."

Ivy rolled her eyes. "Back off Peter, killing the human will not solve anything."

"He has a name you know." Leo said from across the room. Leo was different from the others, while they were all tortured by their existence as vampires he reveled in it, his old life had left little to be desired. "Casper, can we call the guy Casper please?" Casper turned to smile at him for his kindness but stopped at the sight of him. His eyes were like a cat's and Casper could see his fangs from under his top lip. "I'm sorry but I'm the baby here and all this talk about mortals and humans is making me thirsty." Casper became uneasy again, this only reminded him of the great danger he was truly in at the moment. He was in a room full of people who would like nothing more than to kill him where he sat.

"Do you need a moment Leo?" Ivy asked, leaning forward slightly.

"No I'm fine." he said, his face relaxing back to normal.

"Who will they send?" Nora asked glancing down at her hands, her pixie blue eyes brimmed with sadness.

Ivy shrugged. "If we're lucky they'll send Angelo, he's very familiar with the area and I have known him a long time, he would go easy on us."

"And if we're not lucky?" Grace asked, everyone turned to her with a disapproving glance. "What? Someone had to ask, we aren't exactly in the position to live only in best case scenarios."

"If we're unlucky," Ivy began, sweeping the room with her eyes to look at them each directly. "It'll be Eva."

A shutter moved through the room at the sound of the name. "What's wrong with Eva?" Casper felt the need to ask considering it was his life that was in jeopardy as well.

"Imagine a really pissed off Judge Judy with fangs." Grace said.

"That's and understatement." Mollie mumbled.

"She is very old," Ivy began to explain to him. "One of the oldest I have ever seen. She is very traditional in the way of our kind. She believes that we should live entirely separate from the humans and that they are nothing but food. If she comes here, you will die no questions asked."

Casper swallowed hard. "Thanks for sugar coating it."

"What good would that do you, I am simply presenting the situation to you the way that it is." she said with a sigh.

Just then in the midst of the tension the phone on Ivy's desk began to ring. They all jumped at the sound. "Stupid," Ivy said reaching down to answer it. She opened it slowly and pressed her ear to the speaker. "Hello."

"A human Ivyana? A human!" the angry voice screamed from the other end. It caught her so off guard to hear it, it was a voice she had not heard in centuries. She dropped the phone, luckily Alex grabbed it before it hit the ground. Ivy found her chair behind her and eased into it, in a moment Grace and Mollie were at her side, but Ivy barely noticed them.

"Hello," Alex said into the phone. "Ivy is not quite herself at the moment, can I take a message?" They all looked up at him, what a ridiculous thing to say, Alex shrugged them off, phone edict was not his strongest asset.

"Who is it?" Grace asked Ivy, ignoring Alex entirely.

She turned slightly to Grace, her eyes still wide with amazement. "It's Rudolph." her voice was so quiet she thought perhaps the human had not heard it.

She was wrong. "Who's Rudolph?" Casper asked. "Is he one that will kill me?"

"Rudolph was Ivy's creator." Leo said from behind. "And perhaps the greatest prowler of all time."

Ivy snarled at that. "He is not a prowler! Not anymore! No he gave up the side of the innocent and forgotten rogues to become one of Them."

Alex came shuffling back in. "He heard that, he wants to talk to you."

Slowly she took the phone from it and put it back to her ear. "Ivyana how could you let this happen?"

"I didn't let anything happen Rudolph, I did just what I was trained to do. I took in the rogue and tried to help her, how was I supposed to know that the human would come, let alone kill the rogue?"

"You have a seer Ivyana, he should have seen this coming." Rudolph hissed.

Ivy rolled her eyes and said, "You know it's not an exact science." She glanced up at Alex who must have known what she was talking about because his eyes were focused out and away. Alex was what was called a seer, he was supposed to be able to see the future. Unfortunately it did not always work the way she had hoped. Alex could sense things that were going to happen, but not always clear pictures. He could tell mundane things like when the weather would change or if one of their cars was about to break down, but he could also sense the presence of other vampires much sooner than any of the others could and could tell when a human was near, it made his resisting drinking right from the source even harder. Like all of them with "special" abilities chances were Alex had always had them in some form. Alex had been a high ranking Confederate officer in the American Civil War, she assumed that these "instincts" he'd always had made him rise through the ranks faster. He had been injured severely and unfortunately on enemy territory. Part of him prayed for death as he lay there in the makeshift hospital, for if he died from illness at least he could not be tortured by the yanks. He did not think anyone suspected him, which was a blessing, all save one woman. She was nurse and there was something about the way she looked at Alex that made him uneasy, something in her eyes said she knew something, something she shouldn't know.

One day after he had been there about two weeks he decided to confront her with his suspicions. "Why do you look at me like that?" he demanded.

"Like what?" she asked the words like velvet as they rolled off her tongue.

"Like you know something." he said, eyeing her carefully. He had always been good at reading people, very good in fact, and there was something wrong with this woman.

"What is there to know?" she asked, the music in her voice calling him closer to her. He had never noticed before but she was shockingly beautiful. Her straight, black hair lay like a river down her back and her honey color eyes sparkled like the sun. She was the palest person he had ever seen and yet it made her even more beautiful in his eyes. "Oh," she said, pulling him back to reality. "You mean besides the fact that you fight for the other side?"

He nearly gasped aloud, but the pain in his side kept him quiet. "How-how do you know that?" he asked her instead.

"I know a lot of things my friend." she smiled and pushed the light brown hair from his eyes, the feeling of her cool hand on his feverish brow sent a chill through him. "I'm Emily."

"Alexander." he said, his eyes locked on hers in a curious

way, he had never met a woman like her before.

"So, Alexander," Emily said with a smile. "I'd be happy to keep your secret for you if you would only do one little thing for me."

"What would you like me to do?" Alex asked, his voice hopeful.

"No, no. No questions just agree." she said her smile wide across her perfect white teeth. He contemplated for a moment and then nodded. She could destroy him if she wanted, nothing she could require could be worse than that. She seemed elated at his agreement and it was then he knew something was wrong. Her eyes began to change and she seemed to grow a new set of teeth. Before he had the time to scream or even react at all she plunged her teeth into the side of his neck. She drained him straight down to the last drop in a matter of only minutes. When she was done she dropped his lifeless body on the cot where he lay and said, "Thank you that's much better." But then something came over her as she watched him. She did not want to kill this one, and she didn't know why. She grabbed the knife from his belt and cut open her hand letting the blood drip into his mouth, he was her first creation.

After a few days she realized that she did not want to take care of the newborn she had created so she ran him out to the west, farther and farther from where they had been and then she left him. He traveled days alone without seeing anyone, not a soul, and his body grew weary and tired. He lay on his back under the shade of a tree, his body had already had too much sun, thank god for the tree, and waited for the end to come. But it was just when things seemed their darkest that an angel came to him with a satchel of blood. And that angel was Ivy.

"He should have known that the human was coming in time for you do whatever you had to do to subdue the rogue. I taught you better than this!" Rudolph shouted through the phone.

"I am sorry." Alex said from a crouched position in the corner, his head in his hands.

"Do not apologize." Ivy commanded. "You have done nothing wrong." And in her mind she echoed it again *Nothing*.

"Yes he has Ivyana!" Rudolph shouted over the phone. "Why keep him around if he isn't going to do what he was designed for?"

"Stop it!" she shouted back. "This is my family and you will not criticize them!"

"Family, bah! I never had a family and I did just fine." he said, pride spilling out through his tone.

"Until me right?" she asked, her voice deep and angry. He always tried to keep up the shield that he had always worked alone and that she was just his assistant. The fact that he always left out was that in the hundred years she spent with him they captured and saved more rogues than he had in the three hundred years prior. She had the instincts, she had the natural skill for the job. So it really shouldn't have surprised her when she decided to leave him for the New World he chose to become one of Them. He could never be the same prowler without her.

"Do not make this personal Ivy," Rudolph said with a sigh. "Face it, you and your team made a mistake."

"What do you want Rudolph?" Ivy asked rubbing her eyes with her thumb and index finger.

"I wanted to inform you that We are not happy and We will be sending someone to evaluate the situation." Rudolph said, his tone all of a sudden very official.

"Who? Who are you sending?" she asked, this would determine their fate for sure.

"Well, We were just going to send Angelo but I feel that I may need to accompany him now." There was a smile in his voice, she could hear it clearly.

"No, that will not be at all necessary." she urged, if her heart still beat it would be racing.

"Well I have always wanted to see the United States, it seems like a perfect time, and these decisions are not for you to make anyway." he nearly laughed.

"Do not joke with me Rudolph." Ivy hissed. "You promised I would never have to see you again, you agreed."

"Well things do change my dear. See you soon my love." he said as the phone clicked off.

Ivy shut her own phone and through it across the room where it shattered into a million pieces against the wall. "Damn it!"

"What's happening?" Grace asked.

Ivy glanced up at Alex who was staring back alone. "We're getting Angelo." he said.

"What's bad about that?" Mollie asked.

"He's not coming alone." Alex said again.

She tried to block the thought from her mind, perhaps if she didn't say it or think it, it wasn't real, but she thought it anyway. *Rudolph.*

A gasp sounded around the room, which just confused

Casper further. "What? What?" he asked, the misfortunes of being the sole human in the room beginning to toll on him.

"He's coming here? Like here, here?" Leo asked his eyes growing wider. "Has he ever even come to America."

"No," Ivy said quietly, so low she barely thought the others could hear her.

"What does this mean?" Peter asked. "We've never had a high ranking one of Them come here."

"He's not coming because of the case." Alex said with a shake of his head. "He's coming because of Ivy."

"Why would he do that?" Nora asked, turning to Ivy. "I thought you left things on bad terms."

"We did." Ivy said simply. Her eyes shifted up to Casper, brimming with anger she sneered, "You've ruined everything." She sprang quickly from her seat and said, "Much to do everyone They will be here tomorrow, right Alex?"

"Between three and four tomorrow afternoon." he said, disappointed that now his thoughts were coming in so clear.

"Well, Nora I'm sure you have things to do and Mollie I believe you have a shift coming up." Ivy said her hand on the doorknob.

"Ivy I can call out, if you need me here to help-"

"No," Ivy said sharply. "We will go on with our lives as normal, besides with our guests coming tomorrow it might not be a bad idea to replenish our supplies."

"All right, I'd best be going then." Mollie said passing Ivy out the door, but before getting too far she had a particular, much needed thought for Ivy, *We'll get through this Ivy. We're a family and no matter what happens we will always be a family.* A smile came upon the face of every vampire in the room, even Peter, at this thought because each knew it to be true.

"Thank you Mollie." Ivy said aloud. Mollie smiled back and grabbed her keys from the counter and was on her way.

Nora approached her then, her pixie features wretched with sadness. "I'm so sorry Ivy, this is all my fault."

"Well, I'd be lying if I said you didn't have something to do with it, but we'll get through it. Come back tomorrow and we'll face it together. All of us."

"I will." Nora said with a smile. She turned to Casper a final time before leaving and said, "I am sorry Casper and I'll do what I can to get you out of this."

"It's not your fault Nora, please don't blame yourself, I shouldn't have come back here without talking to you first." Casper said with a smile trying to ease his friend. She simply smiled and went on her way.

Ivy kept her eyes forward but had a thought for Leo. *If I give you a task can you handle it?*

Anything. he thought in response.

Take the human-Casper, she corrected knowing how the first term affected him. *I don't care what you have to do to keep him busy, just do it. You are the youngest of our clan so I trust you would be the most in touch with him.*

"Consider it done." Leo said with a nod. He was very loyal to her, more so than any of the others, for he was the only vampire that she had ever met who was grateful for his transformation. Leo turned to Casper and said, "Let's go."

"Where are we going?" he asked, terror in his eyes again.

"We're just going to go upstairs, I promise you everything will be fine." Leo said with a roll of his eyes.

"No offense man, but weren't you the one who just a few minutes ago was ready kill me?" Casper asked, trying hard to inform rather than provoke him.

"Momentary relapse, won't happen again." Leo said with a smile grabbing Casper by the arm.

As they walked up the tall winding staircase Casper asked, "She just wanted me away from her didn't she?"

"Pretty much." Leo said with a nod. "You have no idea how out of sorts she is with the thought of Rudolph coming here."

"Why is it such a big deal? She wasn't a rogue right? Shouldn't she like love her creator?" he asked with a shrug.

Leo laughed aloud. "Oh kid you have so much to learn about vampires."

"Why don't you inform me then, why does she hate this guy so much?" he asked.

Leo shook his head as he pushed open the door to a room upstairs. "Nope, not my story to tell, mainly because I don't actually know the story, it's not one she shares. You want to know that one you'll have to ask her yourself." The room was huge with a giant bed and three large, plush chairs. "Pop a squat." Leo said plopping down on one of the chairs.

"Pop a who and a what now?" Casper asked with a laugh.

"Take a seat smart-ass." Leo laughed back.

Casper sat in the chair next to Leo and let out a sigh. "Fine then, how do you fit into this whole mixed up group? You seem a lot more laid back then the rest."

"Well," Leo said, running a hand through his short blonde hair. "I guess it all starts with how I was created?"

"What do you mean?" Casper asked, turning slightly to see him better.

"Well, most vampires consider their creation to be a curse, like it makes them a monster. For me, becoming a vampire was my salvation." He glanced up at Casper, whose glance was beckoning him to go on. "Okay, I'm sure downstairs you heard me say I was the baby of the group, very much the truth. I was created in 1987. I was a pretty hardcore drug addict. It started out innocent enough, pot and beers with my friends. Then one day one of them brought by ecstasy, a week later it was coke and before I knew it I was begging on the street corner just to get enough money for a fix.

"My parents kicked me out when I was sixteen. I hated them for it, but in retrospect I guess I can't really blamed them. I would have taken everything they had. If I could revisit one thing from my human days if would be my parents, just so I could apologize. Everyday I was killing myself and I didn't care, it was a horrible existence, I honestly hate to think about it most of the time because it's not me anymore. It's the part of me I never want to be again.

"I was twenty-two years when it happened. How I lived that long I'll never really know. I was lying in an alley in Seattle, the needle still my arm, I was too strung out to even remove it. There was this cop on patrol who saw me and approached me. He was getting ready to call it in, take me into the precinct and then to jail with me, but he stopped. I don't how I remember it but he asked me one question. 'If you could do your life over, would you?' I started to cry and nodded. He paused for a moment, I guess truly contemplating whether or not to do it and then his eyes changed and he opened his mouth to the most beautiful set of teeth I'd ever seen, equipped with two very big fangs. He dug them into my neck and drained the blood, when he was done he fed me his and I woke up the next morning and I was this."

"It seems like you had a creator that cared." Casper said.

"He definitely did." Leo said, the greatest amount of gratitude in his voice.

"Then how did you end up with Ivy? I thought she only took in rogues." Casper asked, slowly he was beginning to understand the rules of their culture.

"I was a rogue of sorts. The cop, his name was Eric, couldn't take care of me like a creator is supposed to. He had a job and a life and needed to keep a low profile to maintain it and a newborn would just really mess that up for him. He had never created anyone before which is why when he called Ivy and explained my situation to her she took me in without any penalty to him. I can't tell you how grateful I am that she did that. And I've been with her ever since."

"How does that work?" Casper asked.

"What?"

"Why did you get to stay? I'm sure she had a lot of rogues who come through here, how does she choose who stays?" Casper asked, pulling one foot up onto the chair.

"Well, a rogue will stay for as long as they need to in order to be able to live among the humans, many if given the choice would never leave so she has to make the cut off somewhere, but for those of us who stay there is always a reason. We all have a special ability that she can use in someway."

"Like what?" Casper asked, intrigue pushing him farther and farther.

"Well, like Alex is a seer, he's supposed to be able to see the future and has killer instincts about his surroundings. Gracie is a mover she can move things with her mind, comes in very handy. Mollie doesn't technically have a special ability but she is a doctor so she has really easy access to blood, which with the way Ivy requires that we live comes in mighty, mighty handy. Right now she's working as a medical examiner, easier to get the blood no questions asked. As for me I'm the brute strength which is much needed when taking down a newborn, because when you're first reborn you're stronger than ten vampires so that's pretty much the service I provide."

"You forgot about Peter." Casper said.

Don't you dare tell him. Peter's voice echoed in Leo's head. "Fine." Leo mumbled.

"That's another thing I've been wondering about." Casper said shifting his weight. "Can you hear thoughts."

"Yea." Leo said simply as if they were talking about something as mundane as the weather.

"Can you hear mine?" Casper asked, trying to think of nothing at that moment as if to swear off the overwhelming sense of privacy violation.

"Nah, just each other and any other vampires, but no humans. It's sort of our own communication network." Leo tried to explain.

"So can you hear any vampire anywhere?" Casper asked, his curiosity carrying him away.

"No it doesn't quite work like that. The farthest away we've been about to go and still hear each other is about three miles." Leo said.

Jesus Christ Leo! Just tell him everything why don't you! Peter thought, the voice in his head angry.

Stop being so dramatic or I'll drop a bookcase on you. Grace thought back.

Ha-ha very funny, but seriously don't tell the human everything. Regardless of whatever you all think of him I am not quite ready to trust him. Peter thought, his inner tone only a little lighter.

Casper. Alex and Grace both reminded him at the same time. Peter said nothing else.

"Anyway," Leo said aloud trying to push out the voices in his head. "We can't hear all vampires but we can sense them coming and once they come into range of course we can hear them."

"Well a bunch of you have special abilities, can any of you hear humans?" Casper asked.

Leo shrugged and said, "I'm sure that there are ones like that. I've never met one, but trust me that doesn't mean anything. I'm still the baby remember."

"Are you really considered a child? You said you were created in 1987, that makes you over twenty years old now." Casper asked, his inquiring mind wandering, he had never thought of vampires like this before.

"Well think about it for a second Casper." Leo began to

explain. "Just in our family before me the next closest is Mollie and she was created back in World War II, before that it was Grace in 1907, Peter and Alex in the 1800's and Ivy's five hundred years old." He began to laugh and said, "So yea, I'm still kind of considered the baby around here."

"Well that makes sense I suppose. So when do you switch to not being a baby anymore?" he asked surprised how at ease Leo made him feel.

"I guess when we have a new vamp join the family. I'll be the baby until then." He smiled and moved to the other side of the room. It was a trademark of the vampires to be able to sit still indefinitely, but Leo was nothing if not unique, sitting still for too long was near impossible for him. He had the least trouble recalling his human behavior. "But I'm not complaining, I like my position. I get away with the most."

That's for damn sure. Alex thought, the voice in his head laughing.

Ha-ha leave your opinions to yourself smart-ass. Leo echoed back in response, a laugh of his own hidden in his voice.

"How happy do you think Leo is to get a new pet?" Peter asked Ivy as she bustled around the house, preparing it for Their arrival.

"I suppose that is how he sees him. I just hope he does not get too attached, who knows what They will decide to do with the human." Ivy said pulling the human memorabilia from the walls. She knew that They did not have much tolerance for reminders of their human lives. The most important things for her to get rid of were human interpretations of vampires, they most definitely hated that. So off the walls came the posters, the books, the movies and anything else that need come down.

Peter leaned against the wall behind him. "He will, he always does get too attached, to everything. Do you remember the puppy fiasco?"

Casper's a human not a pet. Grace felt the need to remind them.

I'm quite award of that, am I the only one not allowed to joke in this family? Peter asked, his voice serious and angry.

Drama queen, drama queen. Grace said with an internal sigh. *Sorry but calling the human a pet isn't funny.*

Cut it out, both of you. Ivy demanded. And that was the end of it. She really did feel like their mother much of the time.

"What's the matter with you?" Peter demanded, his voice tense. He pushed the curly dark hair away from his eyes and waited for her to answer.

"Do you really have to ask that? He's coming here. Here, to my territory." Ivy said, anger boiling up inside her. She ripped the thick book in her hand in half. "Damn it!" she shouted, throwing the two pieces across the room.

"First your cell now a book, keep this up and we won't have anything left in the house." Peter said with a laugh.

"There is nothing funny about this Peter." Ivy said, her voice deep and gruff.

"You know if you took a mate he might back off." Peter said, beating the dead horse once again. He hated that she rejected him and had never been able to let it go.

"Peter, how many times must we go through this?" she asked, her voice low and tired. She didn't have time for this now, nor did she really ever want to address it again.

"But think about it." he said quickly moving to her side just as fast. "Think how great we could be together. You with your ability to calm and sooth the newborns, it makes you a natural prowler, and me with my abilities, we could be the most amazing team. And we'd be together forever." He placed a cold hand upon her cheek, of course she felt no difference. "I do love you."

And that was where he lost her. Not because she did not believe in love, more because she knew it wasn't true. She leaned back, pulling her face away from his hand. "No you don't." she said with an overly dramatic sigh. "You love what I could do for you, but it has nothing to do with me."

He shook his head and slammed his hand into the steel table, leaving a dent in it. "Sorry." he grumbled. "And you're wrong, you're very wrong."

"Fine, it doesn't matter anyway." she said placing her hand on the underside of the table, pushing slightly upward and fixing the dent. "As my creator he has first claim to me and he staked that long ago."

"And yet he does not enforce his claim on you. You have been apart for four hundred years." Peter said, his tone almost whiney.

"Do you think he comes here just to lay justice upon the human? Do you really believe that?" she asked, knowing it wasn't true. His voice on phone had given that much away. He was coming to reclaim her. But after the way they parted, he must also know that she would never go freely.

"But it has been so long." Peter said, his tone becoming defeated, his dark eyes falling. Even he knew the rules as far as creators and their created. If Rudolph were to come and demand Ivy leave with him she would have to do it. It was not required that she be happy about it, it just must be done.

She shrugged, running a hand through her long red hair. "Old feelings die hard I suppose. He always tried to convince me that the reason he changed me was because I was dying, rubbish. It is true he did not want me to die, but his motives were selfish, he wanted me to himself. Which is why he made no attempt to stop me when I-" she paused, unable to say it at first. Killing her husband and his lover had plagued her for centuries. "When I killed them. If my husband was dead I could truly be his. I know that's how he saw it." She shut her eyes and tried to push out their faces. Peter could feel her anguish and placed a hand on her shoulder, she quickly wriggled away and said, "Please take down the rest of this, just put it under the floorboards. I need to rest." With that she moved like a flash up the stairs and through the double doors to her own bedroom.

She had designed after a pictures she had seen in a *Better Homes and Gardens* Magazine in 1947. The walls were painted a pale pink and her four poster bed was enhanced by the white lace canopy that lay atop it. Her furniture was all made from dark mahogany wood which may have clashed with her color choice, but it didn't bother her much. She did truly love this house, more than any other one she owned. Due to the fact that they could not stay in one place for too long they had matriculated many homes. Once everyone whom they had known had died in a particular place they were more than welcome to come back to it, which is why they never sold them. This house had been easy to maintain because it had belonged to one of her most trusted rogues. The house had been Mollie's.

Mollie's story was heartbreaking to say the least. She had lived what Ivy affectionately called the cotton candy life. She had married young, at the age at seventeen, her husband's name was Henry. With his own two hands Henry built the house where the vampires now lived. Things had been joyous and happy and Mollie thought they could never end. Too soon she thought such things, because then America joined the second world war and Henry was among the first to sign up.

"Don't worry my love," he had told her, trying his best to comfort her. "I will come back. Nothing could ever keep me from you."

While she had tried to be strong her tears now fell freely. How could she say goodbye to him? "I want to believe you, but I'm so frightened."

He kissed her sweetly on the top of her head and said, "Don't be frightened, no matter what happens I am always with you." And with that released her and boarded the bus that would take him away.

"I love you!" she shouted after him.

He stopped and turned once inside the door. "I love you too, and I'll see you soon." he shouted back to her.

How she wished it would be true, that he would come home and they would begin right where they left off. But it would not happen. Henry would not come home. After only two months overseas he was killed by a stray bullet in combat on the streets of Germany.

Everyone she knew tried to comfort her but quickly found their attempts to be futile. She did not want their comforting. Every morning she would curl herself up in a blanket in the rocking chair on the front porch and she'd stay there until dark. She was glad her husband had built their home so far in seclusion, it meant fewer visitors. The isolation did not last forever. Finally about few months after Henry's death Mollie's sister felt the need to confront her.

"Are you going to sit in this chair forever?" she asked sitting on the cold wood floor next to her sister.

"Let it go Irma." Mollie said shaking her head slowly.

"Henry would not want you to live like this. This is not living Mollie." Irma urged trying to bring back the sister she was missing.

Mollie turned slowly toward her, her eyes laced with tears. "Don't you dare tell me about my husband. You don't know anything about it."

Irma sighed and took her sister by the hand. "The whole family is worried about you baby sister. Come back to us." She rose to her feet and walked back to her car. There was nothing more that she could say now. Mollie watched her go. The tears that had brimmed her eyes now spilled over onto her cheeks. She knew that Irma was right, this life is not what Henry would have wanted for her. She needed to change it.

The next day she signed up for the red cross.

"This wasn't exactly what I meant." Irma said on the day Mollie was to leave.

"If it was important enough for Henry to fight for, then it's important enough for me." Mollie said with a smile. She wanted to promise her older sister that she'd be back and that nothing would happen, but she couldn't bring herself to do that. Those were the kind of promises that Henry had made her and she could not give her sister the false hope that Henry had given her. "I love you." There were simple words, but in them stood everything, the most powerful goodbye she could have ever offered Irma.

Irma began to cry and embraced her sister in a strong hug. "Please be safe."

"I'll do my best." Mollie whispered placing a kiss against her sister's cheek. The train whistled for her, it was time to go. She squeezed her sister's hand a final time.

"I'll miss you!" she called from the window of the train and waved goodbye to her sister. She settled back in her seat and spun her wedding band around her ring finger. What lay ahead she did not know, but she was ready to embrace it whatever it might be.

They stationed her in Italy, a hotspot area for the war. She worked steadily and learned so much about medicine. She watched amputations and surgeries and held the hand of many a man while he took his last breath. It was interesting to her the things they would say in their last moments. Always holding her hand tight they would plead for their wives, most for their mothers. They would ask for absolution. They would simply say they were sorry, as if through her the message would get where it needed to go. Some said nothing, just held her hand.

The ordeal should have been harder on her than it seemed to be, but it was like she was designed for it. She made a promise to herself. When-if she got home she would go to medical school and become a doctor. She did realize that the idea of a woman becoming a doctor was a ridiculous concept, but maybe she could use her widowhood as an excuse to get her along. She shrugged off the idea, she would never use her husband like that. She'd find a way on her own.

So many faces passed before her, all seeming the same, all the same until him. She had never seen anything like him. He was absolutely beautiful. His face seemed like it had been carved from marble and his skin was so pale she could nearly see through it. His short blonde hair was sticking up in every direction and his dark eyes sparkled to life when he saw her. He had no physical injuries that she could see but he was in tremendous amounts of pain. "Where does it hurt?" she asked, her voice as sweet as she'd ever been to any soldier.

"Everywhere!" he shouted, but it came out like music.

She sat down on his cot next to him, something she never did, too close. She took one of his hands in hers, shivering at its smooth, cold texture. She ran her other hand through his hair. He suddenly became incredibly still as she touched him, it was nearly frightening. He locked his eyes on hers and would not move them. "What is your name?" he finally asked her.

"I'm Mollie, what's yours?" she answered with a smile.

He smiled back, revealing the most amazing set of blinding white teeth. "I'm Samuel." he said, his voice literally operatic.

And the rest of the night she stayed like that, holding his hand and easing him through the pain she could not locate. It was on her short break in the early morning hours that something went wrong.

"Mollie!" Samuel shouted in the dark.

Mollie moved as fast as her legs would carry. "What is it?" she asked, instantly checking him for injuries. A single tear roll down his cheek as he stared at the ceiling. He pointed to the cot next to him. "I think the young man next to me has died."

Mollies attention switched quickly. James Philips was only in with a simple gash to the head, he could not have died. His face was chalky white and his eyes were unresponsive and for the life of her she could not find a pulse. She shook him gently and said, "Wake up Jimmy, wake up." Finally she stopped and settled on the stool next to his bed and held his lifeless hand. She had not been there for him in his last moments. For the first time she let the feeling of death around her sink in, she cried and cried. It was only at the feeling of hands on her shoulders that she stopped. Samuel was sitting up, his voice devoid of its original pain and replaced with a new, more sadness than anything.

"You're up." she said simply, wiping the tears from her cheeks with her free hand.

"I feel much better now." he said sadly, his eyes looking down on the young man next to them. He looked down at the arm that Mollie now held and examined what he hoped she couldn't see, the two small puncture wounds on the young man's wrist.

Mollie released James's hand smiled at Samuel. "Everyone has their time to die Samuel, unfortunately Jimmy's was now."

He knew that she had meant it to ease his pain, if only she knew that it was Samuel who had ended the poor boy's life, she would not feel the same then. He let out a sob, he hated the monster that he was and hated that he had to kill a hero just to survive. Mollie put a hand on either side of his face and tried to sooth him. "Sh," she urged. "It'll all be fine."

His eyes flashed open and mixed with the tears they sparkled like diamonds. She was lonely, she was beyond vulnerable and in that moment she didn't care. She encircled him in her arms and held him there tightly. At first he didn't know how to react, he'd never been so close to human before, not since he'd been changed in the war before. At first he felt he needed to push her away, she was too delicate for him, he feared he would destroy her if she stayed so close. But in that moment he didn't care either. He kept in mind his abnormal strength as he held her, he could not hurt her.

It did not take long after that for Mollie to fall in love with him. He taught her how to laugh again, something she thought she'd never get back after Henry died. He held her like she would break in his hands, he looked at her like she was the only woman in the world, and he kissed her like he could never let her go. After two months he could wait no longer.

"I love you, you know." he said one day as they walked hand in hand down a street in Venice.

"I know." she said her eyes focused downward. He thought perhaps that was all she would say, disappointment ran through him quickly. But she was no finished. Emotion caught in her voice as she said, "I love you too. I didn't think that would possible after my husband died, but I do." He stopped her then and turned her toward him and held her gently in his arms. "And I just dream of being with you for forever." she said, her voice muffled in his thick wool jacket.

"Is that what you would really want? Me forever?" he asked, hoping for her to give him one particular answer.

"Yes, I do." she said, a smile growing on her face as she said it.

"What if I told you we could have forever, are you saying you'd really want it?" he asked, if his heart still beat it would have been racing.

She looked up at him and nodded. "Yes I would."

He smiled back and took her by the hand and led her quickly through the back alleys of Venice, she was confused but continued to follow. They were back, in what seemed like no time at all, at Samuel's hotel. "Come inside." he urged. She trusted him so she followed. When they were safely inside he smiled and said, "Just remember that I love you." She furrowed her brow but did not speak, even though she was growing afraid. His put his hands on her cheeks and smiled, absorbing their warmth one final time. Then in a moment that was too fast for her to see he changed to the predator inside him and thrust his fangs into her throat.

She awoke later a new person, she could feel it. Everything was wrong. Her eyes moved quickly around the room, so fast that it normally would have made her dizzy, but no such effect now. She found Samuel on the other side of the room staring at her. "Don't be afraid love." he urged softly.

"What have you done to me?" she demanded, her voice so different as it left her mouth.

"I know I should have told you about this sooner Mollie, but I didn't want to scare you." he said, smiling. The smile repulsed her.

"What are you?" she said, her voice frantic and frightened.

He saw no need to beat around the bush. "I'm a vampire." he said simply, holding her gaze.

She was quiet, her eyes wide with terror. She thought back over everything, everything they had been through and tried to find some clue she missed to prove this. Everything settled back on the day she had met him and all thoughts led back to Jimmy Philips. She gasped aloud, shocked at the lack of relief the action gave her and said, "You killed him."

Because he could read her mind he knew instantly who she meant. "Yes." he said, his eyes focused downward.

"Why would you do this to me?" she demanded, a sob lost in her voice.

His head snapped up and he said, "I thought you wanted to be with me forever."

"As in a lifetime." she said, repulsed by him now and he could feel the change. "How could you think I meant this?" *Monster! Monster! Monster!* she thought in her head.

He moved back to the other corner of the room. "I thought you'd be happy. I thought this would be what you'd want." he said, sadness in his voice.

"I want you to get away from me, and I never want to see you again." she commanded, as if she were the creator here.

It broke his heart to hear her say such things and as her creator he could have refused, but he didn't want to cause her anymore pain. He left her alone in the room and called Them for help. Luckily the American prowler was in Italy tracking one of the rogue creators, she would take her. And Mollie stayed with Ivy from that time on.

Ivy. Grace thought from the other side of the door.

The thought nearly startled Ivy out of her deep, dreamless sleep. "Come in Grace." she said aloud.

The child entered sheepishly, she knew how Ivy hated to be disturbed. "I'm sorry to disturb you Ivy."

"Not a problem Gracie, come on in." Ivy said sitting up on her bed. She glanced out the window, she slept longer than she normally would, the sun was going down. "What can I do for you?"

"Well," Grace said sitting on the edge of the bed. "I know how important everything is tomorrow and I know that you'll probably need me here all day to help and I really shouldn't be asking for this at all but-" she paused for a minute to look into Ivy's eyes, who was patiently waiting. "I have an exam tomorrow morning that I really don't want to miss but you can tell me I have to and I totally will."

"Sh," Ivy said placing her hand atop Grace's. "You will go and take your test tomorrow. Just come back right after, I don't want any of our lives to change, we will continue the way we always do." She smiled at the girl who seemed elated by her answer. Grace was by far the youngest of the group, having only been changed at the age of sixteen so she attended college in every place they lived. Unfortunately for her she could never pass for old enough to attend grad school, but she had racked up many bachelor's degrees.

Grace threw her arms around Ivy's neck and said, "Thank you so much Ivy."

"You're welcome dear." Ivy said returning the embrace.

"Leo man can I ask you something?" Casper asked him, his voice breathy and absent.

"What's up?" Leo asked, stretching his arms above his head.

"I don't want to sound pushy or anything, but um I'm really hungry." he said with a sigh.

Leo sat up quickly and said, "Oh, didn't think about that. I'll be back in a minute." *Family meeting downstairs.* he thought to everyone else.

"Ok," Casper said, flummoxed only slightly by his quick exit, he was beginning to grow accustomed to their flightiness.

All six vampires gathered around the dining room table. "What's the big emergency Leo?" Mollie asked as she walked in the door, back from her shift. She placed two huge bags in the refrigerator, the only part of the kitchen they ever used.

"There is something we overlooked with having the human here." he said with a sigh, how could he ever forgotten something so obvious?

"What?" Ivy asked.

"We have to feed him." Leo said.

A hush settled around the room as if each of them was too only realizing this for the first time. "Well who can cook?" Peter asked.

All eyes started with Ivy, as the mother figure of the group they all assumed she could cook. "Please," she said with a chuckle. "I had servants to cook for me my entire life, I'm out."

They then turned to Leo, being the youngest of the group

they assumed he would have to at least have some experience. He laughed out loud. "Only if going to Taco Bell counts as cooking."

Finally Mollie sighed and said, "I can cook for the human." For some reason they had all forgotten about her. "What? I was a 1940's housewife of course I can cook, it's just been a while."

"Perhaps you could take Casper grocery shopping with you, that way you know what he likes." Leo suggested happily.

Idiot! Peter thought. "Yea let's allow the human to leave, what so he can run away from Mollie once he's out of here."

"He won't run," Leo said, holding his ground strongly. "I trust him."

Naïve child. Peter chided in his head. *How stupid can you be?*

"Stop that!" Ivy bellowed. "I will not allow one human to break up my family. You will act civilized or be punished." *Do I make myself clear Peter?*

Crystal. Peter thought curtly, his stare cold and angry.

Ivy turned to the rest of her family and said, "Mollie you will take the human out, but I will talk to him first."

"Ivy!" Peter protested, jumping out of his chair.

"That's final Peter." she said, her voice a curt as his had been. She rose from her seat at the head of the table and scaled the stairs quickly.

She gently pushed the door open and there he sat, she knew it was because he was hungry but the paleness of his skin scared her for a moment, almost as if he had somehow become one of them. "Something wrong Ivy?" he asked her.

"No," she said pulling herself back to reality. She moved in her graceful matter toward him and sat in the chair beside him. "I'm not sure yet if I can trust you. Leo assures me that I can, but I am still on the fence about it."

"You can." he said simply, looking down at his hands. "I would never tell anyone about you. I'm too fascinated to ever do that."

She ignored his latter comment for another time. "Well I'm going to give you a chance to earn that trust." He was quiet, beckoning her on. "We don't eat, I'm sure you know that, but we also don't ever entertain humans here so there is no food. Mollie is the only one with any real experience cooking so she'll take you out and go shopping."

"Ok." Casper said, trying to find the test of loyalty in this task.

Ivy moved much closer to his face and said, "If you try to flee from her I promise you that I will personally take it upon myself to track you down and take you out all on my own, I won't need Them to help me. Do you understand?"

That was it? He had to stay with the vampire and not try to flee? He could do that. "Absolutely."

"Do not betray me, you will regret it." Ivy said, her voice strong and cold, but as he examined her face further she truly looked like a lion cub trying to be tough, he did understand that she really was the full grown lion, but she still looked liked the cub. He smiled. "What's funny? I like a good laugh." she said, her face still close to his.

"Nothing." he said quickly retreating his smile.

She smiled slightly and said, "Mollie's waiting for you

downstairs." She arose from her knees with barely a move and was out of the room and down the stairs before he could even stand up.

"Aren't you coming." Mollie said suddenly from the door, her voice only slightly impatient, but he appreciated that she was trying to hide it. He looked her over once, he had not really had the time yet to examine them all. She was much curvier than the other woman, but also much taller. She had long brown hair that a wave to it, it looked like a river running down her back. He looked up at her face. It was rounder than Grace or Ivy's, but it was perfectly proportioned, they were all perfect. Her unnaturally red lips were full and her eyes were actually violet. "Well come on then," she said. "I don't have all day."

He popped up as quick as he could, but she still beat him out the door. "Damn it." he muttered to himself.

He met her in the garage, it was incredible! It must have housed thirteen cars, how had he not noticed it before. She opened the driver's door of a red 1965 mustang convertible. He stood by and gawked at it, mouth wide open. "What's the problem?" Mollie asked with a sigh, ready to drive.

"This is the most beautiful thing I've ever seen." he said, almost with a tear in his eye. "How do you guys afford all this? There must be a million dollars worth of cars in here."

Mollie laughed, she was shaking she was laughing so hard. "I guess we don't think about it anymore. When you have a seer, like Alex, it's easy to predict changes in the economic market. It's quite possible we're the richest family in the world." She climbed into the car and turned back and said, "Oh and this is just what we have at this house."

"You have more than one house?" Casper said getting in the car next to her.

"Yea, I think at last count we have seventy-two." she said pulling out of the garage and zipping down the long driveway.

"Seventy-two! Why so many?" he asked, twisting in his seat to see her fully.

"Well we can't stay in one place forever. Since we live among people they would notice the fact that we never get older. So every ten years we pick up and move. We leave the house the same and a few decades later we'll come back."

"That sounds miserable." Casper said with a concerned look on his face.

"Yea," she said, her eyes focused forwarded. "I wish we didn't use this house, but it's big enough for all of us." She could tell from his gaze that he wanted her to explain further. She sighed and said, "This is the house my husband built for me."

"Oh," he said turning back forward in his seat, he hadn't meant to pry.

"It was a long time ago." she said zipping around sharp corners as if they were nothing at all. "Ivy did the hard part."

"What do you mean?" he asked, folding his arms across his chest, the chilly night air beginning to take its effect.

"Well, I was working as a nurse overseas in World War II when I was changed and of course I was handed over to Ivy because I was an American rogue. The army of course sent my family notice that I was missing and after a while presumed dead. Ivy bought the house, but my sister wouldn't give up so easy. She came by every day demanding that Ivy sell it to her, she said she just couldn't lose that last bit of her sister. I can remember sitting inside the door, Alex usually holding my hand as I heard her beg. Ivy was stronger than anyone as she apologized for my sister's loss but insisted that Irma not come back or else she would have to involve the authorities. It's not like she could have let in her in the house, not with me sitting inside the door." Her grip on steering wheel increasing. He sat patiently, not wanting to interrupt her thoughts. "And the worst part of all of it was in the beginning she smelled so good to me. It took all of them to hold me down, against my own sister."

"It wasn't your fault. Instinct is all." he said trying to console her.

She smiled and shook her head. "Thanks, I wish that made it better."

Suddenly she put the car into park, they were already there. He looked around the parking lot. "How did we get her so fast?" he questioned.

"Um, I'm a fast driver." she said with a smile, he didn't need to know she never dropped from ninety miles an hour the entire trip.

She grabbed a cart and smiled, it brought back good memories from her human life. She loved to cook for Henry. "So what do you like?"

"I don't know, do you have anything you prefer to cook?" Casper asked, trying to be polite.

She smiled and started tossing things into the cart. "I can help you know, with the cooking." Casper said, he ran a hand through his hair and said, "My girlfriend was never much of a chef, so I have a little experience in the kitchen."

"That'd be great." Mollie said with a smile. "I am a little out of practice."

They walked silently through the grocery store, grabbing this and that. People would stop and stare at them, at Mollie, she was so shockingly beautiful it did not surprise him that they stared, but she didn't seem to notice. Living among people this way for so long she must have become accustomed to it.

There was a question he had been wanted to ask her, but had put it off, it was rather personal. "I have a question." he said shoving his hands in his pockets.

"Shoot, it's not like we have any secrets now." Mollie said grabbing one of the last things they would need.

He waited until the elderly woman in the aisle turned the corner. "I know you're a doctor, how do you handle that? All the blood. I mean I assume you didn't always work in the morgue."

She sighed aloud. "No, I was a surgeon in the sixties and seventies actually, but we were still relying on both blood from the source and purchased blood at that time. I switched to the morgue when Ivy opted for blood from the source, taking it from the morgue was just easier, no questions asked. But as far as the before then is concerned Ivy is phenomenal teacher. She taught us such control, more than any other vamp I've ever met. I'm not saying it wasn't hard to control, especially when I did one of my residencies as an E.R. doc. But you learn to deal with it." she said getting in line with the full grocery cart.

"Wow, you sure are stronger than I ever could be." he said with a shake of his head.

She smiled and leaned in to whisper in his ear, "You don't

know your own strength until it's tested. You've stayed rather calm in a house of vampires who have not tasted blood straight from a human in over thirty years. Trust me, that's strength in itself."

"Thank you Mollie." he said with a smile. He looked down at the full cart and said, "Is there something that I can contribute to this? I feel bad having you pay for it all."

She tousled a hand through his hair and held up a platinum credit card. "Our food bill has been shockingly small the last few years, I think it's ok." He smiled and helped her put the items up on the belt, she was shockingly faster than he was. She glanced up at him a few times and then finally had to ask, "How old are you Casper?"

"Twenty-five." he said, his eyes still focused down on the cart.

"Really," she said looking at him curiously. She had been frozen at the age of twenty-two for so long she had begun to lose track of how humans aged. She looked him up and down and would have thought him much older, if for no other reason than the fact that his curly hair was almost completely gray.

"Let me guess, the locks of glory on my head threw you off?" he said running his hand threw them again.

"Yea, I would have pegged you for much older." Mollie said handing the young cashier her credit card, the young man's hand shook as she smiled at him.

"Family curse I'm afraid, my dad went entirely gray at sixteen, but still has all his hair so that's a plus."

"Could you sign here Ms. Lyons?" the very nervous cashier asked handing Mollie the receipt and pen, his hands shaking again.

She smiled and tried to ignore the sound of his increased heartbeat. She returned her card to her purse and handed the receipt back to the young man.

They pushed the cart out to the parking lot and he said, "You're a Lyons too? I thought that was just Ivy." he said as he started to fill the back seat of the Mustang with the bags.

"Well we've always found it easier to just live as a family, that is in essence what we consider ourselves to be anyway. I think we've come down to the conclusion that we're all cousins, except for Alex and Gracie we say they're brother and sister. No one really questions a family, if we were just a group living together trust me people would question, I know this because they have." she said placing the last set of groceries in the car.

They got in the car and drove back, at this point he was completely shivering. She glanced over at him and said, "Oh I'm sorry, do you want me to put the top up? I'm sorry I don't get cold."

"No I'm good, really." he said crossing his arms and trying to keep his teeth from chattering, knowing she could hear it anyway. He glanced around as the scenery zipped by and remembered how quickly they had gotten to the store. He glanced over at the speedometer and his eyes grew huge. "Holy Pete! Slow down Mollie!"

"What's the matter?" she asked, laughing aloud.

"You're driving over a hundred miles an hour!" he shouted, checking his seatbelt to make sure it was locked in place.

"Don't worry, I've never been in a car accident or gotten a ticket. My reflexes are a lot faster than yours, trust nothing bad will happen to you." she said, laughing again.

"What's so funny to you?" he demanded, his knuckles white as he clutched onto the sides of his seat.

"I just find it funny that staying in a house with six thirsty vampires doesn't scare you at all but driving with the vehicle expert in the family scares you to death." she said laughing again. "Come on man I already turned the lights on so that I wouldn't scare you completely."

"You drive with your lights off?" he said, his saucer eyes bearing down on her.

"Yea, it makes it easier to avoid the police." she said pulling into the driveway of the house. "Home safe and sound, just like I promised you." He sat quietly in the car, his hands still clutching the side of the seat as she pulled into the garage and got out of the car. On her own she picked up all bags and went for the door. "Come in whenever you're ready." she said to him with a laugh.

She heaved all the bags onto the spacious kitchen counter and began to unload them.

"Where's Casper?" Ivy asked joining her in the kitchen.

Mollie was still laughing. "He's petrified in the garage. We have a new statue!"

"I have no idea what you're talking about." Ivy said shifting her wait from one side to the other.

Just then Leo came in the room laughing as well. "Come on Ivy, what she means is that Speed Racer here drove like a maniac and scared the crap out of the poor kid."

Ivy sighed, it really shouldn't have surprised her, Mollie would be a drag racer if Ivy would allow it. "Leo darling," Ivy said turning to him. "Could you please retrieve our guest from Mollie's car?"

"My pleasure." Leo said with a bow, holding his sides trying not to laugh.

"Was that totally necessary?" Ivy asked turning to Mollie, trying to suppress a laugh of her own.

"Ha-ha I enjoyed it." Mollie said making room in fridge.

"Dear god woman think you got enough food?" Ivy said examining the spread before her.

"I wasn't sure how long he'd be with us-" she began and then turned and really looked at all the food she realized it was a bit overkill. "Ok so I went a bit food crazy."

"Just a bit." Ivy said with a laugh as the door leading to garage opened. All eyes turned to see Casper flung over Leo's shoulder.

"What the hell happened?" Ivy demanded rushing to his side. "Put him down in the chair."

"He's fine, you can all hear his heartbeat. He just passed out." Leo said putting Casper down in the chair.

Ivy crouched down in front of him and put her hands on his face. "Casper, Casper," she said, rubbing her thumb back and forth across his cheek. He was attractive enough for a human. He had a light set of freckles across his nose and cheekbones, she hadn't noticed that before. She gently tapped her hand against his cheek and said his name again, "Casper."

One eye at a time he woke up. He glanced around and said, "I don't want to drive with her again." He pointed across the room at Mollie.

Ivy laughed and said, "Glad to see you're all right."

"Fine." he said, absorbing her beauty from such a close angle, it was nearly overwhelming.

And for a long moment they stayed like, her hands still upon his cheeks and their faces close together. It was Alex's voice in her head that broke the moment, *Family meeting in the dining room.*

Chapter Six

"What's the problem?" Ivy asked as they all piled into the dining room. Casper of course had no idea what was going on but he was welcomed into the meeting this time around.

"I don't know if it's really a problem." Alex said with a smile. "We should be getting a call any minute from Them."

"Why?" Grace asked taking a seat next to him.

"I can't get a clear view of the exact why, but it looks like there's some problem in The Main City so if I'm right they'll be delayed about a week."

"Main City?" Casper asked.

"Um," Ivy began. "One of those places that can only be found by those who already know where it is. It's kind of like our center of operations."

Just as the final words left her mouth the phone on the table began to ring. "Peter, can you get it?" Ivy requested, taking a step back from the table. Just the chance that it could be Rudolph on the other end was too much for her to risk.

He knew her reasons and picked up the phone for her. "Hello," he said. *It's Angelo*, he thought setting off a sigh of relief for Ivy. "All right, we will see you then." He clicked the phone shut and turned to his family. "The seer is apparently good for something."

"Ha-ha you're hilarious." Alex said with a roll of his eyes.

"Alex was right?" Ivy asked, trying hard not to show her surprise.

"Yea Alex was right, big shocker." Alex said with a shake of his head.

"You know I didn't mean it like that." Ivy said to Alex. *I didn't,* she reassured.

I know. Alex thought and smiled.

"Anyway," Peter said, pulling the attention back to him. "Angelo said it'll be at least a week before they can get here and we need to wait."

Ivy sighed and said, "Well Casper it looks like you'll be with us for a while."

"If it means I can put off being killed by your creator I'm quite ok with that." he said with a smile.

Mollie narrowed her eyes and said, "I don't get it, you say something like that and you smile but you passed out because I drove a little fast?"

"You passed out?" Grace said with a laugh. "I guess I can understand that, she does drive like a crazy person."

"I am a fantastic driver, I just drive fast." Mollie said defending herself.

"Anyway," Ivy said glancing around at her boys. "I don't think any of the guys clothes will fit you. We could probably go shopping again tomorrow-"

"Or you could just take me to my apartment." Casper interrupted. All eyes in the room turned to him and were silent for a minute.

"That could work." Leo said with a shrug.

"No that could not work!" Peter yelped back. "Seriously am I the only one with a brain here? I think it was a stupid idea to let the human leave with Mollie in the first place, now you want to send him home?"

"Not to stay, I can just get some of my stuff. I don't want to put you all out anymore, I've already put you through enough."

"Well that's for damn sure." Peter said, his tone filled with its usual sarcasm and gruff. "But we can't very well let him go alone and I for one have to work."

"I'll take him." Ivy said with a smug smile flickering across her face. Everyone's eyes moved from Peter to Ivy and back. "I mean I work from here. I'll handle it. Does that solve your problem for you?"

"Whatever you want to do Ivy, you're the boss." Peter said with a roll of his eyes, leaning back against his chair.

"That's right sweetheart, I am the boss." Ivy said. The room was silent, and the tension grew so thick it was almost visible in the room.

"Anyone else find it ironic that you, a family of vampires, hold all your meetings in a dining room?" Casper asked, hoping to break the tension, and for a moment he feared it had backfired, none of them even changed expressions, just stared at him. Finally Ivy started to laugh and laughed hard, slowly the others joined in, even Peter cracked a smile.

"Oh, thank you for that Casper." Ivy said, her laugh beginning to subside. "And tomorrow morning you and I will go to your apartment. For now, everyone get some rest, it has been a long day."

"Come with me Casper, I'll get you something to eat." Mollie said with a smile. Once in the kitchen she said, "I'm rather tired, think we can do something simple tonight?"

"Fine with me." Casper said peering through the hoards of

food that they had bought. "I think we might have gone a little overboard."

"Yea, but it's ok." she said with a smile. She pulled out a few things and began mixing in a bowl. Absently a smile grew across her face as she cooked.

"You really like this kind of stuff don't you?" Casper asked heating the oven.

"Yea," she said, making no attempt to hide her smile. "Some of the greatest times of my life were in this kitchen. Cooking Thanksgiving dinner for my family or just dinner for my husband and I. I love this kitchen, I miss this."

He nudged her with his elbow. "Well I guess it's good I'm here then, gives you a chance to do what you like."

"Way to find the silver lining of the situation." she said sliding a perfect omelet off the skillet onto a plate. "Here you go." she said handing it to him with a fork.

"Thanks." he said taking it happily from her, he had forgotten for a moment how hungry he was. He was finding it harder and harder now to remember what they were and that at any moment, if he were to do something as simple as get a paper cut, they could kill him. The more time he spent there the more he forgot that and seeing the smile on Mollie's face just from cooking him eggs made it even harder.

Later that night Ivy heard a lot commotion coming from the living room. "What's going on?" she asked as she passed Alex in the hall on his way to the living room.

"Come and see." he said with a smile.

In the living room there was a chess board set up. Chess games were always to the death with the family. It was very difficult, because having a strategy was hard, especially when your opponent knows your next move as you think of it. Grace had always been the champion at the game, no one could ever beat her. But now she had new companion and she could not read his mind.

"You're going to play Casper?" Ivy asked Grace as she set up the super board (four boards put together).

"Yes I am." Grace said setting up the pieces.

"Why?" Nora asked, she had decided to stay that night.

"She wants to prove she's not a big cheat." Alex said jumping up on the hutch behind Casper.

"Get off that, Mollie's husband built that." Ivy commanded.

Alex rolled his eyes, "Yes mom." he muttered and jumped off. Leo sat behind Grace, ready to watch. Chess had never been Leo's strong suit, and Grace never had a problem taking him down, no surprise that he would be rooting for Casper.

"Ready?" Grace asked with a smile, her hands under her chin, she didn't need them to play.

"Born ready." Casper said, returning the smile. Grace held her smile and moved her first piece with her mind. "Show off." Casper muttered, Grace heard it of course and snickered to herself, she'd enjoy this. And then it was like lighting the pieces moving so fast, back and forth like a tennis match. Grace's forehead became creased, she was overly focused, while Casper remained calm. It went on for twenty more minutes, the other four gathered round the table watching intently. Finally Casper got a smile, the most perfect of smiles. He raised his eyes to Grace's and made a final move and then the word that Grace never thought she'd hear against her came out of his mouth. "Checkmate." It was over, he had beaten her.

"How-how did you do that?" Grace said angrily, examining the board for her mistake.

"Oh I was the state chess champion three times in high school, did I forget to mention that?" he asked with a smile.

"You hustled me!" Grace shouted back.

"No, no," Casper said with a laugh he tried to suppress, he was still playing against a vampire after all. "If I was hustling you there would have been money involved. I just beat you."

"Finally!" Leo shouted, his hands in the air. "I knew you were a cheat."

"I am not a cheat!" she grumbled under her breath, her teeth gnawing together.

"Cheater, cheater, pumpkin eater!" he sang out.

Suddenly she switched to predator mode and lunged at her brother. Leo retaliated in predator style. This was dangerous, Ivy knew neither had eaten all day, and the human was very close. *Nora, take Casper upstairs please.* Ivy thought. Nora nodded and grabbed Casper by the arm, taking him upstairs. Casper went quietly, he was learning not to ask questions, he figured there had been a conversation he hadn't heard, in their heads.

Ivy switched to predator mode and jumped between the two. "Pull back, now!"

Leo was playing, but Grace was angry. Grace was who she was worried about. "Back off Grace." Leo began to get the vibe now, he switched back to normal.

"Gracie, calm down." Leo said, trying to comfort his sister.

"I am no cheat." Grace said, her fangs bared.

"We know that." Ivy said, in her most soothing voice, but she stayed in predator mode, she needed to be ready if Grace lost it. "I need you to back off."

"I'm really sorry if I hurt you feeling sis," Leo said, his voice genuine. "I didn't mean to. I love you, you know?"

Grace's eyes softened and she said, "I know."

"Ok, ok good." Ivy said with a deep breath. "Go into the kitchen and have a drink, I think you could both use it."

Leo smiled and said, "Come here squirt."

She smiled and jumped on his back, they really were like brother and sister.

Ivy went upstairs to relieve Nora and Casper. "Disaster averted." she said with a sigh once she was in the guest room.

"Should I have let her win?" Casper asked, feeling terrible about causing tension in their family.

"Of course not, Grace is just a bad loser apparently." Ivy said with a smile. "I sent them to get something to drink, I think they needed it."

"Mind if I join them?" Nora asked. "I haven't had the time today." *Which is making the human smell even better.* she added in her head.

"Sure, go ahead, please." Ivy said, urging her former rogue to go. Once she was gone she turned back to Casper and said, "That was pretty incredible down there. Grace has been with me for over a hundred years and we've had a lot rogues come through here and no one has ever beaten her."

"Well, thanks. Chess was kind of the safe thing when I was growing up." he said with a smile.

"What do you mean?" she asked.

He paused for a minute, not sure if he wanted to tell her, but she had told him about her husband, he felt the need to share something from his past with her. "My dad was a drunk and not a good drunk. He lost every job he ever had, which is why I started writing so young. I published my first book when I was sixteen just to pay the heating bill." He looked up at her, but she was waiting patiently for him to finish. "He used to beat her, my mom, so badly. If she didn't make something he wanted for dinner a certain way, or he didn't think the house was clean enough, he'd beat the hell out of her. So I did everything I could to make him come after me instead. And what sucks the worst is it wasn't always like that. He didn't always drink or hit us."

"What made him start?" she asked, they seemed to have no secrets now.

He was quiet for minute and she just waited. "I had an older brother. He was murdered when I was ten, he was only seventeen years old. My dad just couldn't take it." He glanced up and she had a hand to her mouth, waiting, she wouldn't interrupt him now. "I'm sure you're wondering how chess factors in?" he said with a laugh. "Um, when he was sober, which wasn't often, but when he was he would play with me. He taught me and Zach, my brother, from a very young age how to play and I always knew later when I would come home from school that he was sober because the chess board would be set up on the kitchen table. We didn't speak while we played, but they're by far the best memories I'll ever have with them."

"I'm sorry about your brother, Zach did you say?" she asked, glancing over her hands at him.

"Yea, Zachary Lennox." he said. "It was a long time ago, I don't really dwell on it anymore."

"And your parents, do you still see them?" she asked.

He shook his head slowly. "No, when I was twenty I tried to convince my mom to leave him, that we could go, I'd saved enough money that we could go away and leave him."

"But she wouldn't go?" Ivy asked.

He shook his head. "No she wouldn't. She said that she loved him and that she couldn't leave him. So I left, I couldn't stay there and watch him slowly kill himself and her. I used to send her money, but I knew she was giving it to him, so I stopped. She still sends me a birthday and Christmas card and the occasional letter, but I haven't seen her in about five years. And I could probably go the rest of my life without seeing my father again."

"I'm sorry." she said looking out the window and away from him. "I can vaguely remember after my mother died how miserable my father was. He started gambling and it changed him, so I guess I understand where you're coming from. My father didn't hit me, so that I can't understand, but he did marry me to an abusive man so he could keep his honor."

"Well I guess you get to join the shitty father's club, we have jackets." he said with a smile. She laughed, a tear in her eye. The moment was sweet and perfect, something they could share even though they were hundreds of years apart.

He did not sleep soundly, even though he was on a very plush bed. He couldn't clear his head enough to sleep for long increments. The time alone gave him the opportunity to really think about his current situation. He worried what would happen when They came. Would they let him go? He doubted that. Would they kill him? Make him one of them? He didn't know, but for some reason he couldn't bring himself to worry just then about it. That alone frightened him. He also figured the lack of sleep could be linked to the fact that he worried that at any minute Peter would come in and kill him just to save the family some trouble. He didn't like Peter, that was for sure, but he could see that he truly loved his family and would do anything to save them. That did not mean however that he was not afraid that he would kill him, Casper was far from family.

The next morning when he awoke the house was silent, almost eerie. He wandered down the stairs to the kitchen, his clothes wrinkled and worn, he'd be happy to get some clean ones. He walked down to the kitchen where Grace was standing by the counter drinking from a coffee cup and reading the morning paper. She glanced up and said, "Good morning Casper."

"Good morning." he said back, stretching his arms up and out over his head. "What are you drinking?" he asked, motioning to her cup.

She just stared at him for a moment and said, "I'll give you three guesses but I hope you'll only need one."

"Yea stupid question." Casper said with a laugh, running a hand through his hair uncomfortably.

She lifted her hand and drew a line in the air with her finger, the refrigerator opened. "Mollie made something for you before she left." She slowly drew her fingers in toward her and a plate floated out from inside. He grabbed it.

"Thanks." he said peering down at the plate. "That's a pretty great power you've got there."

"It's nice, it's made me kind of lazy though, never really have to do anything physical for myself." she said pulling another vial of blood over to her. "I've got three classes today in rooms full of humans, I always liked to be prepared on these days." She tipped the midair vial over and the contents fell into her cup. "It was hard to control at first, but I've had a lot of time to focus it."

"How long exactly?" Casper asked taking a bite of the dish Mollie had made him. Berries! Very good.

"I was changed in 1907, you do the math." she said with a smile.

"Do you hate it? Being a vampire I mean?" Casper asked taking another bite.

She shrugged. "That's hard to answer. I hate a lot of what we are, we're the monsters from childhood stories, I can't say I love that. However, I could not be happier with what it has done for me."

"What do you mean?"

"Well, I came from pretty bad circumstances before I was a vampire and now I have twenty-five college degrees, trust me in that sense I'm beyond grateful to be a vampire."

"What kind of circumstances?" he asked taking the final bite. She bowed her head and he realized he may have crossed a line. "I'm sorry I didn't mean to pry."

"I just don't want you to judge me." she said, wringing her

hands together.

He placed a hand atop hers and said, "Never."

She smiled a little, only a little and sighed. "I always knew I was different. When I was a child, I'd get angry the room would shake, I guess that's where my ability first came from.

"I was living in Omaha, Nebraska when it happened. I-I was working with my mother, for her actually, in her brothel." She glanced up at him to see his repulsion, he had none. "I didn't want to do it, but it was what my mother told me I had to do so I did. I was only twelve when I started. The first few times I cried through it, all the girls did. Then became cold to it, I was just a whore, my body a machine and I let the whole process become robotic to me. I was disgusted with myself, but it's what I was.

"Then one day a man came into town and came to our house. He was unnaturally beautiful and the way he looked at us was like we were food-" she laughed humorlessly at that. "All the others were so scared of him and none would go with him. So who does my mother volunteer? Of course it was me.

"She told me to stop complaining when I said I was afraid of him. She called me a baby and told me to 'get upstairs and do it already'. Motherly love right? He was waiting for me when I got there, the smile he gave me with such perfect teeth frightened me further, but I did my best to brush it off. I went and did what I had to, he didn't say anything while I did and when it was done I waited for him leave, they always just leave, but he wasn't done. He looked me over a moment, my exposed naked body and I felt more filthy than I ever had. And then something happened to him, his eyes changed and before I could understand what was happening he bit me and drained me, unlike his other victims he decided that I was pretty enough to be his mate. So he changed me. Only he didn't realize how much work a newborn would be, so just like that he left me. He left me alone."

"What happened? How did you end up here?" Casper asked, his head balancing on his hand.

"One of Ivy's former rogues, Patricia-Jane or as she's called now PJ, found me and kept me alive until Ivy could come and get me." she said her hands folded in her lap.

"I'm sorry that happened to you." Casper said, unable to find words to truly show his feelings.

She shrugged and let her cup glide on air to the sink, she turned the faucet on from across the room and rinsed the cup. "I try not to think about it much, it's done and this is my life now."

"What was his name? The one who changed you?"

She closed her eyes and breathed the name, she had not said it in a long time, "Felix." she shook her head and said, "Thank god for Ivy though, I don't know what would have happened to me without her."

"She seems like a pretty amazing woman." he said glancing down at his hands.

"She truly is." Grace said, glancing down as well.

"Do you know what happened between her and Rudolph?" he asked, hoping maybe to get an answer this time.

Grace shook her head. "No, that's not one she shares."

"That's what Leo said, what I can't understand is if you can read each other's minds then why don't you all know about it."

She sighed, trying to gather her thoughts. "Let's see if I can explain this to you. We have three levels of thought, the best way I can explain it to you is to divide them in colors. White thoughts are the little everyday things you think, anything you'd freely say aloud. All of those we can hear. Then there are gray thoughts, those come in grainy to us, they're things you might be embarrassed to admit but you end up talking about them even if you change some of the details, but we can't hear those anywhere near as clearly as the white thoughts. And then, there are black thoughts. Black thoughts are the most private and usually, no pun intended here, darkest thoughts you have. Things you would never tell a soul. Those thoughts we can't hear at all. The memory of whatever happened between Ivy and Rudolph is a black thought. And we also in our family have a mutual respect to stay out of each other's minds as much as possible."

"Gracie," a voice suddenly said from behind. Ivy. "Doesn't your class start in about twenty minutes?"

"Damn it!" Grace said jumping up from her seat and running at a nearly invisible speed to get her things and go out the door.

"Ready?" Ivy asked, turning back to Casper after watching Grace leave.

"Yea," he said grabbing his jacket off the back of his chair. "Want to take my car?" he asked trying to be gracious.

She tried to hold back her snicker, but she failed at it. "No I think we'll take mine." They walked into the massive garage and she pulled out the key for a Bentley and it led them to a Bentley Azure.

"Oh my goodness," he said, a hand to his mouth. "It's more beautiful than the mustang."

"My little toy." she said with a smile.

"Nice toy." he said with a frown as he got in the passenger seat. "Why don't I have toys this good?"

"You haven't had five hundred years to gather a bank roll." she said with a smile. She pushed the button to put the top down. "It's a nice day today, is the top down ok for you?"

"Yea it's fine for me, but it doesn't bother you at all?" Casper asked, he had been curious about this for a while now.

"Do you mean will I burst into flames?" she asked with a laugh, pulling her sunglasses on her face.

"Well yea, I guess so." Casper said clicking his seatbelt, hoping not to have a repeat of the events of the day before.

"Total myth, about the flames." she said with a smile, tying her red hair in a ponytail. "Too much will make us really sick, but other than that no effect from the sun."

"What about silver?"

"Nope," she said with a smile.

"Garlic or crosses?" he asked.

"Nothing, and some of us are very religious." she said.

"Mirrors?"

"Completely visible in them." she said.

"Holy water?" he asked grasping at any final straws.

"Just gets us wet." she said smiling again.

"Wow, you just devastated everything I ever knew about vampires. You do still drink blood right?" he asked with a grimace.

"Yes, we do still drink blood. And as far as everything you know about vampires, who do you think came up with the myths?" she asked.

"You?" he asked.

She laughed, "Well not me specifically, but vampires."

"Why?" he asked.

"Think about it Casper, if we create a bunch of lies like vampires can't be seen in mirrors or if you splash holy water on us we'll burn to the ground then it's much easier for us to defend ourselves against allegations of being vampires."

"That makes sense." he said nodding his head, running his hand through his gray hair.

"Are you really only twenty-five?" she asked as she watched him run a hand through his salt and pepper hair.

"Yea, I know it's deceiving but I swear it be the truth." he said with a smile. He looked out the window and realized that they were at his building. "That was fast, are you a crazy driver too?"

"Yea, I can just distract you better from it." she said with a laugh. "Mind if I come in with you? The sun's becoming a little much for me."

"Sure, come on in." he said getting out of the car, pulling his keys out of his pocket. Thoughts began to run through his mind, had he cleaned, had he done the dishes? After staying at a home as beautiful and regal as hers he felt embarrassed by his, he didn't want to be embarrassed in front of her.

They climbed the stairs, well he climbed, she seemed to float and got to his apartment. "Do you have a roommate?" she asked when they were at the door.

"No, why?" he asked putting his key in the door.

She put her hand on his to stop him. "There's another heartbeat inside." They both stared at the door for a moment. He pushed the door open for her and looked back at her, she wasn't moving. "What's the problem?"

"You're going to laugh at me." she said, scratching the back of her neck nervously.

"I wouldn't dare." he said with a smile.

She laughed a little and said, "You have to invite me in."

"Really? That one's true?" he asked.

"The pope feared us back in the thirteenth century and made an agreement with god that we would not be exposed for what we are as long as we stayed out of homes we weren't invited to." she said with a shrug. "It sounds silly, but I can't come in unless you invite me in."

He smiled and said, "Well won't you come in?"

"Thanks." she said walking through the door. They had both almost forgotten about the other heartbeat inside. His smiled faded once they were inside and he saw the owner of the unknown heartbeat, it was Gloria.

"Hi." she said softly, her hands folded in front of her. Her eyes quickly jumped to Ivy. "Who's this?" she demanded.

Casper rolled his eyes and said, "Gloria this is Ivy, Ivy this is my ex-girlfriend Gloria."

"Hi." Ivy said, her voice filled with more music than normal.

"Yea," Gloria said trying to keep her cool. "Can we talk?" she asked turning back to Casper.

"Ivy, my room's in the back, can you wait for me there?" he asked.

"Yea." she said pushing her hands into her pockets and moved to the back of the apartment.

"What are you doing here?" he demanded. "You shouldn't be here."

"I made a mistake Casper, haven't you ever made a mistake?" she asked, her voice almost pleading.

"I can't do this now, you have to leave." he said moving for the door.

"What so you can be alone with that girl?" she said her voice nearly chocking on the word at the end.

"Why do you have to jump to that?" he asked as he rubbed his eyes in frustration.

"It sure didn't take you long to find someone else. Where'd you find this whore, on a street corner?" Gloria asked with a huff, her hands on her hips.

A low growl came from the bedroom, that was enough for Ivy. She zipped up from the bedroom to Casper's side. She placed her arms around his neck and in a flash moment, that was too fast to allow him to process she had closed her eyes and was kissing him. He wasn't sure what was going on, but he didn't care, he kissed her back. Slowly she pulled back, her arms still around his neck, his still around her waist. "Hurray up honey, we'll miss the plane if we don't leave soon." She turned and flashed her perfect teeth at Gloria and said, "He's taking me to Aruba! Can you believe it?"

"No, I can't." she said grabbing her coat and walking out the door.

Casper watched her leave and realized his hands were still around her waist, he dropped them quickly. "What was that?"

"I don't like it when people insult me, I figured pissing her off was better than killing her." Ivy said with a giggle. "Sorry I would have included you in what I was going to do, but you can't read my mind."

"No, it's ok." he said, his voice actually cracking, she was not moving away, in fact she closed the little space between them, and she waited.

"You ready to go?" she finally asked after two solid, long, minutes of holding her position.

"Well I haven't packed anything yet." he said.

She smiled and dropped something into his hands. He looked down at a full duffle bag. "Done." she said.

He shook his head and laughed to himself. "I doubt I'll ever get used to how fast you do things."

"You'd be surprised," she said, a smile still on her face and still standing almost too close. Suddenly her face fell and she muttered, "Bitch."

"What?" he asked, surprised.

She rolled her eyes and growled under her breath. "You're little girlfriend just keyed my car."

"What?" he asked moving to the window and sure enough Gloria was standing next to Ivy's Bentley running a key across the beautiful coral blue paint job.

Ivy sighed and said, very matter-of-factly, "Now I'm going to go kill her."

He blocked her exit to the door, like he could really stop her. "Let's not please."

Her eyes had already changed to predator. "Oh come she insulted me and I didn't kill her, but she messed up my car. I think

I've earned the right to kill her."

"You don't kill people, not anymore remember?" he said.

Slowly her eyes switched back to normal and she pouted, "Stop being the voice of reason, that's my job."

"Let's go home." he said putting a hand on her shoulder. She smiled and shook her head. "What?" he asked.

"Mollie's right," Ivy began. "You are crazy, you haven't screamed once."

"Why would I? I'm not afraid of you." he said with a shake of his head.

"Perhaps you should be." she said moving around him and down the stairs.

She was waiting for him in the car when he finally got down to her. He threw the duffle in the back. She had the top up on the car, she'd enough of the sun for one day. He got in the car and glanced over at her, trying to resist the impulse stare. She looked ahead. He snapped his seatbelt into place and she hit the gas.

"What did I say?" he finally asked after they had been driving for a few minutes, her eyes still focused forward.

"What's the matter with you?" she demanded, taking a turn at ninety miles an hour. "We are killers Casper, we've killed more people then you can imagine and you're not afraid. There are vampires coming here that may very well kill you and you're not afraid. What is wrong with you?"

"I don't think you'll hurt me. And as for the others, I guess I'll cross that bridge when I come to it." he said quietly, crossing his arms across his chest.

"I've murdered people you know." she so quietly he almost

didn't hear her.

He sighed. "Ivy you can't think about it that way, food remember-"

"No! That's not what I mean." she shouted back at him, her voice bouncing off the walls of the car. "I've murdered people, not because I needed their blood but because I just wanted them dead."

"Why?" he asked, gawking at her now, he wasn't sure if he wanted the answer. He didn't think he'd like where the conversation was going.

She pushed harder on the gas pedal and car accelerated faster and faster. She had nearly forgotten he was in the car. "If it wasn't for them this never would have happened to me. I could have lived a long life, with my son-" she said, wishing she could have the word back.

"You had a son." he said surprised, he had not expected that. "Who did you kill?"

"My husband and his lover." she whispered, tears glistening at the corners of her eyes. She never shared this detail of his past, it was a black memory and she liked it that way. "I murdered them both, without a bit of remorse. And don't you ever assume just because my family and I have trained ourselves to not drink blood straight from humans that we are safe. We are murderous animals, and even the most well trained creatures can turn back to their natural states in an instant. Don't ever forget that."

The last minutes of the car ride were completely silent and that silence was nearly deafening. As they pulled into the garage Ivy became confused. "What are they all doing home?" she asked at seeing the sight of all the cars of her family in the garage.

What good is having a cell phone if you don't have it on? Grace was lecturing to her in her head. She pulled her phone out of her purse and turned it on. *Seven missed calls.* it read.

Sorry. Ivy thought back. "Let's get inside." she said aloud to Casper.

"What's going on?" she asked once they were inside, everyone was of course gathered in the dining room.

"We just got off the phone with PJ she'll probably be calling back in a minute." Grace said, running a hand through her short black hair.

"What's the problem?" Ivy asked, taking her seat at the head of the table.

"She and a few of the locals have a rogue subdued in Seattle, she's waiting for your orders." Alex said, leaning against the far wall.

Ivy picked up her phone immediately and dialed PJ's number. "Patricia Jane," she said as PJ picked up the phone. "Tell me what's going on."

"I got a call from Leah at six o'clock this morning and she a few members of her family have a rogue cornered in their home, but of course they're not equipped to handle him."

"Any idea who the creator is?" she asked, PJ was silent. "PJ?"

PJ sighed and said, "I'm about ninety percent sure it was Emily."

Ivy nearly fell off her chair. "Another? So soon?"

"Of course I can't be completely positive, but Leah is sure

she saw her in the city yesterday." PJ said.

"I'll send two of my people out as soon as I can." Ivy said with a sigh. This was bad, very bad.

"I'll be waiting for them." she said clicking off the phone.

"What?" Peter asked leaning his elbows on the table.

"The rogue," Ivy began. "They think it's another Emily creation."

Alex nearly fell. "Why? She's been dormant for so long and now she created two rogues in a week! What the hell is this?" He threw his fist in the wall leaving a gaping hole.

"Calm down." Ivy said, suddenly at his side, her hands gently on his shoulders. This was the time she was like their mother, these were the times they needed her most. "Calm down." she said again, her voice soothing and the most musical it had ever been. Being a prowler she had the ability to bring on a sense of calm to those around her. "Calm down." she said a final time, easing him into a chair, running her hand over his light hair. He breathed deep in and out, even though it really had no effect it seemed to help him.

She turned back to the rest of her family. "Because of the sensitivity of this particular case I want to send two of you. Mollie and Peter."

"When do we leave?" Mollie asked. That was the greatest thing about her family, if she told them to jump they would say how high.

"As soon as possible. You should take the Aston Martin, it'll get better speed." Ivy said.

"You have an Aston Martin too?" Casper asked, his voice

like that of a child who has last year's toy. "Life is so unfair."

"Afterlife's not always so great either." Peter said with a smug expression.

Casper shrugged and said, "Touché."

"There's a lot to do." Mollie interrupted.

"We'll start getting ready." Peter said, getting up from the table, he placed his hand on Alex's shoulder and just stood there for a moment. He didn't say anything, he didn't think anything, he just stood there for his brother.

Within the hour Mollie and Peter would be on the road. With Mollie behind the wheel they'd be across the country in only a few hours. If they were just headed across the country they would have run, it would be faster, but knowing that they had to bring back a newborn they had to bring the car.

A moment later a knock sounded at the door. "Who's that?" Ivy asked, looking around the room, everyone was already there.

"Damn it, did anyone call Nora to tell her about the delay?" Grace asked. They each looked around at everyone else, no one was taking responsibility.

Ivy sighed and went for the door. "Nora," she said when she opened the door.

"What?" Nora asked. "Am I late? I'm sorry." she said her voice becoming panicky.

"No, no," Ivy soothed. "We forgot to call you. There was a problem in The Main City and They were all needed. We've delayed about a week."

"Thanks for calling." Nora said with a grimace.

"Please come in." Ivy said with a smile.

"Where's everyone else?" she asked as she walked through the door.

You've got to come see this. Alex was laughing in his head.

"I think they're in the living room." Nora said, following the sound of the snickers.

In the living room Grace had a copy of Casper's book and was performing a dramatic reading.

"Why are you doing this?" Casper asked with a grumble, trying to grab the book from Grace's lightning fast hands.

"Call it payback for the chess game." she said with a smile.

"Just because I beat you?"

"Pick your battles." Leo mumbled.

Grace flipped the book open and began to read. The scene she read was inherently romantic, one of the few scenes of its kind. By the end Grace's plan had backfired and she was crying while reading it. "That was beautiful man." she said, drying the tears from her face.

"Thanks." he said, running a hand nervously through his hair.

"It really was." Ivy said, looking at him intently now. He stared back with the same intensity and they did not lose each other stares. As if to break the moment, the telephone started to ring, Alex rushed to the kitchen to and picked it up.

Ivy, Peter's on the phone. Alex thought.

"I think they've arrived in Seattle, I've got to go talk to Peter." she said jumping up from her chair and rushing to the kitchen.

She reached the kitchen where the others were. She took

the phone from Alex. "How was the trip?"

"We made it in record time, she drove as crazy as ever." he said, no hint of sarcasm in his voice.

"Are you with PJ?" she asked.

"Yes, we've seen the rogue, he's a big guy but it shouldn't be a problem, Ian's here so he should be able to help us keep him contained."

"Ok, keep me updated." she said with a smile in her voice, she truly did love Peter, he was a good vampire and someday would make a good prowler if he needed to be.

"Good night Ivy." he said.

"Good night Peter, give my best to Mollie and PJ and her family."

"I will." he said clicking off the phone.

Ivy clicked hers shut as well and sighed, just another day in the life of a prowler. She wandered into the kitchen where Leo and Grace were sitting. She opened up the fridge and pulled out two vials of O negative, her favorite. She poured them into a glass and sat with her family.

"Where's Nora?" Ivy asked.

"She decided to head home." Leo said with a sigh. Grace and Ivy smiled at each other. It was obvious to see how Leo felt about Nora, but being so young to the vampire life he wasn't sure how to ask the one hundred and fifty year old vampire to be his mate and since it was a gray thought she couldn't sense it for herself.

"Just ask the girl, the worst she can say is no, and we'll be gone from here in a few years anyway." Grace said.

Leo put his head in his hands and said, "Don't say that. I like it here."

"You know the way it works, we can't stay in one place forever, they'd know." Ivy said with a smile. She put and hand on his shoulder. "Think about it my boy, she might surprise you." She sighed aloud and said, "It's been a long day, I think I'm going to try to get some sleep."

Chapter Seven

Her sleep was dreamless as always, but it was more peaceful than it usually was. Something about her talk with Casper had put her at ease and something else in it had bothered her, but for the life of her she couldn't figure out why. About two hours into her sleep a hand came upon her shoulder.

"Ivy get up." Alex urged, shaking her shoulder.

"What's wrong?" Ivy asked, panicked at the urgency in his voice.

"Peter's on the phone you have to talk to him now." Alex said, his voice shallow and frightened. She popped up from her bed and ran down the stairs for the phone.

"Peter," Ivy said frantically into the phone.

"Ivy I'm so sorry, I didn't mean for this to happen." Peter said with a cry over the phone, she had never heard this from him before.

"What happened Peter?" she demanded.

"The rogue got away from us, he overpowered Ian and got away from him. Mollie's faster of course so she went after him. She caught him in an alley, he was about to kill a human, she knocked him out of the way, but the human got scared. We finally caught the rogue and subdued him, but Mollie-" he couldn't finish.

"What happened to Mollie?" Ivy shouted into the phone.

"She got arrested." Peter said, his voice meek and quiet.

"Arrested? How-how could you let that happen? You were supposed to protect her! I trusted you!"

"I'm sorry Ivy, I'm so sorry." he said with a sob.

"Let me think, I'll call you back." she said her head in her hands as she clicked off her phone. "Get the family, call Nora and wake up Casper." she said to Alex who was at her side.

Within only a few minutes the five vampires and one human were around the dining room table. "I have very bad news."

"What happened?" Grace asked, tears running down her face. Leo put his hands on her shoulders, trying to console her.

"Mollie's been arrested." Ivy said her head in her hands.

"Oh god." Leo said with a gasp.

"What?" Casper asked, he knew that getting arrested was a problem, but he didn't understand why it seemed to be the end of days to them.

"Think about it Casper," Ivy said, her eyes sad and lost. "She's a vampire, how long will she last before she kills someone and she's exposed for what she is. What do you think will happen to her? To us? To all vampires if that happens."

"What do we do?" Nora asked, she may not have been part of the family, but this was an issue that effected them all.

Ivy took in a deep breath and said, "Alex, Leo and Grace start running. Grace and Alex you both have law degrees, pose as her counsel, find some way to move a few vials of blood to her, as much as you can without being noticed. Leo you beat than newborn into submission. Nora you stay here and wait, I don't know how long we'll be and if They show up I want someone to be here. Casper and I will go by car and meet you there in a few hours. Go to PJ's first." They all stood up and she said, "Wait." They all turned back to look at her. "We are a family, we will get her out of this, we'll save her and we'll get through it together." They huddled together, in a group hug, Casper stood on the outskirts, watching the family. "Casper, get in here." Ivy said, her cheeks stained with tears. He joined in with them and felt as if he was part of their family unit. It had been only two days, but it already felt like a lifetime and he was happy to be there.

Grace, Leo and Alex left then to run across the country, they would be in Seattle in about two hours. Nora held down the fort and helped Ivy quickly fill the car with everything they would need. Coolers of blood to keep the more traditional vampires away from Casper. Food for Casper and clothes for them all.

"Please be careful." Nora said as Ivy and Casper got in the car. "And bring her home."

"We will." Ivy said. "I promise."

"I have a question." he said after they had been on the road for a few minutes.

"Shoot." she said, her eyes focused on the road.

"Well, when you get arrested you go through the whole processing thing, like fingerprinting, how does that work considering Mollie's like eighty-five years old?" he asked.

"I have friends in many places, you can't comprehend how many vampires are actually out there. One of which is in the FBI and he changes out aliases every few years, along with our fingerprints. When we get Mollie out I'll call in a favor and he'll do it again for us."

"Oh, ok." he said staring out the window. "Why did you bring me? You could have run with the others and left me with Nora."

"No I could not. If They found out I left you pretty much

alone that would just make all this worse." She licked her lips and said, "I also wanted to be the one to prepare you."

"For what?" he asked.

"PJ and her family don't exactly live like we do." she said with a shrug of her shoulders.

"What are you talking about?"

She sighed and said, "They drink from the source."

"Oh," he said, finally understanding. "Ok, what-what does that mean for me?"

"You just need to stick very close to one of us at all times. We won't hurt you, you know that. Just don't ever be alone with one of them." she said.

He swallowed hard. "Ok, I'll remember that."

"What are you going to do? To get out Mollie I mean." he asked, folding his arms across his chest.

She sighed. "This is new for us, believe it or not, but we'll have to break her out. It'll involve all of them to do it, myself included. Alex to see sense the humans around us. Me to convince the guards to let us in, Grace and Leo to break and move some things and Peter, well you'll get so see what Peter can do."

"You all are so cryptic." he said with gruff tone.

"You'll find out soon enough. He'd kill me if I told you before you could see it for yourself."

"Again, so cryptic, it's annoying." he said, his face squished up with annoyance.

She smiled. "I won't lie though, it is nice for once to spend some time with someone who doesn't know everything you're thinking."

"Glad to help." he said with a wave of his hand. He glanced out his window, trying to place where they could be. Of course she was going a million miles an hour, but it seemed like they were in a dessert. He glanced down and could ever see the pavement anymore. "Are we even on the highway?"

She shook her head. "Nah, roads just slows me down. This way is much faster." He checked the lock on his seatbelt again and gulped down hard. Ivy laughed. "Mollie was right you know, we are really safe to drive with, our reflexes are so much better than yours."

He made the mistake of looking over at her speedometer, just under two hundred miles an hour. "I didn't even know these cars could go that fast." he said beginning to sweat.

"Mollie is to thank for that." Ivy said, reaching quickly around her seat for a bottle of water. She tossed it to Casper and said, "Drink that." He had gone so pale, she feared he would pass out again. "Look Casper, you're perfectly safe. If it wasn't for the fact that my girl's in trouble, I'd slow down. I promise we'll go slower on the way back." Casper took a few deep breaths and sipped the water mechanically.

Meanwhile in Seattle

Leo stayed back with PJ and her family to strategize and wait for Ivy and Casper. Alex and Grace however changed into more business like attire. Grace did her hair in a tight bun and put on a pair of fake glasses, anything to make her look older, it was the biggest curse for her, sixteen forever. Finally when they were ready they stuffed their sleeves full of vials, the cool temperatures of their bodies keeping the blood cold. Grace kept each vial still in their coats with her mind. When they were with Mollie, whether it be a handshake or if need be a hug, she would move them to her. That was their biggest objective today until Ivy could be there.

They walked into the precinct where she was being held and were immediately approached by two officers. "Can I help you?" the shorter rounder one asked.

Alex extended a hand to him and said, "My name is Alex Philips and this my associate Grace Skylar, we are Mollie Lyons representation." The aliases were a hazard of the job, the family had assumed there would be speculation, if something like this ever happened, if they all had the same last name.

"Do you have identification?" the taller leaner officer asked.

"Of course." Alex said with a smile handing over his.

Grace extended hers and officer smiled, his hand lingering a second too long on hers before he took it. Pig. "Aren't you a little young to be an attorney?"

"No," Grace said matter-of-factly, her sweet pixie features pointed down angrily.

"Ok," the leaner officer said with a chuckle examining to the two ids for a moment. He handed them back. "Let me take you to one of our interview rooms, I'll bring her to you."

"Thank you very much officer." Alex said, with a polite smile, flashing his brilliantly blinding teeth. The officer smiled back awkwardly and led the way for them.

A few moments later her thoughts came into focus. *Here she comes.* Alex thought. The officer opened the door and said, "Ten minutes."

"Thank you officer." Alex said. He turned to Mollie and

thought, *We have vials of blood in our jackets, when we shake you hand Grace is going to move them, so don't let go right away.*

Ok. Mollie thought, so elated to see her brother and sister. So he extended his hand to shake hers and Grace moved each vial as fast as possible, securing them all in the front of her bra, most logical place.

I'm going to hug you, move mine a different way. Grace thought moving toward Mollie. Once again she moved each vial as quick as possible down the back of Mollie's shirt and securing them in the back of her bra. She released her and took a step back. *Done.* she thought.

They each settled into the chairs around the table and kept mindless legal chatter with their mouths, while the real conversation was in their heads.

Ungrateful human! Mollie shouted in her head. *I save her and then she implicates me in coming after her.*

Were there any other witnesses? Grace asked.

Peter. Mollie thought. *But that's it.* She shifted uncomfortably in her seat. *What do we do? Where's Ivy?*

She's coming with the human by car, she should be arriving at PJ's soon. Once she's there we'll develop a more cohesive plan. Alex thought with a sigh.

And Leo? Mollie thought.

Back at PJ's, probably taking a bite out of Peter by now. Grace thought with a grimace, she didn't relish in the thought of her brothers fighting.

It's not Peter's fault, it's not anyone's fault. Mollie thought, her head in her hands. *You have to get me out of here, I can't be in here.*

He smiled and said aloud, "It'll be ok, we'll make it ok."

"I believe you thank you for coming." she said with a smile

We love you sister. Grace said as they stood to leave, taking Mollie by the hand. *Always.*

"Thanks Gracie, for everything." Mollie said releasing her sister's hand.

They left her then and prayed they would not search her, which they did not. They sped back to PJ's house and could begin to hear Ivy's thoughts, she was there.

Ivy and Casper had just arrived. The family bigger than Ivy's, from what he could see their were ten. A woman came out of the house, her hair white as snow and her eyes the palest blue, she almost looked like a ghost. She rushed quickly to Ivy and hugged her tight. "It's good to see you PJ" Ivy said with a smile.

"Good to see you too Ivy, I just wish it was on better circumstances." PJ said releasing Ivy. She smelled the air and turned slightly to look as Casper with hungry eyes. *Dinner?* she questioned.

"Absolutely not. Make sure the rest of your family understands that too." Ivy commanded.

"Of course." PJ said with a smile. *No one touches the human,* she thought for the family. They all nodded, continuing with whatever task they were   currently doing.   She turned to Casper and said, "I like the hair."

"Thanks." he said running a hand through his gray curls. "Premature graying."

PJ laughed and said, "I understand that. My hair completely

white by the time I was twelve."

Casper smiled and said, "I was fifteen." The two shared a smile and Ivy began to think maybe PJ could be trusted with Casper.

Leo emerged from the house then and smiled when he saw them. "Boss, you made it." he said.

"Casper, go inside with Leo if you don't mind." Ivy said turning to Casper. *Do not let him out of your sight.* she thought for Leo. He nodded and patted Casper on the shoulder, leading him inside.

"Do the rules apply about being invited in here?" Casper asked Leo as he was lead inside.

Leo laughed. "She told you about that? No, the rules are a little different when it comes to fellow vampires, the agreement between the pope and God only protects mortals."

"Where's Ian?" Ivy asked turning back to PJ with a serious look.

"He's not back yet, he decided to go hunting, knowing that the human was coming." PJ said a curious look in her pale blue eyes.

"Can you ask him to stay away. I can't risk him hurting the human." she said, her tone very serious.

"Sure I will, but I don't think he would. He took the extra precautions not to." PJ said, curiosity pushing to ask more questions than she should.

"I just need him not to be here." she said, her tone annoyed.

"Ok boss, I'll make sure." she said moving out from the garage to get better reception on her cell phone, Ian must have been too far away to hear her thoughts.

Ivy walked up the stairs into the house. Peter was sitting at the kitchen table, his head in his hands. She slammed a hand down on the table and he looked up instantly. "I'm so sorry." he said sadly.

"I'll deal with you later." she said, her voice dripping with anger. *Can you all join me in the dining room?* she thought in her head.

Quickly they all gathered around the enormous prop in the dining room, Casper safely nestled between Leo and Ivy. "We need to come up with a plan."

"Why should we listen to you?" a flaxen haired girl said from the opposite side of the table. "You're not our creator and I for one am not one of your rogues."

"But I am." PJ said glowering at the young vampire. "And I am the head of our family so you will listen. Is that understood Amber?"

"Yes ma'am." Amber said settling back in her chair.

"I'm sorry Ivy continue." PJ said.

"Thank you, I believe you have a police officer in your family." Ivy said, glancing over at PJ who motioned to one of her members. A tall man stood up next to Leo. "It's good to see you Eric." Ivy said with a smile.

"Eric? Like your creator Eric?" Casper asked leaning over to Leo.

"Yep, like his creator." Eric said with a smile for Casper.

"What can you tell me?" Ivy asked folding her hand atop the table.

"I've already switched shifts for this evening with another officer so I'll be the only one on duty, along with my captain unfortunately, he will be the only problem. Sometimes I think he's the vampire, never sleeps when on duty."

"PJ we're going to need some cover." Ivy said with a smile.

PJ smiled and said, "Got it, been a while since I've done any serious fog."

Casper was confused, Leo leaned over and said, "PJ can change the weather." Casper nodded his head in understanding.

"Peter, you find your own way in and get to Mollie and wait for us to get there." Ivy said her voice cold, she was still angry.

"Understood." Peter said.

"What does he do?" Casper grumbled to Leo.

"Wait and see." Leo said with a smile. No one was going to tell him.

"Grace and Leo you're the muscle." Ivy said. The two smiled at each other from across the table, something told Casper they'd had to be "the muscle" before.

"As for the rest of you," Ivy said. "I want you patrolling outside the police station to make sure that we don't get interrupted. Use your imaginations if we get an uninvited guest, I won't ask questions." *You just don't touch my human.* she added in thought. The room increased in tension a little, even among her own family. Ivy's overwhelming protection of Casper was growing more intense than may have been necessary and her family especially couldn't figure out why.

"We understand Ivy, don't we?" PJ asked her family, and they nodded.

"When does your shift start Eric?" Ivy asked.

"Eight thirty and everyone but the captain will be gone by ten." Eric said.

"By ten fifteen the air will be thick with fog." PJ said.

Ivy glanced at Peter. "Then I'll get Mollie, take her a vial of blood, she'll probably need it by then. Then I sneak out of the cell grab Mollie's file which will be waiting conveniently for me on Mister Police Man's desk and scurry away while waiting for the power twins to invade and bust her out."

"By ten thirty Leo and I will be inside, Leo will, pretend of course, to subdue Eric and then actually subdue the captain-" Grace began before being interrupted.

"Or you could just drain him." Amber said with a smile.

"No," Grace said meekly.

"Why, because your mother tells you, you shouldn't do that. Ridiculous, it's what we were made for." Amber said, a smile of superiority on her face, it was not a hidden fact that she disliked the human race.

Ivy was about to defend Grace, but Grace needed that from no one. "No, we can't kill him because he needs to live to tell the tale so that no one can implicate Eric as having anything to do with this." Grace said with her arms crossed.

"Exactly." Ivy said, agreeing with her girl. "So let's get ready to go."

Everyone stood up from the table as PJ grabbed Ivy's hand. "Ian is outside Ivy."

"No! I told you to keep him away." Ivy hissed.

"Why? I don't understand why." PJ said in hushed tones so

the others wouldn't see.

"I'm worried about him around my human." Ivy said simply.

"He's not a rogue anymore Ivy, he's been around for fifteen years. What's going on with you?"

She glanced up over PJ's shoulder at Casper and said, "Just keep him outside for a minute."

Ivy walked over to Casper who was having an in depth conversation with Leo about how he'd beaten Grace at checkers, but it was not the same story that Ivy had heard, he had said it was not something he talked about with anyone.

"Casper can I talk to you for a moment?" Ivy asked, interrupting their conversation.

"Sure." he said turning to her. "Can you give us a minute Leo?"

Keep Ian outside. Ivy thought privately to him.

Ok. Leo thought without question, even though his eyes looked confused.

"What's up?" Casper asked once everyone was out of hearing range.

"Casper, do you remember when we were talking about chess and your father?" she asked softly biting her bottom lip.

"Yes," he said, confused by her tone.

"Do you remember what you told me about your brother?" she asked, pulling her knees up to her chest.

"That he died?"

"No, not just that he died. You said he was murdered." Ivy said, the need to clarify important.

"Yea, so what?" he asked, an inquisitive look on his face.

"Did they ever find your brother's body?" she asked her face more pained with every second.

"Well, no but after a few years they just presumed him dead. Where is this going Ivy?" he demanded.

"Did you brother ever go by another name, something other than Zach?" she asked, avoiding his question.

"Do you know something about his murder? Do you know who killed him?" Casper nearly shouted.

"Answer the question Casper." she commanded him.

"You're not answering mine!" he yelled back.

"I'm trying to." she said softly, trying her sooth him with her musical voice, that worried him more than soothed.

"No, I don't think he ever went by another name." he said, after thinking for a long moment.

"What about a middle name?" she asked.

He searched his brain for a moment as if he couldn't remember, it had been a long time. He looked up at her and said, "Zach's middle name was Ian." She didn't even blink, she had already known the answer. "Damn it Ivy, what's going on?"

"Why do you think you write about vampires Casper?" she asked, her voice low and breathy.

"What the hell does that have to do with anything!" he screamed at her.

"Why do you think you write about them?" she asked again, her tone the same.

His shrug was agitated. "I don't know, I guess I always liked them, I don't know. What does this have to do with Zach!"

Her expression didn't change, her eyes remained just as

sad. "You don't think maybe you had a connection to them that you never knew?"

"What the hell are you talking about! I didn't even know they really existed before two days ago." He was on his feet now, pacing back and forth in front of her.

"Are you sure?" she said. She could see that he was about to break, his eyes glistening with tears of frustration. She could almost feel the tears in hers. She closed her eyes and thought, *Leo let him in.*

"Thank you I can actually go in my house now." a voice said sarcastically and annoyed from behind them.

"I'm sorry Casper, I didn't know." she said before the owner of the voice came into view.

Casper got up from his chair and waited as the man came around the corner. He nearly fell back in the chair, he could not accept the face that he saw. He was a very tall man, taller than the rest. He had broad shoulders and olive colored skin. His eyes were nearly black but sparkled bright. And his hair was salt and pepper, just like Casper's hair. "Zach." he murmured, the sound almost inaudible.

The young man froze in the doorframe, unable to move, he too was shocked. "Casper?" His eyes darted quickly to Ivy. "What is this?"

"I didn't know." she said shaking her head.

He hadn't changed, hadn't aged a day. "Zach, what-what's going on? What's happening?" Casper said as he began to hyperventilate.

"Cas-" Ian said taking a step toward him.

Casper raised a hand, as if to stop him. "No, no, we had a funeral for you. This isn't real, this isn't real."

"Casper." Ian said softly, tears in his eyes. "My Casper. You're like a grown-up."

"Yea, it happens." Casper said, still unable to accept what he was seeing. "You haven't changed at all."

The vampire laughed and said, "Yea it happens." He glanced back at Ivy and asked, "How do you know Ivy?"

"How do you know Ivy?" Casper retaliated back.

"Well, I was a rogue." Ian said simply.

Casper flipped around to Ivy. "Did you know about this?" he demanded, his eyes angry.

"Of course not. I remembered Ian of course and after our conversation about your family I started thinking but I wasn't sure." she said with a sigh.

"What happened to you Zach? We thought you were killed." Casper said.

Ian tilted his head to the side and said, "Casper, look at me, I was killed. I'm not Zach Lennox anymore, I'm Ian."

"No, you're Zach, you're my brother." Casper said, the walls seeming to crash in on him. He had spent the last fifteen years thinking his brother was dead and now here he stood in front of him looking the same as if he had never left, he was still only seventeen.

"Can I jump in here for a minute?" Ivy asked, standing up from her chair. "There are things about us that you can't understand Casper. When we become vampires we lose our human side, over time we forget who we even were. I can't see my husband or my father's faces anymore. I can't remember what they sounded, what they smelled like. I can't remember what my wedding dress looked like or what I wore when we buried my mother. Your brother still remembers you, you can't imagine how glorious and painful that is. I teach them to separate themselves from the human that they were, I've never had a vampire who got to see their family again-"

"Except for you right!" Casper screamed at her. How dare she keep this information from him. She knew that Zach was his brother and she didn't tell him. "You went back and killed your family!"

Her entire face fell in that moment of betrayal. She couldn't cry. She couldn't scream. She could only stare, her mouth hanging open with shock. "You bastard." she muttered, zipping away from him. "Get ready to leave!" she screamed to everyone else.

"What about Casper?" Leo whispered.

"I don't care. Feed him to the dogs if you want. I don't care." Ivy nearly sobbed, her voice absent of all its music. "I don't care."

Ian stay here with him, make sure no one hurts him. Leo requested. He glanced over at Casper and his face fell into anger.

"Leo-" Casper began.

Leo raised a hand to stop him and shook his head. "Don't you dare talk to me."

"How could you do that?" Ian demanded.

"Do you even know the story?" Casper asked with a roll of his eyes.

"Do you?" Ian asked, his voice full of disgust.

"She killed her husband." Casper said, sitting back down in the chair behind him.

"Because he killed her, because of him she was condemned to be this, to be the monsters that we are. I could never blame her for what she did, but do you know why she tells us the story at all?" Casper shook his head, beginning to feel meek like a child scorned. "She wants us to see what a huge mistake it was and to keep us from hurting anyone that we knew in our human lives. She said she has never regretted anything more in her life or afterlife than killing her husband. Do you know how many times I wanted to sneak into our house and kill dad while he slept? That woman stayed with me every time I felt like that so that I wouldn't have the regret she has. She is an amazing creature, how dare you insult her." he said walking in four big steps to the door.

He wanted to go and find her and apologize, or go after his brother, but he knew neither one wanted to see him.

It was time for a rescue mission. The clock had just tolled ten and it was time to roll in the fog. Casper stood off on the sidelines in view PJ, Ivy and Ian. PJ smiled and rubbed her hands together vigorously together and jus as she promised a slow roll of fog moved in around them. "Whenever you're ready Peter." she said, holding the fog steady.

Casper glanced around looking for Peter who was standing by the right side of the building. He watched Peter intently waiting for something to happen. He was not going to miss this. Ivy walked up beside him.

"There's a hole in the left wall it will lead right into her cell, give her the blood and get the file then wait for Leo and Grace." she commanded simply.

"I got it." he said softly. Today was delicate, both because he was in trouble with her for Mollie even being here and because of what Casper had said to her.   He didn't want to upset her further. "I don't think he meant it. I think he's just confused."

Her face was angry when she looked up at him. "Well I didn't ask you did I?"

"No," he said shaking his head looking back down at the ground.

She lifted his chin with her hand, tears brimmed the edges of her eyes. "Go get my girl." she said simply.

He smiled slightly and gave her a sharp nod. He took a step back and a deep breath in. slowly his body began to contort and change and get smaller and smaller, when it was finished a mouse lay on the ground where Peter had stood. Ivy held out her hand and he scurried onto it. She tied a vial of blood around his small torso with a strap of leather.

"He's a mouse!" Casper exclaimed from across the street, quiet though so to not attract attention.

"Yep." Grace said, her eyes focused forward, she was mad at him too. "He's a shape shifter."

"Gracie don't be mad at me." Casper said, his heart hurting, regretting every word he'd said to Ivy.

"You have not earned the right to give me pet names." she said, the corners of her mouth turned down. She glanced over at Casper and his sad eyes both annoyed her and made her pity him. "Look dude, you are rare among us. You actually have the ability to think before you speak, we don't have that. The minute we think something the rest of us know it, you don't have that problem. Why would you say those things to her?"

"Now's not the time Grace." Leo said, his voice harsh, too harsh for it to belong to Leo.

Grace sighed and turned back to Casper. "We'll talk more when we have Mollie back."

"Ok." he said sinking back a bit. His brother stood behind him in the shadows. Ian's only job that night was to make sure Casper didn't get himself into trouble, seeing that Ivy wanted nothing to do with him.

In the meantime Peter wandered through the passages that the mouse-size hole allowed him. He finally saw the light and found himself at the top of a cell, but not Mollie's. *I thought you said this would lead to her cell.* he thought to Ivy.

It should have. Ivy thought, running through her mind trying to determine what could have gone wrong, she could visualize the tunnel just as it was. Maybe they moved her, she couldn't be sure. *Well, can you get to her?* she asked.

I'm not sure I'm about eight feet off the ground, and trust me that's even higher when you're only three inches long. he thought, only an edge of panic to his voice.

Peter? Mollie thought.

Oh! I forgot I could talk to you. Peter thought a bit of jubilee to his voice now.

Where are you? You sound so close. Mollie thought.

I'm at the top of a cell, it just isn't your cell. Peter thought peering his little nose over the side of the hole. It was a long drop.

Change into something that can fly then. she thought.

You know that's not how it works, I'd have to change to me first. he thought, trying to ignore the height he was at.

Well then jump. Mollie thought. *It's not like it can kill you.*

Yea but it can hurt. Peter thought.

Stop being a baby, she needs the blood. Ivy thought.

He rolled his eyes and took a deep breath and leaped from the high level to the ground and landed with a thud. *Ow.*

Baby. Ivy thought. Peter ignored her and wandered out of cell from which he began. He examined his surroundings, the captain was nowhere to be seen luckily. He glanced up at the desk in front of him where Eric was sitting smiling at him. *She's over there Stuart Little.* Eric thought, his grin from ear to ear

Ass. Peter thought back, his voice in a grumble.

I could have given that to her. Eric thought motioning to the vial of blood tied to his back.

My job! he thought back his little eyes narrowing.

Um guys, I'm still in here. Mollie thought from the next cell. Peter turned and moved into the cell. She scooped him up quickly in her hands and untied the vial just as fast. "Bless you." she whispered to him. She placed him back on the ground and gobbled the vial's contents. "Much better." she said with a deep breath. Peter transformed back into himself and quickly into another creature, something a little larger so that he could carry the file. A tabby cat. He walked out of the cell and followed Eric's eyes to a file sitting on his desk. Peter glanced in the direction of the captain's office. He moved quickly out of the cell and toward Eric's desk. Unfortunately on the way there he hit another chair causing it to fall over. At lightning speed her ran under Eric's desk and held steady there.

"What's going on out there?" the captain asked from inside his office, his voice sleepy and distant.

"Nothing Captain." Eric yelled back. "Keep it down in there." he shouted at Mollie for effect.

"Bite me!" she shouted back.

Anytime. he thought, a smug grin upon his face.

She rolled her eyes and thought, *Anytime now Ivy.* As she did Peter jumped up on the desk and grabbed the file, then back under the desk to wait for the others.

Ivy turned to Grace and Leo, "You know what to do. Grace you break the bars and get Mollie out, Leo you subdue Eric and the Captain, and may I repeat that, subdue, don't forget your strength and kill him."

Leo rolled his eyes. "Yes mom I got it."

"Just bring her back safely." she said her arms crossed over her chest. Grace and Leo made their move to police station and Casper moved to Ivy. She could sense his presence as he approached and her voice was callous when she spoke, "Not now Casper."

"Zach told me what you did for him, when he wanted to kill my dad." he said, stuffing his hands in his pockets.

"I did that for all of them." she said, her eyes focused toward the station, keeping her thoughts inside the heads of her family. "I never want any of them to live with the regret I feel. We aren't supposed to be able to dream, but I do, I see them every time I shut my eyes to sleep, and I will for the rest of eternity. I never want any of my children to feel like that. And for you to say what you said, you have no idea how much that hurt me."

"I'm sorry. I was just angry." Casper said, his eyes still angled down.

"I really didn't know it was him. Even if I had, I couldn't tell you, everything about my training for them is letting go of the human side. It's too much to hold onto that."

"I understand, I'm so sorry. I can't begin to explain that to you." he said. "Please accept my apology?"

Her eyes focused forward, her expression unchanged and she said, "I'll think about it."

Suddenly the thoughts of four of the other members of her family came rushing urgently into her head. Her head snapped up as they all came running out, Mollie among them. "Let's go! Let's go! Let's go!" Leo was shouting.

"What's the problem?" Ivy asked as Leo scooped up Casper so that they wouldn't have to slow down.

"What happened?" Ivy demanded as they ran at turbo speed.

"Well I knocked out Eric and the Captain as I was told and then Grace snapped the bars."

"So why are we running?" Alex demanded, having just rejoined his family.

"Because the genius cop didn't tell us that snapping the bars would cause an alarm to go off." Grace shouted as they ran.

I forgot! Eric shouted in his head.

They rallied back at PJ's home. Mollie had her head in Ivy's lap. "I'm glad that you are safe." Ivy said, running her hand through Mollie's hair.

"Thank you for coming for me." she said keeping her hands close to her face. "I was so afraid."

"I'll always come for you. You know that." Ivy said with a smile. She looked up at Peter and asked, "Where is the rogue?"

He didn't speak at first, rather glanced up at PJ and her family member Amber. "Ask them." he said.

"What's he talking about?" Ivy demanded.

PJ, with her arms across her chest, turned to Amber and said, "Amber, why don't you tell Ivy what happened to the rogue?"

"Well, someone tell Ivy what happened to the rogue." Ivy said pulling herself back into the conversation.

The golden-haired girl looked uncomfortable for the first time since Ivy had met her. She shifted her weight from side to side and said, "We handled him."

"What does that mean and who is we?" Ivy demanded, moving Mollie's head off her lap and standing up to face the girl.

"He nearly exposed us all, he got one of your own in very dangerous trouble." Amber tried to justify.

"I will not ask you again, what did you do?" Ivy demanded.

"We killed him." she said softly.

"Goddamn it!" Ivy shouted, the sound almost like a sonic boom, the girl before her shaking. "Under whose authority did you do such a stupid, reckless thing!"

"My own ma'am." she said, her eyes downward.

"Did you know about this?" Ivy shouted looking at PJ

"I did not, and I promise that proper punishment will be delivered." PJ promised.

"Oh I know it will be." she said turning back to Amber. "Who did you do this with?"

"It doesn't matter, I was the ringleader, I will take the fall and all responsibility." Amber said straightening her posture.

"Very noble of you, but I asked you for the names." Ivy demanded, the girl was quiet. At lightening speed she was only inches away from the girl, one hand around her neck. "And do not try to bury it deep in your mind, I can see clearly your gray and black thoughts if I want to, so you *will* tell me. Now."

"Megan and Simon." she muttered, so quietly that if Ivy were not a vampire she would not have heard it.

"PJ bring me these two." Ivy said, her voice cold and her eyes still locked on Amber.

"We're here." a young dark-haired man said from behind PJ, a girl with a shaved head beside him.

"What you did, what the three of you did is inexcusable and unforgivable. I am the prowler In this area. I decide what happens to rogues, not you. You are children in comparison to me, babies. I should hand you over to Them and not think twice, Eva would have something to say about your antics. Vampires killing vampires is unacceptable." Their faces grew panicked, there was nothing more frightening to a vampire than that. "But I'm not going to do that. What I am going to do is punish you in house and I will make PJ enforce it." She said glancing over at her former rogue. "You are not exempt from punishment either, as head of your family you should have known everything they were doing." She did not protest. "They will not kill a human for next ten years. They will survive either on the blood of animals or blood you buy but they will not kill a human for a decade." A grumble of disgust rang out among the three vampires.

"You are in no position to complain." PJ hissed to them. "I understand, I will take part in this punishment as well. You are right, they are my responsibility I should have been in control."

"I think that's best." Ivy said turning back to her family. "Perhaps we should head home."

"Ivy the sun just came up, stay until tomorrow. Please." PJ said, her focused downward, somewhat ashamed.

"Fine." Ivy said sitting back down with Mollie.

Are we talking to Casper yet? Leo asked in his mind.

You're a grownup you can make your own decisions. Ivy thought.

We all kind of were wondering Ivy, Grace thought. *You are our leader, if you're still offended by him, still mad at him then we are too.*

"I'm not ecstatic, but no I'm not angry anymore." Ivy said aloud with a smile.

"So could I ask him to do me a favor?" Leo asked.

"Sure, what favor?" Ivy asked.

"Let me ask him first and then I'll tell you, promise." he said and then in thought added, *Please stay out of my head until I ask him.* She nodded and smiled, she could do that for him.

Leo found him a few rooms over sitting with his brother. The two were quiet as they sat staring at one another. "Ian, would you mind if I talked to Casper for a moment?"

"Sure." Ian said raising to his feet and gliding out of the room, happy to have even a moment away from the awkwardness of the situation.

"Are you talking to me again?" Casper asked, his face sad.

Leo half-smiled and said, "You're like a puppy, who can stay mad at a puppy?"

Casper smiled back and asked, "What can I do for you?"

Leo sighed and sat down next to him. He pulled a crinkled envelope out of his jacket pocket and stared at it while he spoke. "Remember when I was telling you what I would do if I could do one thing over for my human life?"

"You would tell your parents you were sorry." Casper recalled.

Leo smiled, "Yea. Well about ten years ago I wrote this letter," he motioned down to the envelope. "Inside telling them that I was ok and you know how sorry I was, but I could never bring myself to send it. But being here, back in Seattle, I guess I was just wondering if-"

"If I could take it to them?" Casper finished for him.

"Yea," Leo said, emotion catching his voice. "I thought maybe you could talk Ivy into going with you. Come up with some story about what happened to me and I could watch from somewhere close by, just to see their faces one more time."

"I'll see what I can do." Casper said with a smile, taking the envelope from Leo's hands. "Let me go do some schmoozing with Ivy, I need to for multiple reasons, I might as well add this to the list."

"No need." Ivy said turning the corner, her fiery red hair bouncing as she walked. "You've got to know I'd do anything for you."

"Thanks." Leo said, exhaling a deep breath.

Casper and Ivy stood on the front steps of the house, Ivy in a ridiculously oversized hat, who knew how long they'd be in the sun, she wasn't taking any chances. As they stood there, just before knocking on the door Ivy took a good look at Casper, in a way she never had before. His short gray hair curling the ends, the gray made him look older, while the curls made him look like a young boy. His face was fresh, and always happy and it still shocked her to think that he was only twenty-five years old. He had an old soul, that much was obvious. And then there were his eyes, dark pools that seemed endless to her. She had never seen him like this before. "This is a very selfless thing you're doing for Leo." she stated.

He knocked twice on the door. "I'm pretty ok guy." he said with a smile. A few long moments passed. *She's not going to answer is she?* Leo thought from across the street in the bushes where he stood waiting with Mollie.

He no sooner had this thought then the door opened. An aged woman stood before them, her glasses half way down her nose, her short, gray hair perfectly set in tight curls. "Can I help you?" she asked, her voice as musical as any human they had ever heard. Leo listened intently through Ivy's thoughts and cried at the first sight of his mother in over twenty years, Mollie stood and held his hand.

"Mrs. Harlow?" Casper asked.

"Yes, I'm Annie Harlow, what can I do for you?" she asked taking a step outside.

"It's about your son Mrs. Harlow." Ivy said.

Her entire expression changed at that. Leo feared that it would be a look of hate or even disgust, he could not have been more wrong. "My Leo?" she asked her voice breathy.

"Yes ma'am." Casper said with a smile.

"He's alive?" she asked and Casper nodded. She put a hand to her chest and said, "Praise be to god, my boy. Come in, please come in."

Ivy glanced over at him and Casper asked for clarification, she need permission. "Both of us?"

"Of course," she said moving inside. "Tom! Tom!" she called out into the house. The two stepped inside to what looked like a picture from a magazine. The walls were painted a butter cream yellow and on the walls hung old pictures, they could see the ones of Leo, what a cute child he'd been, a head full of blonde curls, curls he must have gotten from his mother. The furniture was all very plush and blue. They could see through to the kitchen which was set up with all stainless steel appliances and a dark mahogany table, set for three, almost as if they expected Leo back. And there was a smell, so distinct that it seemed more like a treasured memory than a scent. It was like apple pie mixed with fabric softener and meatloaf in the most pleasing of ways.

"Yes Annie?" a man's voice said as a burly, bald older man came walking up the stairs.

"Tom honey, these two people have news about Leo." she said a joyous tear in her eye.

"My boy, my boy is alive?" Leo's father said turning to Casper and Ivy.

"My name is Ivy Lyons and this is my associate Casper Lennox. We work for a chemical dependency rehab clinic in Orlando, Florida. Your son was a patient there about twenty years ago now he practically runs the place." Ivy explained, sitting on the plush sofa in the spacious living room.

"He's sober then, I never thought I'd see the day." Mrs. Harlow said.

"Yes ma'am, for over twenty years now." Casper said with a smile.

"Where is this place? I want to see him." Mrs. Harlow asked, holding her husband's hand tightly.

"I'm afraid that's not possible." Ivy said.

"Why not? If he's sober why can't we see him?" Mr. Harlow demanded.

"It's part of the recovery. He needed to start anew." Casper tried to explain, his explanation not far from the truth. He reached into his pocket and pulled out Leo's letter. "He wanted me to give this to you. He wanted me to tell you how sorry he was. Sorry that he broke your heart and sorry that he disappointed you."

"My baby could never disappoint, but the boy he was when we had to kick him out wasn't my son." Mrs. Harlow said her eyes filled with tears and she glanced down at the perfect hardwood floor. "Can you answer me one question?"

"Anything." Ivy said, reaching across the space and taking the woman's hand, the woman did not falter at the cold, abnormally smooth feeling of her skin.

"Is he happy?" she asked, a sole tear rolling down her cheek.

"Yes ma'am, he is. And he loves you both so much and he just wanted us to let you know that he's alive and safe, and I promise you he's happy." Ivy said smiling brightly at her.

"Thank you, both of you." Mr. Harlow said, trying his best to contain his own emotion.

Casper shared an emotional hug with his mother, one that was symbolically meant for Leo. They walked slowly out toward the shrubbery across the street. Leo and Mollie were sitting on the ground, Mollie's hands clamped tightly around his and he was crying, harder than Casper had ever seen anyone cry. In a flash instant Leo was on his feet again and his arms wrapped around Casper's shoulders. He held him tightly, perhaps too tight, but he didn't say anything at first. "Thank you, thank you, thank you." he said over and over again.

"It's ok Leo, it's ok." Casper said patting Leo on the back. "You're hurting me just a little bit."

He released him instantly. "Sorry, I forget sometimes that you're not one of us."

"It's all ok now, all ok." Casper said with a smile.

He looked at the girls who were both crying now. Leo fell into Mollie's mothering arms and Ivy wrapped hers around Casper. She turned her head to the side and placed a powerful kiss on his cheek. "All is forgiven." she whispered in his ear. He hugged her back happily and knew it was the truth. He also just relished in the fact that she was close to him and that he could touch her and it was all right.

As the sun began to go down Ivy's family said their

goodbyes to PJ's family. Ivy hugged her former child and said, "No matter what happens I will always love you."

"That is good to know. I am sorry to have disappointed you. It will never happen again." PJ promised and anyone could see she meant it.

She placed her palm against PJ's cheek and said, "Remember the punishment, but consider the disappointment forgotten."

PJ smiled and said, "Yes ma'am."

The family packed Ivy's car and said their final goodbyes. "I made a decision today." Leo said to his family.

"And what's that?" Alex asked loading the final cooler into the trunk of Ivy's Bentley.

"When we get home I'm going to ask Nora to be my mate." Leo said a happy smile on his face.

"That's fantastic!" Mollie said, her smile from ear to ear.

"And about damn time." Peter said from beside them.

Leo's smile only grew wider. "Yea, something about seeing my parents, and how even now after so many years they're still so happy. I want that. The worst thing she can say is no right?"

"She won't say no." Ivy said from behind. They all turned to look at her. "Just make sure that it's what you want. Forever is a long time."

"I don't know what you mean, why wouldn't I be sure? I mean I have only been thinking about it since we moved here" Leo asked shoving his hands in his pockets.

"Consider it a mother like worry. I just want you to be happy." she said patting her hand on his shoulder.

"Thanks boss." Leo said. "Ready to go home?"

"You all get started, Casper's working out some things with Ian, I'll see you all at home."

"Ok," Grace said waving a final goodbye to PJ and her family.

Ivy watched her family as they began to run, and all too quickly they were out of her sight. She got into the car and waited for Casper to finish inside.

"I'm sorry that I left you alone with him Casper." Ian said looking down at his hands. They were sitting across the glass kitchen table.

"It's not like you meant to do it Zach." Casper said, knowing what was going on. His brother was saying his final goodbye.

"You know I can't see you again right? I can't keep in touch." Ian said, his eyes still focused away, almost as if he didn't look up at Casper none of it was real.

"I figured as much." Casper said looking down at his own hands. "It was good to see you though."

"Kid you have no idea. When I was first changed I asked Ivy every day if I could just go and check on you and she told me that I couldn't, but that everything would be ok."

"How could she know that?" Casper asked.

Ian shrugged. "I don't think she did, just trying to make me feel better I guess, but it helped." He looked up at Casper, who looked back at him. "It was very good to see you for myself."

"It was good to know you're alive, in a sense anyway." Casper said with a laugh.

"Yea, I think Ivy's waiting for you." Ian said standing up from his chair. "Take care of yourself."

"You too." Casper said staring at his brother. "Can I give you a hug?"

Ian smiled and embraced his brother. He held his breath as he did it, he didn't need his final memory to be of the appealing scent of his only brother.

Casper met Ivy in the car, where she was still waiting patiently. "Are you ok?" she asked after he clicked his seatbelt.

Casper shook off the tears rising up behind his eyes and said, "No, but I think I will be."

"Good." she said with a smile.

They were on the road for over a half an hour before Casper spoke again. "So Peter's a shape shifter huh?"

"Yes he is." Ivy said with a smile. "Crazy isn't it?"

"Yea just a bit, so how does it work? Can he just change into anything?" Casper asked.

"Only things he's seen before."

"What about other people?"

"No, humans are far too complex. Simpler creatures, cats, dogs, mice, cows so on and so forth. This is a totally separate thing from him being a vampire, he could do this when he was a human."

"That must have freaked out his family." Casper said trying to imagine what his mother would have done if he suddenly became the family pet.

Ivy's expression changed, sadder. "I'm guessing no one's really told you about Peter have they?"

"No," Casper said turning a bit in his seat to look at her.

Ivy licked her lips and said, "Peter's a little older in body than the rest of us. He's about thirty years old. He's grew up in the Midwest, Montana I think, he was born in 1770 I believe. He and his family were farmers, they died when he was young, influenza. He kept his farm running on his own for a long time, another farmer and a family came into town when he was in his early twenties. He gave them a place to stay on their journey across the country. They stayed with him for about a month, with them was their daughter, Beth.

"He loved her the moment her saw her and when her father decided it was time to leave Peter got so scared, he couldn't imagine never seeing her again. So on the day that they were to leave and continue west Peter asked Beth's father if he could marry her instead and her father agreed. They were so happy together. I can see it in his memories, the black and gray thoughts, I know you know about that. They had two beautiful children, a little girl named Sarah and a boy named Alan. Peter was a great father." Ivy's face fell. "And then she came and ruined everything for them.

"Her name was Lola. She arrived at his home, their farm pleading for shelter for just a day or two. She'd been traveling in the sun for over two days, not a safe situation for a vampire. Beth set her up on a makeshift bed and she slept, regenerating. She made Peter uneasy around his children. They way she looked at them was like they were something to eat, and obviously he had no idea that that was what they looked to her. So on the day that she changed him Peter sent Beth and the children into town so that he could get rid of her without them there. God, if only he could have known.

"He tried to tell her is was time for her to go, just to get her to leave. She wasn't having it. She bit him and drained him, killed him. From what I understood when I captured her she could only see his children when she killed him and that's why she changed him, so that he could see them again. She left, she changed him and she just left." Ivy was so disgusted as she said this that she could have spit. That vile was one of the worst she'd ever encountered.

"The years past and Beth got scared, she got older, Alan and Sarah got older, but Peter didn't. He would sneak off for days at a time and feed, just so he wouldn't hurt them. He said the worst part and the reason why he would be gone for so long, away from them, was because of everyone in his family he was so attracted by the scent of his daughter. I was alerted about him. I have been a prowler for five hundred years and I have never seen a newborn so in control of his urges. The fact that for years he was able to lay next to his wife and live among his children and not hurt them, you can't understand how impossible that is.

"I went for him and he fought me, but I took him away. I think he knew how impossible his situation was and he didn't want to hurt them. There's a black thought that he has, and you can never tell him I told you this, but it's just Beth's voice over and over again calling him a monster.

"I understand that Peter's a hard ass and difficult to get along with, but remember what's happened to him, I think it puts it in perspective."

"More than you know." Casper said settling back in his seat. He'd never seen Peter like that. Peter had always been the one who seemed most likely to kill him over anyone else. "I never would have thought that of him."

"Most people don't." she said, she ran a hand through her dark red curls and sighed. "He is a good man, he had a good life and unfortunately afterlife has been hard for him. You aren't born that cold, it comes with experience and Peter has not had the best of experiences."

He shifted uncomfortably from side to side and decided this was he perfect time to ask a specific question that he needed answered. "What about Nora?" he asked.

"What about her?"

"I've known her since I was sixteen and now I feel like I don't know her at all. She's one of your rogues, I was just wondering what her story was." he said, sitting back and waiting for her to answer.

She sighed in deeply and said, "Nora is special."

"I don't know what that means." Casper said with a shrug.

"I'm sure you've heard of the rules of who to kill if you must kill a human. You kill someone who won't be missed, Nora was one who would be missed.

"She was the daughter of a New York Senator in the early 19th century, the most proper of ladies. She married young, I think she was only sixteen. He was a rich banker and everything her parents would have hoped for. There was only one problem in her fairytale life, Nora was miserable. It's not like her husband, I'm pretty sure his name was George, ever hit her or anything, he just completely ignored her. Much like my husband, he didn't touch her or give her any affection at all. You can't imagine as a woman how hard that is to handle. Feeling like you're so undesirable your own husband doesn't want you-" She paused for a moment, her hands gripping harder on the steering wheel. He shook his head, he could never imagine any man being so blind as to not see her as attractive, she was the most beautiful woman in the world to Casper. The softness of her deep emerald eyes that were like pools he could get lost in forever. The gentle curl to her crimson red hair that spilled down her shoulders and back like a river. The gentle curve of her bone structure under her milk white skin. She was the most gorgeous creature that had ever been created. How could anyone not want her?

"Anyway, he used to leave her every night and go somewhere, just like my husband. So she followed him one night and what she found out was something she could have gone her entire life without knowing. Of course she hoped deep down that she was being ridiculous, that he had enough respect for his wedding vows to not be with another woman, but she was also smart enough to know that it was a possibility. He led her to an inn at the center of the city-"

"So he was meeting another woman?" Casper interrupted.

She turned her head toward him and shook her head. "No, not another woman."

It took Casper a moment to process what she was saying, she kept her eyes off the road and stared into his until it kicked in. "Oh god." he said, flipping back to looking out the windshield. "He was meeting a guy."

She nodded. "Yes."

"That must have killed her." he said with a shake of his

head.

Ivy sighed and said, "I can't even imagine."

"So, what does that have to do with her becoming a vampire?" Casper asked.

"George got scared, especially when Nora ran away. His lover told him not to worry, he'd handle it."

"I've heard things like that before." Casper said glancing out the window at the trees that zipped by, they were out of the desert now.

"Being a vampire he could get to her quickly, he'd heard her heartbeat, knew her scent, he could find her. And he did. He nearly ripped her throat out when he took her down. And he looked at her and said that killing her was too easy, she should suffer forever. And so he changed her."

"What makes her special?" he asked, so deeply saddened by Nora's ordeal.

"She did something, something I have never known a vampire to be able to do."

"What?"

Ivy paused and took in a deep slow breath. "She killed her creator."

"Well obviously vampires can kill other vampires-" Casper began.

"You don't understand," Ivy interjected. "Your creator can tell you to do anything and you have to do it, no matter what. So I'm sure that any vampire would command their creation to stop from killing them. So the power that she has is indefinable. It's intimidating and a bit frightening."

"What aren't you saying?" Casper asked twisting to look right at her.

"Just be careful around her. I know she's your friend, but just be careful, that's all I'm going to say." she said, her eyes focusing back forward, the conversation over.

He shifted back in his seat and closed his eyes to sleep. Living in the home of the carnivorous vampires had caused him to lose much of his sleep. And in what seemed like a blink of an eye they were back at Ivy's home, all the way across the country. He decided that it was better he just not ask about the speed at which she traveled. Nothing good could have come from that.

"Nora's car is here." Casper noticed as they pulled into the massive garage.

"Yea, Leo had something important to ask her." Ivy said with a smile that may have been a grimace, he couldn't tell, as she put the car into park. She glanced out through the windshield at the key scratch on the hood, she'd have to have Mollie fix that.

Inside Nora was sitting with the family talking about the trip to the other side of the country. "Thank god you're all right." Nora said patting Mollie on the hand.

The room fell silent and all the faces of the family turned to Leo. "Everyone, could you give me a moment to talk to Nora please." he asked, his voice a bit shaky. Nora knew something was off, especially considering the thoughts around her. Alex was thinking, *It was a one eyed, one horned flying purple people eater.* Grace was thinking, *Yellow bus, yellow bus, yellow bus.* Over and over and over. And much was the same for Leo and Peter. The other three left the room leaving only Nora and Leo in the room.

"What's going on Leo?" Nora asked, her head whipping back around to look at him. He was smiling brightly at her, and knowing Leo she decided this was no call for being on edge.

"I want to talk to you about something." Leo said sitting down on the plush couch beside her.

Nora pushed her corn-silk colored hair behind her shoulder and focused her eyes on Leo. "Shoot." she said with a smile of her own.

"I know I'm young, I know that you're a hundred and thirty years older than I am and that you could probably do better than me." His eyes glanced down, if his heart was still beating it would have been racing. "But from the minute I first met you three years ago I just fell in love with you." Her expression softened, it was not what she had expected. "At first I was attracted to how gorgeous you are. Your eyes, your hair, every valley and mountain of your face, I close my eyes and you're what I see. I shouldn't be able to dream anymore and yet when I sleep I dream of you. And then as we got to know each other I fell harder. You have a heart, metaphorically speaking of course." he laughed and she smiled, that was the Leo she knew. "A heart unlike anything I've ever known." He leaned forward and took her hand and she did not recoil. "My human life was a nightmare, a nightmare I put upon myself. But I was thinking that maybe my afterlife could be everything humanity wasn't for me. So I was wondering if you, the amazing creature you are, would consider being my mate and spend forever with me."

She was quiet for a long moment, still holding his hand. Her eyes seemed unfocused, like she was thinking so hard. He got nervous and a bit embarrassed thinking he'd made himself a fool. "I'm sorry." he said trying to stand up. She forcefully pulled him back down with more strength then even she realized she possessed. She took his other hand and smiled. Her hands moved up to his face and she ran her thumbs back and forth across his cheeks. She moved closer to him and brushed her lips gently against his. Even with over one hundred and fifty years at a vampire she was still quite inexperienced with such things. Her smile sweetened and she said, "My first marriage was loveless and miserable. I never thought I could open my heart again, but I think I can with you."

"Are you saying yes?" Leo asked, placing his hands over hers.

She nodded and said, "I suppose I am." He smiled and put his hands behind her head and pulled her into him. He kissed her deeply and sweetly with all the love he'd always had for her.

"Mazal tov!" Alex shouted coming through the door the rest of the family in toe, Casper and Ivy among them.

Ivy walked up to Nora and embraced her happily. "I suppose you'll be in my family after all." The tone in her head was much quieter, only Nora would be able to hear is, *And don't you dare hurt him.*

Nora smiled and said, "Wouldn't dream of it."

Grace grabbed Nora by the arm and said, "We have to start planning! We have a few days before They come we can have a full ceremony."

"I suppose, if it's all right with Ivy." Nora said turning to the leader of the family.

"Of course, I would have nothing less for my Leo." she said her voice proud, with only a hint of protectiveness.

"Perhaps I could have a white dress?" Nora said, her voice with the sound of a question.

"Did you not have one at your first wedding?" Mollie asked tying her chocolate hair in a knot at the base of her head.

"No, that was a frivolity that my father thought unnecessary. We had all the money in the world but he wouldn't even pay for a wedding dress." Nora said with a shake of her head. "I'd just like one."

"I'm sure we can do that." Ivy said with a smile.

Nora glanced over at Leo who was smiling at her. "Anything you want."

"So are you getting married?" Casper asked as he and Leo decorated the foyer of the house for the ceremony.

"Not exactly." Leo said jumping up and hanging the flowers on a high rafter. "It's more like an eternal commitment. Marriage is a very religious institution and we have issues with the Christian church so we just created our own ceremony."

"But Nora wanted a wedding dress." Casper clarified.

"Yea, that's her human side holding on. It's hard sometimes to let go of the things you really wanted and never got. If it makes her happy I'm glad she's getting it."

"You seem really happy." Casper said with a smile handing the flowers to Leo for him to hang.

"I am." Leo said smiling back at him. "For lack of a better term I royally fucked up my human life and it's like I got a second chance, so I'm doing everything right. And spending eternity with Nora is just right to me."

"I wish I could be so sure with things." Casper said, his eyes falling downward.

"Hey man, you have to remember that I would be a middle aged man by now and it took me this long to find happiness. Give it time, you'll get there." Leo said as he hung the last of the flowers. He ran a hand through his spiky blonde hair and said, "Looks pretty good doesn't it?"

"Looks good to me." Casper said leaning back and looking at the display before him. The foyer was covered, floor to ceiling, with daisies of all colors. They were Nora's favorite flowers and the entire event was to make Nora happy.

"I like that one." Grace said smiling at Nora in the floor length white gown. Nora was on her twenty-fourth dress of the afternoon. Mollie, Ivy and Grace went along to be supportive of the soon to be newest member of her family, that supportiveness was running dangerously low.

"Should you really wear a white one?" Mollie asked.

"Why?" Nora asked, moving away from the mirror and back to the dressing room, time for another dress.

"Well you have been married before right? I know when my sister got married after her first husband died she wore an ivory colored dress." Mollie said with a shrug. "I'm just saying is all."

"Two things," Nora said with a bit of a snap. "One it's not technically a marriage, it's a commitment. Two the white dress is a sign of purity and I am still a virgin."

"You are?" Grace said, her sea blue eyes popping open and her jaw falling slack, Grace of course had lost her virginity at the age of twelve and she had never even been married.

"No, my husband didn't have any interest in touching me." Nora said pulling on another dress. This one more of an eggshell, just to humor Mollie.

"I can understand that." Ivy said pulling her knees up to her chest.

Nora emerged in the off white dress that looked so glamorous, almost like an antique. "That's beautiful Nora." Grace said with a smile.

"You think so?" Nora said turning slowly in a circle smiling at her reflection.

"I do." Mollie said. "I think this is the right one."

"I might agree with you." Nora said glancing from side to side. "It's pretty good isn't it."

"How are we doing ladies?" the nervous saleswoman said to them creeping up slowly from behind. Not all humans were as easy going around them as Casper, and these were humans who didn't know what they were.

Ivy opened her wallet and pulled out her platinum credit card and handed it to the woman. "We'll take this one."

"Well I'm not completely sure." Nora said looking back at Ivy.

Ivy smiled, almost smugly and said, "Well, I am paying for it and I think we all agree that it's the right one."

"Fine, I suppose it is, I'll just go and take it off." Nora said walking back to the dressing room, her voice a little like timid, like a child.

"Did you have to do that?" Mollie asked, shifting her weight to the side.

"Do what?" Ivy asked.

"You were kind of rude boss." Grace said moving over to the seat with Mollie and Ivy.

"I'm sorry what exactly was rude about buying her the seven thousand dollar dress?" Ivy asked crossing her arms across her chest.

"That's not what we mean Ivy." Mollie said with a shake of her head. "It's just you didn't really ask if she liked it or not. You just decided and that was the end of it."

"It's my money, I think I should have at least some say in how it is spent." Ivy said, crossing her arms across her chest, not appreciating the tone from her family.

"I thought you said we should think of it as our money? Like the family's money?" Mollie said glancing up at Grace. "I thought you liked Nora."

"I love Nora." Ivy defended herself. "That's not it at all."

"Then what?" Grace asked placing her hand gently on Ivy's shoulder.

"Nothing, its nothing. I'm just being silly, protective of Leo I guess." Ivy said with a smile. She knew that her fears were unjustified, she knew Nora very well, better than pretty much anyone in the entire world and while Ivy knew that Nora could make Leo happy there was something about her that she did not trust. There had been a reason why she hadn't kept her in the family, but it was more of a gut instinct rather than anything with evidence.

"That's understandable I guess, he is your baby after all."

Grace said with a smile.

Nora emerged from the dressing room, the dress back its garment bag. "Thank you for the dress Ivy." she said with a smile.

Ivy smiled back and said, "Nora I'm sorry if I was forceful before, if you want a different one, you're more than welcome."

Nora shook her head, her soft yellow hair moving like a wave as she did so, and said, "No, I was looking at it in there and I think you're all right. It is perfect."

"Is there anything else you'll be requiring ladies?" the uneasy saleswoman asked handing Ivy back her credit card. Ivy hated it when humans became nervous around them. Their heartbeats raced and this particular human had an extremely appealing beat and Ivy was hungry. Her eyes began to change, as much as she resisted.

"No that will be all." Nora answered for her flashing her brilliant set of teeth, nearly blinding the poor girl.

Grace rummaged through her purse and secretly pulled out a vial and handed to Ivy. "How long had been since you've eaten?" she asked as Ivy popped the top and as discreetly and gobbled down the contents.

"Not since yesterday morning." she said, sighing in sweet relief.

"That wasn't exactly smart." Mollie said handing her another from her own secret stash. "You knew we'd be around humans today."

"It's been a busy few days for her. I'm sure any of us could have made the same mistake." Nora justified for her.

"That must be it." Ivy said moving quickly to her feet. "Let's go I can smell an entire bridal party on their way in."

At the house the boys had changed into their suits and were ready for the ceremony.

"Thanks for letting me borrow this Alex." Casper said, buttoning closed the sleeve on the suit. "I didn't think to bring a suit with me." Alex began to laugh, his hazel eyes brimmed with tears because of it. "What?" Casper demanded.

"You shock me a little more every few minutes." Alex said with a shake of his head.

"Why?"

"Because dude you still don't seem to grasp the situation you're in with us. You act like we're just normal people." Alex said straightening his tie.

Casper picked up a brush and ran it through his hair. "And you all act like you're not people at all."

"And you forget that we're not. We're not human anymore, most of us haven't been for a very long time." Alex said, his eyes angled downward.

"I think you're more human than you even realize." Casper said, trying to comfort him.

"Why?" Alex said with a humorless laugh. "Because you believe the lie? Because I can act human? Let me explain something to you, I have had over a hundred and forty years to practice being human and to be able to handle living among humans, but you have not idea how mouth-watering your heartbeat is, or when your cheeks flush, or when your breathing quickens. Even with all my practice it still takes everything in me not to break your neck and drink all your blood. Don't forget that, especially not with Them coming, They're not like us. They will kill you and not think twice about it."

Alex had been acting strange all day, they all had been, but especially Alex. "What's the matter with you man?" he asked.

He shook his head. "Nothing. The girls are back, we should get downstairs." Casper didn't speak just followed Alex down. Something was wrong with him, but Casper just couldn't place it for sure.

"Give us ten minutes and we'll be ready to get started." Ivy said to Alex and Casper when they reached the bottom of the stairs, just inside the front doors of the house, her voice somber and somewhat unfocused. "Is Leo ready?"

"I'll go check." Casper said walking away towards a room across the house.

When he was out of hearing range Ivy whipped back around to her seer and said, "What do you see?"

Alex sighed and shook his head. "It's all really fuzzy. The only thing that I can see clearly is that They'll be here tomorrow and it's not just Angelo and Rudolph."

"Who else?" Ivy demanded, her voice breathy and panicked. This was far from a good sign, the fewer vampires there were in one place the better.

He kept shaking his head. "It's hard to tell, but there are a lot, not all of them from Them. The Africans, the Chinese and the Amazons along with many others, but they come later. I can't tell for sure, I'm sorry."

"It's okay." she said, running her hands through her red hair. "For now let's not panic the others, bury it in, don't think about it.

We'll cross this bridge together soon."

"Okay," Alex said his eyes flicking up to the double doors behind them that led to the outside. "Here they come." And as the words left his lips the doors opened. Ivy had noticed in the past few days Alex's skills had grown much sharper and defined, more than they hand in the past hundred years. Casper being there, the rogue from Emily, Their impending arrival, the vision of all the vampires at her home. It had to be connected, she just couldn't figure out how.

Chapter Eight

"Is it all right with you that I'm joining your family?" Nora asked as Ivy buttoned up the back of her epic gown. She moved at human speed, savoring the moment, she knew there was much she and Nora needed to talk about.

"Why are you asking?" Ivy asked fastening the last button.

"You seem distant today, like something's wrong." Nora said sitting down at the vanity for Ivy to do her hair. Ivy was quiet, she wanted Nora to continue. "I've always wondered why you didn't invite me to join the family, the strength I have, it's a lot like the power Leo has, but you invited him to join the family and not me."

Ivy sighed as she ran a brush through Nora's blonde hair and said, "You have a different spirit from Leo. You're very independent and Leo needed more structure. He wanted a family, I always got the vibe from you that it wasn't what you wanted. Apparently I was wrong. That and I think you needed to start out on your own, or else you would have been too tied to me and that is not what I wanted for you. That's all." She moved at a much quicker speed to pin up her hair.

Nora reached up and forcefully grabbed her hand, Ivy could almost feel pain as Nora pulled Ivy around to face her. "I love him, I do. I want to be in your family, I always did." She kept her grip just as tight on Ivy's wrist as she said, "And I love you, like the mother I miss."

"Easy goes it, you're hurting me." Ivy said resting her other hand on Nora's slowly easing her grip loose. She put her hand on Nora's cheek and said, "I know all this, trust me I do." She smiled and Nora smiled back. "Let's get downstairs."

The family was waiting for them at the bottom of the stairs. The boys all decked out in designer suits and the girls were lovely. Mollie had on a burgundy, tight knee length dress, with her brown hair flowing down her back. Grace had on a canary yellow floor length free flowing dress with her short black hair slicked back. Ivy walked down the stairs with Nora in her antiqued wedding dress. Ivy wore a tight, floor length evergreen dress that matched her eyes in color. Leo stood at the head of the group and took Nora's hand when they reached them, the smile on his face spreading from ear to ear. He was so happy.

Nora and Leo held hands and smiled at each other and all turned to look at Ivy. "Today is a good day, today I bring two of my children together forever. Eternity is a long time to spend alone, which makes this union all the more joyous. Leo," she said turning to her boy. "Do you take Nora to be your partner forever and promise to love and cherish her above all others for all days of your existence?"

If it was possible Leo smiled wider and said, "Absolutely."

"Nora," Ivy said turning to her. "Do you take Leo to by your partner forever and promise to love and cherish him above all others for all the days of your existence?"

Nora's face was more serious than Leo's had been as she said, her voice just above a whisper, "Forever."

There was a silent moment of reflection and Alex broke the silence, "Dude, kiss her." A low rumble of a laugh sounded among the group as the two shared their first true kiss. The family applauded and then embraced their new sister. "Welcome to family." Ivy whispered when it was finally her turn.

"Happy to be here." Nora said, her voice different, indefinable really.

"Does anyone else find it ironic that the baby was the first to take a mate?" Grace asked with a laugh as she embraced her brother and newest sister. Of course Peter's face fell, if he had had his way he would have a mate.

"I'm just lucky I guess." Leo said glancing down at his mate. He sighed and swept her up in his arms and said, "Well we'll see you all later."

The family groaned and Peter said, "Anyone up for a family outing?"

Everyone quickly grabbed their things and Grace grabbed Casper's arm and hurried him out the door. "What's the rush?" Casper asked, confused by their urgency.

"Have you ever heard people having sex in a nearby room and you can't get away from it?" Peter asked bluntly.

"Um, yea I guess so." Casper said clicking his seatbelt inside Alex's jeep, the girls had gone in Ivy's Bentley.

"Now imagine it with two insanely strong vampires." Alex said backing out of the garage. "Suffice it to say that we would like to keep our distance from that." He laughed then at the vision in his head, "Ivy's going to have to buy a new headboard."

Peter laughed and said, "Yea we all learned our lesson with Victor and Bianca."

"Who are Victor and Bianca?" Casper asked.

"They were members for the family about a century about. They joined us just a little while after Grace did. And they decided to become mates and on the day of their ceremony when they consummated things, we all stayed in the house. What a mistake that was." Peter said with a laugh.

"They were part of the family?" Casper said, he didn't really understand why it surprised him, but it seemed like there couldn't be anyone else in their family, like they could only be the group they were.

"Yea, for about thirty years I guess, only three or four of that after they became mates." Alex said his eyes focused on the road.

"They left?" Casper asked.

"Obviously." Peter said with a roll of his eyes.

"Well what I mean is why?" Casper asked.

Peter sighed and said, "We've had a lot of people come in and out of the family. There's a reason why she refers to her rogues as her children. She raises them and most of the leave when they reach, adulthood let's call it. A few stay with her and join the family, I think we're proof of the that. But things still can change, Bianca and Victor loved each other and wanted to be their own family. And while things can become different from what we become accustomed to, we always love them just the same."

"Is that what you all have been so worried about?" Casper asked with a laugh in his voice.

"What?" Alex asked, turning a bit to look back at Casper.

"Are you worried that Leo will leave you guys with Nora?"

"No." they said in unison, a laugh of their own in their voices.

"You say that like it's preposterous, but you just said that others have left your family for just that reason."

"Trust me man, you don't know Leo well enough. He'd give

up anything for Ivy and the family, he'd even give up Nora."

Casper settled back in his seat and glanced out the window as they pulled into a parking lot. "We're going to a restaurant?"

"You have to eat don't you?" Alex asked hopping out of the jeep.

"Well yea, but what are you guys going to do?" Casper asked getting out as well.

"Perfect our acting abilities I suppose." Peter said running a hand through his dark curly hair. "It's Ivy's idea."

The girls were already inside sitting in a massive booth at a vacant corner at the back of the restaurant. "Hello boys." Grace greeted. They each had a drink in front of them, Casper motioned to the glasses and Grace smiled. "Playing the part Casper dear, playing the part."

The boys piled into the booth with the girls and they were silent. Of course they could all hear the thoughts in each other's minds, Casper was on the outside. "Ok what aren't we saying?" Casper asked with a sigh.

"Mollie," Ivy said folding her hands atop the table. "Ask him."

All eyes turned to Mollie who sighed and said, "I was wondering if you might be able to do something for me Casper?"

"What?" he asked.

"Well, I was thinking about what you did for Leo in Seattle and I was wondering if you could do that for me?" Mollie said, wringing her hands together under the table.

"What do you mean?" Casper asked.

"My sister Irma still lives nearby and she never got any closure with me, I just died on her, they never even had a body to bury." Mollie said, trying to hide the emotion in her voice. "I was wondering if maybe you could go to her house and I'll write a letter or something like Leo did."

"But we also said Leo was alive, I don't think we can tell her that you're still alive can we?" Casper asked.

"No, maybe you could be from some agency with the military and you found a letter or something, I don't know, something." she said, her voice nearly pleading.

"I don't mean to be disrespectful, but why don't you have one of your family do it?" Casper asked.

The family smiled and Ivy said, "Well Irma has seen all of us before, and me especially she probably wouldn't want to see ever again."

"Irma didn't handle it well, the fact that I had my will changed to give Ivy, a woman she had never met, my house and everything Henry and I ever owned. It took years before she stopped coming by," Mollie practically whispered, her eyes focused down. "I don't what was worse, her coming back constantly or her not coming at all."

Casper reached his hand across the table and put it on top of Mollie, her eyes fluttered up to see his lopsided grin. "For you, I'll do it." he said holding his smile.

She smiled back. "Thank you Casper."

"New conversation," Alex muttered. As he did the waitress walked up to the table.

She wore a horrid bubblegum pink uniform, her frizzy blonde hair tied in a messy knot behind her head and her makeup looked like she'd done it in the dark. She smiled brightly and said, "Hello there boys, what can get you on this fine day?"

Alex and Peter both asked for a glass of water and that was it. Casper glanced around and saw that the girls all had water. "Can I have a cup of coffee?" he asked.

"You want anything to eat?" Ivy urged.

"Can I get a bacon egg and cheese sandwich on a bagel?" Casper asked beginning to hear his stomach rumbling and he assumed all his counterparts could hear it as well. "And a stack of pancakes, and a fruit cup, and maybe a few sausage links."

The woman smiled and said, "Sure baby, and my name's Darla if you need anything else. Or if the rest of you decide you want to order something?" She paused for a minute waiting for one of them to speak up, but when they didn't she sighed and walked away.

"Hungry?" Grace said with a giggle.

"Well I haven't really eaten anything, I guess I just forget when I'm around all of you." Casper said, crossing his arms across his chest. He glanced around at their glasses of water. "Can you guys really drink that?"

"We could, it would just involve throwing it up later though." Alex said swirling his finger around in the water. "We don't have a digestive system that works likes that."

"Well how does it work then?" Casper asked, leaning his head on his palm.

The five of them glanced around at one another and then Ivy let out a laugh and said, "I have no idea."

"Then how do you know you can't eat food?"

All eyes jumped quickly to Grace. She rolled hers and said,

"Yea real subtle guys." She sighed and said, "They all just had the instinct that they couldn't eat anymore and while I had it I chose to ignore it. I tried to eat for weeks, the food would literally turn to ash in my mouth and any drink would burn as I swallowed it, but I wouldn't give in. Giving in was like I was admitting that I wasn't human anymore and finally I was actually sick, it took two days for me to cough up everything, which is not an easy task considering we don't have a gag reflex."

Ivy tucked a piece of Grace's short black hair behind her ear and said, "But you got through it just fine."

Grace smiled at looked over at Ivy, "Yea I did, because of you."

"What did you do?" Casper asked, not meaning it to come across as rude.

"My job involves more than just teaching the newborns the rules of being a vampire. You have no concept how overwhelming and terribly horrifying   becoming this is." Ivy said with a shake of her head, he was so human. "It's true, some vampires turn out just like Leo, ecstatic that this happened to them, but that's about two percent of the whole. Pretty much everyone is scared out of their minds and hates the thought of being a monster, at least initially. Many learn to embrace it, after all there's nothing you can do about it, but some need more encouraging than others." Her voice began to waver off, she wasn't sure she was talking about Grace anymore. *Stay out of my head.* she warned the others and all their eyes darted away.

After a long awkward moment of silence Darla, the waitress came back with Casper's coffee. "Sure there's nothing I can get all of you?"

"You'll get a fine tip if that's what you're worried about?" Ivy snapped.

Darla was taken aback, she had not expected the cute redhead of the group to have such a temper, "No sugar I-"

"I'm not your sugar," Ivy barked back. "You're a child in comparison to me."

Darla shifted her weight from one hip to the other, she wasn't getting the hint to leave. "Well how old are you, you don't look like you could be more twenty five and let me tell you dear I crossed that bridge a long time ago."

Under the table Ivy twisted her fork into a tight spiral and so desperately wanted to scream out that she was five hundred years old, just to see how the woman would react. But she didn't do that. This had nothing to do with Darla, it was about Ivy and what she still couldn't accept about herself. She took in a deep breath and looked up at the waitress with an honest smile and said, "Never mind it's not important. Sorry I snapped at you."

Darla smiled too, much a part of her job, but it seemed genuine enough. "Not a problem, let me know if there is anything I can do for you."

"What is going on with you?" Grace demanded as Darla walked away. All eyes turned to Ivy, but she looked at Alex.

"Tell them, tell them what you saw." she commanded of him. He stared at her for a moment, this really wasn't the place or the time. "Tell them Alex."

"Um," Alex began with a bit of stutter. "It seems as though They will be here tomorrow." Casper swallowed hard, and the others stopped breathing for a moment.

"Well we knew that this had to come." Mollie said with a sigh, her hands under her chin.

Ivy's eyes were still locked on Alex and she would not release him from her gaze. A part of her wanted him to reveal everything, but a bigger part wanted to know what he was hiding. While she was usually able to read the thoughts of all vampires no matter what they tried to hide there was something that Alex was hiding. He looked nervous, swaying back and forth, the most random of thoughts going through his mind, the rest of the family began to notice. A slight break in the tension came with the delivery of Casper's food. Darla paused momentarily, apparently not aware of any tension at all. "Now seriously, one of you must want something." she said, shifting her weight from one hip to the other, truly flummoxed with the fact that none of them were eating. Ivy snapped her knife under the table, frustrated with Alex, with Darla, with the sound of Casper's knife and fork on the plate, with the heavy breathing of the people two tables over, she couldn't know for sure, but it wasn't just the knife that snapped at that moment. Her eyes changed and her fangs emerged, a mistake she never made in public. A part of her panicked, but a bigger part didn't care at all. She turned to Grace, closet to her who opened her purse and pulled out two one hundred dollar bills and handed them to Darla. "Keep it please." she said pushing Ivy out of the booth and away from the room

"Oh honey I can't do that, this is an insane amount of money." Darla tried to argue. Then she made a mistake, she grabbed Ivy by the arm. In the instant that Ivy flipped around, ready to kill the waitress that irked her in a inch of her sanity Alex was by her side, too quick for human speed, but that was far less conspicuous that Ivy sucking the blood of a human in a room full of witnesses.

"Just keep it woman and be grateful." Alex hissed at Darla as he walked passed her, nearly carrying Ivy under his arm. *The rest of you go back to the house in the jeep.* Alex thought for the family.

"Are you all right to drive?" he barked at her when they were outside.

"Well you're certainly not driving my car!" she shouted back. "Give me the damn keys!" No one was around them, even if there were it really wouldn't have mattered then, at abnormally fast speed he threw them to her and she caught them without a pause. They got in the car, and all too fast, zipped out of the parking lot.

"What the hell is wrong with you!" he was shouting at her as she weaved in and out of traffic, ignoring the sound of the honking horns. "We were in a crowded room, surrounded by humans and you do that! How could you, you put us all in danger. She jerked the car hard to the right and into an abandoned parking lot.

In a flash she had him by the jaw, pushed up against the window, startling him. "You listen to me now. I don't know how you're doing it but you're blocking something from me and I demand to know right now what it is. Your place in the family depends on it."

He was quiet, starring at her. She knew what he was doing, he was trying to judge if she was serious. *What! What won't you say?* she demanded, and then aloud she said, "This is me Alex, what can't you say to me."

Even though she held his gaze, he found the strength to pull away. "You're not going to like it."

"From the way you're acting, I doubt I would." she said, crossing her arms and waiting, they weren't leaving until she had the answers she required.

He ran a nervous hand through his light hair and licked his lips, twice. "I think I know what They're going to decide about Casper."

Her arms fells down into her lap and her jaw went slack. Casper's punishment had completely slipped her mind, too much had happened in the past days. "Rudolph's going to kill him isn't he?" she said her voice so sorrowful that it even surprised her. A tear sprung to her eye at the thought of Casper dead.   And even worse, even the idea of Rudolph being the one to do it made her skin nearly crawl off her body. But Alex was shaking his head. "That's not what I see." he said, his hazel eyes sad.

"Well what could be so bad you'd go to all this trouble of hiding it from me?" Ivy asked pushing the mounds of red hair away from her face. It was then that she saw it. Alex relaxed his vision so that she could see what he found so terrifying. Her hand flew to her mouth and she gasped, "No. No it can't be." Alex was looking away. The vision was simple, Casper standing in an unfamiliar place, somewhere she'd never seen, everything about him was the same with one important difference. He had the eyes of a cat and fangs. In Alex's vision, a vision of the somewhat near future, Casper was a vampire. "This can't be right." she said, her voice frantic and nearly angry. Angry at Alex, angry at Rudolph, angry at Casper. Stupid boy, why did he ever come there, enter their lives, it would have been better if he just stayed away. But that thought nearly killed her, how tragic she thought of life if she had never actually met Casper. He was a breath of fresh air in their family. He was so different fro any other human, so completely different. She cared for him, she couldn't deny that now, but it wasn't until that moment that she truly discovered why. Casper never once saw her as the monster she was so convinced she was. "But you're vision could be wrong." she said with an orphan sob.

Alex was put aback a bit by the emotion, it was more than Ivy showed for anyone. "It is always possible, I mean until recently I was usually never right."

Ivy nodded slowly. "We're going to go with that thinking, because what your vision portrays, that can't happen. It can't, I won't let it." Without another word she nearly jammed the car back into drive and they were back on the road.

"Where are we going?" Alex asked, clutching his seat as she took a sharp corner at ninety miles an hour. "Ivy?"

"Home. I want to be home." she said, her voice meek and quiet, emotion still rattling her loose, loose of even her sanity. She tried to put her mind on anything else, but the only thought that would surface, the only picture she could see, were the eyes. Casper's eyes if he were like her, a damned monstrosity.

"Why do you see yourself like that Ivy?" Alex demanded, slamming his hand down onto the center console of the car, leaving a dent there. "You have had more time than all of us to cope with what happened to you, but you still don't accept it-"

"I accept it fine," she snapped back. "I accept that I am a monster and there is nothing I can do about it, but I would not wish my fate on anyone."

"I can't understand how you can think like that and do what you do." he said shaking his head. "Your entire life is comprised of teaching vampires how to live with what's happened to them and yet you can never accept it for yourself. There is nothing wrong with us Ivy, we're just different."

"We kill people!" she retorted, her speed increasing with ever moment, they would make it home in record time.

"And humans kill animals for there food, what is the difference?"

"You were never a cow or a chicken! You were a person, you were what you killed! Humans were not ever the things they eat." she said slamming her hand against the steering wheel. "And this eternal life, it's not natural, we are the only things that live forever. Humans have no concept how glorious their mortality is."

"Stop the car." he muttered as they drove down the massive driveway. She didn't listen at first and he repeated himself, his voice booming and angry. "Stop the car Ivy." She slowed to a crawl and then stopped. Her hands stayed on the steering wheel and her eyes remained focused forward as he spoke. He shook his head at her. "Stop pitying yourself, you look ridiculous. Yes we kill people, and yes you've murdered people, but you can't go back to your human life. There's no magic potion that will change you back, as much as you wish there was. I too wish this hadn't happened to me, but I made my peace with it, we all did. Perhaps after five hundred years it's about time you did too." He opened the door of the car and got out, he'd prefer to walk up to the house instead of drive. Slowly she released her hands from the steering wheel and grumbled at the impressing her fingers had left behind. She turned the key in the ignition and at a snail's pace rolled up the driveway to the garage. She stayed in the car, unable to move and thought, *Mollie did you write this letter for you sister?*

Yea boss, are you ok? Mollie asked in her head.

Ivy ignored the latter part of the sentence and thought, *Send Casper out with it, we'll do this now.*

Ok. she said her thought curt, the tone of Ivy's inner voice callous and cold. *He's on his way.*

"Are you all right?" Casper asked her as he got in the car. She didn't answer. She pulled the car out of the garage and drove at a human speed, her hands covering the dents in the steering wheel, her eyes focused on the road. They were silent.

It took her only minutes to get to Irma's home, she had driven past it many times in the past decades, checking on Mollie's family as she had done for many of her rogues in the past. It was a little yellow house with green shutters in a devolvement of new townhouses, they had try to buy Irma's house many times over the years, but she hand always refused. She had said it was because the house was her legacy, something her husband had built her, but Ivy knew the truth. Irma always secretly hoped that Mollie would come home and if the house wasn't there, how would Mollie ever find her way back.

Casper got out of the car and walked up the creaky wooden stairs. There was no doorbell so he knocked and waited. It took a few moments but a voice from the other side of the door said, "Just hold your horses, I'm coming." The door slowly opened to reveal a tiny woman, in her nineties most likely, gazing up at Casper. "Can I help you?" she asked.

"Are you Irma Cooley?" he asked with a polite smile.

"Yes, what can I do for you?" Irma asked pushing her wait out the door and onto the porch with him.

"Do you have a sister named Mollie Victors?" he asked.

Her face turned cold. "What kind of sick joke is this? My sister died a long time ago. What do you want? Other than torture an old woman I mean?"

He was a bit taken aback by her tone and her callous glance, her eyes were so cold. "Well ma'am I work for the Second World War historical society," he lied and then licked his lips and continued. "Two days ago I was going through a box of letters that hadn't been mailed and there was one there for you. It was from a Mollie Victors and I looked her up in our database, you were listed as he next of kin as her sister and I just thought you might want to have it." He pulled the letter out of his jacket pocket and she snatched it away.

She ripped open the envelope and pulled out the letters she then pushed it to Casper. "I don't have my glasses, read it to me." she commanded.

Considering the fact that he was actually a little frightened of Mollie's sister he obeyed. He unfolded the letter and cleared his throat and began to read. "My Dearest Sister Irma," he began. "If you are reading this letter, then that unfortunately means, well I think we both know what it means. It means I am gone. I know that you never wanted me to leave in the first place and if you're angry with me I understand, you have every right to be. But I didn't come to this place because of you, or Henry, or even my country really. I did it for me and only for me because I needed something new, a change. I want you to know how much I love you and I will always be there for you, I will look after you for the rest of your days. And that's a promise." Casper swallowed hard and read the end of the letter, "Goodbye forever my one and only sister. I love you. Mollie." He lowered the letter and folded it back up, handing it back to her. "I'm sorry about your sister, she must have been an amazing woman."

"She was." the old woman said holding the letter delicately in her hands. She glanced up at Casper and then beyond him to the car parked on the curb and more importantly the driver behind the wheel. Ivy panicked when the old woman saw her, she tried to play it cool but it wasn't working. She pulled her oversized sunglasses out of her purse and slid them on her face and sunk down in her seat hoping the old woman would just go back in the house. She didn't.

"I know that girl." Irma said passing Casper and walking down the stairs. She tapped on Ivy's closed window and Ivy sat there, pretending she didn't hear. Irma tapped again. Slowly Ivy reached up and pressed the button to roll down the window.

"Can I help you?" she asked, her eyes focused forward and out the windshield, trying her best not to make eye contact. Casper was on the sidewalk rocking back on his heels waiting to see what would happen.

"I know you." Irma said, leaning her hand on the door of Ivy's car.

Ivy didn't move a muscle, very inhuman of her but she feared if she moved even a little she'd break all the nerve she ever had. "I don't think so ma'am."

"No I'm sure of it, you have a face I'm sure I could never forget." Irma said leaning in closer, the aroma from her breath making Ivy's head spin. After a moment longer of staring Irma nearly jumped back. "You-you look just like her."

"Who ma'am?" Ivy asked, her hands tightening on the already battered steering wheel.

"You look just like the girl who stole my sister's house after she died." Irma said her voice sounded just as angry as it had the last time Ivy had seen her.

"That's ridiculous ma'am, you sister has been dead over sixty years, I'm only twenty-two years old." Ivy said, her jaw locked tight.

"Well of course you're not her, I'm not completely crazy. But you look far too much like her to not be related. You must be her granddaughter or something." Ivy kept silent and Irma took that as confirmation. "Well you can tell your grandmother she can go to hell."

"Already there." Ivy whispered to herself, low enough that Irma didn't hear it.

Irma's eyes snapped up at Casper and then back at the letter in her hand. "And what is this? Some sick joke by a couple kids with nothing better to do?" Ivy remained still.

"No ma'am I swear-" Casper defended, but she wasn't listening. She ripped the letter into four pieces and stomped back to her house.

"Get off my property and don't you ever come back!" she shouted as she slammed the door.

Casper got back in the car and said, "That wasn't how I expected that to go at all." He turned to Ivy but her eyes were still focused forward. Once he closed the door she hit the gas and flew down the street. She was completely silent, unable to bring herself to talk or do anything except drive and even that was proving difficult. And then she made the mistake she had been hoping to avoid, her eyes in a flash glanced over at Casper, the human Casper. The wonderful human who saw in her what she could not, the human hiding inside her. She slammed on her brakes and pulled off the road. She broke down into tears over her steering wheel. He wasn't sure what to do or what was going on. He assumed it had to do with Irma, but she had seemed bothered since they'd left so he couldn't be sure. He put his hand on her shoulder and said, "Ivy-"

In a flash that was faster than he could see she had both her hands on his shoulders holding him back. "What is wrong with you!" she was screaming. "Why aren't you repulsed by me! Why don't you look at me like I'm a monster! Damn it Casper, why don't you act human at all!"

He stared at her for a moment and tears ran from her sparkling emerald eyes down her snowy cheeks, even when she cried she was the most beautiful thing he'd ever seen. He shook his head slowly and placed a hand on her cheek, wiping away the tears with his thumb. The warmth sent a chill through her. "You're not a monster, and nothing you could ever tell me would make me think otherwise."

Slowly her eyes began to change and her fangs protruded from under her lip and she said, "Tell me that now, look at me as I truly am and tell me I'm not a monster."

Her face was only inches from his and even though he knew he should be afraid of her, she could kill him, he wasn't afraid. "I'm not afraid of you. You're not a monster, you are the most beautiful thing I have ever laid my eyes on. You're not a monster, you're not." Slowly she changed back to herself, the tears still falling down her cheeks and over his fingers, he was shocked how cold they were. Daringly he placed his forehead against hers and just held there. He closed his eyes and she did the same. "Do you remember when we kissed in my apartment?" he asked his eyes still closed. He could feel her nod against him. "I didn't tell you this before, but that was one of the greatest moments of my life." He swallowed hard and said, "It's all I've thought of since then." Her eyes fluttered open, her forehead still against his. She smiled a bit to herself, what a beautiful creature he was, and what a heart he had. Without thinking, without giving herself the chance to take it back she pushed her chin forward and laid a soft kiss upon his lips. His eyes opened and he looked at her, questioning, she had a smile in hers. With his hands still about her face he pulled her into him and kissed her deeply. She put her arms around his neck and kissed him back, trying to be mindful of her strength, but most of her forgetting about that entirely. He tried to ignore the fact that she was crushing his throat, he wanted this so much, but it got to the point that he couldn't breath at all. "Ivy, Ivy you're hurting me a little." She pulled back instantly, and he regretted saying it.

"Sorry," she said, her voice breathy.

"It's ok, it's beyond ok, in fact ok doesn't even begin to describe it." he said with a smile, that perfect smile, his hands still on her cheeks. "Should we head home?"

Her face fell a bit and she shook her head. "I don't really want to go back tonight if it's all right with you. And to be totally honest with Rudolph coming tomorrow I'd prefer to spend the evening with you. If that's ok."

He moved his hand under her chin and lifted her head. "Absolutely."

There was hotel she had always wanted to stay at but the opportunity, or the need really had never arisen. They checked in and Ivy insisted on ordering room service for Casper, he hadn't eaten all day. His food came and the waiter gave her a once over before leaving, no tip required. She watched Casper eat and when he went to take a shower she ate for herself. She knew that he didn't see her as the monster she still knew she was, but she still didn't want him to see her eat and with their being in such close proximity that night she wasn't taking any chances by not eating.

In the bathroom Casper had turned on the water and pulled out his cell phone. He dialed the number for Ivy's house and waited while it rang. Perhaps she would be able to hear him talking, perhaps not. He didn't know for sure, but her family had a right to know that they were at least ok. "Hello." Grace's voice said on the other line.

"Hi Grace it's Casper." he said.

She sighed in relief and said, "For the love of god where have you been? We've been so worried about you."

"I know, I know but Ivy just didn't want to come back. Did something happen with Alex on the ride back to the house? It seemed to all start after we left the diner."

"I don't know," Grace said. "It's possible I suppose. How did it go with Mollie's sister?"

Casper sighed. "Not too well I'm afraid. I gave her the letter and everything, but she spotted Ivy and accused her of being a descendent of the woman who took Mollie's house and she thought we were just playing a cruel trick on her. But do my a favor and just tell Mollie it all worked out. I think it's best she not know."

"I've got to agree with you there. Mollie was really counting on it. I'll take care of it, and you take care of Ivy, with Rudolph coming tomorrow I guess it's not really a surprise that she's coming unglued like this." Grace said, pausing for a moment. "We'll see you tomorrow."

"Bright and early." Casper said clicking the phone shut.

"How's the family?" Ivy asked from the other room

Casper ducked his head out of the bathroom and asked, "What are you talking about?"

Ivy was smiling, a good sign, at least she wasn't completely angry. "Nice try with running the water, but you forget how heightened my senses are, I could hear you clear as day."

He reached in and shut off the running water. He sat next to her on the bed and said, "Sorry I just didn't want them to worry."

"It's ok, I'm glad you did." Her eyes lowered and she asked, "So how is everything?"

"Fine, I was just checking in really." Casper said with a smile.

"Who did you talk to?" she asked, wringing her delicate fingers together.

"Grace, why?" he asked, turning to look at her more directly.

She shrugged her shoulders. "Oh no reason I was just wondering how Alex was doing. We got into a little tiff in the car coming home, nothing serious of course, I was just wondering."

He placed a hand over hers and said, "If he's mad at you he won't be for long. They all love you too much to stay mad at you."

"I know," she said, still looking down, her voice not matching the confidence he thought she should have.

He found the need to change the subject. "Tell me more about you, before you were changed I mean."

She shrugged. "There's not much to tell I guess. I was really quiet and meek, never spoke my mind." she said glancing back at her hands. "That all started after my mother died. She was an amazing woman who really loved me and after she died everything changed." She pulled her feet up onto the bed, sitting Indian style to see him better, he did the same. "You see my father was a gambler and while my mother was alive she kept him in check with it, how much of our money he spent and so on. Once she died he couldn't handle it, the gambling got worse and slowly I watched everything we ever had disappear. The only thing that we had left when all was said and done was my title."

"You had a title?" Casper asked, his eyes widening a bit.

She nodded. "Yes I was a Duchess." He jaw fell open and she laughed. "It's not quite as impressive as it sounds, there were a lot of them in those days."

"But still, that's pretty amazing."

"Well thank you." she said with a bow of her head. "Anyway, all we had left was my title, I had no dowry left to speak of, he'd gambled that all away. So I was left to marry someone with money but no title, and as shallow as it may sound that was rather embarrassing for me." She shook her head slowly and he waited patiently for her to go on. "My father found a wealthy shipbuilder named Marcus Lecruex. I absolutely hated him. The first day I met him he hit me, put me in my place as he put it, he wouldn't have a disobedient wife. And ultimately he's what brought me here, what made me what I am. Yes Rudolph did the actual changing, but without the beating Marcus had given me I doubt Rudolph would have done for me, he loved me at least that much."

"What happened? Between you and Rudolph? Why did you leave him?" he asked.

She shook her head. "The particulars of that I don't share with anyone, I even try to hide them from myself so I don't think I can tell you all of that. Just saying it out loud is too hard, so don't be offended by the fact that I just can't tell you. It's not that I don't want to I just can't." He patted her hand and smiled, telling her it was ok. She took a moment before she could speak again. "But there were other reasons, other than Rudolph. You can't imagine how amazing and wonderful and frightening the concept of a New World was to us. I had to be there, to see it. Besides I knew of a few of our kind who were planning to make the journey so someone had to go to keep them in check. And after what happened," she shuttered at the memory. "Well it was just best."

"So you came over on-" Casper began.

"The Mayflower." she finished with a nod and smile. "Yes I did, we landed in Jamestown and I lived there for a few years."

"All right I have to ask," Casper said with a grin, that may have been a grimace. "That boat ride was like six months, how did you survive it?"

She nodded slowly, she assumed he'd ask this. "Like I've told you, I haven't always been proud of all the decisions I've made. There were a lot of people on the ship so when some went missing it was simply a case of them falling overboard. I ate as little as possible and enforced the same on those who were traveling along side me. They humans aboard had to suffer so we did too." she said shifting her weight from side to side. "I insisted we stay together for a while but after a few years it was time to move on so we did, moved on and moved apart." She smiled to herself and said, "Five vampires started out in America, now there are over a million."

"There are that many!" Casper squeaked.

Ivy let out a laugh that started from the tip of her toes and moved to the ends of her eyelashes. "Yes, you probably know more of us than you think you do. I have met thousands of them, and of over a million vampires only about six or seven hundred of them are rogues. You see Casper most vampires take the responsibility of changing someone very seriously, you've just only been exposed to the bad eggs of our race."

"Why do it? The way you always make it sound it seems like it's something no one would ever do to anyone." he asked.

She smiled and said, "It's something I wouldn't do, I can't say the same for everyone else. Eternity is a long time to spend alone. Vampires get lonely too, they get lonely enough they create a companion. Again we're a rarity, most vampires end up alone. Families don't happen so often."

"Why?"

"We become very territorial. These are my hunting grounds, you can't have them, things like that. Most vampires can't get past the hunt and need to feed. Families are work, whether your human or otherwise. It doesn't get any easier as a vampire, but I always thought it was worth it. I love my family." She said smiling to herself.

"It doesn't seem like it would be that bad, being a vampire." he said gazing out at the wall, almost as if her were visualizing it.

Her mind instantly jumped to the image of Alex's vision of Casper as a vampire, but she pushed it away as fast as she could. "You don't know what you're saying." she mumbled.

"Well I'm not saying that it would be the most amazing thing ever, but I don't think it would be all that bad." he said leaning back on the bed.

She shook her head and laid down next to him. "I won't lie, it hasn't all been bad. The history I've seen has been pretty amazing. I was there for the Revolutionary War, the end of slavery, the sinking of the Titanic, Civil Rights movement and so many other things. Seeing that has been pretty incredible, of course their were scary parts too."

"Like what? The wars or the Depression?" he asked, his hand laid gently on his stomach.

She giggled. "No, we pretty much were assured to get through that fine. The scariest one was AIDS."

"Can you get it?" he asked, his brow furrowed.

"No, but we didn't know that then, and considering it was coming through the blood and the blood bank, where we buy our food source, we were scared."

"What did you do?" he asked.

"Well, we tried animals for awhile, but again in the 80's they weren't sure if it came from animals or not so we just decided we had go back to normal. Leo was the first I knew to drink infected blood, it wasn't on purpose of course, but nothing happened. We were still careful but we calmed down some."

"Yea I guess, but I still don't think it would be that bad to live forever." he said and she laughed humorlessly. "What?" he asked.

"You humans, you so fear your mortality. You don't know how much of a gift it is until you loose it."

He shook his head. "I don't know though, if I could live with a family like yours forever I think I would give up mortality for that."

Her jaw clenched shut, that image of him with those cat eyes so glued in her mind she couldn't push it away. "Please don't say that." Her eyes were focused up on the ceiling.

He pushed his weight up on his elbow so that he could see her better. "What's the matter?"

"I just don't want you to talk like that." she said her jaw locking down tighter. "Because I swear to you it will never happen, I'll make sure of that."

"Hey," he said putting a hand on her cheek, her eyes still locked on the ceiling. "Hey look at me." Slowly her eyes pulled away from the ceiling and towards him. "I'm sorry if I upset you, I was just kidding."

"Don't kid about that." she whispered, a hint of a smile on her lips.

"There's something you're not saying." he said, his gaze

intensifying. "Tell me, please."

Everything inside her told her to keep it silent, not to tell him about Alex's vision. But something larger, something in his eyes told her she could trust him with it, she could trust him with anything. "Alex-" she began, pausing for a moment. "Alex had a vision about you."

"What did he see?" he asked, coaxing her on.

"You-you were one of us." she said, her vision growing fuzzy at the edges with tears. "You were a vampire."

He had nearly stopped breathing. "Are you sure."

Her face got angry suddenly. "Alex isn't always right, his visions can be wrong, in fact they're wrong all the time. And besides I told you, I won't let that happen. You have my word on that."

He tucked a piece of her hair behind her ear. "Sh, it's ok." He laid his head down next to hers and they just laid there quietly together, and that was how they spent the night, just like that, laying quietly together. He fell asleep at one time and she just watched him. He was so trusting, sleeping next to a creature who could so easily kill him. She could not bring herself to sleep, it was all too fascinating to watch him. The rise and fall of his chest as he was breathing, the smirk on his face as he dreamed, oh how she wished she could know what he was thinking. Then as the sun came up his phone began to buzz on the side table. She reached over and recognized her home number at once.

"Hello," she whispered, at her abnormally low level so as not to wake up Casper.

"Hi, it's Alex." he said.

"Hi," she said getting off the bed with enough ease to not

jostle him at all.

"Look Ivy, I'm really sorry about what happened yesterday-" he began.

"It's ok Alex, really." she finished for him.

"Good, but I am sorry." he said, his voice a little happier than before. "Anyway, when were you all planning on coming back? We're all ready for our guests."

"When should we be back?" she asked.

"As soon as possible." Alex said, a bit of urgency in his voice. "Mainly because I'm not sure when They'll be here exactly."

"All right, we'll be back soon." she said clicking the phone shut.

She sat down on the bed next to Casper and smiled, so peaceful. She put her hand on his cheek, he only recoiled slightly, and whispered, "Casper, Casper you need to get up." He stirred slightly but didn't wake, and a large part of her didn't want to let the moment end. There was something about this human, this simple ordinary man that made her feel alive again. She pushed the gray hair from his eyes and he mumbled something she couldn't quite hear, she waited to see if he would say it again. "Ivy," he mumbled softly, she stopped breathing, keeping incredibly still. He was dreaming about her. "I-I" he mumbled softly with more music than that of any vampire and she waited. "I love you." Her heart nearly exploded in her chest. He loved her. What did this mean for them? For her? She shifted her weight away from him, she had to think. Did she love him? She had always promised herself that after Rudolph she would never love again, but what did she feel for Casper? It was true that when she was near him she felt more human than she had in centuries. But perhaps what she admired most about him was that he saw her as more of a human than anyone had in centuries. He looked at her like she was beautiful, like she was the only woman in his sights and he had an old soul that seemed familiar to her. So, did she love him. The more she thought about it the more she realized that it was true. She did love him. Tears sprung to her eyes, mixed with happiness and overwhelming sorrow. She was capable of loving again, and she loved someone who would never hurt her, she could see that in him. But, what a horrid fate this would be. It would never work. He would get older, he would die. She never would. She had to swallow her tears, that's not how she wanted him to wake up. She closed her eyes tightly and waited a moment, she leaned out and caressed his cheek softly and said a little louder, "Casper, you have to wake up."

His eyes slowly fluttered open and he smiled. "Good morning."

"Hi," she said with a sad smile. "We have to go, you need to get up."

He cocked his head to the side. "Are you all right?" he asked.

She looked down and nodded. "Yea, it's just a big day I guess."

He raised himself up on his elbows to the point that he was almost too close to her face. "You're lying."

Sighed aloud and said, "Did you know you talk in your sleep?"

He fell back down on his back, recalling his dream suddenly.

"What exactly did you hear?"

"Is that really how you feel?" she asked, dodging his direct question a bit.

He sighed, choosing his words carefully. "You're different from anyone I've ever met. You put your family above everything else and you're just lovely, inside and out. You're everything I wish I was. So yea, I guess that is how I feel."

She stared at him for a moment, absorbing what he had said. At lightening speed she put her hands on either side of his face and kissed him sweetly. She released him suddenly and shook her head. "You're so stupid." In the next second she was at the door. "I'm going to go check out, I'll see you in the car." And then she was gone. He laid his back against the bend and pinched the space between his eyes in frustration. Perhaps he was stupid.

The drive was quiet and uncomfortable. She kept her hands in the conservative ten and two position and he kept his hands folded in his lap. The tension between them was so tick you could cut it with a knife. As the entered the mouth of the driveway he grabbed her hand and said, "Stop the car for a second." She always seemed to stop the car here, for a moment she kept driving, but after a second of reflection she eased the car into park. She kept her hands on the steering wheel, it was already formed for them. He sighed and said, "We need to do this now, because I know once we get back to the house you'll get as far away from me as you can." He looked over at her to see if she would say anything, but that wasn't happening. "What's going on with you? I tell you that I love you and you don't say anything."

"You didn't actually say it. You just didn't deny it." she

whispered.

"Well then fine," he said grabbing her by the shoulders and turning her to look at him. "I love you. I love you. I love you."

It didn't take much effort for her to pull herself away, her hands back into position. "Would it mean anything to you if I said you shouldn't love me? That loving me was the worst decision you could make?"

"No." he said with a smile. "Besides, I don't really think we choose these things." His face dropped a little. "What about you?"

"What about me?"

"Come on Ivy," he said, hoping he wouldn't have to actually ask. "Do you love me?"

She gripped the steering wheel as tightly as ever. Not telling him was the best way to go, but saying nothing only validated what he wanted to hear. "I can't love you." she mumbled.

"But do you?"

Stubborn human. "It doesn't matter, I can't."

In his human stupidity he put his hands on hers, as if he could overpower her and pull her hands away. To humor him she let him move her hands. "Stop thinking about what's important, or what your duty is and just say how you feel for once." he demanded.

"I can't tell you that. I can't tell you what you want to hear. Don't you understand that? Why can you not understand that? Why can't you understand anything you're supposed to?" she demanded rubbing her head in frustration, she never thought humans could be so irritating. "Look, just forget about it. What you want is impossible."

He banged his hand against the door and car actually shook for moment. "Goddamn it Ivy! For once in your life just say what you actually think, not what your duty tell you, or what even common sense tells you, just tell me what you think."

He waited for her to answer, but she was so inhumanly still that he thought she'd never move again. How desperately she wanted to tell him what she felt. How much she wished she were human and their lives could be that simple. How seeing him hurt her inside because they could never live happily ever after, never. But even with all this in her head, all the reasons why she knew she couldn't tell him an overwhelming part of her was urging her to just tell him and let the chips fall where the may, but as these whimsical thoughts entered her mind a voice came along with it. *You have to lie to him.* Alex's inner voice said, nearly making her jump from her skin, for a split second she had forgotten about their telepathic abilities with each other.

What are you talking about? she snapped back, her body still remaining painfully still.

You have to tell him you don't love him. Please. Alex thought, his inner voice pained.

I don't know what you're talking about, her inner voice nearly whispered.

And as she thought this a different image popped into her mind, a more disturbing vision of Alex's came flooding in. It was of Casper again, but unlike the last, Casper was not a vampire anymore. There was someone standing over him, over his limp lifeless body. He was as pale as they were and his heart was not beating, but he was not a vampire. He was dead. She couldn't see the face of the vampire standing over him, but he had a familiarity to her, something she couldn't put her finger on. Slowly the man turned and her breathing stopped entirely. It was Rudolph, Rudolph was going to kill Casper. He had blood and fire in his eyes. *Please just tell him you don't love him, it's the only way you can save him. Rudolph will kill him to keep him away from you and keep you for himself. You know he will.*

She blinked her eyes hard, she couldn't let that happen to him. She opened her eyes slowly and whispered, "No, I don't love you." The words burned as they left her lips, but the pain was necessary, she knew that.

He shook his head and said, "I don't believe you."

She flipped forward and turned the key in the ignition. "You can believe whatever you want. You're a good friend Casper, but I don't love you." She pulled the car into the garage and cut the engine, but neither was quick to move.

"You know if we go in there now everything that happened yesterday, everything that happened between us is over." he said, crossing his arms across his chest.

She gently released the steering wheel and turned to him slowly. She tried to hide the sadness in her eyes, but she knew it wasn't convincing, she smiled sadly and said, "I know." She unbuckled her seatbelt and got out of the car and he followed a moment after.

"Hope you had a fun evening." Peter said coldly as she walked in the door.

She rolled her eyes and said, "Not now Peter, not now."

"Well while you were off doing whatever it is you were doing with the human we were all here getting ready for Them. I thought you were supposed to be our leader, what's the matter with you?" he demanded.

Anger bubbled up inside her. In a moment quicker than she could think she had her hand around Peter's throat and she was holding him against the wall. She lifted him off the floor and held him there. His eyes were shocked, as if he never expected her to be able to do something like that.

"Ivy what are you doing!" Grace shouted as she came running in the room and the others followed. Ivy ignored them. She pushed him further up the wall and increased the pressure on his throat. While he did not need to breath to live, cutting off the ability was still uncomfortable and her grip was probably causing him pain.

"I am the alpha," she hissed through her teeth, her eyes changed and full of fire, baring a her fangs at him. "What gives you the right to talk to me like that? You will never, ever do it again!" His eyes were wide and frightened, she had never done this to a family member before. She dropped him to the ground and turned to her family, still with the face of a predator. Casper hovered in the doorway, afraid to come in. "How long until they're here?" she asked, her eyes darting away, but the question obviously meant for Alex.

"About ten minutes." Alex muttered.

"Fine then, what are we standing around for?" she said, her eyes returning to normal. "Get ready." They scattered quickly and Peter was the first to get up and out of the room.

It'll be ok boss, you had to do it. Mollie thought, her inner voice sympathetic.

Stay out of my head. All of you. she thought, her inner voice cold and angry. She couldn't stand in the room with them and just wait. She zipped up to her room and shut the door behind her. She slid down against it and rested her head back against the door. She knew that Mollie was just trying to help her, make it easier, but she didn't need that now. She didn't want to think about any of it.

Chapter Nine

The moments ticked by too fast and then there was a soft knock on her door. "Ivy They're here" Grace said softly. She sighed aloud. Part of her was glad her heart no longer beat, that was an extra stress that she didn't need. "Alex sees them headed down the road now, you should probably be downstairs when they get here."

I'm scared Gracie. Ivy thought, a single tear running down her cheek.

Grace ran a hand down the doorframe and said, "I know you are, but we'll get through it as a family, always as a family."

Ivy smiled at that and pushed herself up against the door. She opened it slowly and Grace was smiling on the other side. "Did I hurt Peter?" she asked.

Grace grinned even more. "I think you scared him more than anything else."

"Well perhaps it wasn't all bad then." Ivy said with a humorless laugh, no matter how hard she tried she could not make this situation funny. She shook her head and said, "It's been four hundred years since I've seen him Gracie."

"At least he won't look any different, can't be shocked that way." she said with a smile. "I can't really help you here, it's a situation I've never been in, none of us have. All I can tell you is that I'm here for you, we all are."

They're here. Alex thought from downstairs.

Ivy took in a deep breath and wished for that moment she was human so that it could give her some comfort, but of course it didn't. She smiled to Grace who walked down the stairs in front of her. She took in everything her senses could give her. The sound of her families inner voices as well as the pounding sound of Casper's heartbeat, it was faster than normal. He was nervous too. She had almost forgotten that he had anything to be nervous about, this whole endeavor was really (well officially at least) about him. She could also hear a new set of thoughts, a familiar voice she had not heard in decades, Angelo. He was outside, pulling into their driveway. And while she couldn't hear his thoughts, he was still blocking her, she knew he was there. She could smell him. The scent stopped her dead on the stairs. *I can't do this.* she thought, her grip tightening on the railing, she could hear the would splintering to pieces beneath her hand.

"Yes you can." Mollie and Alex said together aloud. Their faces were so confident. Nora and Leo stood together by the door, Casper at their side. The other four at the base of the stairs waiting for her. She glanced around at them, all of them, her family and realized that it didn't matter. There was nothing that Rudolph could say or do that would change the way these people felt about her. That realization made her walk down the rest of the stairs.

"We're going to have to fix the railing." she murmured to Alex as she passed him.

He grinned and said, "No problem."

She walked slowly to the door, the only other time she had ever been this nervous in her life was walking down the aisle at her wedding, but this was a different type of dread. She reached the door and laid her hand gently on the handle, she didn't want to break another thing in her house. "You'll be fine." Leo said from the side, but she couldn't turn to look at him. She closed her eyes a moment before she turned the handle and pushed the door open. The sun was especially bright that day, perfect. A dark SUV was zooming up the winding driveway. All breathing stopped. The car stopped in front of the house. She thought she would fall over. The windows were deeply tinted, a must have for vampires, but she could not see inside. The driver's side door opened and the owner of the thoughts she could hear emerged. It was always a sight to see a black vampire, they were so mesmerizing to look at. You could tell what their race was, but it was as if they had been covered in powder, everyone got paler when they became a vampire. The last time she had seen him he had dreadlocks down his back, now he was shaven bald. She smiled at him, forgetting entirely for a moment about the passenger. "Angelo." she said.

He flashed his brilliant teeth at her and said, "Ivyana, it is good to see you." He encircled her in a hug and she welcomed it happily. "Of course I wish it were on better circumstances." he added, that pulled her back into the moment.

She pulled back and said, "I agree with you there." Her eyes looked passed him at the car, was he ever coming out, the suspense was killing her.

Then she heard the sound of the passenger side door click open. She released Angelo who quickly zipped away into the house. She really wished she weren't alone for this, but she knew it was the best way. She held her breath as a dark figure stood from the car. She could only see the back of him at first. He had cut his dark hair short, but it still curled at the ends as she remembered. Slowly he turned and their eyes met for the fist time in four centuries. His dark eyes were full of pain as he gazed at her, as if he had been dreading this moment as much as she had been. Tears welled behind her eyes, he was as beautiful as the day she'd left him. She could feel the tension that rose between them and what was the hardest for her resist was the urge to forget the past and rush into his arms again. She broke her gaze away, remembering all the reasons that she should and yet she could still feel his eyes on her.

"Ivy," his deep voice sang, pulling at every fiber of her heart. "It is good to see you."

"Rudolph." she said simply, staring intently at the tire of Angelo's car, anything to not look back at him.

In a flash he was standing in front of her, blocking her view of the tires. "Just look at me for a moment." he was saying, standing uncomfortably close. "Just for a moment." he said again, he dare not touch her yet for fear of further rejection from her.

Slowly she dragged her eyes up to his eyes, those dark sparkling eyes. She could only hold his gaze for a quick moment before pulling them away. "I can't." she said zipping into the house. She nearly fell over the members of her family inside the door. She sighed and said, "Do none of you have any sense of privacy?"

"Not when it comes to you and Rudolph we don't." Leo said with a smile. *Are you ok?* he asked in his head.

No. she thought walking past them. Casper grabbed her arm as she tried to pass and held her there. She stared into his eyes and so desperately wished she could read his thoughts. His eyes were not filled with the anger or even hate that she expected, but rather concern and sympathy. He made it all about her, never about how he felt. She had openly rejected him and yet he was still thinking all about her. Always about her. She pulled her arm away and went to her office and closed the door. *Just give me five minutes.* she thought to the outside, she took their silence as an agreement.

She took her five minutes and gathered her emotions the best she could. When she emerged from her office the vampires were sitting around the dining room table. She took her place at the head of the table and asked, "Where's Casper?"

"Rudolph told him to go sit in the kitchen." Mollie said from beside her.

"Well we are discussing him, I thought it inappropriate for him to be in the room." Rudolph said. "Besides he's a human, he's our food. It would be like their kind including a chicken in on their conversations." he was laughing.

"It is no way the same thing and you know that." Ivy growled, her eyes focused on a knot in the wood in the table.

"Fine." he said quietly. "Then let's just address the issue." He adjusted himself in his seat and said, "There are only two options available, we either kill him or make him one of us." His voice was so cold. The family fell silent, a cold hush among them.

Ivy slammed her fist against the table, her mind jumping to both of Alex's visions, and hissed, "No, that won't happen."

"The human killed a vampire Ivyana, that's not something we can take lightly." Angelo said, being one of Their oldest members he was very set in the idea of vampires first humans second.

"I understand that Angelo, but can those really be the only two options." Ivy argued, tying back her red hair with a rubber band, preparing for war, the images of Alex's visions still flashing in her mind.

"What would you have us do Ivyana? Let him go free?" Rudolph asked, swinging his legs up onto her table, his boots splattering mud all over it, she cringed.

"That's exactly what I'm suggesting." Ivy said with a smile.

Rudolph rolled his eyes. "Be serious Ivy."

"I am." she said, sweeping her bangs away from her face. "We have spent several days with him. He's unlike other humans, he understands us, he's comfortable with us. He won't tell anyone what he knows."

Rudolph cocked his head to the side and said in a condescending voice, "Dear, sweet Ivy what is the first rule in our world."

"Don't patronize me Rudolph." Ivy said with a gruff tone. "The first rule is not exposing ourselves to the humans and I understand that, but this is not your average human."

"She's right there." Leo said with a laugh. "He thinks we're completely normal."

"Even when we talk about our food supply he doesn't cringe." Grace said.

"When he killed the rogue he barely even flinched." Peter said with a shake of his head, still unable to believe that.

"And as far as killing the rogue was concerned, he thought he was protecting Ivy, not hurting April, but even so the rest of us froze and he acted. It was rather incredible for a mortal." Mollie said with a smile.

But Rudolph wasn't paying attention to them at all, he was

staring at his creation and her alone. He cocked his head in the other direction and said, "Get out, all of you. I want to talk to Ivy alone."

The family glanced at each other and then stood. Ivy rose from the table as well and said, "Stay." They settled back into their chairs.

"I told them to leave." Rudolph growled, they rose again.

"And I am the head of this family and I told them to stay." she said, folding her hands atop the table. She turned to her family and said slowly, "Sit down."

"Ivy," Rudolph said in his creator's voice, sweeping through her like a wave. "Tell them to leave." he commanded.

While every fiber of her body willed her to refuse, she could not fight the strength of her creator's demands, but she could also not admit defeat aloud. *Wait outside.* she thought sadly. The family rose and left the room, each member giving her a sympathetic smile as they passed her. It was a moment to be grateful for not having a pulse, for while she was mentally nervous, left alone with Rudolph, she didn't have the added effects of a racing heartbeat.

They sat across the long mahogany table, on the two far ends, and stared at one another for a long moment. The silence between them so booming, so loud that she thought it would deafen her and surely drive her mad. Then, in a flash moment that was nearly too quick for her to see, he flicked his wrist against the table and sent it flying into the wall, splinters of the wood flying everywhere. In another instant he was croutched down before her, her body trembling with a sudden fear. What of she wasn't exactly sure. She had never been scared of Rudolph, but perhaps it was what she was feeling, seeing him again that truly had her spooked. He put his hands on either side of her chair, forcing her to look at him. His eyes were full of fire. "You have feelings for a human?" he demanded.

She dragged her eyes away and muttered, "I don't know what you are talking about."

He grabbed her forcefully by her chin and said, "Do not lie to me! You would not be defending him so strongly if you did not have feelings for him."

"I'm defending him because he did nothing wrong and even if he did I refuse to believe there is no punishment other than death or eternal damnation." she said with a shake of her head. She was not going to back down now.

"That's not it and you know it!" he shouted, she realized then that the fire in his eyes had not been anger but rather jealousy. He caught her head in her hands and held it there. She had missed that feeling, of his skin on her skin. It had been a long four hundred years. He placed his forehead against hers and for a moment she forgot everything that had ever happened between them. For a moment, a single moment, she wanted her old life back, her life with him. But it only lasted a moment, for in the next she remembered why it was she hated him so much and she pulled away.

"No," she said softly.

He sighed, his eyes falling and biting his bottom lip. "Will you never forgive me? For something that happened so many lifetimes ago?" he asked, the jealousy in his eyes replaced with sadness.

She shook her head and said, "How could you ask me that? After what you did? Were you ever human? Because I find it hard to believe that any person could not understand the gravity of what you took from me." She pushed herself free from him and said, "For now, as far as Casper is concerned give us a few days to prove to you that he is different. You owe me at least that much."

For a moment he was silent, pausing, thinking. Then he sighed and said, "Fine, I'll give you two days. Then I pass my judgment on the human."

"Thank you." she said pushing through the door and tasting the sweet air that was not filled with the scent of him. She passed by Mollie and said, "Put them in the two guest rooms on the far side from Casper, I want to keep them far away from each other." They nodded to her. *Is he still in the kitchen?* she asked in her mind.

Yes. Nora replied, smiling at her. Ivy had to hand it to her, she really was trying to fit in with the family, but something was still unsettling about her.

Ivy wandered into the kitchen where Casper was sitting patiently at the kitchen table eating a sandwich. "What's the verdict?" he asked calmly, making her laugh, he was most definitely different from any other human.

"Well," she began taking a seat in the chair next to him. "They want to either kill you or damn you for forever."

He swallowed a large bite of his sandwich and said sarcastically, "Well that's just a bit unsettling."

"I've gotten him to extend his final judgement for two days so that he can see how different you are." she said.

"What difference will that make?" he asked, taking another bite.

"We have to prove to him, somehow, that you won't reveal

what we are to anyone." she said with a sigh, realizing the near impossibility of what she was trying to accomplish.

"I can tell him that." Casper said.

Ivy laughed a bit and said, "Unfortunately it doesn't work that easy. Rudolph has been morphed into a tradtionalist vampire, you're nothing but a steak dinner equvilant to him. Just telling him won't do anything."

"So what do we do?"

She rubbed her forehead with one hand and said, "That's a very good question, I'm not exactly sure yet."

"Are you ok?" he asked, sliding the plate away from him, and reaching for her hand.

She jumped up from the table and moved to the door. "I'm fine," she said zipping back from the door. Alex's vision of a dead Casper was still in her mind, she couldn't torture herself, she couldn't let the warmth of his skin touch her icy exterior, it would break her. She had to protect him without getting too close, it was the only way to save him.

"It's ok you know." he said, breaking her entire train of thought.

"What are you talking about?" she asked, pulling herself back into the moment.

"It's ok that you don't feel about me the same way I feel about you. But I still want to be your friend, even if you don't love me." he said with a smile. "Maybe you were right, it never would have worked anyway."

It felt like he had plunged a dagger through her heart. She should have been releaved, she knew that, but she wasn't, not even close. However, having him in her life in some way must have been better than not at all, at least it was what she was hoping for. She smiled and said, "I would like that too." He smiled back at her.

She walked through the hallways to the living room where Alex and Leo were playing chess. "Alex, do you think I could talk to you alone for a moment?"

"Sure," he said with a smile. "Peter and Angelo have been dying to jump in here."

"What can I say," Angelo began, taking Alex's seat. "I love the way you all play this."

So Peter and Angelo took over where Leo and Alex had left off, as if the game had not even paused. Alex and Ivy wandered outside. "Are you doing ok?" Alex asked her. "I can't imagine how hard it is for you, having him here."

"I'm fine." she said, crossing her arms over her chest.

"What did you want to talk to me about?" he asked.

"One of your earlier visions." she said. He waited for her to continue. "About the numerous vampires that should be here."

He shook his head. "It's still there, the vision I mean, I just can't pin down an exact timeline."

"The vision hasn't changed?" she asked.

He shook his head. "No, but it's becoming more vivid all the time, I guess we're getting closer."

"Really that's the best you can do?" she asked, scratching her head.

"Sorry." he said. "Let me know if there's anything I can do for you."

"Well actually there is one thing." she said, turning to face him.

"Name it." he said with a shrug.

"Have the vision again, vividly enough so that I can see it and analyze it a little bit." she said with a sigh. He smiled and closed his eyes and she did as well, visualizing the faces of each vampire in the vision. Her eyes flashed open and she said, "Blanche and Vincent are standing next to each other in your vision."

"Does that mean something?" he asked.

"Well, Blanche and Vincent have been, for lack of a better term, mortal enemies for the past millennium. Why would they be standing together in your vision?"

Alex shrugged. "I don't know."

There had to be a reason, nothing was coincidence. Whatever was coming, whatever Alex's vision was portraying, it was something big, something the likes of which had never been seen before.

The entirety of the family, and their guests, gathered in the family room, the dining room was out of the question considering that the table was now in nothing but splinters. In order to prove to Rudolph that Casper was not a danger to them, Ivy had set up a chess tournament. She had thought that putting him a situation where he had no choice but to interact with the others and truly be what she knew him to be. He was good at their game, better than anyone she'd ever seen.

She had it set up that two pairs would go against each other at a time. The first match up was Angelo against Peter and Casper against Nora. Quickly the games comensed and Rudolph watched Casper's every move, analyzing how he interacted with the vampires, but more importantly his skills. Rudolph was a proud individual and he had no interest in being beaten by anyone, but especially not by a measly human. So he watched intently as Casper plowed Nora into the ground, beating her nearly as fast as they had begun. Casper laughed and so did Nora, he leaned forward and kissed her on the cheek and Rudolph was astonished he'd get so close to her. Ivy gauged his reaction and smiled. Quickly the games progressed, Casper and Rudolph dominating their opponents. Finally it came down to only the two of them.

"All right boys, this will decide our champion." Ivy said, pumping a silly drama into her voice. She smiled and patted Casper on the shoulder softly, making him smile and Rudolph cringe. The intimate moment nearly made him ill with envy, even though he would never say it aloud.

"Ready?" Casper asked. Rudolph's response was wordless, more of a grunt. The game began with such intensity, no one dared to utter a word. For Casper it still seemed to be a game, just fun, like they all were to him. For the vampire it was a very different game. It was a battle that he had to win. Slowly Ivy noticed that this may have been a mistake. She had hoped that it would be a way for them to all come together, but now she saw that if Rudolph lost it would only ensue more hatred towards Casper. Their hands moved like lightening as pieces moved and fell and then finally the word came from Casper's lips that Ivy had been dreading, "Checkmate." his smile stretched from eartoear. Ivy could nearly feel the anger coming from her creator. In a swoop that she knew was too fast for Casper to see Rudolph threw Ivy's priceless, glass chess set across the room, shattering it against the wall. In an instant just as fast Ivy knelt down beside the broken pieces, it was only thing of her human life she had taken with her. The set had belonged to her father. She held a few of the shattered pieces in her hands and shook her head.

Grace knelt down at her side and thought, *I'm so sorry Ivy.*

"It's fine." she said coldly letting the pieces hit the floor again. She stood up and locked eyes with Rudolph. "You stupid child." she muttered walking past the table and into the kitchen, the girls followed.

"What just happened?" Rudolph asked Leo and Alex, his teeth clenched as he hissed the words.

"You just destroyed her most important possession because you lost a game." Leo said without emotion following the girls into the kitchen Alex close behind him.

Rudolph turned slowly back to Casper, his eyes narrowed and said, "How did you do that?"

"Do what?" Casper asked.

"How did you, a measly human, beat me at anything." he said with a laugh. "Ridiculous."

"And yet I still beat you, ridiculous as it might be." Casper said, leaning back against the chair.

"You pompous child." Rudolph said with a huff. "You think you are anywhere near the level that I am? I have centuries on you."

Casper nodded, processing this. Then he stood from the

table and walked toward the kitchen, while he did he said, "And yet she likes me more."

Rudolph clenched his fists and his jaw. Angelo sat in the chair vacated by Casper and said with a smile, "Well that went well."

Rudolph sighed and said, "I hate humans, perhaps that's why we eat them."

"He can play chess, you have to give him that." Angelo said, buttoning closed his jackets.

"I suppose his beating me isn't reason enough to kill him is it?" Rudolph said with a smile.

"Not from my experience, but we do have to consider all the facts and probably make a decision soon. I mean we can't stay here forever." Angelo said. Rudolph looked away, Ivy instantly popping into his mind. "Not a good idea my friend, going down that path again. I mean you remember how well it worked last time."

"It wouldn't necessarily be like that again, I mean that was a long time ago, centuries ago." Rudolph said.

"Yea, because she seems so over it." Angelo said, laughing. "Look my friend you did something that no human could ever forgive, and even after so much time as a vampire you have to agree she's more human than anything else."

"I suppose you're right, I guess I just never figured she'd be this angry for so long." He said glancing down at his hands. "I mean it was just one human."

"Yes but a rather important one, how is it that I'm more in touch with my human side and your over a hundred years younger than I?" Angelo asked with a laugh.

Rudolph shrugged. "I don't know what to tell you, perhaps I was never really human to start with." he said as the phone in his pocket began to buzz. "Hello."

"It's going to be ok." Mollie said running a hand across Ivy's red hair.

"I know." Ivy said, her knees pulled up around her chest. "I'm being silly, it's just a chess set."

"It's much more than that." Grace said, holding her hand. "It was important to you, it's all right to be upset."

"Yea I guess you're right." Ivy said glancing down at her hands.

"I'm sorry Ivy, maybe I should have just let him win, then he wouldn't have broken your chess set." Casper said patting her shoulder.

"Don't apologize Casper, it was actually worth it to see Rudolph brought down a peg." Ivy said with a smile.

Just then Rudolph came walking through the kitchen door. "Well speak of the devil and he shall appear." Mollie hissed.

Rudolph rolled his eyes and said to Ivy, "Ivyana I need to borrow your seer, it is most important."

Ivy motioned to Alex who followed Rudolph out the door. *Wonder what that could be about?* Grace thought to her family. The others shrugged.

No. They could hear the thought from the other room. All of the their heads snapped up at the sound of Alex's inner voice, Casper's head followed, knowing he had missed something. "No!" this time it was verbal. The family was on their feet in an instant and out the door to the dining room, Casper close behind them. In the dining room Alex was pacing back and forth so fast that he was wearing down the carpet.

"What?" Ivy demanded, her hands on her hips, all her attention focused on her creator.

"It can't be, it can't be." Alex was muttering over and over, too low for the human to hear, but the vampires heard every word.

What is it? Ivy asked in thought, now focused on her brother. *Tell me.*

He stopped dead, so fast he nearly fell over and said, "Emily. She's in the area and she's getting closer."

"I don't understand." Ivy said glancing between Alex, Angelo and Rudolph. "What is he saying."

"Alex," Rudolph said, beckoning him on to explain. "Tell her."

Ivy turned to her boy and hated the pain she saw in his eyes. That horrid woman had ruined him in so many ways. Anything about her threw him into a downward spiral. She hated to see him that way. "Tell me Alex."

"She's organizing some kind of army, you know her, she hates humans. Thinks we should push them into the darkness and we should take over the outside world. She wants to put her ideas into practice, create newborns and overthrow the old ways of vampires and destroy enough humans that we scare them into submission."

"That's ridiculous." Grace said from behind. "She can't do that."

"Emily has never exactly been one to respect the rules." Angelo said, leaning against the wall, a worried look upon his face.

"Just think about who created her, I think if anyone could do this she could."

"Who created her?" Casper asked, his inherent curiosity taking over again.

"Cosmo Leona." Peter said with a sigh, appeasing the human was becoming second nature.

"You say that like I should know who that is." Casper said with a squint of his eyes. He rest of the group eyed him curiously. "Should I?"

"Well obviously you do, I thought everyone knew who he was." Mollie said in a confused tone.

Ivy rolled her eyes, this was of such little importance now. "I'm sure he does know who he is, just not as Cosmo Leona." She turned to Casper and asked, "Casper who is the most famous vampire you can think of."

Casper thought for a moment. "Well Dracula I guess." Ivy smiled and nodded her head. "Holy cow!" Casper exclaimed. "Dracula is real?"

"Sort of." Ivy sad. "Cosmo is who the character is based on anyway. By far one of the most powerful vampires to ever live, and one of the oldest. His choice to create Emily was no accident. He only creates vampire who could be of equal or greater power and Emily is by far his greatest creation."

"Then we take care of her the way we took care of him." Rudolph said jumping into the conversation.

"You killed Dracula?" Casper exclaimed again. His gaze darted back between Ivy and Rudolph like a child with new toys on Christmas.

Ivy slumped down on a chair crossing her arms across her chest and shrugged. "He had to be taken care of."

"He had a plot much like Emily does now," Rudolph began, "and while I do personally agree that we are far superior to your race I also realize that there are far many more humans than vampires and it would be all too easy for them to find our weaknesses and use them against us. We have to stop her."

"So you were all there when Dracula died?" Casper asked, the same goofy grin on his face. In response Rudolph and Angelo raised a hand plus Ivy, Peter and Alex. "Wow." Casper said with a smile. Rudolph eyed the human carefully again, how queer a person, so entranced, not a bit of fear in his eyes.

Suddenly Ivy's head popped up and she turned to Alex. "Your vision." she muttered.

"What?" Alex asked, taking a step toward her. "What vision."

"Of the gathering of vampires here. A group unlike I've ever seen, even when we took care of Cosmo. It was getting so close this must be it." She darted her head around to Angelo and said, "You have to see this." She grabbed Alex by the wrist and took him over to where Angelo was standing, true it wasn't necessary to take him that close, but Ivy felt the compulsion anyway. "Show him." she ordered. And together they all watched the much clearer vision of hundreds of powerful vampires, so many faces that they recognized, so much familiarity.

"Good god," Angelo muttered when he had seen enough. "I've never seen so many in one place."

"This will be the battle of all time I fear." Rudolph said, his eyes glancing away. "I think we'd best start making contact, getting the others here."

"Why here?" Ivy asked crossing her arms. "I'm sure there's somewhere better to do this."

"She's in the area and you live on a big piece of land in the middle of nowhere. Where would be better exactly?" Rudolph asked.

Ivy shrugged. "I suppose nowhere." She sincerely did not want this gathering and imposing turmoil at her home especially with Casper there. She didn't want anything to happen to him. Inevitably Alex's disturbing visions of what could happen to Casper flashed through her mind, this gathering of carnivorous vampires was not exactly the safest place for him. She shivered at the thought of either of outcome.

"What about why you came here?" Ivy asked, narrowing her green eyes at Rudolph. "What will you do with Casper?" She was hoping that he was say that Casper was of no consequence, that there were more important things to worry about.

Rudolph glanced up at Casper and said, "We'll deal with him when this is done."

"You want him to stay here when it will nearly be a convention of vampires?" Ivy said with a shake of her head.

A bit of a smile spread across Rudolph's face as he cocked his head in Casper's direction, his eyes still locked on Ivy. "I could kill him right now if you'd like. That would be quite fine with me."

"I'd rather take my chances with the vampire convention." Casper chimed in.

Rudolph smiled brighter. "Well the man has spoken." Rudolph said standing up quickly and leaving the room. "I need a few of you to come and help me." Leo and Nora followed him out the door.

Ivy rolled her eyes and turned to Casper, concern plaguing her face. She glanced into the dining room, they would need a new table. "Casper, will you come with me, I need to go buy a new dining room table."

Casper nodded and said, "Sure Ivy, I kind of wouldn't mind getting out of here for just a little while." Casper hopped up and moved toward the garage door quicker than any had seen him move. In that moment Ivy remembered that he was human and this may have been a much more frightening situation for him than any of them had realized.

The car ride was silent, they decided to take Peter's pickup, there would be no fitting a large kitchen table in her little car. Casper was the first to break the silence, "He's a little frightening."

"Yea I know." she said, her eyes focused on the lines of the road. "He has that effect on people."

Casper licked his lips and asked the question he'd been avoiding. "What happened to the table Ivy?"

Ivy was quiet, her eyes still focused on the quickly moving lines. "He doesn't mean it, he just goes too far sometimes. Doesn't know his own strength."

"Did he hurt you?" Casper demanded.

Ivy laughed humorlessly, "I'm not so delicate Casper, but I appreciate the concern."

"You didn't answer the question." Casper said with a smile.

"He didn't hurt me Casper, I promise. He just shattered my table." Ivy said with a sigh.

"Are you ever going to tell me what happened between the two of you? What he did?" Casper asked, the question had been bothering him for a while.

"No." she said curtly, increasing her grip on the steering wheel.

"It's really that bad?" he asked.

"You have no idea." she muttered through her teeth.

"I should probably let drop right?" he said.

She cocked her head to the right and said, "That would be good."

"I probably should then." Casper said looking out the window.

She swiveled her head to look at him and said, "But you don't plan to do you?"

He turned his head back toward her and was smiling. "Not so much. I like a mystery."

"I hope you enjoy being disappointed then." she said her grip increasing further.

"Please don't break Peter's truck, I think he'd find some way to make it my fault." Casper said staring at her hands. Slowly she released her grip. "Just a hint, that's I want."

Ivy shook her head slowly. "You are stubborn, you know that right?" Casper just continued to smile. "The first rule of being a vampire is to take people of no consequence. That's all you get."

"Ok," Casper said stewing over that. "Ok."

They couldn't pull into the parking lot fast enough for Ivy. In a flash moment she was out of the truck and up to the store, Casper had to sprint to catch up with her. Luckily there was no one around to see her. She had to move at human speed once she was inside the door, much to her dismay. Of course she could have carried the heavy table out by herself, with one hand, but being that she was surrounded by humans she had to let Casper help her. Together they loaded the table onto the dolly and paid for it. She let Casper steer the dolly out into the parking lot and then they waited for no witnesses as Ivy hoisted it into the back of the truck with no effort at all.

"I wish I could do that." Casper said when the two got back in the truck.

"It's not a fair tradeoff trust me." she said turning the key in the ignition.

Casper clicked he seatbelt and said, "You keep saying that, but it still looks pretty appealing to me."

"No, it's not. You'd have to live it to really understand." Ivy said pulling back onto the main road. "You know how people say you never really appreciate something until it's gone?" Casper nodded. "Well, that same logic applies to your mortality. Everyone fears death until it's no longer an option. Trust me you don't want this."

He didn't say anything more, he had no interest in aggravating her further. But in his mind he wondered what it would be like, to live forever. He could see his brother again anytime he liked, he'd never grow old, he could see everything that the world would become. And, if he really wanted to, which he couldn't deny otherwise, he could stay forever with Ivy. He could watch over her and out for her forever and perhaps one day he could take her as his mate. It was all possible, but impossible too. Ivy had made it clear that she would never let that happen to him.

As they pulled into the driveway Ivy could already sense the presence of many more vampires than had been there when she left. "Listen to me," she said to Casper. "We're not all so warm and fuzzy, there are plenty of vampires who will kill you faster than you can blink. Make sure that you are always with one of the family, I don't care if you have to pee, you take someone with you."

"Ok," Casper said, taking her seriously. Her tone let off how important it was.

They hoped out of the truck and Ivy hoisted the massive box containing the pieces of her table onto her should and said, "Stick close to me." Casper did as ordered. They walked into the house and Ivy placed the box in the middle of the dining room floor. *Put it together for me will you, and watch him*. She thought to Alex and Peter. They obeyed. "Stay in here with them okay?"

"All right," Casper said with a smile, kneeling down with others to put together the table.

Ivy wandered into backyard where some very familiar faces from her past had gathered. PJ had already arrived with her family, which she had figured would happen, around her were others of Ivy's children. Barbra and Ellen who had come to her together and were still together, traveling through the darker parts of Canada and Alaska, anything to avoid the sun. Blanche, who was one of her earliest conquests, was there too. Her blonde hair was cropped short below her chin, she was as beautiful as the day she'd left. Then there was Ivy's rebel, Milo. He was covered in tattoos from head to toe and with the hard skin of a vampire that was quite an endeavor to go through. She approached her children and said,

"Hello kids."

"Ivy!" Ellen cried, jumping on Ivy and nearly knocking her to the ground.

"Honey, honey," Barbra gently urged her partner. "Personal space babe."

"Sorry," Ellen said, releasing Ivy slowing, a bright grin across her face. "You look so incredible."

"Ellen I don't look any different." Ivy said with a smile.

"Oh, well you do to me." Ellen said tucking Ivy's red hair behind her ears. "Perhaps it's just the time that's lapsed."

Ian shoved his hands in his pockets and leaned in toward Ivy. "Is Capser here?"

Ivy smiled and said, "He's in the dining room with Leo and Peter." Ian smiled back and walked quickly in the direction of the house.

"Look at my girls!" Alex shouted from across the lawn, another familiar face next to him. Vincent, another of Ivy's first vampires. At lightening speed Alex was at their side, scooping Barbra up into his arms and spinning her around. They had joined Ivy around the same time.

"It's good to see you too." Barbra said, laughing as Alex spun her.

Vincent did not hurry over to them. Ivy glanced back at Blanche who was rolling her eyes. The two had never exactly gotten along, Ivy was never exactly sure why. Finally he reached them, one hand shoved in the pocket of his jeans the other running through his dark brown hair. Blancher had her arms crossed across her chest. "I thought you were damned." she muttered when

Vincent was close enough to hear her.

"Well, hell was full so they sent me back." Vincent said with a smile, his still focused away. "But the devil does send you his regards."

Blanche rolled her eyes again and said, "Whatever, I'm going in the house."

When she was out of hearing range Ellen punched Vincent in the arm. "Ow," he said. "It's good to see you too."

"What is it with the two of you?" Ellen demanded. "You guys have never gotten along."

Vincent shrugged. "I don't know ask her."

Ivy walked toward him and encircled him in her arms. "It's good to see you my boy."

"You too boss." he said hugging her back.

"Where've you been recently?" Milo asked shaking hands with Vincent. "You always had the best adventures."

"I've been in China, I actually brought two people with me." he said, shoving the other hand in his pocket.

"Who?" Ivy asked, scanning for thoughts, finally finding two not in English.

"Ping and Lulu." Vincent said. "They're in the house with Rudolph."

"Rudolph was kind of sketchy on the details boss, what's going on?" Milo asked.

"Yea he kind of just told us it was an emergency and we had to be here." PJ said tying back her snow white hair.

Ivy sighed and said, "We have another Cosmo."

There was deafening silence that settled among the group.

Unlike Casper they were all very well aware of who Cosmo was. "Oh god," Ellen muttered. "That's no good."

"Who?" Barbra asked.

Ivy turned her attention to Vincent. Slowly he rolled his head back and said, "Emily. God how could I not see that?" Vincent was a seer, just like Alex, in fact he had been the one to live with her family until they attained Alex.

"It's all right Vincent, we didn't even see it right away." Ivy said patting his arm. "Or maybe Alex was pushing it out, I'm not sure."

"That's possible." PJ said. "I mean he isn't exactly fond of the woman."

They were all quiet for a moment, but Milo was the one to break the silence. "Ok I'm just going to ask." he said throwing his hands up and looking at Ivy. "Ivy do I really smell a human?"

Ivy nodded slowly. "Yes, there is a human here, he is a guest."

Milo pondered this for a moment and said, "And guess wouldn't possibly be a substitute word for lunch would it?"

"Not even close." Ivy said shaking her head. "No one touches the human, he's under our protection right now."

"And under mine," PJ said. "He's Ian's brother."

"Understood." Ellen said, wrapping her arm over Barbra shoulders. They stared lovingly at each other, and a bit of pain settled in Ivy's stomach. She dreamed she could let herself feel that way openly again. She had had that feeling twice before, once with Rudolph and once with Casper, and a deep part of her knew that it would never happen again.

"Good, I will be making it clear to everyone once they're here, which I'm thinking may be soon." Ivy said.

"You can hear them too?" PJ asked. There was a swarm of voices that were growing louder and louder.

"I think we should go inside with the others." Ivy said walking back toward the house at an even pace, the others following behind her.

She met Rudolph by the front door. "They're here." he said pointing down her driveway at what looked like a swarm of bees moving toward them.

"My god." Ivy muttered. She felt a warmth next to her that could have only belonged to one person. She looked over at Casper, who was staring out at the swarm too. He was as pale as she was. She reached down and took his hand, purely out of her mothering instinct. She leaned in and whispered, "I will not let anything happen to you." He must have been assured because he glanced down at her as he was squeezing her hand and nodded slowly. He let out a deep breath and closed his eyes. When he reopened them they had their sparkle back. She patted his hand in hers, but did not release it. She could feel Rudolph's eyes on her, burning on her face. "There are so many."

"We needed a lot," Angelo said from beside Rudolph. "Many of them were around the last time this happened, they remember the force needed to take a power like this down."

They reached her door and gathered in her backyard throughout her house. Ivy kept her hand clamped on Casper's hand, unable to let him go. Finally she released him, realizing that she was probably hurting him and turned her back to go in the house.

Ivy turned back to her family for a moment and thought, *Keep him with one of you at all times. Understood?* They all nodded in response. Grace grabbed Casper by the wrist and pulled him over with her where Peter would be training with her.

"What are you doing?" Casper asked.

"Keeping an eye on you." Grace said as she took her stance against Peter. The two lunged at one another, as they did Peter transformed into a cat and reappeared on the other side as himself again. "Come on you can't do that."

"Hey you've got to be prepared for anything kiddo." Peter said with a smile.

"I'm not a child you know." Casper said from the sidelines.

"If you would like us to set you free into the crowd of carnivorous vampires who would quicker kill you than anything please be my guest. One less thing I have to worry about." Peter said with a devilish grin.

"He doesn't mean it." Grace said, rolling her eyes.

"You don't speak for me." Peter said with only a hint of a sneer, a smile hiding underneath.

"Yea well someone has to." Leo said from beside them with a laugh. He had matched himself up against PJ. While Leo was incredibly strong, PJ was agile and could outrun him, his perfect opponent.

"Where's Nora?" Casper asked looking around for her.

Leo shrugged. "I don't know, she didn't tell me where she was going, just that she had something important to take care of."

"Bad timing isn't it?" Mollie asked from next to them. "I mean in the middle of all of this."

Leo shrugged again. "I don't know what to tell you but she couldn't get out of here fast enough."

"That's strange," Alex said as he faced off against Mollie. "Even for Nora."

"Thanks man." Leo said with a roll of his eyes. "Anyway I'm sure she'll be back soon."

But Alex wasn't so sure. Something was off about Nora, something he had always sensed but could never put his finger on and now it seemed wrong to suspect her of anything, she was the mate of one of his brothers. But something was wrong, he knew it. He felt a hand on his shoulder and spun around to strike at the assailant. Ivy grabbed his hand in mid-swing and the two locked eyes. After staring at him for a long moment she said, "Come with me a minute."

As Ivy and Alex watched away Mollie turned to Grace, "What do you suppose that's about?"

Grace shrugged. "Not a clue, those two have both been kind of weird the last couple of days."

"Yea I guess if something was wrong they would tell us." Mollie said.

Grace simply shrugged again and said, "I guess so."

"Hey are we going to practice or are you two just going to talk?" Peter asked stepping in between them.

The girls rolled their eyes and went back to practicing. After about an hour Grace became tired and sat down to watch Mollie take on Leo. Peter sat down on the ground beside Grace to watch them battle. Her eyes scanned the crowd to see who else she may have overlooked, it had been so long since she many of them. Her eyes settled on one vampire who was slowly approaching them, his eyes settled on Mollie. Grace nudged Peter in the ribs and motioned to the man. "Peter, is that who I think it is?"

Peter, who had been focused on Mollie and Leo, swiveled around to look at the man. For a moment he was silent, just gawking at the man. "Yea that's who you think it is." He looked over at Mollie. "Of course I don't know how happy she'll be to see him."

The man got very close and Peter decided to keep Mollie from being completely surprised. "Moll," he began.

"What?" she asked turning around, practically falling over the man.

"Hi Mollie," the light haired vampire said.

Her eyes grew large and her mouth hung open. He grabbed from falling, but his hands were still protectively on her arms. "Samuel?" she said.

He smiled. "It's good to see you Mollie."

She had not seen he created since the day she told him to leave and that she never wanted to see him again. She wrapped her arms around his neck and he accepted the embrace happily. He sighed and said, "It is so good to see you."

She could not bring herself to pull away. "It's good to see you too."

Finally they separated, only slightly though. He was smiling brightly, his dark brown eyes sparkling. "You look beautiful, as always."

"Thank you." she said, finally pulling all the way back. "What are you doing here?"

He looked at her quizzically and said, "I'm here for the party. I remember the last time this happened, with Cosmo, I figured I could lend a hand."

Slowly Mollie was shaking her head and said, "I can't believe how good you look."

Samuel shrugged. "I haven't changed."

"So, what have you been up to?" Mollie asked awkwardly. She wasn't exactly sure what she should say to him.

"You mean over the past sixty years?" he asked with a laugh.

She shrugged. "Yea, I guess so."

"Not much really, just moving from here to there. I just got back from serving in the war."

"You're good at that." she said running a nervous hand through her wavy brown hair.

"Yea." he said, stuffing his hands in the pockets of his jeans.

The two stood there awkwardly for a long moment. Mollie glanced up and realized that her family had skipped out, leaving her completely alone with Samuel. She bit her lip and said, "Samuel I'm so sorry."

"About what Mollie?" he asked, his brow furrowed.

"About the way I treated you when you changed me. I know you just were trying to help, but I was so scared. I didn't mean the things I said to you." she said, pain pouring from her voice.

He stared at her for a moment, unable to believe what was hearing. "Do you mean that?" She nodded. "I always thought you hated me."

She shook her head feverously. "I could never hate you." She reached out and took his hands in hers, she leaned in close to his ear and whispered, "I love you. That never changed."

He ran a hand through her hair and cradled her head. "I've waited a long time to hear you say that."

It had been so long since Mollie had been happy, she had lost both the men she'd ever loved. But now, now she was getting one back, and she could not allow the experience to pass her by. She wrapped her hand around his neck and pulled him close. As she kissed him she could feel him smile, she was smiling too. She pulled him tightly to her, never wanted to break the embrace. "God how I've missed you." she murmured into his neck. They held each other close for a long while. It was right this way.

Her family looked on from across the yard. "Did you know he was coming?" Grace asked Peter.

Peter shrugged. "I figured he might, but I couldn't be sure. She deserves this though. It's been too long since she's been happy."

Meanwhile inside the house Ivy pulled out a chair around the kitchen table and motioned for Alex to sit. A few of the new arrivals past by the door of the kitchen but Ivy motioned for them to move on. Once they were alone, or at least as alone as they could possibly be in a house full of telepathic vampires with exceptional hearing, Ivy said, "All right spill. What's the matter with you."

Alex rubbed his hands together for a moment, looking at the floor, not wanting to say. She lifted his chin with her finger and said, "Don't make me read your mind."

He smiled without a trace of happiness and asked, "Do you think there's anything strange about Nora?"

Ivy settled back in the chair and asked, "What do you mean?" Of course she did feel something, she always had but she wasn't about to reveal her speculations to Alex without first knowing what he was thinking. And since there was the mutual understanding around her family that they did not read each other's minds without permission Ivy waited patiently for Alex to tell her.

He licked his lips and said, "I keep getting these flashes of her, nothing really lucid or clear, but there's something unsettling about it. She has fire in her eyes that is beyond disturbing." He looked down at his hands, wanted to hold back the rest.

She cocked her head to the side and asked, "What aren't you saying."

He kept his gaze locked on his hands, knowing that just a quick glance at her would make him spill everything. "She's Leo's mate, I can't." he said through a closed throat, his voice hoarse.

"Alex, what is it?" Ivy pushed, fighting the urge to just take it from his mind. But the need became unnecessary as he showed her himself. He was right, they were simply flashes, not full visions, but it was enough to set Ivy aback. For what she was saw was the fire in her eyes as she faced off against another vampire. And what was the identity of that vampire that made it the hardest to swallow. It was Ivy.

"How long have you been seeing this?" Ivy demanded.

"For a while." he muttered.

"How long is a while?" she snarled.

"He's my brother Ivy, I couldn't bring myself to think that she was really capable of that because she was with our Leo. I was hoping that the vision would change or maybe just go away, but it didn't." he said, his voice meek like that of a child.

"I can't believe you hid this from me." Ivy said shaking her head. "Do I need to start just randomly going through your thoughts to know what you're hiding for me? We have the respect in this family that we don't intrude into others thoughts, but doing this, hiding this, betrays everything we stand for in that respect."

"I'm so sorry, I didn't mean to." Alex said, pain radiating from his voice, disapproval was something no one ever wanted from Ivy.

"Why can't you see anymore of it?" she demanded, folding her arms across her chest. "Or is that just all you're willing to show me?"

"Aw Ivy," Alex said in a wounded voice. "Of course not, I don't know why I can't see anymore."

Vincent get in here. Ivy thought. Within a matter of seconds he was in the kitchen with him.

"What can I do for you boss?" he asked with a smile, clapping his hands together.

Ivy's face was cold which banished the happiness from Vincent's. "I need you to help Alex clarify a vision. I need to go and address the mass of vampires in my backyard." Ivy said as she arose from her chair. She stopped at the doorway, but didn't turn around as she addressed Alex. "Don't come to me until you have some answers." His silence was considered an agreement.

She wandered out into the backyard where all had gathered. It was incredible to her that in such a short amount of time so many had arrived. She assumed that the urgency They had put on the situation had something to do with the speedy arrival. There were vampires from every stretch of earth, from every continent, from Siberia to the equator. Hundreds of vampires gathered in one place, something unlike she had ever seen, something unlike anyone had ever seen. Her gaze passed a very nervous Casper and she remembered what she needed to say. "Can I have your attention everyone." she said in a normal voice, everyone could hear her fine. When she knew she had all of their attention she said, "I would like to start by thanking you all for being here. In a moment I'll turn it over to Rudolph who will brief you further on the situation at hand. But considering you are at my home I will need to lay down a few ground rules." There was a grumbling among some of the crowd. Many of these vampires were nomads, living by no one's rules but their own, barely even observing Their laws. So the thought of having to following Ivy's rules would not sit well with many. "There is no hunting here, we have in stock enough blood to feed you all and one of my family is a doctor so we can get more if the need arises, if you feel the desperate need to actually hunt we limit it to only animals." The entire congregation grumbled this time, cold human blood and/or animal blood was anything but ideal. "I realize that this is not what most of you would like to hear, but there are far too many of you to not attract attention with a hunt. And I believe the basis of all of this is to elevate attention from our kind. Secondly, I'm sure all of you by now have sensed the presence of the human." A hum arose around the crowd. "Nothing will happen to this human, that must be universally understood. He is a guest among my family and it is a boundary that none of you will cross, it is a problem you do not want to bring upon yourself. If you make it your problem, I will make you mine." The hostility in her voice rose the hostility among them all.

Rudolph stepped up next to her and said, "It is also an order from Us. We are the ones to pass judgment on this human, it is not your place to do so." While she could have handled it on her own in that moment she did appreciate Rudolph's help, anything to keep them away from hurting Casper. There was a feeling of consensus around the crowd and it eased Ivy's apprehension. "Now that we have that settled," Rudolph continued. "We have little time to prepare, according to the seers we have only a few days before Emily makes her way here. Surely she has a seer by now and knows what we're planning. Continue your training and I will let you know of more information as it comes to me."

Ivy glanced up at her house as Vincent emerged, he locked eyes with Ivy and thought, *Any chance I could borrow Miles and Laura?* Miles and Laura were two other seers. She looked up and spotted them, they had heard him too. She nodded to them and they moved toward Vincent and then into the house. She glanced up across the lawn at Mollie and Grace staring at her.

What's that about? Grace thought.

Ivy sighed and thought, *Once I know you'll know.* The two nodded together and went back to their work.

"Are you all right?" a voice said from behind.

She closed her eyes and said, "I don't know Rudolph."

"Please look at me." he whispered.

She shook her head. "Not now Rudolph, I can't do this now." she yelped through a closed jaw. He always picked the most inopportune moments. She whipped around at a vampire's speed and hissed at him. "Why can't you just leave me alone, why? Things will never, ever be what they were, I will never love you like I did. Why can't you just accept that? Why?" He didn't speak, but he did grab her forcefully by the arm and lead her away. Hundreds of sets of eyes followed them, but Rudolph leveled them with a gaze which turned them back to their tasks. All save one set of eyes, belonging to the only heartbeat in the crowd, he could not break his worried gaze away from her.

Rudolph led her deep into the woods that surrounded her home. He whipped her in front of him. He dug his hands deep into her dark red hair and held her head in his hands. At first she tried to struggle away but slowly allowed herself to be held by him. He closed his eyes and settled his forehead against hers. "I'm sorry." he murmured after several moments.

She shook her head, her eyes open and focused on him. "It doesn't matter."

"I didn't know that you would feel this way about it, I swear I didn't." he pleaded with her.

She pulled his hands away from her face and said, "How could you not know? You killed him."

"It was for your safety, everything's always been about you." he said reaching for her again.

She pulled away quickly and a sob escaped her lips. The tears would come soon. She couldn't even think about this without crying. "How on earth could that be for my own good? He was my son, you killed my Steven."

"He kept looking for you, asking so many damned questions. Ivy he never would have stopped. If he had found you and found out what you are, we would have had to kill him anyway."

Her hands clutched as fists at her sides, so tightly that her fingernails pierced her skin and own scarlet blood began to flood down her hands and drip into a small puddle on the ground. "So you just decided to beat him to it. Kill him before it was necessary. I would have made sure he never found me, I would have moved to the south pole to keep him safe."

"It wasn't meant to hurt you, never to hurt you. I only ever did anything to protect you." he urged, trying to make her understand.

She clenched her jaw so tight she thought her teeth would shatter. "No," she hissed. She raised a hand a sliced across his face, cutting his cheek with her razor fingernails and smearing her own blood across his cheek. "You did it to isolate me from everything that was important. You took away the one thing that made me human, that kept me connected to who I was. You wanted me just for yourself, you selfish bastard." She raised her arm to hit him again and he made no attempt to move, he knew he had earned it. But another hand grabbed her arm before she could strike Rudolph. She turned to see Alex holding her arm and Grace and Mollie not far off in the distance. They would always be there for her. "What!" she shouted.

Alex shook his head and said, "You don't want to do this."

"Let her." Rudolph said with a husky voice, he was nearly on the brink of tears himself.

Alex ignored him. "We need you two to come back to the house anyway. The other seers and I have found out something." He released her arm and walked back toward the direction of the house. Ivy took a last painful glance at Rudolph before turning toward her girls. They each took her side as she sobbed and looked down at the blood on her hands. The wounds would heal quickly, one of the benefits of being a vampire, but the scars would last forever, another way he had imprinted himself on her. Grace ran and hand across her hair.

"How much of that did you hear?" Ivy asked them in a hushed tone.

They exchanged glances and Mollie said, "As much as you wanted us to." Ivy threw her arms around Mollie and cried into her shoulder.

"We're so sorry Ivy." Grace said.

She wiped the tears away from her eyes and shook her head. "It doesn't matter anymore."

"Sure it does, it always will." Mollie said with a sympathetic smile.

Ivy pulled herself away and walked quickly, but no faster that a quick human speed. But she needed her space. She needed to get away. She just needed to not be there or anywhere anymore.

Chapter Ten

She wanted to walk away and leave it all. He had reopened a wound that she had never wanted to revisit, Rudolph had killed her only child, destroyed her family. She wanted to run and keep running until she hit the ocean and even then she'd find a way around it. But something stopped her in her tracks. For the longest time, before she really embraced her role as the prowler, she considered Steven to be her only family. But now, the more she tried to think that the more the faces of Peter and Leo and Alex and Grace and Mollie and all her children before them flashed past her eyes. Steven would always be her only child by blood, but he was by far not the only thing that mattered. Her family mattered, her way of life mattered, the others like her mattered and as much as she was trying to resist it, Casper mattered. She turned around and walked back toward the house, she'd sort everything out once this was done. Once they'd gotten Emily, she was after all the main objective.

She arrived back at the house and everyone was in a twitter. There was a nervous buzz. Angelo grabbed her by the arm and hissed, "Where the hell have you been? We've been looking for you everywhere."

"What's going on?" she asked.

Angelo sighed and said, "The seers together were able to make a rather clear vision. The way they see it Emily is going to win, both the full battle among us all and her battle against you."

"That can't be possible." Ivy whispered shaking her head.

"We also have about twenty minutes until they're here."

Angelo said, glancing around nervously at the others. But Ivy had stopped listening, in fact she was walking away quickly, searching for the heartbeat among the crowd. She had to hide him, keep him from this. She spotted him on the far side of her yard standing with Peter, at lightening speed she was beside him.

Ivy where have you been? Peter thought. *The girls told me what happened, I'm sorry.*

She ignored him and grabbed Casper by the wrist and led him toward the house, so fast she nearly lifted him off his feet. "Ivy," he said tried to get her attention. "Ivy remember I can't move as fast as you." But she still ignored him, she had to get him safe. Finally she got him in the house, her frantic pace beginning to scare him more than he already was. She opened the door to the creep cellar and pulled him down the stairs. "Where we going?" he asked with a tremble in his throat.

"You need to be safe." she muttered pulling a cord to turn on the swinging light bulb at the bottom of the wooden stairs. She released his arm and began scurrying around the room at a speed he could barely see.

"Ivy are you okay?" he asked reaching out for her arm.

She stopped dead where she was and whipped around to look at him, tears streaming down her marble cheeks as she shouted, "No Casper! No, I'm not all right! I'm rather far from all right!"

"Okay, okay." he said in a soothing voice. She was pacing back and forth again, her speed rapidly increasing. "Do you want to tell me what happened?"

She stopped again, this time facing the wall, away from him.

"Do remember when you ask me what Rudolph did to make me hate him so much?" she asked, trying as hard as possible to keep her emotions at bay.

"Yes." he said, trying to speak as little as possible, letting her carry the conversation.

"He-he killed my son." she said meekly, running a hand across her face.

"What?" Casper muttered.

She turned slowly toward him, a sad smile on her face. "Steven could never accept that I had just disappeared. He looked everywhere for me and after my husband died he became the duke and it was easy for him to get people to help him. So many tried to discourage him and stop him, but he never would. He knew I was still out there, he never lost the connection to me. And the greater the search got the more nervous Rudolph became. He began considering moving us away, but while anonymity is important among our kind Rudolph had spent far too much time establishing himself as the alpha in our community there."

"So he killed your son instead?" Casper asked from the stairs where he had sat.

She nodded slowly. "To him that was the better decision, rather than let him get any closer." She closed her eyes, remembering the awful day. "When he came home that night I knew something was wrong. He smelled all wrong, too familiar. And when I asked him where he'd been he said he had just been taking care of some business. That I shouldn't worry about it. And a part of me just knew, a few years later I left and never looked back. Things would never be like they were between us. He killed that."

"You said you lived together?" Casper asked, not really wanted an answer to his next question. "Like you live with the family?"

She smiled and shook her head. "Not exactly Casper."

"Oh, I understand." he said bowing him head.

She sighed and sat beside him on the stairs. "You have to understand Casper, I loved him for a very long time. Even when I was still human, when I was married. A part of me probably always will love him, but too large a part is dominated by what he did, and even nearly half a millennium later I can't forgive him."

Casper shrugged and looked away. "I mean it doesn't matter to me, you and I are just friends right?"

She smiled without any trace of happiness and said, "Casper look at me." Slowly he turned his head to look at her sad face. She ran her hands through his salt and pepper hair and held his head still.

Ivy, it's time. a voice upstairs thought.

"Not yet." she said aloud, unable to keep it, or the sob that came with it, inside.

"What?" he asked, placing his hands on her wrists.

"I couldn't mean it, it was just to protect you." Ivy said with a cry.

Ivy don't. Alex's inner voice warned.

"You couldn't mean what?" Casper asked, concern pouring from his voice, his thumbs moving across the smooth planes of her wrists.

She shook her head. "That I didn't love you. I don't know what it is about you, but I do. It doesn't even make any sense to me."

He put his hands on her cheeks and said, "It doesn't have to make any sense."

Ivy. the voices upstairs said again.

Ivy let out a sob and closed her eyes. Casper just watched her, unable to find any way to help her. Suddenly she opened her eyes and said, "I might not come back from this Casper, you have to understand that."

"What are talk-" he began, but she cut him off.

She started shaking her head and said, "Sh, just listen for a moment. If anything happens to me, I won't be here to protect you from Rudolph, but I promise the family will take care of you."

"Can't I help? In any way?" he asked.

She shook her head again and said, "No, the best thing you can do is stay here, try to plug up the door if you can and keep the windows closed, your scent won't get to them that way." In a moment she couldn't control she crushed her marble lips to his and kissed him for a long moment, probably too long considering he began gasping for breath, but still made no attempt to pull away. Finally she bit her lip and pulled away.

He kissed her forehead and said, "I need you to come back."

She closed her eyes as he held his lips against her head. "I'll try my best." she said. Finally she uncoiled her hands from his hair and stood. "Stay safe."

"I love you Ivy." he said as she turned to leave. It felt like a goodbye and he was so helpless to do anything at all.

She wanted to say it back, but she thought it would break her last bit of sanity to do so. So instead she simply smiled and turned away. On the other side of the door her family waited. She locked the door and said, "I just don't want to talk about it."

She stepped outside with her family and a creepy sensation settled over her, they were all dead silent. Ivy scanned the crowd for Rudolph and found him quickly. "What's going on?" she asked him in response to the silence.

His stayed fixed on one spot, the same spot as everyone else. "They're here." he said.

Ivy looked out at the spot too, emerging from the woods was a pack of newborns, blood in their eyes. There must have been a hundred of them, with their ungodly strength this would be a battle indeed. At the head of their pack was a small cluster of seasoned vampires. Those who had chosen to follow Emily. Emily was at the head of them all, her long raven hair swinging at her hips, her golden eyes already in predator mode, she was taking no chances. Ivy could feel Alex's fear and anger from across the yard, she turned to him and leveled him with a glance, no rash movements now. Her family stayed huddled together. Slowly Emily headed toward Rudolph and Angelo, and of course Ivy. She stopped only a few yards before them, her troupe standing at attention behind her, her own mindless army.

"Emily." Rudolph said with a sharp nod.

Emily was smiling brightly as she said, "Rudolph it has been far too long." Slowly she turned to Ivy and smiled brighter. "Oh, and Ivy, it is good to see you too. Have you been taking care of my creation, I'm sure he's close by, I can sense him. Where is dear Alex?" she asked her eyes scanning the crowd.

"Leave him alone." Ivy commanded.

This only caused Emily to smile brighter. "Oh, hit a nerve have I? You know I could just order him to come to me."

"That won't be necessary." Ivy said, with a shake of her head. *Come here Alex.* she thought. Slowly and hesitantly Alex moved toward them. He stood behind Ivy as if she were a shield to protect him.

"Hello child." Emily said to him, her smile increasing. This was a game to her. Alex offered nothing but a nod, he didn't even look at her. That did not please Emily. "Look at me." she ordered in her creator's voice. The wave moved through Alex up to his eyes making him focus on her, evil Emily. "Say hello to your creator." she ordered.

"Hello," he murmured just above a whisper.

Ivy looked at Rudolph, urging him to end this. He took the hint. "You certainly did get here fast. Create a seer?"

Emily's smile returned and said, "I had no need for one."

"Then how did you know?" Angelo asked.

She turned to Ivy and said, "I think Ivy might know, and maybe Alex too."

"What is she saying?" Angelo asked Ivy and Alex.

"I have no idea." Ivy said with a confused look. Rudolph scrutinized her further, she turned her attention to him. "I swear."

"No," Emily said with a laugh. "Get out here." she said to no one in particular it seemed. They all turned their attention to the crowd in front of them as a far too familiar person emerged from the crowd. All breathing stopped.

"Nora!" Leo was shouting instantly at Ivy's side. "What are you doing with her?"

Nora shook her head. "Darling don't you understand that Their way of thinking is so backwards. We should be dominating the humans not the other way around."

"I was lucky to find one of yours who was willing to help me," Emily said to Ivy. "It was just too easy for her to set the plan in motion."

Suddenly it all became clear. "You planned it all." Ivy muttered. "Bringing Casper here, you knew what would happen with the rogue here, that she would attack him and start all this. You knew."

"Yes I knew, it worked even better than I would have planned." Nora said with a smile. "I was going to bring you to him myself, but somehow he found your book on his own and he came to me."

"Why Casper?" Ivy demanded, hissing through her teeth.

Nora smirked. "Because I knew how desperate he was too work, desperate enough to latch onto you and need to meet you to discuss it."

"Nora I don't understand what you're doing. Why are you doing this?" Leo asked, the tone of his voice torn and hurt.

Nora stepped away from Emily who made not attempt to stop her. She reached for his arm but he pulled away. "Leo, I love you."

"I don't think I believe you." Leo said, turning away. "I feel like you only are with me to get to Ivy."

She shook her head feverishly. "That's not true Leo, it's not true. I loved you long before I even met Emily." She glanced back at Emily and smiled. "But you have to admit that she is right, we shouldn't bow to the humans, roll over and take it. We need to dominate them." She put her hand on his cheek as he closed his eyes and said, "Join us."

Slowly his eyes rolled open and he asked, "Are you asking me to choose between you and the family?" She just stared at him for a moment. "That's no decision at all." She smiled at him and took his hand, but he pulled away and stepped behind Ivy. "My family will always come first."

"Leo." she said her voice breathy, a sob hiding under her voice. She went to reach for him.

Enough. Emily's inner voice hissed, but Nora didn't move. She turned slightly to Ivy and hissed, "You ruin everything. I hate you."

Ivy crossed her arms across her chest and said, "I think you did enough of that yourself."

Nora was slowly grinding her teeth together, fighting off the change to the predator mode. "You don't know anything."

"I took nothing from you, you just changed." Ivy said in a sad voice. How could she not have seen this?

"You'll pay for this, you will." she murmured to Ivy. Emily looked at her quizzically and did not have time to stop her before she spoke. She turned to the rogue army and said, "She has a human here, a real living, breathing human. She wants to protect him, even puts him above her own family." The rogues buzzed. An angry look spread across Emily's face.

"Nora, stop." Emily urged.

"No," Nora said defiantly. "They should know, they should know that there's a vampire here who defies her own kind for them, humans."

Ivy slowly shook her head. "What happened to you? You were always one of my favorites, one of the successes."

"People change." Nora said, her voice cold, a voice so different from the Nora she knew.

"I never would have thought you would change like this." Ivy said. "I'm so disappointed."

In a flash Nora turned to the predator side and pounced at Ivy. "Who are you to judge me?" Ivy switched to predator mode too to fight her off. Nora slashed at her and Ivy bobbed away. And that was all it took, Nora took the first move which gave Rudolph all he needed to pounce at Emily, he wanted the glory of taking her down. And then everyone began to run into battle. It was just the way Alex had seen it, starting with a battle between Nora and Ivy and leading to a victory by Emily's side. It couldn't happen that way. Ivy flipped Nora onto her back and pinned her against the ground with her forearm.

"Go ahead," Nora gasped from under the pressure of Ivy's arm. "Do it. Kill me. You know you want to."

Ivy shook her head. "No Nora, I don't want to." A single tear ran down Ivy's cheek and caused a confused look to cross Nora's face. In one quick motion she snapped Nora's neck, as she did she whispered, "But I have to." She looked up and locked eyes with Leo, standing only a few feet away. "I'm sorry my boy." she muttered.

Leo said nothing at first, merely stared at Nora's decapitated body. He knelt down beside Ivy and took his mate's body in his arms, he was silent. He picked her up leaning her head against his shoulder. A fire had started on the other side of the yard, he was silent. He carried her toward it, ignoring everyone who walked or ran by him. He held her still for a moment in front of that fire and held her close. "I don't understand my love." he whispered into her ear. "How you could do this, how could you turn against me like this?" He closed his eyes for a moment and then kissed her forehead. "I love you." he said before throwing her into the fire, the only way to dispose of a vampire body. He rubbed the tears away from his eyes quickly and had little time to mourn as he was attacked from behind by a rouge. Being that it was Leo he took him down instantly.

Emily was overwhelming Rudolph, she was stronger than he had anticipated. "Imagine," she said with a smile. "Me taking down one of the infamous Them. Who would have ever thought it." Suddenly she was blindsided from the right.

"You don't have him yet." Ivy said crouching in front of her, in full predator form.

But rather than be angry as Ivy had expected her smile only grew. "Now this is what I was really waiting for."

"Why me?" Ivy asked, as curious and interested as Emily was.

"You're famous my dear, more so than any of them. The prowler who cares. And lord knows you've taken in more than one of mine." she said, it was clear she was talking about Alex. "He's prettier than I remember. Perhaps I will take him after all." Ivy flipped her over with all her force onto her back. She began to crush Emily's throat with the palm of her hand.

"He is everything he is in spite of you. You're just the bitch who tried to destroy him." Ivy hissed. Despite the fact that Ivy was crushing in her throat Emily continued to smile.

"Feisty, I have been waiting for this for a long time." Emily breathed through a nearly broken windpipe, luckily for Emily not a necessity for a vampire to live.

"I don't understand, what is it about me?" Ivy demanded pushing down harder.

"They listen to you, every vampire in the world in this country is tied to you in some way. I get you on my side and I can win over so many." Emily muttered. Ivy was pulled off her guard a bit, just enough for Emily to take control again. She put her knee in Ivy's chest and pined her down at her shoulders.

"Why would I ever do that? Join you?" Ivy said with disgust.

Emily smiled brighter, her honey eyes sparkling as she leaned down to Ivy's ear, "Because maybe I'll take him away and force him to stay with me. How much do you care for him Ivy, enough to sacrifice yourself to save himself from me."

Ivy stared into her eyes. Was she serious? Suddenly Emily's face twisted in pain and Ivy saw a familiar face behind her head. Alex leaned down to Emily's ear and said, "She'll never have to make that decision you horrid bitch." Emily slumped over and Ivy could see the stake sticking out of her back.

"Not again." Ivy murmured as she squeezed her eyes shut as Emily burst on top of her. Slowly she opened her eyes, the stickiness of Emily's blood all over here. "Nice shot." she said to Alex.

He extended his arm to her to help her up. When she was on her feet she noticed that Alex's hand was shaking. "Alex." Ivy said.

A tear fell from his eyes. "I killed her Ivy, I actually killed her. It's done, it's over. She's gone."

Even though she was disgusting, she wrapped her arms around him and he welcomed her happily. He glanced around at the surrounding battlefield. "I think it might be over. "Ivy I think it's over." Ivy straightened up and looked out too. Only a few of the rogue remained standing and they had been cornered and imprisoned by some of the others. The bonfire in the middle of her lawn would be difficult to explain, considering how high is was now, thank god she lived in the middle of nowhere.

"I thought we were supposed to lose." she said to Alex.

Alex shrugged and said, "I guess we got it wrong."

Just then Grace came running toward them smiling. "Thirty-two! That's right all on my own I took down thirty-two."

"All on your own? Or with the help of your powers?" Alex asked.

Grace huffed and said, "Why do you want to take this away from me?" Alex laughed. Grace looked Ivy over and said, "Damn, you get staked again?"

"Something like that." Ivy said wiping the gunk away from her face. "This is disgusting."

"What happened to Emily?" Rudolph demanded walking toward them.

"She's dead." Ivy said simply.

"Who killed her?" he demanded, offended that it wasn't him.

She glanced up at Alex and nodded. "My boy here."

"You killed your creator?" Rudolph asked, intrigue laced in

his voice as his focused flickered between Alex and Ivy.

"Yes, she was kind of distracted trying to kill Ivy so she didn't notice me." Alex said with a shrug.

"We won?" Rudolph asked, his eyes focused now completely on Ivy, a smile flickering across his lips.

"We did." Ivy said smiling back.

Mollie and Samuel came running up to them then. Ivy had not seen him yet. "Samuel?" she said.

"Hello Ivy." he said with a nod and a smile.

Ivy glanced down at their hands which were intertwined. "Reconciled have we?"

"I actually really need to talk to you." Mollie said with a smile. *In private.*

Ivy nodded and said, "Let's go inside, I need a shower."

"We'll hold the fort down here." Grace said with a smile.

She led Mollie toward the house which was surprisingly undamaged. The walked up the stairs to the bathroom and Ivy got in the bathtub. "What did you want to talk about?"

Mollie was wringing her hand together quickly. "It's about me and Samuel."

"Okay, what about you?" Ivy asked, rinsing off her hair and face."

"He's asked me to be his mate and I've said yes." Mollie said with a smile.

Ivy peered around the side of the shower curtain and said, "That's fantastic love, I'm happy for you. Is that all you wanted to tell me?"

Mollie ran a nervous hand through her wavy brown hair and

shook her head. Ivy kept her eyes focused on Mollie and waited. Mollie took in a deep breath and said, "When this is over and Samuel leaves, I'm leaving with him."

Ivy absently reached for the faucet until she could turn it off. "What?" was all that Ivy was able to muster.

Mollie shrugged. "You'll be able to find another doctor easily."

"You say that like it's the only reason we keep you around, which you have to know isn't true." Ivy said wrapping herself in a towel and sitting on the side o the tub.

Mollie shrugged again. "I know that, but I think it's time for me to move on. I'm ready, being with you for the past sixty years has been everything to me and you've prepared me to go." A tear escaped her eyes. Ivy wiped it away with her thumb.

"I love you, you know that right?" Ivy asked and Mollie nodded. "If this is what you want I'll support you all the way. I know you love him, you could never hide that from me. Know that you taking a mate doesn't mean you have to leave."

Mollie smiled. "I know that, but Samuel is much more of a nomad, and I think he's a little threatened by our family. I'm ready to start my own, finally."

Ivy encircled her tightly in her arms and the two shared a good cry. "You'll be a great leader, just keep in touch with me."

Mollie nodded beside Ivy's head and whispered, "Always."

Ivy wiped away her tears and said, "How long till you go?"

Mollie's face fell. "Tonight."

Ivy bit her lip, fighting off more tears. "Do you want me to help you tell the others?"

She shook her head and said, "No I can do it, I would appreciate you being there though."

"Of course." Ivy said with a smile and hugged her girl again. Family left, it was not the first time, many had left before, that didn't make it any easier. She assumed this was how any mother felt when her children fled the nest. It was sad, but she was happy for Mollie. If anyone deserved this kind of happiness it was Mollie.

Ivy redressed, Mollie had taken her close to burn them. As she was walking back down the stairs she suddenly realized she had forgotten about Casper. She went to the door of the basement, but Rudolph beat her there. "Not yet." he said.

"What do you mean? He's been down there for hours." Ivy said with a furrowed brow.

"Mollie just brought him some food, we're going to discuss him first." Rudolph said.

Ivy rolled her eyes. "We just settled one problem, can't we take a break?"

He shook his head. "Not right now."

Ivy sighed. "Fine I'll gather the family." She went to move around him but he grabbed her arm to stop her.

He was shaking his head. "No Ivy, just you and I are going to discuss it."

Ivy cocked her head to the side, confused. "Ok, what about Angelo?"

"I'm taking the lead on this. I asked him to stay out of it." Rudolph said.

"Why?" Ivy asked, wary now of whatever it was Rudolph was plotting.

He sighed and said, "Can we just go somewhere private and talk."

She didn't want to, she really didn't, but she also didn't see any other choice. So she led him to his office. Smugly he sat in her chair and she had to sit on the other side of the desk. "Okay, what was so important it had to be said in secret?"

He was smiling now, not the best sign. "You did a good job today, handling the whole situation."

"Thank you?" she said, more as a question.

"I mean it you did." he said.

"And thank you, but what does this have to do with Casper?" she asked.

"Nothing, I just wanted to pay you a complement before we talked about him." Rudolph said with a sigh, another bad sign.

"Just say what you need to say." Ivy urged coldly.

"I don't like him." Rudolph said bluntly.

"Well that's obvious." Ivy said with a humorless laugh.

"And I especially don't like you around him."

"What does that mean?" Ivy asked.

"I'm a jealous man Ivy, I think you probably know that. I don't want to share you, not at all." he said, crossing his arms across him chest.

Suddenly and uncontrollable Ivy began to cry as the vision of either a dead or vampire Casper flashed across her eyes. "What are you going to do?"

"I'm going to give you the choice."

"What does that mean?" Ivy demanded.

"I want you for myself, I'm not going back to the Main City,

I'm staying here with you. And if I can't have you no one can." The sound of those words sent shivers down her spine. "So, you get to choose, either you send him away, anyway you know how and you stay with me, or I kill him."

"You can't force me into loving you again Rudolph." Ivy said with a quiet sob.

"No, but I can try." he said getting up from the desk. He ran a hand across her shoulder, sending a shiver through her. "I give you an hour to choose before I choose for you."

She settled her forehead against her desk and cried. The choice was simple, she knew that. She couldn't let Rudolph kill him, she loved Casper too much for that. So why was it so hard for her to choose it? She didn't wanted to be with Rudolph, but she wouldn't let him take Casper. She would rather be living miserable life while knowing that Casper was alive than miserable because she knew he was dead. She wiped away her tears and walked from the room, everyone was gathered in the back yard, it already looked as if nothing had happened. The fire was dying down, and all the vampires were gone, every one. They were not creatures who hovered or overstayed their welcome, they came for their objective and now they were gone.

Rudolph had let Casper out of the basement and he was now in the backyard with the others. They were all sitting in a semicircle around Mollie. Ivy walked up behind them for support.

"What's up baby sister?" Peter asked her.

Mollie smiled. "Well let me start by saying home much I love you all."

"I don't like that as a beginning." Grace said with a panicked look.

Mollie just held her smile. "The last sixty years have been so incredible, we've done so much together and you are the best brothers and sisters I could have ever asked for."

"But," Leo said, his voice sad and cold.

"But," Mollie began. "I think it's time for me to move on. I'm going to be leaving with Samuel."

"What the hell are you talking about?" Grace demanded.

"Gracie, it's okay." Alex said.

"No it's not, you can't leave, you belong with us. You're our sister. He can't just come here after sixty years and take you away."

"Gracie he's not taking me away, I'm going willingly." Mollie said with a soothing voice, trying to calm her sister. Samuel stood by her side quietly. Mollie bent down in front of the crying Grace and said, "I will always love you, you are my sister forever. I'll keep in touch, it's just time for me to move on, start a new adventure."

Grace looked up at her and said, "How can you leave me here with all these boys?"

"Thanks." Ivy said from behind.

"You know what I mean boss." she said, still facing Mollie. "I don't what I'll do without you."

Mollie smiled. "Sure you do sis, you'll continue being amazing you. You'll keep going to school and learning everything you can and I'll stay in touch with you, I promise. I also promise that you'll see me again. Nothing could keep me away from you." Grace could say no more, she simply pounced at Mollie and encircled her in a vicious hug. Mollie laughed and held her tight.

Leo locked eyes with Samuel and thought, *That's my sister, break her heart and I'll break your neck.* Samuel smiled and nodded in understanding.

The whole family stood up and hugged Mollie, losing a sister was nothing they were happy about, but they loved her and if this was what she wanted then this was what she would get. A tear ran down Ivy's cheek. *I need to talk to you all about something. And we need to discuss it without Casper.* They glanced at one another nervously, and without understanding. Ivy glanced up at Rudolph who was smiling, he knew her choice.

Samuel, Mollie thought. *Think you can keep Casper busy for a bit.*

Absolutely. Samuel thought. "Casper," he said aloud, grasping Casper's attention. "I was wondering if maybe you could help me load some of Mollie's things into my truck."

Casper looked at him confused for a moment, the gaggle of superhuman vampires and he wanted the human's help. But who was he to disagree? "Sure," he said walked with Samuel across the yard.

"What's up boss?" Mollie said, for what could be the last time.

"It has to do with Casper's sentence," Ivy muttered, her arm still protectively around Alex. Instinctively they all glanced up at Rudolph who instantly looked away. "We have to leave him." A silent sob left Ivy's lips and all the faces of her family fell even Peter's face. "So, I'm going to take him for a drive and take him home. When I get back, have his bag on the front porch, if he wants it he can come for it. Otherwise, pack up what we want to take from here and I'll tell you where we're going when I get back."

She could see that some of them wanted to protest, they weren't ready to leave, but they knew it was necessary. They all nodded and Ivy sighed. *Samuel, you can bring him back whenever you'd like.* Ivy thought. Within moments the two were walking back, her eyes locked on the gray haired Casper. She smiled sadly, but refused to cry, she wouldn't let him know yet that anything was wrong.

"Casper," she said to him with a smile. "Do you want to go for a drive?"

He smiled and said, "Sure, I'd love to."

They climbed into her Bentley and away they drove. For a good spell of time they were completely silent, he assumed she just didn't want to talk. It had obviously been a hard day for her. "Are you all right?" he finally asked.

"Yea," she said quietly. "Just a long day."

"I can't believe what happened with Nora." Casper said shaking his head.

"They told you about that did they?" Ivy asked pulling into the parking lot of the local mall, only about a block from Casper's apartment.

"Why are we stopping here?" he asked, glancing around.

"I have to talk to you about something." Ivy said calmly and coolly, she could not get emotional here, not now.

"What's wrong?" he asked placing a hand on her shoulder. She shrugged it away.

"Rudolph and I got to talking earlier." she said, her eyes focused forward.

"Oh," Casper said turning back in his seat.

"Yea," she said.

"What did you talk about?" he asked, crossing his arms.

"We've reconciled." she said quietly, he bit his bottom lip and waited. "In fact he's staying with my family."

"What? He's staying here?" Casper demanded.

"Yes." Ivy whispered.

"There's something not you're not saying to me. Tell me Ivy." he demanded. "You owe me that."

She closed her eyes tight, the tears were coming. One escaped. "Let's take a walk."

"What? No." he said simply.

She turned to him, her eyes full of tears. "Please, just a few minutes."

"Fine." he said getting out of the car.

They walked silently for a moment, there was a small park next to the mall. "Will you please tell me what's going on?" Casper asked.

She stopped dead and looked down at the ground. "We're leaving Casper."

His face fell. "What does that mean?"

"Exactly what it sounds like, we're leaving and we're not coming back." Ivy said, she had wanted to just drop him off and avoid this conversation, but he was right, she owed him more than that.

"Where are you going?" he asked, a bit of panic in his voice.

She shook her head. "I can't tell you that."

"Why not?" Casper said. "How will I know where to find you."

Ivy took in a deep breath and just looked at him and waited for him to figure it out. "Oh, I see, you don't want me to find you."

She started shaking her head. "It's now what you think."

"Then what is it?" he shouted, anger and pain mixing in his voice.

"It's your sentence." she muttered, tears falling from her eyes.

"What? My sentence, how is this my sentence?" he asked.

She sighed aloud. "Rudolph won't share me, he gave me a choice."

"What choice?" he asked, placing his hand gently on her crossed arms.

"Either make you go away or kill you." she said with a sob.

"What?"

"He said that if he couldn't have me no one could, he'd kill you before he'd let you have me. I love you too much to let that happen." she said with a sad smile.

"I'm not scared of him Ivy, you don't have to do this." Casper pleaded. "Please don't do this."

She put a hand on his cheek and he closed his eyes against the coolness. "You should be afraid of him, and yes I do have to do this, because I love you. I won't let anything like that happen to you."

He placed his forehead against hers and closed his eyes. "Don't do this, we'll get through it together."

She shook her head. "You don't understand Casper. We're leaving today. Right when I get home."

"What?" he said a little more forcefully.

"The family's packing up the house right now. We'll be gone

right when I get home." she said with a sob.

"Ivy," he pleaded. "We can get around this, I'll-I'll talk to Rudolph we'll figure out something."

"Do me a favor, keep living your life, don't let it stop you. That would be horrible for me." she said rubbing her thumb across his cheek.

"Ivy-" he began, his eyes filling with tears.

"Sh, sh, just listen to me for a second." she said moving both her thumbs across his warm cheeks, making a memory of the feeling. "You will never age for me in any way. I will always have you in my heart Casper. I love you, but please, don't come looking for us. You won't find us, we're good at hiding and I don't want you to waste your life like that. I'll take away all memory of us from this place. You'll be able to forget us, I promise." She crushed her icy lips against his and held there for a long moment, another memory to make.

He held her wrists, he never wanted to let her go. "Don't do this, I love you. Please."

She kissed him again sweetly and released his grip. "I'm sorry. Take care of yourself." She kissed him a final time and then at a speed that was too fast for him to see fled back to her car.

She cried the whole home, she made it there in record time. When she pulled into the driveway and collapsed over her steering wheel. Grace pulled her from the car. "Sh, it's okay. It's okay."

"I need you to drive my car, I can't do it." Ivy said with a sob.

"Sure, Rudolph can drive my car." she said with a smile.

They hugged Mollie goodbye for a final time and said that they would see each other soon. Oh how she hoped it would be true. The family loaded into the cars and Rudolph pulled Ivy aside. He opened his mouth to speak and she cut him off. "No. You don't speak to me right now. In fact, I'll let you know when you can talk to me again." And he said nothing more. She got in the Bentley next to Grace and they drove away. She looked back at her home, her home for the past ten years and said her silent goodbyes. She looked out at the front porch, they had left his bag like she told them. He'd be by soon, sure he could beat them before they left, but of course they'd be long gone. She closed her eyes and muttered her final goodbyes to him and her life there. She loved him so much, enough to let him go for his own good. It broke her heart, but it saved him and to her that was all that really mattered.

Just as she had predicted, twenty minutes later Casper arrived at the house. He saw his bag on the front steps and panicked. He ran through the front door and panicked again at the eerie silence inside. "Ivy!" he screamed, he ran through the dining room, everything was gone. "Ivy!" In the kitchen he pulled open the fridge, empty. The bookshelves had been cleaned out, the closets in the bedrooms emptied. Everything was gone. They were gone. He wandered into Ivy's office and sat on the chair behind her desk. The computer was gone, all the books, everything that made the room what it was, was gone. He looked down on the desk and saw an envelope. He picked it up, his name was on it. Inside was a key with a note attached. *Keep the house, it's yours. Love Mollie.* He held the key in his hands, he would return it to them once they found them, because he would find them, he had to.

Chapter Eleven

And so the days passed and turned to months which turned to years. He searched and searched but just as Ivy had promised he hadn't found them. The real challenge in it all was how to go about looking for them in the first place. It wasn't exactly like he could file a missing persons report for the undead or hang fliers reading "Have you seen these vampires." He remembered back to what Mollie had told the first day about the seventy two houses they owned and since they were all probably under different aliases it would be impossible to find them that way. Ivy had stopped publishing under her pseudonym so no more books came out that he could find. Ivy was right, they were experts at hiding. Every few months he would return to the home in Maryland, just to see if maybe they'd come back there. They never did.

After a decade of searching he lost all hope. He returned home and decided to stay in Mollie's house, she had left it for him after all. He set up the house for himself, bought and new computer. He sat down to write, missing a lost friend he had not seen in many years, but nothing would come. He had to face it, he wasn't the same person anymore.

He opened the door slowly, he wasn't really in an entertaining mode. "What Michael?" he said to his old friend with sleepy voice.

He held up two cups and said, "I brought coffee."

Casper smiled and took a cup from him, walking away from the door and letting Mikey in. "What can I do for you?" Casper asked him.

"Well," Mike began. "Belinda and the kids are spending the weekend with her mom in New Jersey so I thought I'd stop by and see you for a bit."

Casper just stared at him, he was the worst liar. "I'm fine Michael, I'm not hanging from the rafters yet."

"I mean I just wish I understood what happened to you. Ten years ago you were this happy vibrant guy and then it seemed in like a couple weeks you just changed forever." Mikey said with a sigh. "I just worry about you man." He leaned back against the chair and said, "Like how'd you get this house when you haven't published a book in over ten year?"

Casper sighed and said, "How many times are we going to go over this Mike?"

Mikey took a long sip from his cup and shrugged. "Until you give me an answer I actually believe I guess."

"The people I met here became my friends, practically my family and they're going to be gone for a good few years so they told me I could live in the house until they come back. So I'm not paying anything for it, it's not really mine." Casper said with a sigh.

"Fine man, if you say so." Mike said with a laugh. "I just worry about you."

"You worrying about me got me into this mess." Casper mumbled under his breath.

"Huh?" he asked.

"Nothing." Casper said, taking a swig of the coffee.

He appreciated Mikey's worry, it was the marker of a good friend. But it got him thinking of everything left undone in his life. He missed Ivy and her family, but it got him thinking more and more about his own.

He stood outside their door for about five minutes, unable to bring himself to knock. "Stop being a baby." he muttered to himself as he raised his fist to knock on the door. He began to regret the decision and considered fleeing, but before he could the door opened, stopping at the chain.

"Casper?" the voice on the other side murmured.

Casper smiled slightly. "Hi mom."

At lightening speed she nearly tore the chain off the door. She hoped up into his arms and crushed him close to her. She looked, smelled, and felt just how he had remembered. "Oh my goodness." she cried into his jacket. "You're so grown up."

He chuckled. "Yea mama, just a little."

She reached down and grabbed his hand. "Well come inside, come inside."

He put his hand on the doorframe to stop himself. "Wait a second mom, is he here?"

She smiled sadly and said, "Just come inside Casper, I'll explain."

He hesitantly released his grip on the doorframe and walked into his old home. It was as if nothing had ever changed, everything still in its place. She motioned toward the couch for him to sit. "So, it's been a long time Casper."

He nodded slowly as he sat. "About fifteen years now."

She looked at him in disbelief. "My god, has it really been that long? How old are you now?"

"Thirty-five." he said with a sigh, barley able to believe it himself.

"My goodness." she said shaking her head.

"How've you been mom?" he asked awkwardly. He had expected it to be so hard.

"Good, good." she said, crossing her legs.

He finally needed to ask. "Mom, where's dad?"

She licked her lips slowly and said, "He's upstairs. Your father's a little different than you remember."

"What do you mean?" Casper asked.

His mother sighed and said, "A few years after you left your father got into a bad accident."

"Let me guess he'd been drinking." Casper interrupted.

She nodded sadly and said, "Yes, yes he was. The accident crushed his spine and left him paralyzed."

"So is he in a wheelchair?" Casper asked, his voice filled with more curiosity than concern.

She shook her head. "No, because the extent of his injuries he's been in bed since I brought him home ."

"How long?" he asked.

His mother sighed and said, "About thirteen years I guess. He's been sober that long too."

"Really?" he said. He never thought he would hear that his father was sober, it wasn't something he ever saw as being in the cards. "How?"

"Well, with his being completely at my mercy for once I cut out all alcohol. He didn't really have any choice. He couldn't get up and walk away, or hit me again. He's so different now."

"Sorry if I'm not jumping for joy mother." he said his voice cold.

His mother reached out and patted his hand. "I can never expect you to forgive your father, I can't make that decision for you. What he did was unforgivable, and I think you made the right decision by leaving."

"You think so?" he asked.

"I do." she said with a smile. "I also think you should go upstairs and talk to him. Tell him you hate him, you love him, whatever you want. I think it would do you both a world of good."

"I don't know if I can do that mom." he said staring down at his hands.

She placed hers over his and said, "I know you *can* son, the question really is will you?"

He truly didn't want to, he had always sworn that he would never see his father again, but then a thought crossed his mind. If he wasn't there to see his father, why was he really there. Ivy had taught him to face the things that scared him, and perhaps that's why he did come, to face what scared him the most. His father. He began to nod his head slowly and said, "Okay mama, okay."

She smiled and took his hand. They walk up the stairs together and paused outside a door at the top of them. She squeezed her son's hand and said, "Don't be afraid." They were the same words he used to tell him in dealing with his father when he was a child. He took in a deep breath and walked in behind his mother.

"Alan, there's someone here to see you." his mother said once they were inside the door.

"No one but the doctor ever comes to visit me." his father

said, his eyes focused on the television. His voice sent shivers down Casper's spine.

"Sorry to disappoint." Casper said from behind his mother.

The old man's head flipped to the side and his eyes grew large at the sight of his son. "Casper? Casper is that you."

He nodded curtly and said, "Yea dad it's me."

He patted the bed frantically and said, "Please come sit boy."

Casper shook his head. "No dad I think I'll stand." It was nearly frightening to see his dad sober, like he literally was a different man.

His father nodded slowly. "Okay, okay I deserve that."

Casper looked back to see that his mother had slipped out of the room. They were alone. "Mom said you're sober."

His dad nodded. "Thirteen years." he was smiling, something inside of Casper twisted.

"Yea but you had to get into an accident for it to happen." Casper said leaning up against the wall.

"Yes, I did. No one else was hurt thank god."

"Yes thank god for that." Casper said, the corners of his mouth turned down.

"Son, you can try and pick a fight with me all you want but I'm just happy to see you. I won't fight with you because everything you say will be right, I've been very wrong in my life, especially where my family has been concerned. I know that."

Casper sat in a chair that was pushed up in a corner and said, "You are different, that's for damn sure."

His father chuckled. "Yea I guess I am. Once I didn't have

the alcohol in me anymore I got to see my life for what it was, and I have never been so disgusted. What I did to your mother, and you and Zach, there's no excuse for it." His face had turned very serious. "I don't expect you to forgive me Casper, but just know that I am sorry, more than you'll ever know, and that I do love you."

"Dad, I just think it might be too little too late." Casper said with a sigh.

His father nodded slowly. "And if that's how you feel that's completely fine. I just want you to know how I feel."

This was such a different man. This wasn't the father that beat him or his mother, or chased his brother away. This man was, for lack of a better word, pitiful. A man who saw a lifetime of abuse and anger and finally regretted it. His father had done horrible things to him, but this wasn't the same man anymore. Did Casper really have it within him to stay mad at this man? He inched his chair closer to his father's bed. "You can't imagine the hell you put us through."

"Yes I can Casper, I put you through enough to get this as my punishment. The rest of my life on my back with the wife I battered for so long completely in charge of everything I can do. I deserve nothing better."

"I'm not going to lie, I agree with you." Casper said, crossing his arms over his chest.

"See we can agree on something." he father said with a pained laugh.

Casper sighed deeply and said, "Dad you have to understand what you did. I used to be so scared for mom, I swear to you the only thing that kept me here as long I did was because I didn't want to leave mom. But then you pushed me too far, you pushed Zach too far too. You lost us, you killed any relationship we could ever have."

His father nodded slowly. "I understand."

"We can't have a relationship, but I think I came here to forgive you. And to give you the goodbye I never gave you before." He leaned down and kissed his father on the forehead. "So, I forgive you dad. Goodbye."

"I love you son." he said as Casper walked from the room. It would have been preposterous to believe that going and seeing his father would make all of the problems of his childhood go away. Nothing can be fixed that easily. Casper and his father were beyond broken and nothing would fix that, but it was good to clear the air.

He met his mother at the bottom of the stairs. His kissed the top of her head and said, "Bye mom."

"Goodbye Casper, thank you for coming." his mother said with a smile. She was used to her boys leaving. If only he could tell them that Zach hadn't died, he would sure it would bring them peace, but obviously he couldn't, because he couldn't tell them what happened. He waved a final goodbye to his mother as he climbed into his car.

It was a quick drive to his house, he hit his breaks halfway up the driveway, there was an unfamiliar car parked in front of the house. He pulled his car into the garage. He unlocked the door from the garage and stepped inside, very carefully of course. He grabbed the first blunt object he could get his hands on, in this case an umbrella. He walked quietly through the empty kitchen toward the dining room, he could hear someone inside. He sucked in a deep breath and ran into the dining room and hit the assailant in the head. The young man whipped around and grabbed the umbrella from Casper's hand. "Ow." he said simply, bending the umbrella in half. The man's eyes turned to cat's eyes and fangs protruded from under his lips.

"Damn it, another vampire." Casper muttered under his breath.

"It has been a long time since I have been this close to a human." the young man said.

"Hey!" a familiar female voice shouted from the living room, coming toward them. "Leave Casper alone."

A smile grew across Casper's face and said, "Mollie!"

"Hello Casper." Mollie said with a smile encircling him in her arms. "It is so good to see you."

"What are you doing here?" Casper asked, so glad to see his old friend.

"My family and I were just passing through, and so since I knew we were coming through here I told Samuel I wanted to stop by and see you."

"You have your family now, that's just what you wanted." Casper said with a smile.

The young man who had destroyed Casper's umbrella cleared his throat behind them. "Oh," Mollie said, forgetting that he was even there. "Casper, this is Trey."

Trey extended a hand to Casper and said, "Nice to meet you man, sorry about the umbrella."

"Oh it's okay," Casper said with a laugh. "Sorry about your head."

The two shared a laugh. "Mollie was right. You are a strange human." Trey said.

"I haven't heard that in about ten years." Casper said, running a hand through his gray hair.

Just then Samuel and a young woman walked into the room. "Hello Casper," Samuel greeted shaking his hand.

"Good to see you Samuel." Casper said back.

Samuel turned to the young, fair-haired, woman and said, "Casper I'd like you to meet Ruby."

"Nice to meet you Ruby." Casper said with a smile, shaking her hand.

"You weren't kidding Mollie." Ruby said with a smile, revealing her brilliant teeth to him.

"Do you talk about anything but me?" Casper asked turning to Mollie.

"Only talk about the good things I swear." Mollie said with a smile. "Except for maybe your squeamishness when it comes to my driving."

"I don't blame you there," Trey said with a smirk. "She's an insane driver."

Mollie shook her head. "None of you know what you're talking about." She looked up at Casper and asked, "Want to take a walk?"

"Sure." he said with a smile.

They walked through the backyard and Mollie stuffed her hands in her pockets. "Wow, it seems like yesterday I was back here."

Casper shrugged. "I'm sure ten years for you is different than ten years for me."

"Yea," Mollie said with a smile.

"You're family seems really great Mollie." Casper said with a smile.

"They really are." Mollie said proudly. "I mean, I miss my old family everyday of course, but it's nice to have my own."

"So, Trey and Ruby, were they rogues?" Casper asked.

"No, not all vampire families are built that way. They were nomads looking for something more permanent and they found that with Samuel and me." Mollie said.

"Okay I see." Casper said, nodding. "Do they eat like you used to eat. Or better yet do you still eat like that."

Mollie looked at the ground. "No, not really. It was kind of hard to keep up that lifestyle when the other three in your family don't observe it."

"Then why did Trey say it had been a long time since he'd been close to a human?" Casper asked with a furrowed brow.

"I didn't completely turn back to my old ways. We eat animals." Mollie said with a smile.

"That must be almost the same thing right?"

She laughed deep from her chest. "No, not even close. It's rather disgusting actually but better than cold blood for sure."

The two walked quietly for a long moment. Finally, he sighed deeply and said, "So, how are they?"

Mollie sighed and said, "I figured you were going to ask that at some point. I've only seen them twice since I left with Samuel. They're doing good as far as I know, I know they have a new permanent member, she's a doctor, took my place."

"That's great, that's great." Casper said kicking a rock with his foot. "But I think you know that's not what I meant."

"Rudolph's still with them." Mollie said, seeing no reason in tiptoeing around the situation. "I talk to Grace on the phone a lot and she said that he spends everyday trying to get close to her again. Grace thinks Ivy may give in soon."

"Why?" Casper asked.

"She's lonely Casper, and Rudolph secludes her so much that she can't get away from it. And I think you know that a part of her still loves him. From what I understand from Grace, giving in might just be easier for her now." Mollie said.

Casper shook his head vigorously. "That bastard, he couldn't just let her be happy with me."

"And how would that have worked exactly?" Mollie asked, biting her bottom lip, her eyes focused forward.

"What do you mean Moll?"

"Look Casper, I'm by no means a Rudolph fan and I too really wish he'd left her alone, but I don't think you and Ivy ever would have worked." He looked confused, so she sighed and continued. "Casper, she's a vampire, she's five hundred years old, but will be in her early twenties forever. You're already what, thirty-five? Soon you'd look like her father, then her grandfather and then you'd die. What would she do then? How would you expect her to handle that?"

"I had a thought about that." he said, shoving his hands deep into his pockets.

"Enlighten me."

"I was hoping that I could convince her, or one of you to change me at some point." Casper said biting his lip nervously.

"Cas, you know Ivy would never let us do that. You don't want this." Mollie said with a sympathetic smile.

"But look at what you have with Samuel, I want that. I wanted it with Ivy, and I honestly still do." he said with a sad look on his face.

"One of the few, and I mean few, perks to the eternal curse Casper, you have to remember that." Mollie said patting his arm.

"Any chance you know where they are?" Casper asked. She was quiet for too long a moment. "Come on Mollie, I'm exhausted. I've spent ten years looking for them."

Mollie shrugged. "I can't Casper. I swore to Ivy that if I ever saw you again I wouldn't tell you. She's really only doing it for your own good."

He bit down hard on the inside of his cheek. "I wish people would stop telling me what's best for me. I'm a big boy I can take care of myself."

"I don't doubt that," Mollie said. "I mean as far as human development you're older than all of us, but Casper you have to remember that no matter how hard you try, no matter what you read, or how much time you spend with us, unless you are a vampire you'll never understand it you'll never understand us. You have to understand that leaving was the only way for her."

"I get that, I do, but I would have rather had a short life with her and all of you, then a long life alone." he said with a shrug.

"That's sweet, but I still can't tell you where they are. I promised." Mollie said with a sad smile.

Casper sighed deeply. "I understand, but do you think maybe you could do something for me?"

"Sure." Mollie said with a smile.

"Great." Casper said smiling back. "I was just hoping if you do see her again that you could give her something for me."

"Yea, I could do that." Mollie said with a nod.

"Great," Casper said again. "It's in the office."

The two walked back into the house and glanced into the living room. Ruby and Trey had a chess game set up. "Did they not take that with them?" Mollie asked.

"Oh no, they took theirs, that's one of mine." Casper said.

"Do you not want us to use it?" Ruby asked snapping her head up to look at Casper with sad eyes.

Casper smiled. "Of course not, my home is your home." And suddenly a thought came to him that he had yet to consider. "Hey how did you get in here?" he asked Mollie.

"Through the door." Mollie said with a laugh.

"No, no, that's not what I meant." Casper said shaking his head.

"Then what did you mean Mr. Lennox?" Mollie asked.

"What I mean is, how did you get in without me inviting you in? I thought that was one of the rules." Casper said.

Mollie grinned from ear-to-ear and said, "Well, that would be because this is actually my house still, you just happen to live here."

Casper nodded slowly. "That's good to remember."

"What did you want to give me Casper?" Mollie asked with a smile.

"Right," Casper said, being pulled back into the moment.

He walked with Mollie back to the office. He opened the closet. "Don't laugh." he cautioned Mollie.

"Why would I laugh?" she asked.

Casper sighed and pulled out a massive trunk. "This is why."

"That's what you want me to take to Ivy? What's in there?" Mollie asked pointing to the black trunk.

"Letters." Casper said staring down at the combination lock, considering whether or not he should open it.

"Letters?" Mollie repeated.

"Yea," Casper said, a laugh hiding somewhere in his tone. "For the first few years I was so sure that I would find an address for her that I'd have a place to send them. After a while it just became habit." He glanced up at Mollie who was smiling, with pity, down at him. He began to blush and said, "I know it's stupid."

"No, it's not." Mollie said patting him on the shoulder. "It's sweet Casper, really."

"Yea, ok." he said flipping open the lock on the trunk. Inside were hundreds of letters to Ivy. The spoke of everything from how he felt about her, to how much he missed her and her family, to his everyday activities, trying to make it seem like she was included in on his everyday life. "It's kind of heavy." Mollie just stared at him and smiled, a smile of his own grew across his face. "Oh yea I forgot." She leaned over and closed the trunk, then lifted it effortlessly up onto her shoulder.

Trey could you come here a moment? she thought. Trey walked into the doorway of the office and Mollie said aloud, "Could you put this in the car for me?"

He smiled and said, "Sure boss." He hoisted the oversized

trunk onto his own shoulder and strutted easily from the room.

Casper shook his head. "I don't get it." he said.

"What?" Mollie asked.

"The downsides of being a vampire." he said, his head still shaking, the curls in his long gray hair falling around his face.

Mollie rolled her violet eyes and said, "You'll never learn will you?"

Casper smiled, sadness flooding his eyes. "Guess not." Mollie patted his arm again.

Mollie glanced down at her watch and sighed, "Well I think we need to get going."

"Why so soon?" Casper asked, a sad look across his entire face.

She shrugged and said, "We're nomadic, we're always moving on."

Casper hopped up to his feet and encircled Mollie in a hug. "Well don't be a stranger."

"I won't." Mollie said returning the hug. *Time to go.* she thought to her family. They met her at the front door. Casper shook hands with each of them and said his goodbyes.

"Please get that trunk to her Mollie, it's important." he said.

She smiled. "I promise my friend. She'll get it." She hugged him once again, aware of how tightly she held him. "Take care of yourself Casper."

He smiled against her cheek and said, "You do the same."

The family packed into the car and drove away and he missed her instantly. Casper wasn't sure how he ever lived before he knew vampires were real, because now he was so aware of how alone he was. His life was not complete without them, and he wouldn't stop looking, just because Mollie couldn't tell him where to find Ivy didn't mean he couldn't continue the search alone.

Chapter Twelve

"Mollie!" Grace screamed running down the hill toward Mollie's car. It had been six years since she had seen her sister face-to-face. She tackled Mollie before she even had the chance to get out of the car.

"Wow good to see you too Gracie." Mollie said with a laugh. It had been a long drive from Maryland to the family's new home outside Chicago, but the distance was worth it just to see Grace like this.

"It's so good to see you. It's been too long." Grace squealed bouncing up and down, after all she really was only sixteen years old. Mollie looked up over Grace's shoulder as three more familiar faces crested the hill by the house.

"Hey stranger!" Peter shouted a smile sparkling in his dark eyes.

"Hi boys!" Mollie shouted running to greet them, pulling all three into her arms.

Alex kissed her on the cheek then wrapped his arms around Grace. The two finally after so many years admitted to the attraction that had always been there. They were mates now. Grace stroked Alex's arm lovingly and Alex kissed the top of Grace's head. Mollie smiled at them. "What?" Alex asked.

"I believe I was the one who always said how perfect you two would be together." Mollie said with pride.

"You were also the one who said I'd be perfect with Nora." Leo said with a laugh. The family fell silent. Leo rolled his blue eyes and said, "It's been a decade, I'm over it."

"No one believes you." Peter said punching his brother in the arm.

Leo rolled his eyes again. "Whatever." He turned his attention to the young woman walking down the hill. She was slight and petite, her hair was dark with blue highlights. "Oh," Leo said as she reached them. "Mollie, this is Dottie, she's the newest member of our family."

The young woman extended her hand to Mollie and said, "So you're the famous Mollie. It's a real honor to meet you."

"Nice to meet you too." Mollie said shaking her hand. "Are you the doctor."

Dottie nodded sharply and said, "Yep that would be me, I was finishing med school when *it* happened."

"Ah, well it's good to see that the family got such a sweet replacement for me." Mollie said, only a hint of jealously in her voice.

Alex, sensing the impending tension, quickly changed the subject, "So, so what brings you here baby sister?"

"Well my family and I were just passing through." Mollie said with a smile motioning to her car for the others to get out. Grace's face fell, she did not like the idea of her sister having another family.

"Hello," Ruby said with a bright smile as she bounced next to Mollie. Grace mumbled something incoherent and walked back toward the house.

"Gracie," Alex said turning to the house, before he did he shouted back, "I'll be back."

"Was is something I said?" Ruby asked.

Mollie patted her on the shoulder and said, "No, it's not you I promise. I'll be back too." She walked at a brisk pace toward the house.

Leo and Peter turned back to Mollie's family. Peter smiled and said, "We are normal to extent, I promise."

"I'm sure, and I'm Trey." he said extending a hand to Leo.

"I'm Leo and this is Peter." Leo said with a smile.

"And I'm Ruby." Ruby said extending her hand to Peter.

"Good to meet you." Peter said. He glanced around and said, "Well we don't have to wait out here, let's go inside."

Inside Rudolph watched Ivy meticulously while she went about her work. Cleaning had become important to Ivy in the passed years. She was on her hands and knees now scrubbing the kitchen floor. He was sitting on a chair at the small table, his chin resting in his hand, he watched her every move now. She scrubbed vigorously, so hard in fact that she began to peel the paint off the linoleum. Finally she threw the sponge in her hand into the bucket and settled back on her feet. "Must you always do that?"

"What?" he asked, his eyes still glued on her back.

"Stare at me all the time? I'm not going anywhere, you don't have to watch my every move." she hissed softly.

In spite of himself he smiled. "I love when you get angry, you almost bring color to your cheeks."

She rolled her eyes and whipped around to look at him. "You're ridiculous."

"You can make it really easy Ivy, just come back to me." he said with a smile.

She clenched her teeth together so hard she thought they

would shatter. "Then why not just force me if that's what you want so badly? Why continue to torture me like this? It's been ten years, when will you just accept that I don't want what we had back, I don't want you like I one did. When will you just let me be."

The room was silent for only a moment as someone in the doorway cleared their throat. Ivy's eyes shot up and just as quickly she was on her feet. "Mollie," she laughed aloud, pulling Mollie into her and holding her tight against her chest. Oh how Ivy had missed this child of hers.

"It's good to see you too." Mollie said, shooting daggers with her eyes at Rudolph. They all hated him, but especially Mollie, probably because she wasn't there anymore to protect Ivy from him.

"It's okay." Ivy whispered into Mollie's ear. Ivy pulled away and said, "What are you doing here? It's been too long."

"I have something for you." Mollie said taking Ivy by the hand. "It's out in my car."

Mollie nearly dragged her outside by the arm. "What are you doing?" Mollie didn't answer as she pulled open the passenger side door of her car and nearly pushed Ivy inside. She leaned toward Leo, who was standing beside her and said, "Keep Rudolph busy for just a little while." He looked confused, but nodded anyway. She ran around the car and into the driver's seat and pulled out of the driveway.

"What was that about?" Ivy demanded as they pulled onto the main way.

"I just wanted you to be away from him when I told you what I brought you." Mollie said, zipping through traffic at her traditional hyper speed.

"Why would I need to be away-" Ivy began, but cut off mid-sentence, realizing Mollie's meaning. "You saw him."

Mollie kept her eyes focused on the road, both hands on the wheel. She nodded slowly and said, "Yes I did."

"How does he look." Ivy asked, an unintended smile spreading across her face.

Mollie smiled too. "Older."

Before she could stop them tears poured from her eyes. The image of this new Casper flashed in Mollie's mind and Ivy couldn't help herself but to look. "He is older. I could never have seen him as older. I always promised him and myself that he would be the same."

"I'm sorry." Mollie said pulling into a nearly abandoned parking lot.

Ivy's head snapped up. "You said you had something for me, did he give you something for me?"

Mollie smiled and put on the parking brake. She opened the door and got out of the car and Ivy followed quickly. They walked to the trunk and Mollie opened it. Ivy glanced confused at the large green trunk inside. "Is it in there?" she asked.

"Yea," Mollie said with a laugh. "All of it." Ivy looked at her, confused again. Mollie rolled her eyes and said, "Just open it Ivy."

Ivy popped the lock on the trunk and opened it slowly. The breath caught in her throat at the sight of hundreds of letters. "My god." she muttered, lifting one from the box.

Mollie smiled and said, "I think I'm going to take a walk, I'll give you some privacy." But Ivy had stopped listening, she grasped a handful of letters and frantically ripped open one after the other.

They all said much the same thing, how he missed her, how he wanted to find her. And the most recurring item, how much loved her and he would never stop looking for her. Within an hour she'd been through them all, reading so fast she caught only every third word, but the point came across. She found the last letter, dated years before. The words hurt her deep inside.

I'm not writing anymore letters, it seems a bit silly to me now. I'll still never stop looking for you Ivy, I love you too much. You have my heart and you are my life. I know you want me to move on with my life but it's no life without you. I love you. Casper.

She closed her eyes and held the letter close to her heart. "Even when you loved me you never reacted to me like that." a voice said from beside her.

Her head snapped up and an angry scowl brushed across her face, how dare he ruin this moment. "Everywhere? Must you be everywhere?"

"Did anyone really think Leo was going to hold me?" Rudolph said with a laugh.

"Obviously not, but I guess they were hoping you'd get the hint, that I needed to be alone, for just a few damn hours. Just for once, why is that so difficult for you?" she hissed.

He sighed and sat beside her on the bumper of the car. "I started thinking, I guess two or three years ago, about whether or not you really loved me at all." He glanced over at her, but she simply waited. "I began to wonder if all that time in the past you really loved me or just loved that there was an alternative to your husband."

"Then why not leave me alone? Let me get on with my life?"

she asked, neither affirming or denying his accusations.

He shrugged slightly, running a hand through his black hair. "I know that I love you. Regardless of what you think everything I've done is because of you and for. I only killed your son because I thought it would protect you. That's the only reason, no matter what you think."

She sighed aloud and slowly shook her head. "Even if you believe that, which I'm sure you do, how can you ever expect me to forgive it? And if you thought that I didn't love you why didn't you just go away."

"I thought maybe if I stayed around I could make you love me." he said softly.

In spite of herself a laugh escaped her lips. "You can't make someone love you Rudolph, no matter what you do."

He reached around her and grabbed one of the letters. Her first instinct was to grab it away, but she resisted. He didn't open it, but cradled it in his hands as if it could crumble at any moment. "When I walked up here I was hell bent on dragging you back with me."

"What stopped you exactly?" Ivy asked, pulling back her red hair from around her shoulders.

He shrugged again. "I saw the look on your face as you were reading that letter and the only image in your mind was that boy's face. I guess I just let myself accept what had always been there."

"What do we do now?" she asked, resting her chin on her shoulder, her eyes glancing up at him.

He bit his bottom lip and moved in close to her, but she

didn't move. His kissed her forehead. "I'm going to leave. I think that's what you've always wanted."

She smiled and said, "I think that's for the best Rudolph. You should get on with your life."

He smiled sadly and said, "Life's over Ivy, but I'll get on with what I have." He pushed himself off from the car and began to walk away, back the car he'd brought. Before he got too far he turned and said, "Piece of advice Ivy?"

She shrugged. "Why not?"

Rudolph shook his head slowly. "It'll never work with a human, and I know you won't change him. Let him go."

She pressed her lips together and said, "I think you might be right. Thank you Rudolph."

"Anytime." he said climbing into his car. He too knew he was right, but still something about it seemed wrong. In any other situation Casper and Ivy would be perfect for one another. Why not now? Why not?

Ivy grasped the sides of the car for balance, could it be true? Could his clutch on her really be over? She shut the lid on the trunk and then closed the car. She turned around and nearly fell over Mollie. "Was that who I think it was?" Mollie asked.

"Yea." Ivy said with a smile.

"Wow a smile at the mention of Rudolph, that's a first." Mollie said smiling back.

"He's leaving." Ivy said, her smile growing across her brilliant teeth.

"What? Like leaving, leaving?" Mollie asked, nearly giddy.

"That's what he said."

"Why? I mean after all this time why now?" Mollie asked.

Ivy shrugged. "I think he just gave up." She laughed a bit to herself. "It's funny, I always thought I'd be the one to give up and just give into him. It's hard to be alone you know."

Mollie nodded, still smiling. "Yea, I know."

"I forgot, sorry." Ivy said.

"What will you do now?" Mollie asked walking around to get in the car. It was time to go home. "I mean now that you're free?"

Ivy closed her door and said, "Same old, same old. Protecting humanity one rogue at a time." There was a smile in her voice.

"No, I meant, what will you do with Casper?" Mollie asked turning the key in the ignition.

"Nothing to be done." Ivy said crossing her arms over her chest.

"What do you mean? Isn't it perfect?" Mollie asked turning onto the main road. "You love him, he loves you, now there's no crazy jealous vampire in the way. What's the problem?"

"I don't know Mollie, maybe the immortality thing?" Ivy said putting her foot up on the dashboard.

"That shouldn't matter, you could live his whole life with him." Mollie said taking a sharp right turn at a hundred miles an hour.

"Let's say I do that, what happens when people start to think he's my father, or my grandfather. I couldn't do that to him." Ivy said biting her bottom lip.

"To him or to you? Since when do you care what mortals

think Ivy, you avoid them at all cost. If it doesn't bother him it shouldn't bother you." Mollie said taking another fast turn. After a long awkward silence Mollie said, "Fine, well what if Alex's vision came to fruition? What if you changed him?"

"Don't ever say that." Ivy said shaking her head feverously.

"He's too perfect for you Ivy, you can't just let him go." Mollie said with a sigh, pulling into the driveway of the house.

"It's better this way." Ivy whispered. "I can't damn him to what we are, but I it would destroy me to live a full life with him and then have to spend an eternity without him."

"So you're just jumping to the eternity without him, completely alone?" Mollie asked putting the car into park.

"It's too hard Mollie, for everyone." Ivy said wanting very badly to just get out of the car.

"Ivy it's your life, but if you do it this way I think you're just going to make yourself miserable." Mollie said biting her lip. She placed a hand over Ivy's and said, "I'm only telling you this because you're my friend and I want you to be happy."

Get in here please. Peter's perturbed thoughts bellowed to Mollie and Ivy.

They exchanged confused glances and quickly exited the car. Inside the house everyone was in a tizzy. Peter and Trey were yelling at each other while Alex was guarding Grace and Samuel guarding Ruby and Leo and Dottie just tried to stay out of the way. "What happened here?" Ivy demanded.

"She's insane!" Ruby shouted in Grace's direction.

"I'm not insane, you're insane!" Grace shouted back.

"Okay both of you shut up," Ivy ordered. "And I'm going to

ask again, what happened here?"

Everyone was quiet for a moment, no one wanted to slip with another cruel name and anger Ivy, even the visiting family could tell that would be a mistake. Ivy turned her gaze to Leo who sighed and said, "Ruby made the mistake of calling Mollie her sister to Grace and Grace didn't appreciate it."

"So she went predator and lunged at me." Ruby yelled.

Grace crossed her arms and pouted like a child. "She's not your sister, she'll never be."

"Baby now might not be the best time for you to talk." Alex urged, stroking her short black hair. But Grace ignored him and lifted a large cabinet behind Ruby's head.

"Put it down." Ivy hissed and Grace let it hit the ground, the contents inside shattering. "Grace!"

"Sorry." Grace muttered, sinking into herself, what everyone seemed to forget was that no matter how long she was alive she still only had he maturity of the sixteen year old. And girls of that age don't always handle stress well.

Ivy started to move toward Grace, but Mollie stopped her. "Let me Ivy." She walked over to Grace and bent down in front of her. "Gracie, my dear sweet Gracie, just because I have a new family doesn't mean you're not still my family."

"I don't like it." Grace huffed.

"You don't have to, it's okay that you don't, but they're my family now. But remember you're my family forever." Mollie said with a smile.

Grace wrapped her arms around Mollie's shoulders and whispered in Mollie's ear, "I want you back though."

"It's just different now, but you're always my sister, just because I have a new sister doesn't change that." Mollie said, Grace was silent for a minute and Mollie giggled a little. "Do you think it wasn't hard for me to meet Dottie and realize that you have a new sister?"

"It's not the same." Grace muttered, pulling back.

"How is it different?"

"You left!" Grace shouted. "You left us, I stayed. That's how it's different. You went and got yourself a whole new family, leaving us behind, but I stuck with my family. You left." She knocked her chair over and stormed into the kitchen, Mollie followed close behind. Grace pulled a few vials of blood from the fridge and gulped them down.

"That's not fair Grace." Mollie hissed. "Me starting my own life doesn't mean that I abandoned you. I had the right to leave whenever I wanted."

"Well why couldn't Samuel have just stayed here with us? You never would have had to leave. Or is just that we weren't enough for you anymore." Grace demanded. "I've been with Alex now for five years now and we have no intention of leaving, what makes you any different?"

"Who are you?" Mollie demanded shaking her head. "This isn't the sister I remember."

"You changed damn it! You left." Grace shouted.

"Why do you keep saying that! I know I left!" Mollie shouted back.

"Enough." Ivy snapped from the doorway of the kitchen. "This childish bullshit will stop right this second. You two are too damn old for this. Now what the hell is going on?"

"I have no idea." Mollie shouted.

"Neither do I." Grace grumbled.

"Well you're both getting over it, now. You're going to remember that you love each other no matter the circumstances. Do you understand me?" Ivy hissed. The two nodded. "Now hug each other and like it."

The walked toward each other and hugged awkwardly. "I do love you, you idiot." Mollie murmured.

"I love you too dumbass." Grace muttered with a laugh.

"That's better." Ivy said, her arms crossed over her chest. "Remember that. I think you've scared both our families enough for a day."

The girls exited the kitchen, Mollie and Grace with an arm around one another, to rejoin their families.

Casper did his best to keep himself busy after Mollie and her family left. He reorganized his books from alphabetized by author's last name to by title. He organized his spices by color. Scrubbed every inch of floor and carpet. Anything to keep his mind off of what Ivy might be thinking when she opened his letters, if Mollie took them at all. He knew there was a chance when he turned his things over to Mollie that she would never send it to her, but he was willing to take that chance.

As he was scrubbing out the area behind the refrigerator a knock came at the door. He lifted himself off his tired knees and walked to answer it. Slowly he opened the door and as he saw the person on the other side he slammed it just as quick. He turned the locks and pushed himself against it. "No!" he shouted. "No, no, no!"

"I gave you the common courtesy of knocking, now let me in before I pull the door off the hinges." Rudolph said with an aggravated sigh, he hated waiting.

"No, I finished dealing with you ten years ago. Haven't you tortured me enough?" Casper demanded.

"Last chance Casper." Rudolph warned, pushing his weight against the doorframe. When no change came from inside Rudolph gripped the door and pulled it off from it's hinges.

"What the hell man!" Casper yelped from the hole left behind. "That's my door."

Rudolph shrugged. "I gave you the option to let me in, you refused. Did you think I was going to go away?" He laughed and stepped around Casper into the house.

"Don't you need my permission to come in?" Casper said harshly, keeping close on Rudolph's heels.

"My previous invitation was never rescinded, no problem." Rudolph said with a smile.

Casper rolled his eyes. "Your rules have more loopholes than any I've ever heard."

"No such thing as a perfect society Casper." Rudolph said sitting on Casper's new couch in the living room.

"What are you doing here?" Casper asked, his hands defiantly on his hips.

Rudolph smiled. "I swear Casper, if I didn't have such reason to hate you I'd actually admire you."

"Thank you?" Casper said hesitantly, it didn't really sound like a compliment.

"Seriously, I don't like many people, you should be pleased." Rudolph said, his smile growing.

"Thanks I'll keep that in mind. What are you doing here Rudolph? Did you think that I didn't get a bad enough punishment the first time around? Taking away the only thing that mattered? What do you want to take now?" Casper asked.

Rudolph nodded slowly. "You're right, I was a little brash in my decision, but hey I never did learn to share when I was a human."

"Well thanks for that, but what are you doing here?" Casper asked again, an edge to his voice.

"Did you know that I'm descended from royalty Casper?" Rudolph asked. Casper offered no response, just stared. "Perhaps that's another thing that attracted me to her, we were both of noble blood, we belonged together. But anyway the sentence I gave you had nothing do with you and everything to do with me, if I couldn't have her, no one would. But I've realized recently that she'll never love me again, what I did to her, to her son, she could never forgive me for that. And then there's you, even when I thought she loved me she didn't look at me the way she looks at you. She loves you Casper." Casper still stared. "So, I left. I'm leaving her alone."

"What does this have to do with me now?" Casper asked finally, his eyes still locked on Rudolph.

Rudolph bit his bottom lip. "It would never work, I'm rather assured of that. You're a human and she's a vampire, a vampire who would never change you. And even if she could, would you want her to?"

Casper thought for a moment. "I think I do."

"Let me tell you something, if you hesitate, it's not what you want." Rudolph said shaking his head. He settled back against the couch and said, "But that's not my decision to make. I've put Ivy through enough, I want her to be happy. You make her happy."

"What are you telling me?" Casper asked, rubbing his eyes in aggravation.

Rudolph reached into the pocket of his jeans and pulled out a slip of paper. He handed it to Casper. "This is where they are, a town outside Chicago. I'm going home, back overseas to the Main City. The decision is yours now, I don't want anything to do with it anymore." And with that he zipped from the room, too fast for Casper to see. Casper held the small piece of paper with the scribbled address in his hands and stared at it. After ten years of searching could it be that easy? He lowered himself down the couch where Rudolph had just been and his eyes stayed focused on it, he couldn't believe it but he was having doubts. Should he go? Live the fairytale he'd dreamt of for so long now. Or should he just leave her alone, not give the chance to make the hard choice. But then her face flashed before his eyes, the most beautiful face in the world and he realized he had to go. Even if she wouldn't change him, just living his life with her would do fine. That would be enough for him. He'd go as soon as he could, but he had something he needed to do first, the right thing.

It had been ten years since he'd been there, but it was like taking the steps home, implanting in his brain. He pulled up in front of the little yellow house with green shutters. His things were all packed up in the back on the car, he wouldn't be going back to

Mollie's house. He walked up the creaking wooden stairs and knocked on the old door. A young woman answered. "Can I help you?" she asked.

"Hi," he said, not expecting anyone other than Irma, Mollie's sister, to answer. "I'm looking for Irma Cooley."

The young girl stepped outside onto the porch with Casper and said, "I'm her granddaughter. She's not doing very well, she's rather old. What is this about."

"Please, Miss Cooley, I have something your grandmother will want to see for herself." Casper said, his look serious.

She hesitated for a moment, cautious as anyone should be to a stranger. But finally she opened the door. "Only a minute." She led Casper up the stairs, looking back constantly to make sure he was still there. She knocked softly and opened the door to a bedroom. The frail old woman lie in the bed, barely able to keep her eyes open. "Grandmother," the young girl said. "There's someone here to see you." She turned to Casper and said, "I'll be back in a minute."

"Thank you." Casper said with a smile as the girl left the room. He sat in the vacant chair beside her bed and said, "Hello Mrs. Cooley, you probably don't remember me, but we met once, about ten years ago."

Irma's head rolled onto its side and her eyes widened to look at him. After a moment she said, "You came here about Mollie."

Casper smiled. "Yes ma'am."

Irma's face was not so happy. "I thought I told you I never wanted to see you again."

He nodded slowly. "Yes ma'am you did, but I have something for you that I think is rightfully yours."

"What's that?" Irma asked.

Casper bit his bottom lip and reached into his pocket and pulled out a key. He rested it in her hand and said, "I think Mollie really wanted you to have this." She looked confused as she eyed the key. "What's it to?"

"The house." Casper said softly.

Irma's eyes fluttered closed, then opened again. "Mollie and Henry's house?"

He nodded. "Yes ma'am."

"Why now?" Irma asked.

"The house was giving to me and I'm leaving town. Rather than selling it and giving it to a stranger I thought you should have it." Casper said.

She reached up and touched Casper's cheek. "Thank you."

"My pleasure." Casper said getting up and walking away. The young girl was outside the door. Casper smiled at her as he left. He got in his car and began to drive. It felt right, giving Irma the house. Mollie had left it to him, she said that it was his, but it didn't feel that way. It meant too much to Irma.

He put the coordinates for Ivy house into his GPS system and began the drive. He started thinking about what he would say to her when he got there. Would she be happy to see him or would she just want him to leave? It was a risk he was willing to take, but it scared him nonetheless. It was a long drive, over seven hours, but it was worth it. The house was easy to find, big and secluded from everything, the perfect place for a family of vampires to hide. He pulled up the long driveway and spotted the oversized garage, the perfect place for their play things. He parked his car in front and stepped out, instantly nervous for some reason he couldn't pin down. Before he could even get to the stairs leading up to the porch the front door flew open. They must have heard his heartbeat, or maybe just his car. Grace emerged from inside, exactly the same, not that he should have been surprised. He knew they didn't age. "Casper?" she muttered.

"Hello Grace." he said with a smile.

Slowly she took the stairs, one at a time like a little girl, she kept her gaze locked on him as she floated toward him. "Casper? Is that you?"

"Yea, it's good to see you Gracie." Casper said wrapping her up in a hug.

She put her hands on either side of his face and said, "You look so much older."

"It happens sometimes." Casper said with a laugh.

The front door opened and the men stepped out. "Casper Lennox?" Peter said with a laugh. "How the hell did you find us?"

"Hi Peter." Casper said shaking Peter's hand, a little frightened by his happy demeanor.

"You look great Casper." Leo said pulling Casper into a strong embrace, nearly crushing his ribs.

"You look the same." Casper said with a breathless laugh.

Leo pulled back, letting Casper breath. "Sorry man, it's been a while."

Suddenly everyone heard the door open behind them and

all breathing stopped. The family turned to look at her, but Casper couldn't bring himself to move. Finally, after a long moment of silence he turned and saw her standing at the door. She was as lovely as he had remembered, in fact his memory did not do her justice. The family had pushed themselves to the sides, leaving an open path between them. "Casper," she muttered, her voice airy and breathy, almost dream like. At first he thought his feet would not move, that he'd been literally petrified by her, but the moment soon past. It had been ten long years. He crossed the distance between them in three steps. He paused only slightly in front of her before digging his hands deep into her red hair, she closed her eyes embracing the feeling of his warm hands. He rested his forehead against hers and they stood there in silence for a long moment, just being together. Finally, when he could take it no more his crushed his lips against hers and happy tears sprung to her eyes. She ran her hands through his gray hair and his hands moved around her back. Finally he pulled back, only slightly, when he was in need of air.

"You have no idea how I've missed you." he said, kissing away a tear that had fallen down her cheek.

She rubbed her cheek against his and smiled at the tickling feeling of his stubble. "I think I can imagine." she said back. She pulled back just far enough that she could stare deep into his light blues eyes. "How did you know where to find us."

"Rudolph." he said with a smile.

"Rudolph? My Rudolph?" she asked, her brows pushed together. Casper nodded. "Why would he do that."

Casper shrugged and said, "He told me he just wanted you

to be happy."

Ivy pulled him into her and kissed him again, embracing the warmth of his body that she missed so much. "I'm happy." she whispered in his ear. She kissed his cheek and held him close, never wanting to let him go.

Later that night the family was sitting around the large dining room table. "So you're Dottie?" Casper asked the newest member of the family.

"Yes, I'm the new doctor." Dottie said getting a laugh from the family. "I must say Casper, you're older looking than I would have thought."

Ivy rolled her eyes, she was holding Casper's arm, which was around her shoulders. "Is it just because of the gray hair?"

"No," Dottie began. "I mean that's part of it I guess, but you just look older than I thought you would."

Ivy glanced up at him and smiled. "I think he's perfect." she said and he kissed her forehead.

"Gag." Grace said smiling, leaning her head against Alex's.

"Say what you will, I'm happy." Ivy said squeezing Casper's arm.

Suddenly a cat ran across their feet and into the next room. "You have a cat?" Casper asked in a perplexed tone, he'd never thought of them as animal people.

The family laughed aloud and Ivy said, "No that would be Peter we have mice."

Shut up. Peter murmured in his head. *O! Found one!* He could deny the nature of the animal when he was one. He morphed back to himself and wandered in with the family. "Mice are good eating, the blood's really not that bad."

"Did you get rid of it? I really don't want a dead rat in my kitchen." Ivy said with a roll of her eyes.

Peter rolled his own and said, "Yes mom I took care of it." Everyone laughed. "What did I miss."

"Nothing but goo-goo eyes." Grace said with a smile.

The family grew silent and watched Casper and Ivy, the reunited lovers. And slowly the family moved onto to other things, but Casper and Ivy just stayed together on the couch, holding close to one another. Hours later Ivy bit her bottom lip and stood up, taking Casper's hand. She didn't speak, and neither did he. She led him up the stairs and into a large room at the end of the hall. She closed the door behind them, it was a bedroom, Ivy's room. She walked up close to him and took his hands in hers. He was shaking, "What are you nervous about?" she asked, her voice soft and musical.

He smiled. "Nothing, I just, I missed you." He rested his forehead against hers. "And I always wanted this."

Her eyes were open, watching him. "I'm just afraid I'll hurt you."

He put his hands on cheeks and shook his head. "You could never hurt me. I know you couldn't do that."

"Sometimes I forget my own strength in any activity, I would just never forgive myself if I hurt you."

He kissed her cheek. "It's okay, it's okay."

She held her breath and murmured, "Just don't move for a minute." She reached her hands up under his shirt, running her hands up his stomach and chest. The cold of her hands sending a shiver through him, but he didn't move. He lifted his arms and she pulled the shirt off over his head. For a long moment she just stared and he back at her. Hesitantly she reached down to the first button on her blouse and slowly unsnapped each. As she unbuttoned the last one she slowly pulled it off her shoulders.

"You're amazing." he murmured, lost in the beauty of her.

"Casper," she began, grabbing his attention back to her. "I've never done this with someone I love. I'm scared."

He slipped his hands around her neck and cradled her head in his hands. He kissed her cheeks, her eyelids, the tip of her nose and left a long sweet kiss on her lips. "Don't be scared, I'll take care of you." And she knew it was true. She threw her arms around his neck and let him take her, mindful of her strength so that she would not hurt him and she trusted him to do the same.

They fell asleep with their arms around each other, but the sleep was short lived for Ivy as it was for most of her kind. She laid her head on his chest and allowed herself to be hypnotized by his breathing. She kissed his stomach and grabbed her robe from her closet, she needed to eat. She wondered down to the kitchen where Peter was sitting at the table.

"Hi boss." he said with a smile.

"Hi Peter." Ivy said back pulling two vials of blood from the fridge. They were running low, Dottie would have to restock soon.

"Are you all right?" Peter asked looking down at the glass in his hands. She did not have to read his mind to know what he meant. Peter cared deeply for her, that was obvious, he would rather die than see anything happen to her.

She smiled and said, "Yes Peter, I'm fine."

"If he hurts you I'll kill him." Peter said seriously, running a hand through his dark curly hair.

But Ivy couldn't help but smile. "Yes dear, I know. But he won't hurt me. I wish you could see that."

"Well what are you going to do with him?" Peter asked. "Keep him a human, make him one of us? I want to know you're being smart about it."

She kissed the top of his head and said, "I don't want to think about it right now. I just want to enjoy what we have in this moment. This moment's all that matters."

"Just be careful." he urged.

She patted his shoulder and moved toward the door. "I promise."

Ivy walked back into the bedroom where Casper was sitting up in the bed. "I thought maybe you'd left me." he said with a smile.

She smiled back. "No, no I didn't." She looked him over once and stayed in the doorframe. "Be honest with me a moment will you?"

"Of course." he said sitting up a little straighter.

"How badly did I hurt you?" she asked, her arms crossed over her chest.

He cocked his head to the side and said, "Not bad at all, I promise you."

"I think you're lying." she said as she stared at the bruises forming on his arms. He grimaced as he pulled himself up. She floated to his side and examined his torso closely. "If you're fine then sit up straight." He tried and then eventually gave up. She melted onto his shoulder. "I knew it was a bad idea, I'm so sorry."

He kissed the top of her head and shook his own feverously. "You did nothing wrong. It was the first time Ivy, it's okay, you didn't hurt me badly. It was better than I thought actually."

"So I didn't hurt you as bad as you thought I would?" Ivy said, disgusted with herself.

"No, no, that's not what I meant." Casper said biting his lip. "I love you and I'm so happy this happened. I mean it."

She put her hands on his cheeks and said, "I love you too." She rested her head on his shoulder and he put his arm around hers. She only sat there for a moment before she began to feel the itch to move. "We should probably get up now."

"Ivy, come on it's okay." Casper said biting his lip.

She smiled, but didn't raise her eyes to look at him. "Oh I know, I'm just not the lay in bed all day kind of person. Lots to do." She stood up and dressed quickly. "Take your time though, I'll see you downstairs when you're ready."

And then at a speed too quick for him to see she was gone. He rested back against the headboard and sighed. "Well that went well." he murmured sarcastically.

Down in the dining room the family was assembled around the table, the traditional meeting place. "What's going on?" Ivy asked, perplexed by the meeting she wasn't invited to.

"We didn't want to wake you boss." Leo said looking down at his intertwined fingers.

"Still doesn't answer my question, what's going on?" Ivy

asked again.

Ignoring her Alex said, "Here it comes."

Ivy looked down and noticed for the first time the phone sitting in the middle of the table. Just as Alex had said it began to ring. They each looked at one another as Ivy rolled her eyes. "For god's sake." she said. She reached down and snatched the phone up. She opened in and lifted it to her ear. "Hello." she said.

"Ivy?" a familiar voice said on the other end, nervous and shaky.

"Rudolph? Rudolph what's wrong?" Ivy asked sitting in a chair between Grace and Peter.

"Ivy I messed up." he said softly.

"What does that mean?" Ivy demanded. What trouble could he have brought to her now.

"I got back to the Main City this morning and I had to give a report to the elders." Rudolph said, his voice still soft and sad.

"What happened?"

"I told them about the punishment levied against Casper and a few of them were less than pleased." he said.

"You mean Eva was less than pleased." Ivy said with disgust.

"She was one of them." he said.

"Rudolph why do you sound the way you do?" Ivy said, only a hint of panic in her voice.

"I was punished myself for yielding an unworthy punishment." Rudolph said, a shaky laugh in his voice. She waited, unable to speak. "They de-fanged me."

She gasped aloud, sending a shiver through her family.

"Rudolph no, how could they?"

"Eva said that a vampire who can't kill a human doesn't have the right to feed on them." Rudolph said with a hard swallow.

"Rudolph I'm so sorry." Ivy said, her voice muffled by the hand now at her mouth.

"But that's not why I'm calling." Rudolph said, cutting her off. "Because the elders were so unhappy with the punishment so they're sending someone to do what I couldn't."

"What? Who? When?" I've shouted frantically at him.

"I didn't kill Casper or change him, so now They want to clean up my mess."

"It's been ten years! Why would they care now?" Ivy demanded, jumping up from the table, knocking over her chair.

"Ivy you know as well as I do that ten years is like ten minutes for Them, and anyway it's the principle of the thing, they can't look bad in the face of Their community." Rudolph said, swallowing again.

"Who's coming?" Ivy demanded, running her hand over her face.

"Who do you think?" he asked.

Ivy dropped the phone and it shut as it hit the floor. She began running around like a crazy person. "We have to leave, we have to leave right now!"

"It won't do any good boss, you know that. Eva must already be on her way here." Grace said.

"Then we'll just send Casper to Mollie, where did she say she was heading? Arizona? Or maybe we could send him to Seattle to PJ." Ivy said frantically pacing back and forth through the room.

"We send him away that will only make it worse, you know that." Peter said trying to calm her.

"Only make what worse?" Casper asked from the doorway. His eyes darted to each of the family members as they gawked at him. "Only make what worse?" he asked again.

Ivy walked toward him briskly and took his head in her hands. She kissed him hard and said, "We need to get you out of here."

"Ivy." Alex urged, she glanced back at him and he shook his head. "It won't work."

"Ivy what's going on?" Casper asked, his hands on her wrists.

"Um," Ivy began, her hands still on Casper's cheeks. "It's not over Casper."

"What's not?" he asked.

Ivy was silent so Grace decided to speak. "They're coming back for you."

"Why?" Casper demanded, pulling away from Ivy.

"They didn't like what Rudolph decided to do, They're planning to fix it." Ivy said, her hands aching now away from his face.

Casper took in a few deep breaths. "Okay, okay," he finally said, trying to calm himself. He looked up at Ivy and said, "Death isn't the only option." Ivy began to shake her head vigorously. Casper's gaze switched to Alex. "You saw me as one of you in a vision of yours didn't you?" Alex just looked away. Casper flipped back around to Ivy, but she was looking away, her hand gripping the doorframe. "If it's going to happen then why don't we just beat

Them to it."

Ivy snapped a piece of the doorframe off. "No!" she shouted. She turned around and put her hands on Casper's shoulders. "That won't happen. I won't let it."

"Would you rather have me be killed?" Casper asked her, shaking his head.

"Of course not." she said biting her lip. "I won't let her do that, you have my word."

"What if you can't stop her, what if she kills you too?" He put he forehead against hers and whispered. "I just want to be with you. Forever."

"Then be with me, just as we are and I'll handle Eva." Ivy said. "I can't do that to you."

"I didn't ask you to do it." Casper said glancing up at the family.

Don't even think about it! Ivy shouted in her mind. The eyes of the family darted away.

"Don't do that to them." Casper said with a sigh. "Let them choose."

Alex did see it that way Ivy. In a place he'd never seen before, this is a new house for us. Grace thought. *Perhaps we're just fighting the inevitable.*

"No!" Ivy shouted aloud. "No! Don't you dare even think it again! It's not happening."

"Why are you resisting it so much? What could be so bad about us being together forever. Is that not what you want?" Casper asked, he voice growing louder and more angry with every passing moment.

Her eyes were filled with tears when he finally settled to look at her. "Is that what you think?" she muttered. "I'm trying to save you from a damned eternity and you think that it's because I'm trying to avoid being with you?" She took a few steps away. "Interesting." she muttered as she walked out the back door.

After a few long moments of wandering around the backyard he joined her. "I'm sorry." he said softly to her back.

"You don't want this Casper, no mattered what you think this is, it's not what you want. And I'll do anything to protect you from it." she said, her arms crossed over her chest, her face streaked with tears.

"Okay," Casper began licking his lips and shifting his weight. "Okay, let's say then that Eva comes and you're able to convince her to keep me as I am. What happens then Ivy? Do you let me just grow old, because that is what will happen. I'll get older and older, I'll look like your father and then your grandfather. How will you be attracted to me then?"

She smiled in spite of herself. "Attraction wouldn't be the problem trust me. I worried about that too, but it had nothing to do with my attraction to you. You'll always be everything Casper, regardless of how old you get."

"Then what worried you?" he asked, wishing she'd turn around to look at him.

"I suppose," she began, turning around slowly, as if reading his mind. "I worried how I would handle it when you died."

"That is the curse of mortality." he said with a smile.

But she frowned and said, "No my love, that's the blessing of mortality. Trust me, being on the other side I wish I could die, but

I can't, you're lucky enough that you still can."

He put his hands around the back her head, digging his fingers deep into her fiery hair. He laid his forehead against hers and said, "With you, any amount of time it worth it."

She closed her eyes and kissed him, but she was not yet convinced that he accepted what she was giving him. But she would not give in, he didn't know the gift she was giving him, allowing him to keep his life, but she would show him. She had to.

The rest of the day was hurry up and wait. They all sat around the dining room table, no one speaking. "This is so nerve-racking." Grace muttered after a while.

"Imagine if you had a heartbeat." Casper muttered back. A humorless laugh aroused among them. "What happened to Rudolph?" Casper asked, no one had jumped to tell him, however they did tell him he was the one who called.

"It doesn't matter now." Ivy said, her eyes glued to the table.

"Sure it does. Especially if keeping me alive did it to him." Casper said biting the inside of his cheek.

The family glanced around at one another, but it was Peter who finally spoke. "He was defanged."

"That does not sound pleasant." Casper said with a grimace.

"It's not." Alex murmured, a cold chill running through him.

"What is it?" Casper asked, curiosity always leading him.

"It involves pliers, I think your imagination can take care of the rest." Peter said coldly.

"From what I've been learning it's a big deterrent for breaking Their rules." Dottie added.

"Do they come back?" Casper asked, running his tongue across his teeth.

"Do your teeth grow back?" Peter asked sarcastically.

"Can we not talk about this anymore?" Ivy pleaded.

"Sorry," they all said in unison.

"See anything Alex?" she asked. "Any idea when she might be here?"

Alex shook his head slowly. "Sorry Ivy, I can't see anything."

"Try to clear your mind, it would really help if I had a timeline." she said running her hands through her hair.

"I'm trying." Alex said, his voice only a bit defeated.

"I know you are." Ivy said with a reassuring smile.

Suddenly a knock sounded at the front door. "It can't be." In a flash moment all six vampires were on their feet and at the front door, Casper took an extra few moments. Ivy's breathing stopped as she stared at the doorknob. Another knock sounded making them all jump. Finally Ivy grasped the knob, so hard she knew that the imprints of her fingers would be left behind, and turned the knob, opening the door. On the other side was a face that she had hoped to never see again. The being on the other side has skin so thin that it was nearly translucent, a gray color to it. Her hair was raven black and laid near her knees, her eyes were the most piercing blue it was hard to look at them directly. This was Eva. The woman smiled and said, in voice with so much music it could make you cry, "Hello Ivyana."

"Eva." Ivy said simply, trying to keep her mood light.

Eva's face was cold as stone. "Do not be nice to me. I know you are not happy I am here."

"Fine." Ivy said, her own face turning cold.

Eva looked up into the crowd surrounding the front door and instantly spotted her target. Instantly she jumped to her predator mode, but Ivy followed suit. "No." Ivy said simply.

"This is what I have come for Ivyana, do not get in my way." Eva growled, as the other members of the family turned to predators and kept Casper protectively behind them.

"It doesn't have to be like this." Ivy hissed. "You don't have to kill him."

"Perhaps not, but oh how I want to." Eva said with a cruel smile. "Besides, it is not your decision to make. I am an elder, you have no power in this."

Ivy pushed out onto the porch, leaving the family inside with Casper. "What are you doing!" Eva demanded.

"I want to talk to you for a minute." Ivy pleaded, her eyes turning back to normal.

"About what exactly?" Eva asked, slowly pulling her guard down as well.

"It doesn't have to be this way Eva, it really doesn't have to. It's been over a decade and he hasn't done anything. He's kept our secret. I know ten years isn't anything to you, but it such a long chunk of time for them."

"It doesn't matter Ivyana, he broke the rules, he has to die." Eva said simply as if it were nothing at all.

"But he doesn't, if you knew him you'd understand." Ivy urged.

Eva looked her over a moment, contemplating what she was saying. She nodded her head slowly. "Perhaps, let me talk to him then."

Ivy sighed in relief and said, "Thank you Eva, you won't regret it."

Eva smiled too, unsettling smile, but Ivy didn't notice. "I am sure I will not." Eva said in response.

Ivy opened the front door and called inside. "Casper, it's all right, can you come here a moment."

Through the crowd of vampires the sole human walked. He bit his bottom lip, a nervous habit. "Hello." he said to Eva.

"Hello Casper." Eva said back with the same eerie smile.

What happened next was a move that no one saw coming and happened too fast for anyone to stop. Eva reached into the pocket of her jacket and pulled out, of all things, a gun. She fired one shot into Casper's stomach and then returned the gun to her jacket.

Instantly Ivy was at Casper's side. Ivy's eyes flashed up to Eva who starring back with that cold stare she wore so well. "I thought you might cause a problem," Eva began. "So I brought a back up plan."

"You're going to be all right." Ivy said to Casper. Blood gushed from his abdomen. She held her hand against the wound, trying to stop the bleeding and at the same time ignore the smell of the blood. She looked up at her family, and no matter how they tried to fight it, the predator side began to show. "Get inside, just get away all of you!" Ivy shouted at them, they couldn't hurt him, it couldn't end like that. The family did as they were ordered and fled inside the house, as far away from the smell as they could get.

"You have a choice to make now Ivyana." Eva was saying.

"You can either let him die, or you can change him, but it all comes down to you." And with that she was gone, her job finished, leaving Ivy with the choice. Either let the love of her life die or damn him forever, and worse she did not have a long time to choose.

"Change me, make me what you are." Casper murmured, a small trickle of blood running from him mouth. "We can be together forever."

Ivy's glance rushed back and forth from his eyes to the wound and back again. And then in a split moment she made her decision.

Chapter Thirteen

He felt like his was flying, or falling maybe, he couldn't be sure. He only knew he'd never felt anything like it before. He could feel his insides burning and feeling like they were ripping to get out. Was this what it felt like to die? Or was it what it felt like to change? It had to be one or the other. He could hear a loud and unfamiliar beeping sound. Slowly his eyes fluttered open to a room as unfamiliar as the sound. It was bright white, so much so that it hurt his eyes. His throat was dry as a bone. He tried to sit up but was held down by a web of wires.

"Don't try to get up." a soft voice urged from beside him. He glanced over to see Ivy sitting in a chair beside the bed. She smiled at him and he smiled back.

"Where am I?" he asked, his voice dry and scratchy.

"Hospital." Ivy said simply.

"Why? What happened?" Casper asked. "I thought, I thought-"

"I told you I wouldn't let that happen." Ivy began, her eyes darting away. "Eva assumed that I wouldn't be able to take the blood without killing you. She underestimated me."

"What did you do?" Casper asked, astonished that he was still alive.

"I held my breath and put you in my car and drove as fast as I could to the hospital. Dottie came with me to help the bleeding stop. You were in surgery for hours, I was so scared you wouldn't come out alive." she said biting her bottom lip, now was not the time for tears. "And then when you finally got out they weren't sure if you'd wake up. That was two days ago."

"What happened to Eva?" Casper asked.

Ivy shrugged. "She's gone, I don't know. She leveled her sentence, I doubt she'll be back."

"Why did you risk it?" Casper asked letting his heavy head rest against the hard, hospital pillow. "There's more than a good chance I would have died. Why didn't you just change me?"

Ivy smiled and ran a hand through Casper's gray hair. "I told you love, I'll never do that. I want you to live a long life and if you want, I want you to live it with me."

"What about when I die? I'm already dying Ivy, every minute I get closer. How will you handle it? Because I don't want you to have to go through that, I don't." Casper said, swallowing hard.

She reached down and took his hand. "It's a risk I'm willing to take. I just want to live with you, but Casper if you ever feel like you want something more. If you want something different, something I can't give you, I want you to go find it." she said looking down at their intertwined hands.

"Look at me." Casper said simply. She glanced up slightly and he said, "Don't be stupid Ivy. I don't want anyone else." Ivy nodded unsure still. "Do you think there's something you could do for me then?"

She nodded slowly, her eyes falling again. "Of course, anything." she whispered.

His arm was heavy, but he lifted enough to put his hand under her chin, making her look at him. "Would you marry me?"

"What?" Ivy asked, her eyes wide with shock.

"Would you marry me? I want to be with you forever, so I'd

like you to marry me." Casper said simply. It wasn't hard for him, he always thought it would be hard to ask that question, but it was as easy as breathing for him now.

"Okay." She said with a smile.

"Okay?" Casper asked forcing himself to sit up just a little, but the rushing pain in his stomach forced him back down.

She switched from sitting in the chair to beside him on the bed. She took one of his hands in the two of his. "Yea, I want you forever and if you want to get married then I'm all for it."

"But is it what you want?" Casper asked.

Ivy thought for a moment. Marriage had been so far from her mind for so long, but the idea of being married to Casper was different to her. It seemed right. "Yea I do, I really do." She gently pushed herself forward, mindful of his wounds and kissed him sweetly. She ran a hand across his cheek and smiled. She'd follow her instincts because she knew they were right.

He came home from the hospital a week later. Still battered and bruised but much better than anyone had thought he'd be, even the doctors were surprised. One of the lucky things about being a vampire, it made it easy for Ivy or someone else in her family to carry Casper around until he was back on his feet.

They agreed to wait and marry when he was completely back to health. It took a few months but neither minded, they wanted it to be a day for them both to remember happily.

Finally the day arrived when everything came true. Mollie and her family came for the wedding along with PJ and hers, a few of the other vampires came as well, having advance notice gave more of them the chance to come. It added up to be a congregation of about twenty, but Ivy didn't care. Today wasn't about them, it was about Ivy and Casper and everything they had been through to get to this day. The day when their life together would officially start.

"I can't believe how nervous I am." Ivy said, holding a hand over her stomach. The dress she wore was her something borrowed, it had been Mollie's wedding dress. "I mean what do I have to be nervous about?"

"Everyone gets nervous on their wedding day." Mollie said with a smile pinning a magnolia flower into Ivy's hair. "I threw up three times before my walk down the aisle."

Grace and Ivy laughed together. "I was nervous before my ceremony with Alex." Grace said with a smile. "I think it's just normal."

A knock sounded at the door. "Come in." Ivy said staring at her reflection in the mirror.

The door creaked open slowly and a face she thought she'd never see again was smiling at her. "Hello Ivy." Rudolph said.

"What are you doing here?" Ivy asked whipping around in the chair.

He shrugged and said, "I wanted to be here for you today."

She stood and moved toward him quickly, she hugged him close to her and asked, "How have you been? Really?"

Rudolph sighed and said, "It's been a difficult adjustment, living like you do, but I'm doing all right."

Ivy smiled. "I'm so glad to hear that Rudolph."

I was wondering if I could ask you something. Rudolph thought.

A confused look grew across Ivy's face. "Did you just let me read your thoughts?" she asked.

He smiled. "I figured it was about time I let you in."

She smiled brighter. "Thank you. What did you want to ask me?"

"If you would be all right with it, I'd like to give you away." Rudolph said meekly. "I know it probably seems like a strange request, but it would mean a lot to me."

Ivy nodded slowly. "I'd love that Rudolph."

"Are you nervous?" Leo asked Casper as he tied his bowtie.

"No actually, I've been waiting for it so long that I'm just itching to get there." Casper said with a smile.

"You really love her don't you?" Peter asked.

Casper smiled genuinely. "I really do, more than anything."

"I can see that." Peter said with a nod. "I never wanted to before, but I see it now. I think you're good for her."

"Thank you Peter that means a lot to me." Casper said sitting down beside Alex on the couch in the living room.

Ian sat next to Casper on the couch. "I've got to be honest, I never thought I'd get the chance to see you get married."

Casper started to laugh. "Well as long as we're being honest, I never thought I'd see me get married."

Ian laughed too. "I'm happy for you. I know I love Ivy, you sure picked a winner there."

"I think she picked me, I know I'm the lucky one." Casper said with a smile.

Alex, Leo and Peter put their head. "Aw." they all said

together.

"Shut up." Casper murmured, hitting Alex in the head with a pillow.

Suddenly Grace's head popped in the room. "You all ready?" she asked. "Because we are."

Casper and the boys took their places outside with the other vampires. PJ had agreed to do the service for them. The girls all sat in the front row with their men around them. Everyone turned at the sound of Ivy and Rudolph's approaching thoughts. She turned the corner with Rudolph on her arm, her dark red hair was piled on top of her head with a large flower pined at the back. The white lace dress fit her to a tee and the train seemed to float behind. She was lovely. They met Casper and PJ at the front of the crowd. Rudolph leaned in and kissed Ivy on the cheek. He had no final parting thoughts, no words of wisdom or desperate pleas for her to pick him, just a parting smile. It was all he had to give her.

Casper and Ivy looked at each other for a moment, sharing a smile of their own. They turned to PJ for the ceremony to begin. "We are gathered here today to bring two of our close friends together in matrimony." PJ began, her white hair glistening in the sun which she was so nice to bring with her, of course she kept the clouds moving so that the sunlight would not become too much for the guests. "I have known Ivy since my creation nearly two centuries ago and she has been the greatest friend and mentor I could have ever hoped to have. Casper I have known a much shorter amount of time, but I have never seen our Ivy as happy as she is around him. And today we join them forever." She turned to

Casper and said, "Casper repeat after me, I Casper take you Ivy to by my wife, for richer and poorer, in good times and bad, until death do we part."

Casper smiled sincerely and said, "I Casper take you Ivy to be my wife, for richer and poorer, in good times and bad, until death do we part."

PJ turned to Ivy. "Ivy repeat after me, I Ivy take you Casper to be my husband, for richer and poorer, in good times and bad, until death do we part.

Ivy locked eyes with Casper for a long moment and said, "I Ivy, take you Casper to be my husband, for richer and poorer, in good times and bad." She paused for a moment and smiled as she rephrased the last part. "As long as we both shall live."

PJ took the rings from her pocket and said, "Okay Casper, place this ring on Ivy's left hand and repeat after me, I give you this ring as a symbol of my undying love and affection."

Casper slipped the small platinum ring onto Ivy's delicate finger and said, "I give you this ring as a symbol of my undying love and affection."

PJ turned to Ivy and said, "Ivy place this ring on Casper's left hand and repeat after me, I give you this ring as a symbol of my undying love and affection."

Ivy took the ring an slipped it on Casper's finger. "I give you this ring as a symbol of my undying love and affection."

PJ smiled and said, "It is my pleasure to announce that you are husband and wife." She turned to Casper and said, "You may kiss the bride." The two turned to each other and smiled, it had been a long road to get here, but they never looked back. PJ moved the clouds in the sky around so that the sun centered on the happy couple. Casper placed his hands on around Ivy's face and pulled her into him. He kissed her passionately, it was all they ever wanted, and they would have it for as long as they could.

Days turned to weeks, then to months, then to years. Casper stayed and lived with Ivy and her family and they kept up with their work. Ivy allowed Peter to take over more of the Prowler's responsibilities for as long as Casper was alive. Everyday Casper grew older, just the way Ivy wanted. They secluded themselves much from society, but when they did go out they made a point to ignore the stares of others. They didn't matter. Ivy had been so concerned to know what others would think, and now she knew how little importance it held. She held his hand and kissed him in public, she was his wife, the age difference was nothing. And besides, those people had no idea that Ivy was actually the elder in the relationship.

Ivy and Casper lived every day to the fullest. Their lives were so full of love and fulfilled that nothing could have made it better. They spent every moment of every day together. It was one day after Casper's hundredth birthday that everything changed.

It was a Tuesday when Casper died. He always wanted to go easy, painless, after being shot by Eva it was the last thing he wanted. Ivy always slept on Casper's chest, lulled to sleep by the steady sound of his heartbeat and breathing. One this night she was started awake by the stop of both. Her eyes flashed open and she pushed her weight up on her right hand. She gently shook his shoulder with her left hand. "Casper," she murmured quietly, hoping it was a mistake. She shook a little harder. "Casper, honey wake up. Please wake up." She shook him harder and harder and began to scream at him. "Damn it Casper wake up!" Suddenly she let her hand drop from his shoulder and buried her face in his chest and cried softly.

"Thank you for coming." Ivy said, welcoming the guests at Casper's funeral a few days later.

"I thought one of the perks of being immortal was avoiding these kind of things." Leo murmured, death wasn't something anyone liked to see.

"I can't do this." Ivy muttered, trying to swallow a sob as she turned to her family.

Grace took her hand and said, "Yes you can. Casper would want you to do it."

Luckily everyone in attendance was of the vampire persuasion, so there was no need to hold anything back. When everyone was inside Ivy began the service. "Thank you all for coming." she began. "Casper Lennox was the only man I ever loved. He was beautiful in every way to me. He was the first person who saw past what I was and could see just who I am." She swallowed her tears, she needed to keep it together now. "In the past few days I've wondered whether or not I made the right choice, keeping him human. And then I realized that this was about him and not me. He asked me once to change him and now I remember why I didn't do it. Making Casper keep his mortality was the greatest gift I could have ever given him, it was a gift I and none us got to keep. I had over sixty years with the man I loved and will continue to love him until the world ends and maybe then we'll be together again." She smiled to herself. "I can't really be sad that he's dead, that would be an insult to the wonderful time we had. I would rather have had these amazing sixty years together than an eternity of never having him. He was, is and will always be my entire world and have my entire heart. That's enough." She stepped down and let the others make their final farewells, an especially sad goodbye came from Ian, a goodbye from the brother he never thought he'd have again.

They laid Casper to rest under a tree near the house in Maryland, via the permission of Irma's family of course. It seemed like the right thing to do. It was where their entire journey began. It was in the shade of the large ash tree, so when Ivy came to visit she could stay as long as she wanted.

Ivy took back her position as the Prowler, it was her calling after all, and she felt like the greatest disservice she could give to Casper and his memory would be to stop her life. They'd be together again, Ivy could feel it. When the world ended, whenever that was, the two would find their way back. They were kindred souls, meant for each other and it had taken Ivy five centuries to find him. If nothing else it could make you believe in destiny. That everything, from marrying Marcus to being changed by Rudolph, the death of her son, becoming a Prowler, the death of the rogue April, everything, it led to bring them together. The universe does work in peculiar ways after all.

5031397R0

Made in the USA
Charleston, SC
20 April 2010